BOB KNIGHT: HIS OWN MAN

ALSO BY JOAN MELLEN

PRIVILEGE: The Enigma of Sasha Bruce
NATURAL TENDENCIES: A Novel
BIG BAD WOLVES: Masculinity in the American Film
THE WAVES AT GENJI'S DOOR: Japan Through Its Cinema
VOICES FROM THE JAPANESE CINEMA
WOMEN AND THEIR SEXUALITY IN THE NEW FILM
MARILYN MONROE
A FILM GUIDE TO THE BATTLE OF ALGIERS
THE WORLD OF LUIS BUÑUEL (ed.)

BOB KNIGHT

HIS OWN MAN

BY

Joan Mellen

DONALD I. FINE, INC.
New York

Library of Congress Cataloging-in-Publication Data
Mellen, Joan.
  Bob Knight : his own man.

  1. Knight, Bobby.   2. Basketball—United States—
Coaches—Biography.   I. Title.
GV884.K58M45   1988   796.32′3′0924 [B]   88–45377
ISBN 1–55611–100–2

Manufactured in the United States of America

10 9 8 7 6 5 4 3 2 1

Grateful acknowledgment is made for those photographs that appear
courtesy of the Indiana University Athletic Department.

FOR RALPH SCHOENMAN
WITH GRATITUDE

ACKNOWLEDGMENTS

When Don Fine approached me with the idea for this book, I had to consult Bob Knight. Practices at Indiana University are closed to the press. And such a book would be meaningless without his voice. Having heard him tell an Indiana audience, "Nobody else is going to write a book while I'm here unless it's me," I had my doubts about whether he would go along with the idea.

"I have no problem with that" was his reply to my inquiry about doing a book. And so I began.

Not only did Knight make no attempt to influence this book, but he never even asked me for the name of the publisher. There were no rules, no agreements, oral or written, and no stipulations about what might or might not be said, regarding language or anything else.

Bob Knight is so often open and uncalculating, even garrulous, that I think some of his friends were concerned that his privacy would be violated. But he never expressed a word of caution. In retrospect it seems clear that he had decided that was the way it would be, a decision that was implemented from the moment he agreed to open the doors of Assembly Hall to me, despite his friend Father James Higgins' warning, "If you ever trust another writer, you'll go to hell for sure."

"True to you, fair to him," Tom Callahan of Time advised. I hope I have been both.

This book exists by virtue of Bob Knight's great quixotic generosity, but I would now also like to acknowledge some of the other people who were kind enough to grant me their time and their thoughts.

Tough-minded and bemused, Bob Hammel, sports editor of the Bloomington *Herald-Telephone,* helped whenever I asked. Any errors about basketball are my own. Many of the errors from which I was saved are owing to Bob Hammel's gentle persuasion as he set me straight all along the way, right down to Hartford.

I am indebted to the athletic department of Indiana University, most particularly to athletic director Ralph Floyd, for many courtesies and to Sports Information Director Kit Klingelhoffer, who accomplished the impossible for a book writer, given the NCAA's determination that only newspaper and magazine people are worthy of tournament credentials. I would also like to thank Eric Ruden, and Academic Advisor Elizabeth (Buzz) Kurpius for her abiding assistance.

I saw from the first the camaraderie that prevails in the basketball program at Indiana. Coaches Ron Felling, Joby Wright and Dan Dakich taught me a lot, as did Julio Salazar. Bob Knight's secretaries, Mary Ann Davis, B.J. McElroy and Kyle Parmenter were always warm, helpful and cooperative.

To the Indiana players who suffered my presence in their locker room and who talked with me, I am also very grateful.

The Indiana managers assisted me in a host of ways, but I would like to single out Greg Burton and Stephen Trust for being especially considerate and ready with help even when I wasn't aware that I needed it.

For their willingness to recall old times, I thank these graduates of the Indiana University basketball program: Tom Abernethy, Steve Ahlfeld, Quinn Buckner, Jim Crews, Steve Downey, Phil Isenbarger, Steve Green, Ted Kitchel, Landon Turner, Jim Wisman and Mike Woodson.

I am especially grateful to Coach Mike Krzyzewski for his graciousness to me in Raleigh-Durham.

And there are many others whom I would like to thank: Ira Berkow, Brad Bomba, Rita Bomba, Dr. Donald Boop, Pauline Boop, Tom Callahan, Brad Duggan, Gary Eiber, David Ferrell, Tim Garl, David Israel, Father James P. Higgins, Tim Knight, Jeff Marx, Bob Murrey, Robert Quay Norris, Dick Otte, Billy Reed, Satch Sanders, Mark Stephens, Mya Shone, Fred Taylor, Joe Vecchione.

In Bloomington Nancy Salmon, Harry and Maryrose Pratter and Eleanor Byrnes became friends. I thank them for everything. But, most, for the extraordinary interest he took in this project I thank Distinguished Professor Emeritus of History Robert F. Byrnes, my alter ego in Bloomington.

Coach Jay Norman at Temple was a solace and a support, as was my pal Bill Van Wert, who taught Larry Bird freshman English for a few days at Indiana University. I would also like to thank for their good insights those basketball fans-to-be Michael Pakenham, Natalie Robins and Francine Toll.

More than thanks, my deepest appreciation to my agent Jane Gelfman and to Mrs. Judith Burnley of London, England, who, never having seen a game of "roundball", knew the right questions to ask. For her advice about titles I thank Dorothea Straus. I would also like to thank my editor, Susan Schwartz, for her consideration, for her good taste, and for the interest she took in this project.

The dedication reveals the source of my nurture during this unlikely enterprise.

CONTENTS

PART I

1. A MAN WITHOUT A MASK 15
2. A VOICE FROM THE HEART OF THE COUNTRY 20
3. VALPARAISO, INDIANA, POPULATION: 23,000 24
4. THE LITANY 47

PART II

5. THE ART OF BASKETBALL 85
6. SCRIMMAGING 123
7. INTERLUDE: INDIANA CLASSIC 150

PART III

8. THE GAME'S THE TEST, AND THERE'S NO MULTIPLE CHOICE 167
9. LEARNING AS YOU'RE PLAYING 211
10. REPRISE: THE LITANY 267
11. CONCLUSION 280

But that is the way people are. They want talent, which is in itself something out of the ordinary. But when it comes to the other oddities that are always associated with it, and perhaps are essential to it, they will have none of them and refuse them all understanding.

THOMAS MANN, *Confessions of Felix Krull Confidence Man*

PART ONE

CHAPTER ONE

A MAN WITHOUT A MASK

"I want him to go away and say, well, I learned more in basketball than in any class I took at Indiana. Basketball was by far the most educational experience that I had when I was at Indiana. And if that kid says, well, Chemistry 401 was my best, then I want to find out what the hell that guy is teaching in Chemistry 401 because I ought to be teaching it in basketball."

"THE GENERAL," ABC's Dick Vitale calls Indiana Coach Bob Knight, the basketball genius who has won three NCAA championships, the NIT, eight Big Ten championships, the Olympic and the Pan American gold. Yet for most writers covering college basketball his name at once evokes an obligatory reference to: a chair, an LSU fan, a Puerto Rican policeman and, of all unlikely people, the Russians.

Few know him beyond formal press conferences; few have observed Knight's Indiana team at practice.

To paraphrase a scene in which he confronts his team later in this book: Who is he? What is he? Where is he? And does Bob Knight the coach or the man bear any resemblance to the stereotypic profane bully, his mouth open in a shout, his arms up in the air ready to descend upon a student we meet so often on the sports pages.

*   *   *

In fact, his flamboyant public image notwithstanding, Bob Knight is a teacher first, a purveyor of subjects not covered in any known college curriculum. To the chosen few young men who come to him, he imparts deceptively simple and yet invaluable lessons of hard work, self-sacrifice, self-reliance and effectiveness.

Through basketball, a "kid's game," he'll call it, he reveals to his players not only what their particular talents are but how to respect themselves sufficiently to develop them. And he demands what few teachers do: that they ask of themselves nothing less than what he asks of them. He requires that they take themselves seriously, settle for nothing less than excellence, and that through competition they discover the secret of how to live well, how to survive.

Through an unending struggle for perfection in basketball, Knight offers a model for how his players might best conduct the rest of their lives. Winning becomes nothing less than taking yourself seriously enough to demand excellence. Basketball is the activity through which these truths are taught at Assembly Hall, the games themselves their proving ground. The rest of life awaits their application.

The photographs convey a man with his mouth open in disbelief, his eyes flashing in anger, his arms raised to the heavens in exasperation. That is not the man you will encounter in these pages. Nor once you meet him will it be difficult to forget that shrill icon, that caricature, however endlessly perpetuated.

That image vanishes because there's a viable alternative—the man as he is rather than as he's been presented in the media.

This Bob Knight is a man of profound moral significance who has changed for the better the lives of the young men under his charge. If such a description seems uncharacteristic, it's because he will not trouble to help strangers understand. It may be that the deception amuses him, this enormous disparity between appearance and reality. And the misunderstanding grows because he is a man who will neither demand his due, defend himself nor clarify misconceptions.

Instead he defines his existence on his own terms, and, as always, his teaching, his work, unfolds behind closed doors. No doubt you expect in the pages that follow to read a lot of profanity, but you will not. It's not that Knight is never salty, although he's less so than you might imagine. In the environment of sports, even college sports, he would be robbing himself of an effective tool to attract the attention of young male students. But profanity actually occupies a small proportion of his speech. Listen to him in these pages in a variety of situations, at work and at home, at dinner and in the locker room, and because I am there so frequently I realize that he can't be adjusting his language to the presence of a woman, a writer.

There are occasions when, if only for the fun of it, he'll string together a chain of expletives of the most dramatic variety. But such occasions are rare. In trying circumstances, coaching a team playing abysmally, losing a first round game at the NCAA tournament, he is not profane. To present him as spewing forth obscenities at every turn would be simple bad faith.

But there's something else that needs to be said. Most coaches use profanity. They do it in the confines of the locker room while in public they may appear mild, unemotional and controlled. A visitor at practice forces an adjustment, not only of the coach's language, but of his entire personality.

With Knight, there are no such disguises, no masks. He's the same everywhere. Once he amazed a houseguest, Clippers' assistant Don Casey, by suddenly walking into a room stark naked. That's Knight, never cloaking an action in pretense, a man without a mask.

Knight *is* a man obsessed. What drives him is a need, almost indeed a compulsion, that his students grow strong, competent and sure of themselves. He's adamant that in the destructive element of the basketball game, which will become, as Joseph Conrad had it, the deep sea of life itself, they discover how to keep themselves afloat.

He looks at his twelve players sitting before the open lockers, identified with little plaques by the names of those who have been there before them and he asks that they compete. Primarily, they must compete against their own recalcitrance, against the resistance of all students to change, to grow, to think in ways other than they have thought before. Then they must compete against his disenchantment with them as they carelessly fail to do what they can do best, as they fail to be all they can. Never does he demand feats that a player lacks the ability to achieve.

Always he is unrelenting in his insistence that what they can do, they do well, consistently and with increasing flair.

As a teacher he brings to his students his historical imagination as he recaptures for them the exploits of his former players. At speaking engagements, at a restaurant over dinner, but mostly to his team, all those who played for him inevitably reappear. Together they form a visionary company, to be recalled at will. There is a promise he makes to those enduring his constant criticism, which even accompanying praise does not wholly mediate: they know they will one day join that roster, many of whose members turn up at Indiana games, keepers of the flame. Having passed through this crucible of effort, they are now friends of the coach.

Often Bob Knight seems a happy man whose days are full. As he enlarges their lives, so does he reach out to the community, those in distress, illness, old age, recipients of catastrophe, whose lives might be brightened by Indiana basketball—a telephone call from him, a letter, an appearance at a hospital or nursing home. These visits, unheralded and unreported, form an inextricable part of the texture of his days, rich in the presence of people and events, made doubly pleasurable for him by the presence of his two sons, Tim and Patrick, and by the woman in his life. There is something sacred to him not only about family, but about one's personal history, and his is reflected in these pages by the friends of his own youth, by co-workers of his father, and students of his mother some seventy years ago.

With a prodigious memory, alert to all he has done and where he has been, he recounts for players, friends, assistants and strangers the truths he has learned. He insists by the vitality of his enthusiasm that life is worthwhile, which is why his friends are not only gratified by his invitations, but cannot stay away.

He lives by what he teaches. He takes his own life seriously, even surprising the outsider by the unselfconscious pleasure he takes in the achievements of his teams: the Pan American medal, the Olympic gold, Big Ten championships tenaciously extracted, the three NCAA national championships in 1976, 1981 and 1987. He remembers these victories through those who achieved them, his team leaders whose names he has raised to Indiana legend. And so after the 1987 championship he would spend a season talking not only about Steve Alford, but about Daryl Thomas and

Todd Meier too, all three having become the bulwarks of that team.

There is nothing of precision, concentration, effectiveness or hard work demanded by that apocryphal chemistry professor that he will not wrest from his own students. He made that remark at the NCAAs in New Orleans in April of 1987. When he is reminded of it, he half-smiles as he says, matter-of-factly, simply and indubitably, "But I know they don't learn more in chemistry than they learn here. I know that."

CHAPTER TWO

A VOICE FROM THE HEART OF THE COUNTRY

"I'm not difficult to deal with like these people think I am. But, you see, they won't take the time to find out. They're afraid to find out."

ONE HOT SUNNY JUNE AFTERNOON in 1986 in a telephone conversation of no particular significance, a friend asked, "Aren't you watching the NBA finals?" I wasn't. Not only didn't I know which teams were playing, but I hadn't seen a basketball game in years. Idly I turned on the television. And it couldn't have taken three minutes for me to discover a game I hadn't known existed.

You could see it immediately, the player of startling concentration who at once saw the entire floor and everyone on it, knew what they would do, where they would move, what they were thinking before they themselves knew, a player who used this sense seamlessly and unselfishly to create opportunities for his teammates to participate, a player whose own scoring was woven into the texture of how the other members of his team performed. It was that fusion of thought and action that makes basketball a paradigm for the fulfilled life. It was the unselfish team game much vaunted but little seen.

I was no reader of the sports pages and so I had no idea who that player was. The morning newspapers, however, emblazoned his name over half a dozen stories. He was from Indiana. One of the articles referred to a short sojourn at Indiana University. There was a very intelligent coach there, but somehow it didn't work out. I might have seen that coach's name in print somewhere although I couldn't remember in what connection.

I put the pieces together. By some twist of fate, the brilliant coach, practitioner of the team game, had lost the unselfish, creative player who exemplified that game better than anyone who had ever played it.

So when late that summer I saw an advertisement for a book about that coach, I ordered it to find out how that unlucky accident had happened, how the coach who stood for team play had lost the player who best understood how it leads to greatness in basketball.

I read the book. There wasn't a word in it about why Larry Bird left Indiana University. The book itself seemed to be unedited transcriptions of a coach endlessly, furiously criticizing mediocre players. As if aware of its own banality, it would race forward to new displays of temper, only to subside into long descriptions of basketball games, victories and defeats merging toward no particular end.

Nonetheless, I saw through those pages a teacher facing the same struggles with students I faced at Temple University, so I decided to review the book. Unlike most teachers these days (and, I hoped, like me), he would not give up on a single one of his students. He battled with them all, believing they all could learn, not because he was waiting for their thanks, but because he cared. These students weren't mastering Sir Philip Sidney, but "help side defense," and while it may be natural to Larry Bird, it was not easy for them. They faltered. Sometimes they even cried, as my own students will on occasion when they receive a grade lower than B. But he never gave up on them and he wouldn't allow them to give up on themselves, even if it meant shaking them to bring them to their senses.

He also had a larger vision, this teacher. He was helping them to grow up, encouraging them in manners where before they had none. He had also rescued a former player from the depression that was an outcome of a devastating accident. I thought I had seen an extraordinary teacher buried in those pages.

One day in January the secretary of the Temple English Department, Catherine Hence, called to say she thought I ought to know about a telephone message taken by one of her assistants. Bob Knight? Was that important? He had left no forwarding number, but he wasn't difficult to find.

"I just wanted to tell you I really liked what you wrote." There were no introductions, greetings, prefatory awkwardnesses. Nobody's name need be spoken. (Yet when he speaks to his players, when he's teaching, in a given sentence he's likely to speak someone's name not once, but twice. So he assigns responsibility, as in, "There you are, Keith, ten feet away from anybody, not creating problems for anybody, you're just there, Keith, where you want to take it," or, "Dean, look at him walk right over you, Dean.") His voice was as lucid and clear as a cold mountain stream, his pronunciation defiantly middle western, precise, definite, loud, uninhibited, unambiguous, a skeleton key to his character.

"You're a professor of literature?" he chuckled.

There was some more talk. But what I remember most was the energy of his silence: his silence was palpable, more aggressive than other people's words. It made you examine your own words as you spoke them; it never left you in doubt that there was a presence on the other end who would hold you accountable for whatever you said.

At that moment it seemed inconceivable not to suggest that I would like to come to Indiana to write a story about him.

Time passed.

The first time I saw him on television was at the tail end of a game. Suddenly, as he shouted "Ricky!", his voice thundered across the court with such force and velocity that you thought all must be lost, now and forever. So I was incredulous to discover that his team was winning by more than ten points with less than half a minute to play. He was yelling instructions although the game was in fact over. At the time, this seemed utterly inexplicable.

There was no straight line to Bloomington. Delays followed. In one telephone conversation, as the 1987 season drew to a close,

I told him I hoped he would win. This was greeted by the overwhelming silence. I thought then that I had jeopardized my chances, exposed my ignorance, because winning might not be what he was about at all.

I read everything I could find out about him, and the stack of clippings grew. Scarcely a day went by that he was not quoted, mentioned, attacked. There seemed to be three Bob Knights of my potential acquaintance, the affable, friendly, quick-witted man on the telephone, the dedicated teacher I perceived through the book—and this other strident, belligerent person of the newspapers, a person I discovered had just been censored by the Indiana University faculty for physically and verbally abusing his students.

One editor to whom I spoke revealed the certainty with which those who didn't know him concluded what he was.

"I don't like him," the man said. Then, oblivious of the contradiction, he asked:

"What's he like?"

"He was courteous, rather kindly," I began.

"Ah, he's faking," came back the answer. The case was obviously closed.

At last a date was set. It was October 15, the first day of basketball practice. I expected an extensive lecture, spelling out all the rules, for personal behavior no less than for basketball from the coach whom I had read was supposedly an admirer of General Patton and ran his practices like boot camp in the marine corps.

"We just start practicing," he said simply.

The details of my arrival, however, were not left to chance. I would be met, he told me, by someone six foot five inches tall, with sharp features.

"You carry a carnation and have the New York *Times* under your arm," he said in that definite way of his, "and he'll have the *Wall Street Journal* and carry a rose."

CHAPTER THREE

VALPARAISO, INDIANA, POPULATION: 23,000

"Most of us go on to other things."

AT FIRST MEETING he seems a foot taller than the six foot five he is, and his aura can be measured on the Richter scale. Get too close and you experience the sense of danger that comes when you put your hand too close to a fire. You feel as if you're nowhere you've ever been before. Later a professor friend of his, a man old enough to be his father, will confide, "He makes me feel like a boy." "It's very hard to become something if you don't already look the part," Bob Knight will say. In many ways he resembles the stereotype: he's large and commanding, authoritative and definite and physically powerful. You believe that if he had to impose his will by force, he could do it. A tall gray-haired man in the vigor of early middle age with eyes that turn instantaneously from green to grey to hazel—hardly unique and yet there's something about him that defies whatever your expectations might have been. There's also an incipient air of impatience, or even derision, which already insists that there's no time for trivialities.

Look again and it's a pleasant-seeming man in an old blue sweater and a plaid shirt that sticks out in back and wrinkled gray corduroy pants. He has appeared without being announced and now leans against the door with a half-smile on his face. He's long and lean with only a gentle paunch, nothing like the belly-bulging firebrand you've read about. It's obvious that there's too little personal vanity here for him to be considered handsome. When he speaks, it's to tell me I don't have to get dressed up for the speech he's giving in Northern Indiana. He walks with his shoulders thrust slightly forward so that effortlessly he covers great distances, in this case the ramp leading down from his office to the lobby of Assembly Hall. In the basketball office an air of cheerful energy and good humor pervades among secretaries and assistants, and a sign reads, "Everyone Who Visits Here/Brings Happiness/Some By Coming In/Others By Going Out."

The voice is as I've heard it, the accent evoking the sounds of the frontier a century and a half ago. Before we leave, he disappears into the coaches' locker room to change into the costume by which he is known: the red sweater, the blue pants, the black loafers.

On the late afternoon flight in the tiny Indiana University jet to Valparaiso, a steel town more in the sphere of Purdue than Indiana University, he sleeps. He is obviously exhausted, having been "roasted" in Atlantic City the night before, an event hosted by Howard Cosell. ("I told Don King he had to get a haircut or he couldn't play on my team.")

The plane is met by Gary Dunne, an FBI agent friend whom Knight immediately ribs: "You guys did a great job on the Kennedy Assassination. It rivals the Normandy invasion." "Getting needled is part of being here," he'll say. No one escapes. The needling both expresses and wards off intimacy: it's an affectionate way he has of distancing himself from people, rather like a magnetic screen that comes up and down at will. It's part of the world of sports, of course, men ribbing each other. It evokes feelings only to pull back from them; it admits sentiment while at the same time rejecting it. And it forms a barrier between the man and himself, just as sports provide an outlet for emotions and actions our lives may be too pallid to admit. (The needling is also fun for Knight, who will admit to frequent boredom. "That's an absolute needle I give to every FBI guy I've ever met. I stick 'em with that. Have you sons of bitches ever decided to release the facts on the Kennedy assassination? They're sensitive about that; I enjoy it.")

Dunne counters: He'll hang Knight's picture in his office next to Reagan's.

"Not too close," Knight murmurs.

We are bound for the Valparaiso high school gym, which, like so many Indiana high school gyms, seats more people (6,600) than many university arenas. A young reporter from the local newspaper, dressed in white shirt, suit and tie, squeezes into the car. Knight tries to find out what he's supposed to speak about. The reporter has questions of his own.

"What would you like to have written about you?" Knight sinks back into his seat and says, quietly, "Nothing."

And then come the seemingly endless questions: How would he write his job description, how does he see his relationship with his players, what specific characteristics does he look for in recruits? Fatigued, he answers almost in slow motion, and he replies to every one, but when it comes to this: "Of all the teams you've had at Indiana University, could you name an all-time starting five?"

"Yes, I could, but you'll never hear them."

The reporter laughs. Young as he is, he has been schooled to place his need to get the story before considerations of his subject's comfort. Finally he raises the subject of Isiah Thomas. Eliciting no reply whatsoever, undaunted, he wants to know, "Are you as fine a fisherman as I've read you are?" The subject revives: "Damn near as good as anybody!" And, finally, "What are you gonna do when you quit coaching?"

Knight cannot resist this one.

"Become a writer."

He began this ribbing of the press, not with an attack on a writer who wronged him, but as one of those needles bestowed upon one of his closest friends, the sports editor of the Bloomington *Herald-Telephone*, Bob Hammel. How convenient, some might smirk. How sycophantic, others might scoff. And yet behind Hammel's affable exterior and his easy laugh, he is a tough-minded, unsentimental man of principle, more rigid and unbending of purpose than his seemingly less sensitive, more rough-hewn friend. What they have in common is not only the belief that college athletics can be played successfully and honestly at the same time, but also that neither is what he seems.

The incident occurred at a suburban Kiwanis Club dinner in November of 1973 at a Bloomington motel since torn down. Hammel had been at practice and now wanted to go home. Knight invited him to the dinner: "You're going to miss some really good stuff," an appropriate needle for a writer.

Hammel declined. Then, half way home, he turned back and went to the dinner, heading for a seat in the back, hoping he would not be noticed.

During the question period, one of the inevitables turned up. "You're rated third in the pre-season . . ."

"Well," Knight said, "polls come from sportswriters. All of us learn to write in the second grade. Most of us go on to other things."

There was only one writer in the room. Heads swiveled around; everyone looked. The writer, who blushes easily, blushed.

"What exactly is this thing tonight?" Knight asks again.

"It's a ladies' sorority. Haven't you been up here?" Dunne asks him, as if Valparaiso, Indiana, were the capital of the Western world.

"These people up here are basketball fans. Any given home game you get three or four thousand people; they just like their basketball," says the reporter. "Twenty-five hundred tickets have been sold."

"Who else is on this thing with me? Do they have Michael Jackson also?"

"Only you."

He enters the gym and the president of Kappa, Kappa, Kappa, Iota Chapter, a "not-for-profit organization for women whose goal is to further charity, culture and education," is waiting to greet him. He puts his arm around her shoulders and asks what she wants him to talk about. "Inspire us and motivate us," she says. The printed program defines his talk: "Motivation"—Bob Knight.

Inside, the Valparaiso high school band plays. The crowd awaits him, the old, the middle aged and the young, men, women and children. A sign above the podium is emblazoned with the dates of the Indiana championship seasons.

The twenty-two hundred give him a standing ovation as he walks down the aisle with a sheepish smile on his face, ducking his head. All that's missing is "Hail to the Chief." He likes being "Coach Bob Knight," there's no mistaking that. But standing ovations have not made him pompous or pretentious; his notoriety has not led him down paths of narcissism or self-aggrandizement. When I ask him how he feels to be so glorified, he replies, "What pleases me is that it's a recognition of what basketball in Indiana means to those people, the players, the way they conduct themselves. They're probably telling kids, Indiana's basketball players are graduating, they're going to class, that pleases me. What they're saying is that Indiana University basketball stands for something they like." Somehow, I believe him.

II

"Don't you worry about old fat-ass catching you."

He needs no introduction in Valparaiso, and the Tri Kappa is too nervous to say much anyway. "He's gonna cut me off," she says quickly, "so with that, Coach Bob Knight!"

"Reagan should have had you present Bork," he begins. "He might have had less trouble." He's a practiced speaker with a sense of timing not unlike Bob Hope's. "I'm a little bit concerned that you say this affair here tonight will take in more money than your cookbook did. What you ought to do is find better cooks to give recipes."

His subject is Indiana basketball, what happens that the audience might not see on television. He speaks from memory with energy, forcefulness and good humor.

Early on, he asks the audience for a five-second period of complete silence "from the time I say start, 'start!' " only to conclude, "That gives the news media here in attendance something that can be quoted with absolute accuracy."

He invokes the stereotype forged by the press to poke fun at himself. "There have been a lot of distorted images projected of

what goes between players and coaches at Indiana University,"
he says. With play in progress, he asks the audience to picture
him asking Steve Alford, "Steve, would you mind coming over
here a second?" And he questions his star player, "Would you
guys have any objection if I took a time-out here?"

In this parody of Indiana basketball, Alford first confers with
Daryl Thomas and only then returns with his answer: "That
would be fine." The team is down 24 to 10; coach tells them:
should they continue at the present pace, they will "get beat 211
to 63."

Knight now politely suggests to Alford that for two or three
minutes they run the offense that "we set up for this game and
play the defense that we have set up for today's game." Alford
looks around; Todd Meier says, "Well, coach, would you mind
letting us alone for just a moment to talk this over?"

"Sure."

The coach retreats to the scorer's table, where, "fortunately,"
he mocks himself, "they did not put any telephones. That's the
most expensive phone call ever made," he adds, referring to the
NCAA's ten thousand dollar fine at the 1987 tournament for his
bringing his hand down on the phone during the LSU regional
final.

By a close majority, Alford and his teammates vote to use
Knight's offense for three minutes.

"I couldn't have asked for anything more from you."

His point, of course, is the reverse. Coaching does not permit
a democracy. Like any teacher, the coach leads by virtue of his
superior knowledge, wisdom, guidance and leadership. Coach
and players, teacher and students, are separate and unequal.

One of the constants of Knight's approach to Indiana basketball has also become apparent. The anecdote has starred Alford,
Thomas and Meier, all last year's seniors and now remembered
as their team's leaders. As he recounts their exploits, and their
foibles, they become Indiana players once more, participants in
a living history, sharing a continuity with each other and with
those at Indiana now. All have come through the experience of
playing for him stronger and better able to survive in the world
they have since entered.

The members of this endlessly present visionary company are
remembered not for their weaknesses, which can no longer be

amended, but for the seemingly impossible feats they accomplished. The invocation of their names even takes on a religious, a spiritual quality.

It all comes down to recruiting, Knight goes on, describing Randy Wittman's living room, the Wittman who now in the autumn of 1987 still plays for the Atlanta Hawks, and will later be traded to Sacramento, but then he was a senior at Ben Davis High School in Indianapolis. "He's one of the all time great players that I've coached," Knight adds.

He tells the audience not of an NBA star, but of Wittman as a ninth grader at Knight's basketball camp. The formidable, frightening coach, a giant of a man, beckons the boy to his side. "He didn't know what he had done, but he was sure he was in trouble for something."

"Is your name Wittman?"

"Yes, sir."

"Wittman, would you like to come to Indiana when you get out of high school?" The voice is gruff, forbidding. No one would enjoy this interrogation.

"Yes, sir."

"All right. Keep playing and we'll try and see that that happens."

The scene flashes forward to Wittman as a senior in high school with the same coach now ensconced in his living room, reminding him of that day in basketball camp.

"Are you still coming to Indiana?"

"Yes, sir."

"And that," says Knight deadpan, "is the intricacy of recruiting at Indiana. You get the kid when he's a ninth grader, make sure he's afraid to say no to you, and then make sure he stays that way when he's a senior."

He now evokes one of his favorite characters, the mother of one of his top players, who wanted her son to come to Indiana because "she thought I was the next best thing to a convent." Many of the mothers of Knight's former players remain friendly with him; they all receive gifts at Christmas, and tickets whenever they wish, as if they too will forever share in the living history of Indiana basketball. They are not, however, exempt from his needling.

Knight portrays this woman as a mother who wants to keep her son alongside her, innocent of sex, innocent of adulthood as long as she can. "This player and his wife are now about to have a baby," Knight reveals, "and his mother's not sure how that came about." He's providing background to a story about a rebellion of players who want to live off campus, which Knight had permitted up to 1980 only for seniors.

He considers their arguments and agrees. All the parents are notified; none, of course, is more incensed than this player's, with whom Knight makes a deal.

"Have I ever done anything else wrong as far as your son's development as a person is concerned in your eyes?"

Reluctantly, the mother admits he has not, and agrees to a month's trial period. Her son moves off campus. In a month she receives a telephone call from Coach Knight.

"Hi, this is your old friend, Coach Knight."

"I hate to admit it," the woman says immediately, "but you were right. It's much better for him living off campus."

The coach appreciates her having given him that month, adding, "I'll tell you something. You'd absolutely adore the girl he's living with."

The dead silence is interrupted only by the player's father coming on the line: "What the hell did you just tell her?"

"I can't believe you haven't told her about the girl your son is living with. You and I took her to lunch last week." And Knight hangs up the telephone. Slightly ribald, invoking the parental authority the members of this audience would retain over their children, the story strikes at the heart of their concerns, and it brings down the house.

Knight tells another story illustrating how coaches get players to do things. It stars his 1976 championship team and its captain Quinn Buckner, that hero, who inevitably comes to the fore in these events perpetually made legend, the player who walked out onto the practice floor his first day as a freshman and became the team's leader.

Indiana is down a point to Alabama in this story, with two minutes to play in the first game of the 1976 regionals. A fourteen-point lead has been reduced to one. The coach orders Buckner to take the ball out of bounds, and Wilkerson and Abernethy to screen for May, while Benson breaks across the baseline toward the ball. No one in this Valparaiso audience will have trouble with these names, members of that undefeated team.

A time-out is taken.

"I went over everything I wanted and when they told me they understood everything that I wanted, I grabbed Benson by the shirt, I wrapped his shirt up in my fist, and I said, 'Benny, they're going to come down the floor and they're going to get the ball in to their center. Benny, if he gets the ball and scores, I'm going to chase your ass up the turnpike to Bloomington.' "

While Benson is left hanging in the wind, Knight digresses to a game against Texas A&M. In the huddle, Knight has his team chant, "One, two, three, four," the four passes they must make before they shoot the ball.

"May has been playing really well. But he takes a fifteen-foot shot on two passes and misses. We get the rebound and it comes back out to Buckner at the top of the key. I'm playing better on the bench than Buckner has in the game for these ten minutes.

"Buckner's just been chewed from end to end at this time-out and this is what made Buckner great. May is his best friend in all the world. Right in front of me, he puts the ball under his arm, May's down in the corner, and in a voice that everybody in Market Square Arena can hear, Buckner says, 'Goddamn it, make four passes!' "

But however gratifying Knight finds Buckner's assimilation of his teaching, as soon as he hears this comment, he jumps up from the bench and yells over to Buckner, "Yeah, you just better make damn sure you've got somebody counting for you too!" If you listen between the lines, you will hear a teacher whose students are never off the hook.

Knight returns to the story of Benson, Buckner and Alabama, with Buckner taking Benson by the arm, while Benson leans down and nods his head. Back on the bench, isolated from the action, the coach wonders what Buckner has come up with. What has he changed? What will happen?

"Remember, I said I wanted Buckner taking the ball out of bounds. Abernethy takes it out of bounds. So I have a suspicion that things aren't going to work the way I want them to here. I had Benson breaking across the baseline. They put Wilkerson on the baseline. I had Wilkerson and Ab [Abernethy] screening for May. Somehow Buckner's got them screening for him.

"The pass comes in. A kid named T.R. Dunn deflects the pass and it goes to May, the guy I want to shoot. I look up and say, 'There is a just God up there.' May has the ball, he turns, he shoots it, and it goes in." (He can't resist this.) "A play we work on a lot. We draw the defensive man into a position where he can't quite get the pass and just deflect it into the hands of our good shooters and we go on to win the game!"

Knight then takes his Valparaiso audience to the locker room after the game, where Buckner is sitting calmly taking off his shoes.

"Quinn, what'd you tell Benson after that time-out?"

Buckner continues to remove his shoes as if he doesn't hear.

"Quinn, what the hell did you tell Benny?"

Buckner still does not look up. But coach knows that Benson at least will not ignore him, Benson, who now plays for the Cleveland Cavaliers, was always afraid of him.

"Kent, what did Buckner tell you?"

Suddenly a grin lights up Benson's face.

"Coach, he just came right up to me and grabbed me by the arm, and he said, 'Benny, don't you worry about old fat-ass catching you if Douglas scores, 'cause I'll have you before he ever gets off the bench!' "

III

"Don't let me intimidate you."

"You girls don't have to introduce anybody else?" So he begins the question period. "I don't want any dumb questions. We play the Russians on the fourteenth of November, and from that night on, following the game, I'll get all the dumb questions I care to hear until sometime in March."

After this prescient demand, he goes on to mock himself: "So ask me whatever you want, don't let me intimidate you."

Then he orchestrates, it's the habit of command. "What I would like you to do, if you would, is simply stand, and don't face me, but let everybody hear your question. Speak loudly and clearly."

A speaker asks how much playing time Jay Edwards and Lyndon Jones will receive; both were high school stars winning three state championships at a school called Marion. "This guy's a Marion alumnus," Knight informs the audience. "I don't give a damn where you went to high school. That doesn't mean anything to me."

Knight's bluntness might cause discomfort, but the man has indeed asked a dumb question: playing time, of course, is something earned. Even the coach who is treated here as a cross between Paul Bunyan and Davy Crockett cannot know how Jay and Lyndon will develop.

At his peril, the man remains standing. "You ask some question and then you sit right back down," Knight orders.

Of course they want to know about this season's team. Keith Smart is compared to Mike Woodson, who was "the epitome of a real scorer. He constantly looked to drive it, to shoot it, any way he could get it in. That's what I want Smart to think about."

Optimistically, Knight draws a line from Woodson to Smart, as if greater ability would be infused in Smart by virtue of his connection with the visionary company—all team players.

Someone asks about Daryl Thomas and is told he had "trouble finding the classroom and we took what steps we thought we had to take to show him the direction. To a degree he found it, but not to as great a degree as I would have liked, however." In fact, Knight was disappointed that Daryl Thomas did not graduate.

Here in Indiana, north or south, Larry Bird is always on someone's mind, no matter that it's nearly fifteen years ago that Knight recruited him.

The big classes were "just something that he was totally unprepared for," Knight says. And he adds, "I made a couple of mistakes, how I roomed him . . ."

Bird's pride indeed suffered at Indiana. He arrived with a few shirts and a few pairs of pants, so that the clothes of his roommate, Jim Wisman, seemed formidable. Wisman, from Quincy, Illinois, didn't have much, but he had more. Bird took bowling as a physical education elective and one day came back upset that he had to buy special bowling shoes. "I thought I was on a full ride," he said indignantly. The truth was, of course, that he couldn't afford the shoes.

Bird hated the big classes and began almost at once to say, "I'm getting out of here. I can't stand it. There's 260 people in there. How can I learn anything?" Worse, in a scrimmage he was one of the last chosen by his teammates, although he knew

he was better than more than a few, including roommate Wis-
man.

It rankled. And so one night three weeks after he arrived,
and long before basketball season began, he waited until
Jimmy Wisman was asleep and went out onto the highway
with his bag, hitch-hiking back home to French Lick.

Bird the Celtic, his frontier wit transplanted to Boston,
laughs and says, "It was the closet. I was afraid of Jimmy's
clothes." And the elegance that permitted him to disallow Isiah
Thomas's remark about how if he were black, he wouldn't be
special, ("If the statement doesn't bother me, it shouldn't
bother anybody.") notwithstanding, there is no reason to doubt
his present assessment: "If I knew then what I know now, I've
have run right back. Coach Knight and me wouldn't have had
no trouble."

In an aside, Bird added that he got Isiah Thomas off the hook!
"Bird probably shouldn't have gotten him off the hook," Bob
Knight reflects. "It would have taught him a little lesson."

Knight reveals that he appreciates best those players who rec-
ognized that his dominating ways are directed toward helping
them grow strong. Michael Jordan, he tells them, is "the best
player who ever played the game, I can't imagine anybody being
any better than Michael Jordan physically." The word "physically" is not idly added—the most intelligent player, he'll tell his
team was (of course) Bill Russell.

"My experience with Jordan was simply this," he confides.
During practice for the 1984 Olympics, "When Jordan wasn't
playing well, I walked up to him and I grabbed him by the arm,
and I just squeezed his arm. I'd say, 'You're too damn good to play
like this.' And Jordan looked me in the eye and said, 'You're right,'
and he'd play better."

Has he ever hit a player? No. Has he ever touched a player?
There is no self-consciousness about that. The Jordan story has
a parallel in Knight's coaching of Michael Brooks during the
Pan American games of 1979. He was a player who made many
mistakes. One day that summer after one of their morning
workouts Knight ripped him "from pillar to post." Brooks then
walked over and took his free throws, only to return to say,
"I'm twenty-one years old and no one has ever talked to me

like that in my life and I just wanted to thank you." Eight years later Knight remembers: "I love the kid. I just love the kid because of the significance of what we were saying to him, he grasped. He understood."

As for other coaches, his favorite joke on his colleagues involves the original voting on the three-point shot. In the spring of 1982, believing he had the only two kids in the league who could shoot the shot, Knight deliberately voted against it. His strategy was that this would ensure the other coaches voting the reverse.

Outvoted nine to one, with the three-point shot in place, he wins the Big Ten championship. Meanwhile, prior to the season, he had told reporters that there were *three* players in the league who could shoot the three-pointer and he had two of them. Who was the third? He wasn't telling. "I watched us play eighteen games with every kid who thought he could shoot the ball trying to prove to me he was the third guy. It was the best defense we played in fifteen years!" Practical joker meets basketball coach; the man who is a genius at the "kids' game" entertains himself.

"There were more bad shots taken against us that year than any year I've been coaching," he insists. "Out of a gesture of magnaminous appreciation of the friendship of my fellow coaches, at the meeting that spring following the 1983 season, I said, 'I want to apologize to you guys because you were right about the three-point shot. It's a hell of a rule.' And they voted it out nine to one!" By now he has his Valparaiso audience shrieking in delight, for they well know he was never an advocate of this innovation.

("The friendship of my fellow coaches": he knows they recruit against him, describing to prospective recruits how difficult it is to play for him. This season, Digger Phelps, a man Knight considers a good friend, called Eric Anderson, a senior at St. Francis de Sales high school in Chicago with a 3.65 scholastic average, and a future McDonald's All-American, a boy recruited heavily by Notre Dame and Purdue as well as by Indiana. Although Anderson had already made an oral commitment to Indiana, Phelps called to talk him into changing his mind and choosing Notre Dame.

Far from retaliating, after Indiana's defeat of Notre Dame, Knight sat in the locker room explaining to Phelps how David

Rivers had been too easy to guard, and that if he came off the screen in either of two ways, rather than always in the same way, it would make a difference. And it did; it has.

Notwithstanding Phelps' call, justice did prevail. Eric Anderson honored his commitment to come to Indiana.)

There are more jokes. He tells his oft-repeated story of how he came to throw the chair: a grandmotherly woman called to him from the other side of the court, "If you're going to stand up the whole game, throw me your chair!" Someone wants to know whether the baskets should be raised to bring the game "back to the little guy".

He offers a ready answer: "I say, the hell with the little guy," says Knight with gusto. "Let him play golf. Let him play second base. This isn't a game for little guys!"

His voice grows hoarse. At times he seems to draw into himself, abstracting himself from the situation. He is thinking, perhaps, of tomorrow, the first official day of practice. But he summons the energy to make his most important point.

Part father, part teacher, part role model, Bob Knight defines Indiana basketball in terms of what happens to kids. His life's work is helping kids grow up strong. If this audience listens to him, it is because it accepts the sincerity of his mission, and the sincerity of his complete disdain for the business big-time college sports has become.

He begins by replying to a question about drug testing. He's for it. There's applause. He tells the Tri Kappa hostesses, "There isn't a bigger community project, girls, than helping your school system to get funds to drug test athletes.

"Let me speak to you kids for a second," he says. "Parents are beyond help at this point." He invokes Len Bias, the Boston Celtic recruit dead of cocaine poisoning. I "felt no empathy whatsoever for Len Bias, none."

He expects them to be shocked at his callous lack of feeling for the young man cut down in his prime. But there is a larger message for young people here. Len Bias, Knight tells the kids, had "the world by the tail," and he lost everything.

"Each of us is free to make up our minds as to what's best for us as individuals," he argues. "The worst thing that any one of you kids can ever say is, 'I did it because the other kids did it.' "

The "absolute best word in the English language for you kids ever to learn is the word 'no.' 'No' is the best word you can ever learn. No, I won't. No, I can't. No, I don't. No, I'm not." This is Knight at his best, using his success as a winning basketball coach to reach young people, as their parents and their teachers may fail to do.

He pauses. "And if that doesn't work, you call me, and I'll give you a couple of stronger words you can use." Never is the applause greater than it is now. "You are a hell of a lot more important to you than anybody else is, and you have to learn to take care of you because you can change it to 'yes' if you should, but it is damn difficult to change 'yes' to 'no.' "

There's something more he has to say to these kids, and it involves his whole philosophy of teaching. It's about discipline, the mode of the caring teacher. He knows full well that kids do not always appreciate the hard demanding teacher.

"I'll tell you kids something," he begins. "Find someone who'll kick you in the ass once in a while, because that's the person who really cares about you. When that person delivers that kick, don't think about it. Think about the many pats on the head, or the pats on the fanny you've got from the same person. You all have a tendency as kids to focus in on a particular moment when you're probably getting just what the hell you deserve. Think about the times when you've been praised by that guy or that lady who doesn't worry about kicking you in the ass."

He proposes a game. Let them think of the most demanding teacher they've ever had and then the best teacher. "And I'm willing to bet that over ninety percent of you have the most demanding teacher and the best teacher as one and the same person."

He wishes for them: "demanding teachers who are parents, who are coaches, demanding teachers who are classroom teachers and demanding teachers who are friends."

He comes to the end of his sermon.

"Demand a little bit from each other," he says, "but most of all demand something from yourselves, you kids." And the gymnasium is so silent you could hear a pin drop.

A final question comes from a child who wants to know who will write the next book about him.

"Nobody else is going to write a book while I'm here unless it's me. When I write one, you make damn sure your Mom and Dad buy it for you."

The evening closes with his invocation of the line from "America, the Beautiful," "God shed his grace on thee." He says he never wants to hear the phrase "Born-again American." And so he stands there before them as a man proud of what he has built, of who he is and of his country.

Exhausted as he is, he is not yet free to go. The lottery must be called, with Coach Knight standing patiently on the stage picking numbers out of a giant wastepaper basket. Some of the winners will get basketballs which he will then sign; one will get a photograph of Keith Smart making his winning shot, "the shot" which will so haunt him in the season to come.

The audience is now free to ascend the stage for autographs. There are as many in middle age, men and women, grandmothers, and teenagers as there are kids; autograph hunting is not a sport for the young here, and only a few even bother with the excuse that they're doing it for their children.

(A Bloomington feminist requests that Bob Knight sign a sweatshirt for her thirty-year-old son-in-law. Could he use an indelible laundry marker so that it will not wash off? Could he insert cardboard inside so that the signature will not bleed through to the other side? Coach Knight obliges. And the gift is received with due solemnity: "Bob Knight touched my sweatshirt.")

He poses for pictures with someone's wife on his knee, or holding a baby. He signs photographs, caps, programs, Bob Hammel's book about the 1987 championship season, *Beyond the Brink with Indiana,* or paper napkins. Always he asks the name of the person for whom he's signing.

On the sidelines a gray-haired man is annoyed that he has to wait for Knight to sign the basketball he won in the raffle: "Why didn't he do it before all the kids lined up?" he whines.

Knight is about to depart at last, when another reporter wants an interview, and so he stands before the glass doors leading out of the gym for another fifteen minutes. But a beige suede jacket covers the red sweater.

At last he can depart. In the car, he turns on the Giants-Cardinals playoff game. By the fact that the Giants have eight hits and a certain batter is up, he figures out what inning it must be. About the evening, he wants to know: "How many people came? How much did they raise?" Fifteen thousand dollars, he's told.

The pilots are nowhere in sight on the deserted airstrip. "You may have to drive us back to Bloomington," he threatens Dunne, a three-hour journey by car.

But the pilots materialize out of the darkness, and the twin-engine eight-seater lifts off smoothly into the night.

Clutching a box of flies (they knew he was an obsessive fisherman) and one of the cookbooks of the Tri Kappa sorority, he sleeps. When he awakens, it's to rib the pilot. "Hey, Wally," he calls, "is that Indianapolis?"

"Yes, it's Indianapolis."

"I thought it was Kokomo."

Back in Bloomington, he heads for a midnight dinner at a fast-food place called "The Big Wheel." On the floor of his car is John McPhee's *A Sense of Where You Are,* which he has been reading. Bradley for President? The Democrats? "The last time they didn't have anyone, he became president."

With a final thought he sums up the evening, and simultaneously his chronic warfare with all those he deems the enemies of promise. By way of Benjamin Franklin, he offers the following look at a disillusioning world he believes neither he nor anyone else can hope substantially to alter for the better: "If the rascals understood the advantages of virtue, they'd be virtuous for the sheer rascality of it."

IV

"Never gamble and don't hang out with queers."

It can't be news that a deep cultural conservatism still pervades the heartland of America. Bob Knight's Indiana base is founded not on the cultured immigrants from Germany who brought symphony orchestras and the fine arts to Indianapolis and the North.

Rather, his characteristic supporter traces his ancestry to the pre-Civil War Southern migration. These were people from the Carolinas, who settled in Southern Indiana and had little to do with their civilized neighbors; they were a group so fierce that Union recruiters making the mistake of heading south of Indianapolis simply didn't come back. When the great aunt of the leading Hoosier novelist married a bookseller from Louisville, they refused to sell in their shop the novels of her nephew Kurt Vonnegut on the grounds of "taste." Of the raw conservatism of this side of the heartland, Vonnegut muses: "I thought the whole world would be as mean as that and it wasn't." As for why some Hoosiers were so mean—"It was because they lost the Civil War!"

The world in which Bob Knight is treated as folk hero and legend remains uneasy with change. It is rooted in the belief that before duty and moral obligation, personal inclination, the impulse toward happiness, must at critical moments give way. Intellectuals and professionals, distinguished professors and doctors no less than ordinary folk live traditional lives. They go to church on Sundays and raise large families.

Young people marry and settle close to home; for the quintessential Knight basketball player, Illinois to Indiana has been a frequent migration. Living still in Milwaukee (having been a Milwaukee Bucks draft pick), Quinn Buckner, Illinois-born, talks today of moving to Indianapolis. If Keith Smart and Dean Garrett represented departures from that norm, Eric Anderson is a return to the type of young man who has provided the muscle and bone of the Indiana program, from Jim Crews and Jim Wisman to Randy Wittman to Ted Kitchel and Tom Abernethy to Mike Woodson and Buckner himself. At Indiana all these people flourished under the coach, whom they still say reminds them of their fathers and their grandfathers and their teachers.

You have only to cross one state line from the heartland to Ohio, where Bob Knight was born in 1940. With its agriculture and iron foundries, Orrville remains the prototypic small town, population eight thousand. If there is uniqueness to Orrville, it is that it was a railroad town to which blacks were brought to handle the creosote used for making the railroad ties at Kuppers because it was thought to be too toxic for whites.

Here the same values of conformism, moral uprightness and patriotism dwell. Knight, who attended church Sundays as a child, was raised in the same values as his constituency. So it should not be surprising that as he finishes speaking in Val-

paraiso, as he will in hundreds of places large and small throughout Indiana in any given year, he intones in that loud, clear and
defiant voice of his, "America, America, God shed his grace on
thee." He is welcomed as one of them by people whose faith in
America has been unshaken either by Vietnam or by the struggle
for civil rights. "God truly did shed his grace on us," Knight says,
"and I hope we appreciate just what we have."

And yet he is no longer quite one of them. Were he merely an
advocate of received truths, he would not be the folk hero that he
is, one whose aura draws people like a magnet. For he is also a
rebel, a man who would dare speak his mind and stand up for
what he believes despite the consequences. A provincial in his
origins, and so at once recognizable to them, he is no less an
immensely sophisticated man who has seen the world and suffered its ways. Yet he prefers being among people like those with
whom he grew up, sharing the simple pleasures of rural America.
And for those many who chafe under the rigid structure of small-
town life, through his activism he offers vicarious transcendence.

For the acceptance of conformity breeds its opposite; the appe-
tite for rebellion, for outrage, for defiance of the repressiveness
that settles over life led in the predictable lanes. In his fierce
individualism, Knight fulfills for his wide heartland constituency
what they will not do for themselves: he cultivates an independent spirit and implements it through actions that embrace the
risks even as they accept the consequences.

Vicariously through him the Hoosiers, who have raised Bob
Knight to the status of folk hero, exorcise the repressiveness.
Their quasi rebellion is achieved with neither guilt nor bad faith
because while he speaks his mind, at the same time Knight stands
for the very principles they hold dear: justice and self-determina-
tion, honesty and competence, and hard work, the "work ethic"
they still call it. That he will defy acceptable norms of behavior
in pursuit of these principles, that aggressively, flamboyantly and
outrageously he is willing to defy hypocrisy, greed and corruption, wins him to their hearts.

There is a line in Rudyard Kipling's "If," displayed in Knight's
office, which invokes "the will" to hold on, and which expresses
what he loved best about his father, "the strongest-willed man I

ever met." One of thirteen children born in the Arkansas hills and growing up in Oklahoma, Carroll ("Pat") Knight, a freight agent for the Wheeling-Lake Erie Railroad, was a man of few words. Stoicism was his credo, his definition of what it meant to be a man. He would walk four miles every day, to work, back home for lunch and back to work and home again at night. One day he slipped on the ice on the porch, went to work (writing with his left hand this day) and visited the doctor to set his broken right wrist only when the workday ended.

Simple needs, simple desires sufficed. Pat Knight never earned more than eight thousand dollars a year, his son remembers. He owned a total of three automobiles in his life, including one which survived ten years with only eleven thousand miles on it. He would not be a slave to money, to material things, and so paid off the twenty-year mortgage on the first house he ever owned in four and one half years.

He was a man who never told his son he was proud of him, who never once spoke to his son about feelings. His advice to his son was "never gamble and don't hang out with queers." He did once tell Fred Taylor, the basketball coach who had recruited his offspring, that he was "awful glad" Bob had gone to Ohio State since that meant he could come to all the games. (Their father believes that "Pat" Knight's grandsons, Tim and Pat, would not have managed very well with so stern a father as their grandfather was. He makes this point matter of factly, not as criticism, if perhaps implying that in needing praise, approval, affirmation they are softer than the generations which preceded them.) Out hunting one day, Pat Knight suffered a heart attack—a cardiogram confirmed the fact—one which did not prevent him from returning to work, where his wife and family friends descended upon him in a quixotic effort to bring him home.

But if Pat Knight could fend off this crew, he was no match for his strong-willed son, who immediately dismissed his mother and the neighbors. Then he proceeded, in no uncertain terms, to "blister" his father. In response, Pat Knight put on his hat, left the railway freight office, and got into the car—on the passenger side. As his son drove him to the hospital, he did not utter a word. He never worked again after that. He was sixty-four years old.

His wife, Hazel, was a schoolteacher, an old-fashioned schoolmarm who one day in the third grade paddled a pupil named Danny Markley hard with a ruler because he walked on grass where he shouldn't be walking. Once, her son remembers, she paddled him too, but he places his emphasis on that singular: once.

A month before she died, on New Year's Eve of 1987, a family friend remarked to Hazel that she hoped Bob would beat Kentucky. "I hope he behaves," returned Hazel Knight, then in her mid-eighties. She adored her only child, often letting him win at cards. She was so fiercely proud of this son that she once upbraided a friend for being too busy to take her child to a game. She would have taken her son herself.

Hazel Knight never learned to drive, but was dependent on her mother, Sarah Henthorne, who moved in with the Knights before Bob was born.

It was Grandma who taught Bob Knight to make his bed every morning, and it's Grandma's words Knight more often quotes today, as in, "Never tell a lie, then you don't have to remember what you said." It was she who took him to visit colleges, and baked strawberry shortcake for Fred Taylor out recruiting.

She died in her favorite chair. Having driven downtown that day, she had placed her hat and bag and gloves neatly on her bed. Always she was elegant; her hair was set in what they called "marcelled waves," and she would wear a matching suit and hat and gloves, always the most appropriate attire. It was she, this exemplary woman, everyone agreed, who provided the most physical affection to the boy, and whom Orrville people remember hugging his Grandma.

He was not popular with his peers, the child whose mother could not envision him with a broken heart. But beloved as he was by his parents, he was not showered with worldly goods. Through high school he wore khaki pants in which you put metal stretchers to form the crease.

He was different, gifted. He liked adults better than children. His mother was tough on him when she had him in her second-grade class, for much was expected of this unusual child. He was a fun-loving boy, who liked practical jokes. Willful, rambunctuous, at sixteen he watched his neighbor Pauline Boop working in her garden only to grab the garden hose and drench her. Caught at one of his pranks, he would grin sheepishly and blush.

If he was a good student, who could have been a better one had he tried, he also played sports—all sports, for in the world in which he grew up a boy would not do otherwise. It was a culture which at its best acknowledged no separation between mind and body, student and athlete. But sports fascinated him, and were his preference. The lessons he learned from all the coaches of his childhood are as real and alive for him today as they were on the day they were spoken.

So he will remember playing baseball in junior high only for the coach to admonish him for not leading off first base far enough.

"I was never very quick, so the lead I took was very short. This coach said to me, 'Bob, I want to tell you something. You can't steal second by keeping one foot on first.'" Sports becomes a paradigm for all of life, not only a metaphor for excellence, but also a training ground for learning how to cope, to mature, to excel.

As a youth, he must already have been articulate because his Grandma and his dad told him they wanted him to become a lawyer. His dad had said he couldn't understand why you had to go to college to become a coach. Bob Knight wasn't stuck for an answer to that one: "I couldn't understand why anyone as honest as my dad would ever want to admit that he had a son who was a lawyer."

There are light years between the speaker of that remark and the playing fields of Orrville. For in those words you meet the man of the world transplanted back to the heartland, the person who understands Kipling's definition of what it means to be a man, as one who "can bear to hear the truth you've spoken/twisted by knaves to make a trap for fools . . ."

To his constituency, Bob Knight brings news from elsewhere, a knowledge of the wider world in all its infamy. Through his basketball program he has shown them how the principles by which they have all been raised might yet defeat iniquity. That he bears the laurels, the national championships, garnered without cheating, testifies to the rightness and the longevity of these beliefs; that he aggressively and forcefully argues for these principles relieves the pressure of his constituency's thwarted desire to act at times more forcefully themselves. If they, mired in conformity, have eschewed risk-taking, he has not.

You listen to him and you see the warfare between the boy

from Orrville, raised to do "what was right," and the man whose credo is to do what's right, but only as he defines it.

In many ways, he is not a rebel. Too extreme a defiance meets a resurgence of the pull of Orrville. What was written in childhood cannot be erased, not by all the slogans from Patton to Vince Lombardi. The adult feels a loss of self-respect in violating the childhood norms. Too great a departure from what you have always known brings depression, or, perhaps, loneliness, a recklessness that allows you to cast all caution to the winds . . . to throw a chair, to refuse to leave a game after the third technical foul has been called, to use a phrase like "rape is inevitable," susceptible to misinterpretation and then, naively, to challenge a media celebrity not to use it.

You might think of him as Huckleberry Finn, who got stopped before he could light out for the territory. Before he could do anything about it, he got enrolled in high school, where he played sports. Very bright and increasingly savvy, he found himself coaching at West Point.

He's accepted his fate in civilization, but he remains that independent-minded, ornery boy. Every once in a while he goes too far in his orneriness. He may seem wild, even reckless, anything to protect himself from the taint of civilization, which has long since taken over small-town America. Boyish intransigence becomes his familiar weapon. No wonder that he enlists it in frequent patterns. It's all he has to protect himself from those cold nights out there on that precarious platform that he is destined never to escape half-way between the frontier and progress.

CHAPTER FOUR

THE LITANY

"No one ever knows when I'm happy or sad. I cry inside."

"LET'S JUST GO THROUGH the whole litany," Bob Knight said, offering what he had granted no reporter before me. He would even talk about Puerto Rico, a subject which for years he had refused to discuss. I was to assemble a list of every incident of his untoward behavior I could come up with, everything bad that had been written about him, with no restrictions. He would respond to each item.

"Talk to a lot of other people," he ordered. He planned no apologia for his own foibles, but an attempt at discovering what actually happened. It was another of those opportunities which "might be interesting."

*   *   *

They think they know him. He's the one who "scuffled with,"[1] "punched,"[2] "slapped,"[3] "hit,"[4] "slugged,"[5] and "assaulted"[6] a policeman during the 1979 Pan American games in Puerto Rico. Then, at the 1981 Final Four, after some uncomplimentary remarks were tossed his way, he "stuffed" a taunting LSU fan into a garbage can.

Four years later, in the process of losing to a hated rival, another Indiana team, he violently jeopardized life and limb of the players by throwing a chair onto the basketball court. And two years after that—if you believe what you read—incensed at losing to the Soviet National team, rabid right-winger that he is, he defiantly led his team right off the court and by so doing ended the game. He alone of coaches quarrels with officials; he alone is profane; in sum his behavior is worse than that of any basketball coach in America.

No wonder then that his players defect in droves, as the popular wisdom has it. In other programs the students never leave, only in his. And he abuses them. Wasn't it reported how he grabbed Steve Eyl by the jersey during a 1988 loss to Michigan, shoving him several feet down the bench? Sure, he's a legend out there on the edge of the frontier, in the heart of the country that's not even a swell place to visit. In Southern Indiana all they care about is basketball, so they like him because he'll do anything to win a basketball game.

This litany, with variations, is invariably chanted whenever Bob Knight's name is mentioned in print—which is often. Sometimes the frenzied effort to pour forth the litany results in an error. The Puerto Rican policeman may be dumped in the garbage can.[1] Knight, and not the NCAA, suspends Steve Alford for posing for a sorority calendar.[2] When Buddy Martin, a columnist for the Denver *Post*, is questioned about that statement, he replies that

1. *USA Today*, November 23, 1987

2. New York *Daily News*, November 24, 1987.

3. Washington *Post*, November 25, 1987.

4. Philadelphia *Daily News*, November 24, 1987.

5. Santa Barbara *News-Press*, June 30, 1987.

6. *Sporting News*, December 14, 1987.

1. New York *Times*, November 25, 1987.

2. Denver *Post*, April 1, 1987.

he read it in John Feinstein's *A Season on the Brink.* In fact, Feinstein accurately reports that the NCAA did the suspending. After the Russian incident, NBC is reported by several newspapers to be "reconsidering" whether they want to hire Knight as a commentator at the 1988 Olympic games.[3] In fact, Knight had already been offered the job and turned it down. The NBC producer was concealing his failure to garner Knight by suggesting that now they might not want him anyway!

Are hostile sportswriters motivated by malice? What accounts for so many deliberate attempts to smear Knight, lie about him at every turn? Certainly it seems that people are willing to go into print without checking the facts. One might even conclude that he was being treated as a resident scapegoat, a stock Satan destined forever to enliven the sports pages with his antics.

It's also true that having been burned too often, and over the years watching this litany proliferate and multiply, with the attendant inaccuracies, he is no longer accessible to most writers. When then neophyte sportswriter Ira Berkow traveled to Bloomington in 1981 to cover the story of Isiah Thomas's decision to turn pro after his sophomore year, Knight's distrust of the media was already in place. Berkow did not get in to see Bob Knight.

"What I am is really honest with them, and they don't like that," Knight says. Is he then alone among coaches in distrusting sportswriters? "What did you mean by *that?*" Temple coach John Chaney's friend Tony Penne demanded one day a few years ago. "Don't you run a three-guard offense?"

"That's what I tell *them!*" Chaney replied. And when a year later reporters began calling the Temple dorms at four A.M. in search of "the freshman," Mark Macon, Chaney refused them access to Macon for the rest of the season.

Less diplomatic than Chaney or former Marquette coach and now NBC commentator Al McGuire, Knight, with vestiges of the mischievous boy who turned the hose on his neighbor Pauline Boop, taunts his adversaries. "Like after the Olympic Gold Medal game. I pick out about three guys in the press, and I just did it intentionally. I said, 'Hey, why don't you guys come back here with me.' That just infuriates the others."

Knight is also happy to be proven wrong about a sportswriter's

3. New York *Daily News,* November 25, 1987. New York *Times,* December 1, 1987.

willingness to treat him fairly. Years ago Larry Merchant, then of the New York *Post,* just (to use Knight's term) "blistered" him. Knight tells what happened next:

"Then he became a TV guy. There was a crew from NBC to talk to me after we won the championship in 1976 relative to a show for 1977. I go downstairs and it's Larry Merchant! I just say to myself, 'I can't believe I'm doing this.' But I went ahead and did it. He says something and I say, 'Larry, have you ever seen us play this year?' He says, 'No.' 'Have you ever been to one of our practices?' 'No.' 'Then I don't know how you could make a comment like that.'

"I know this will be edited out of it. But it wasn't. I called him later and I told him, 'That was really good that you would leave that in.'

" 'Well,' he said. 'I was wrong.' "

Merchant at once became one of the writers with easy access to Bob Knight.

Nor was this an isolated occurrence. An "undisciplined disciplinarian . . . a coach who orders haircuts while throwing furniture," wrote Tom Callahan in Time magazine.[1]

But two years later, writing about the 1987 tournament, Callahan referred to the litany by invoking Puerto Rico. He wrote: "The officer's story collapses when he swears that Knight called him a 'nigger.' Any other vile expression would be eminently believable. But a legion of young black men can testify that Knight does not think in those terms."[2]

It isn't that Callahan's article was an all-out rave. He also wrote that had Knight played more at Ohio State, "basketball might be a little seemlier today." Judging from Feinstein's book, Callahan adds, "He may be the most profane coach in history." And he concludes that Knight "doesn't have the restraint born of good taste. It's the way he defines himself as a man."

Yet Knight was gratified by that column. A month later he ran into Callahan at the Kentucky Derby.

"Hey, Callahan, what the hell's wrong with you? What's with the article in Time magazine on the NCAAs? That's the best thing I've ever seen anybody write about Puerto Rico and about the only accurate thing. You're a lot friendlier to me lately."

1. Time, March 18, 1985.

2. Time, April 13, 1987.

"Maybe one or the other of us has grown up."

"I think you have more growing up to do than I do," says the coach.

Then he adds, "Why don't you come to Bloomington?"

Callahan has not been "converted." But Knight so appreciates even the single note of fairness that at once he opens the doors to the Indiana basketball program.

For good or ill, sports remains one of the few arenas of experience where there remain leaders, and hence followers, heroes and villains. There are those whom many agree are sportsmanlike people: Larry Bird and Earvin Johnson, for example. And there are unsportsmanlike people, drug users, people who violate the law, coaches who cheat and solicit students to cheat, or who look the other way while others are bribing students on their behalf.

Yet although most writers grudgingly grant that Knight runs what they call a "clean" program, he has overwhelmingly been pilloried in the press, while writers only occasionally report on the endemic cheating in college basketball. Only the Lexington *Herald-Leader* has distinguished itself through its vigilance on this issue.

It may be that, insecure about being relegated to the "toy department" of their newspapers, many sportswriters become uneasy with the notion of the leader who takes command. Admiring a hero who rules by dictatorial methods seems to exclude them from the ranks of intellectuals; it seems unworldly. Yet sports each day brings its heroes, those who excel above others. Sportswriters may compensate for this contradiction by postulating a demonology, villains whom they can criticize, whose very existence reveals that they as writers care more about the real questions than they do about the day's scores.

Paradoxically, they choose their villains not on moral criteria, but on more superficial grounds. Knight's aggressive style offends them. He has attacked them for not knowing the game as well as he does; he has refused many of them access; and they have used their pens to retaliate. Were this not true, surely there would not be so many inaccuracies in the reporting about him. The desire to attack him sometimes outweighs their commitment to accurate reporting. Occasionally a newspaper will retract, as the New York *Times* did after readers were told that Knight threw the

Puerto Rican policeman into the garbage can. More often errors are allowed to stand.

The truth about the press's treatment of Knight becomes apparent when we compare how the events in Puerto Rico were reported—and continue to be reported—with what actually happened.

II

"You do whatever you think you should do."

When he arrived in San Juan with his well-drilled players, Knight agreed to a scrimmage with the Puerto Rican team as a courtesy. Bill Wall, representing amateur athletics for the United States, suggested it. Knight complied, although he rarely practices with a team he will later play in competition.

Afterward, Knight conducted a clinic sponsored by Converse, during which he remarked, "I'm not here to pimp for Converse." He meant, obviously, that he was not there to sell anyone anything. At once the local press labeled him a "racist," suggesting the mood of Puerto Rico—and all of Latin America—that summer.

While the Puerto Rican movement for independence had been waning, there was enormous anti-American sentiment that summer. It was fueled by the brutalities of Somoza's last two months in power, which many saw as fostered and made possible by the North Americans. Anti-American feeling ran high, especially after the June insurrection in Masaya; even General Torrijos of Panama, to whom Jimmy Carter had signed over the Panama Canal, was engaging in strong anti-American rhetoric. There were large demonstrations throughout the Latin American continent on behalf of the resurgent Sandinistas, who would defeat Somoza at last five days after Bob Knight's departure from San Juan.

Because he was highly visible, outspoken and perceived as an American patriot, Bob Knight was a likely candidate on whom Puerto Rican sympathizers with the Latin American revolution could vent their political outrage. It began from the opening ceremonies when American flags were burned, and would last until the conclusion of the championship game.

Accompanying Knight as his assistants were Fred Taylor, who came out of retirement to be "delegation manager," and Mike Krzyzewski, currently the coach at Duke, once Knight's player at West Point and his assistant at Indiana, and at that time the head coach at Army.

In his first game, against the Virgin Islands, with the United States thirty-five points ahead, Knight protested a blatantly bad call. He had thought to himself: the players were letting the officiating affect their play (they had been assessed thirty first-half fouls!). Why not draw a technical to illustrate to the students how futile worrying about calls would be on their part?

When the officials seemed to change their minds about what the call was (they had first called a charging foul), Knight found himself asking for an explanation in English to a Spanish-speaking referee near the Virgin Islands' bench. He had passed the center line that serves in international play as a limit. For this, he was assessed a second technical, which meant expulsion. Hardly exemplary, the officiating was so sloppy that in the confusion the Virgin Islands team never shot a single free throw for his transgressions.

After the game, Knight conducted a press conference out in the rainy parking lot, where he joked about how the cool night air was superior to the steamy arena. The incident did not seem unusual, until the International Amateur Basketball Federation demanded that Knight appear before them the next morning.

There he was told that the technical foul and the expulsion amounted to strikes against him; a third transgression would mean a sanction against him or his team. In retrospect, it seems obvious that those in charge of the games on behalf of international basketball were already reacting to the prevailing mood of anti-Americanism in San Juan that July. While the Latin coaches would put on fiery displays of temper on the sidelines, abusing officials and receiving their share of technicals, it was Knight who was warned about expulsion from the tournament; it was the Americans who were told that their behavior had to be "exemplary."

In the press Knight at once became "temperamental" and "controversial," although in the first week of Pan Am play Knight was not the only coach ejected from games—two others were, also.

The next "incident" came in a game against Brazil. With the

United States out to a fifteen-point lead, a pass came to high
school star and Indiana freshman-to-be Isiah Thomas. Thomas
put out one hand and the ball went off his hand out of bounds—a
turnover. Although he had not yet played for Indiana, he had been
at Bloomington with the rest of the team since May, about thirty-
five days of practice. He should have known better. Knight yelled
at him, as all the players would be yelled at during those games,
Kevin McHale no less than eighteen-year-old Isiah.

Shortly after the turnover, Isiah got the ball on a fast break
and raced down the open floor for a dunk. He missed the dunk.
Meanwhile, coming right behind him had been Mike Woodson
and Michael Brooks, two of the best offensive players in the
tournament. Isiah should have dished it off to either of them—or
laid it up. The failed dunk did not endear Isiah to the coach, no
matter that the United States was leading by fourteen points at
the time.

Before the half, Isiah was still in the game, but Brazil had gone
ahead 38–36. The United States tied the game with less than a
minute to play. Then, just before the buzzer, Brazil got the ball.
One of their players was about to throw up a desperation shot
from twenty-five feet out. There were two seconds left on the
clock. Michael Brooks had his hands up, making the shot even
more difficult when, suddenly, just as the shooter was cocked to
fire, Isiah came up behind him and slapped him from behind,
giving him a two-shot foul. While the Brazilian player made the
two foul shots, Isiah was called over to the side and given the
most bristling lecture of his life. To drive the point home, Knight
benched him for the rest of the game.

The Americans won the game 82–78, but not easily. The Brazilian coach rose from his seat seventeen times to scream at the
officials. But the press wrote only about Knight's "vicious treatment of a high school student." What Knight had seen was a high
school player with bad habits, one about to join his Indiana team
and whose instruction couldn't begin too soon. He wanted to
make it clear he would not tolerate such play. "He got on me
because I was wrong," Isiah said afterward. "And that's the way
you learn. And that's why he's the coach."

"I didn't yell at him that much, did I? What do you think?"
Knight asked a friend later.

"Well," he was told, "I'd put it in the top five."

(In fact, even now, with Isiah Thomas, one of the most successful professional basketball players in the country, Knight occasionally feels the impulse to coach him, to make him better. "We used to play Isiah Thomas in the post," he'll say, "because he was far better in the post than the guy guarding him was defensively. Invariably. I'd play him in the post with the Pistons a little bit just to keep him from throwing the ball away." When Isiah dribbles too much, Knight itches to correct him.)

By Sunday July 8, the games were half over. Having squeaked by Panama, the American team remained unbeaten going into the championship round.

Five minutes before their alloted time at ten in the morning, the American team bus pulled up for practice at Espiritu Santo High School gym. A policeman stationed at the door named Jose Silva told them, "You can't come into the gym until ten!"

"That's fine," said Mike Krzyzewski, "just let us know." It was clear at once that the policeman was bent on asserting his authority. The players were kept on the bus until just before ten.

At ten, practice began, interrupted a short time later by the Canadian women's team chattering as they left the gym. Although the American team was preparing for its game with Canada, no one complained. Knight was putting them through a customary combination of practice and walk-through.

Between 10:45 and 10:50, the Brazilian women's team entered the gym at the far end from where the Americans were now seated on the floor. The players had their notebooks open, and were taking notes from Knight on their match-ups and other details of the game plan. The noise of the Brazilian women talking and laughing became loud and the team could barely hear what Knight was saying. It was clear that the Brazilian women's team had not been required to wait outside, as the US team had been.

"You are either going to have to get them to be quiet or get them the hell out of here," Knight called over to the coach of the Brazilian women's team.

The laughing and talking only increased in intensity.

Krzyzewski went over to the scene of the disturbance. In his calm and controlled manner, he said: "Could you please keep quiet?"

"Hey, man, this is my gym. When you're in Puerto Rico, you do as I say," said Jose Silva in English. "They can come in. They've got a right to be in here. They stay here because I say they stay here."

"You wouldn't allow us in. Now you're allowing them in," Krzyzewski said indignantly.

"What the hell's going on down there?" Knight wanted to know. And now he got up and walked to mid-court, where Silva and Krzyzewski were standing. The American players were sitting against a stage on the baseline forty feet away.

"Who gave you the right to tell these people to leave the gym?" Silva demanded of Knight, shaking his finger in Knight's face. "You don't run this gym. I'm in control. What I say goes." To assert his authority, he stepped closer to his much-taller adversary, who weighed at least sixty pounds more than he did. Three, then four times, Silva shook his finger in Knight's face in a series of stabbing motions. The shaking finger stretched closer, shook again, closer, closer-until Silva poked Knight hard directly in the right eye.

Stunned, Knight ducked his head and raised his left hand, as if to protect himself, to push the policeman's hand aside. Unintentionally, he placed his open hand on Silva's right cheek and gave him a slight shove. It wasn't a smack, let alone a punch, a slug, a hit or an assault. The heel of Knight's hand rested briefly on the fleshy part of Silva's cheek at his chin.

It was a small gesture, a reflex of self-defense, but Silva interpreted it as a blow to his authority, to his very manhood. In rage, he grabbed Knight's arm.

Knight jerked his arm away. "Get your hands off me," he said, and as Krzyzewski stepped between them, Silva, by now out of control, shouted, "You're under arrest!" Again he tried to grab Knight's arm and again Knight jerked his arm away.

"You hit me! This isn't the United States. This is Puerto Rico. You hit a policeman! You're under arrest!" Silva shouted.

"I didn't hit you," said Knight quietly.

Obviously taking advantage of the moment of quiet reason, of his adversary's calm, Silva ordered Knight to the parking lot outside the gym, where he removed his hat and took a nightstick from an unmarked car. Then he touched Knight's nose twice with the nightstick.

"Goddamn you, brother, this is what I'd like to use on you. You want me to use this on you, don't you?"

"You do whatever you think you should do," Knight said.

Raising the club, Silva taunted Knight again, "You just want me to hit you, don't you?"

"You do whatever you think you should do," Knight repeated.

What Silva did was handcuff Knight and put him in the squad car. Then Silva took out a notebook and began speaking to a few Puerto Ricans at the gym entrance. Knight took the opportunity to ask the driver where they were headed and the driver obliged with the address. "Get moving on this," Knight told Krzyzewski as he gave him the address. "Something bad is going to happen."

Silva returned in time to push Fred Taylor away as Taylor tried to get into the car with them. And off they sped to a jail in Hato Rey.

Team captain Mike Woodson said, "Maybe someone better follow the squad car. No one knows what they'll do." Mike Krzyzewski and Fred Taylor did just that, while the players returned to the village in their bus.

That afternoon the charges were dropped. But in the evening Knight was arrested again. Puerto Rico had brought no charges, but Silva had appeared to bring a civil charge against Knight for "aggravated assault," claiming there was a hematoma—a bruise—on his cheek. Two days later he insisted that Knight had hit him on the jaw after he reprimanded Knight for calling the Brazilian women's team "dirty whores" because they made too much noise. He had asked Knight his name to report him to the Pan American games organizing committee, and as he was writing down the name, Knight hauled off and slugged him. (Under oath on August 22 Silva would testify that when he grabbed Knight by the elbow to arrest him, Knight said, "Take your dirty hands off me, nigger.") Now Silva said he had a broken jaw and had to take a leave of absence from his job. He denied that he had ever touched Knight.

That Knight's entire team, in addition to Krzyzewski and Taylor, were witnesses and heard exactly what he said didn't deter Silva from concocting this story. The entire team would later deny that Knight had used racial epithets. It is unlikely that the eight black players would have kept silent.

Knight countercharged, the evidence of his reddened eye obvious and documented by Dr. Tony Daly, head of the Pan American medical group, as a corneal abrasion. But the judge dismissed Knight's complaint, while allowing Silva's to stand (and, even then, Silva's charge only involved a misdemeanor). Meanwhile a trial was set for Friday morning, July 13, with the championship game—which would turn out to be the United States against Puerto Rico—to take place that same night.

During those tension-filled days, Angel David Gonzalez, president of the San Juan Policemen's Benevolent Association, met with the press on Silva's behalf. "We feel there is a reality in this case," he confided, "and that is that there has been a violation of the law. There is a dignity of the policeman's uniform." It was not only Silva as an individual who had come to accuse Knight.

"I've given him all the resources of our organization," Gonzalez revealed. Should the district attorney not charge Knight, he already had plans for the legal division of the Policemen's Benevolent Association to submit the case on behalf of its members in their own right as private citizens.

And his plan, he admitted, was not to have Knight jailed, but to "get the man fired for moral turpitude." Relieved of the misapprehension that Knight was the permanent national coach, Gonzalez corrected himself. He would get Knight fired "here. He will not coach any of *these* games."

It was Wednesday and Silva's wife told anyone who would listen that she had to give her husband food "he doesn't have to chew very much." A doctor had filed a paper that Silva had suffered a "hematoma." Angel L. Tapia, president of the Puerto Rico Bar Association, told reporters that Silva had applied for state insurance benefits.

"It's almost like we're in the middle of a dime-store novel," Fred Taylor said. Meanwhile the Americans proceeded through the games but were unable to practice. Knight worked out plans for the game with Argentina in the police parking lot.

It would appear that Knight's behavior was indeed rather exemplary, that in fact, nothing happened! Why then are we wordlessly treated to Puerto Rico and the litany, and the endless resurrection of the story of Knight slugging the Puerto Rican policeman?

One reason certainly is that the US Olympic Committee would not allow Knight to talk to the press for two days after the incident. The only information available came from Silva and his allies. The American officials were so anxious to avoid charges of "ugly Americanism" that they eschewed not only common sense, but integrity in the process.

Whether or not Silva was influenced by a radical pro-Independence group bent on creating confusion and fanning anti-American sentiment, it seems obvious that the American officials played right into their hands by refusing to allow Knight to tell his story. And fan the flames the local press did.

The atmosphere was now about to turn even uglier. On Tuesday, during a game with the Cubans, with scarcely three minutes left and the Americans out in front, a Cuban guard named Tomas Herrera, twenty-eight years old, walked up to Kyle Macy and, entirely without provocation, hit him in the jaw with a sneak punch. The ball was on the other side of the court; the incident had nothing whatever to do with play.

Herrera then walked over to the Cuban bench and sat down, as if anticipating his punishment. Ultimately he was thrown out of the game, although given his action he could have been charged with criminal assault.

Groggy, Macy had dropped to his knees. He managed to play for another minute and then left the game. He sat on the bench holding an ice pack. In fact, his jaw had been fractured.

A starting guard, Macy had to fly home for medical treatment the next day. No one raised the cry of "Ugly Cubans," nor should they have denigrated the entire country for the unsportsmanlike behavior of one player. But the incident suggests up that once more, large and small, the Americans were being treated as fair game.

By now the Americans were unified against adversity by now. At a team meeting after the incident with Silva, Knight told his players to vote on whether to leave or to stay for the remainder of the games. It was clear that the opponent in the final would be Puerto Rico. Knight suggested that maybe they should all just go home. They didn't have to stay; he wasn't going to make them stay.

After the first count, half the players voted to leave and half to remain. But Kevin McHale and Michael Brooks argued that they had worked so hard during training, as well as having played in a tournament in Italy, that they wanted that gold medal. Mike Woodson, Knight's own Indiana player, agreed. A few others changed their votes then.

As for Silva's suit, there were those who still couldn't bring themselves to take it seriously, like Fred Taylor, who asked Knight every day what color shirt he would be wearing, red, white or blue.

"What the hell difference does it make what color shirt I wear?" Knight finally demanded.

"I just want to wear a different color from you. I don't want anyone remotely to connect us."

Taylor was obviously defusing tension because there were threats. On Wednesday, Knight moved the team to a downtown hotel, using the money he had raised at the practice games. The team had been placed on a high floor in a building without air conditioning.

At this hotel on the night before the final game, two men came up to Michael Woodson and threatened: "We have guns. If the game is close, we're going to shoot down onto the floor."

This remark was sufficient to frighten college students, if not the wry Taylor, who told Knight, "If they throw a grenade, don't expect me to use my body to cover you."

In terms of politics and power, public opinion and the press, the Americans had become the underdogs.

On the morning of Friday, July 13, the judge granted a continuance, postponing the trial. Knight's own Puerto Rican attorney chimed in with, "It's the responsibility of all of us to be prepared for tonight's game—which Puerto Rico is going to win!"

The San Juan *Star* in the morning's paper called Knight "an international embarrassment to his country," his actions "inconsiderate, rude and not a little uncivilized." It called Knight's contention that the case against him was built on lies and anti-Americanism "an act either of abysmal ignorance or acute paranoia." Yet Knight's contention was true.

The championship game against Puerto Rico was billed as the greatest sporting event in the island's history.

Thirteen thousand people crammed into the ninety-six-hundred-seat Roberto Clemente Coliseum. Four hours before game time, people were jammed in everywhere, right up to the out-of-bounds lines on the court. Hard liquor was sold. Leading his team out onto the floor, the captain of the Puerto Ricans unfurled a gigantic Puerto Rican flag, which the crowd greeted by waving thousands of little flags of their own.

It seemed, however, that the Americans would have no trouble. They jumped to a 12-point lead and by the half were ahead 54–39. Then, in the second half, Puerto Rico began to catch up and after two free throws, with 9:35 left, the lead had melted to 73–70. At this point Knight called a time-out.

In the huddle, Knight grabbed Mike Woodson by the front of his jersey, startling him. He had played for Knight for three years and he had never been grabbed like that.

"What the hell's going on?" Knight yelled, seemingly in a rage against Woodson. "Get those guys together!"

Furious himself, but also stung, Woodson began to holler at his teammates. The hysteria of the crowd faded from his mind. All he cared about was never, not ever again being grabbed by Knight like that. The players returned to the floor, a team possessed.

Fear of Knight had released them from fear of the violent, hostile crowd. Cleverly, Knight had chosen as his scapegoat his own player, Woodson, on whose reactions he could rely. It was a stroke of genius. The American players reached back into themselves, instantly transcending everything that had come before—the vicious press, the Cuban who had fractured Kyle Macy's jaw, and now the hostile drunken crowd. Knight was simply being Knight, the man of action for whom passivity is anathema.

Racing back onto the floor, eighteen-year-old Isiah Thomas took an out-of-bounds pass on the fly. He bolted to the basket, got the basket, drew a free throw and sank it. It was the biggest single play of the game. Isiah then hit Michael Brooks for a three-point play and Woodson came up with the third three-point play in a row.

In four minutes Isiah Thomas had three baskets, two assists and a blocked shot, and the lead had jumped back up to 82–72. Later, Woodson would express his pride in baby Isiah, who had a 21-point, 5-steal, 4-assist game. "Isiah played his ass off," Woodson declared.

Refusing to permit his own jeopardy to interfere with his responsibility, Knight led the Americans to victory, as they say in sports, "going away." The final score was 113–94. (Their average age, twenty, the Americans had won nine games, each by an average of 21.2 points against older, more physically mature opponents.)

Remembering the threats, the players were worried as they lifted an elated Knight into the air, an easy target for a sniper. Again Knight was booed, lustily and long. He responded by raising a triumphal fist, which became an index finger, which, he explained later, stood for being number one.

After the medals were presented, Knight was accompanied back to his car by the policemen who had been assigned to protect him. He opened the trunk and to their delight presented them with all the T-shirts, pins and medals he had left. At the same time the superintendent of police in Puerto Rico apologized, expressing his regret for what had happened.

With some of the players still shaken by the crowd's hostility, the team raced out to their bus as soon as they could. Mike Woodson remembers the crowd erupting, and the police using their clubs on the unruly. The team returned by bus to spend their last night not at the hotel, but back in the village with the other athletes.

"Do you want to know my appraisal?" Indianapolis lawyer Clarence Doninger, representing Knight, said. "We better get the hell out of here! Silva now has as many witnesses as you and it's a Puerto Rican judge."

The next morning, Bastille Day, Knight flew back to America. On August 22 he was tried in absentia, having forfeited his constitutional rights by "escaping."

At the "trial" Silva again told the story of how Knight had slugged him as he wrote on his pad. There were no witnesses for Knight, except the policeman at the Hato Rey station, who, of course, had not witnessed the event. Knight was convicted of charges of "aggravated assault," and was sentenced to nine months in prison and a fine of one thousand dollars, although the maximum penalty for a misdemeanor—which this was—is six months and five hundred dollars!

On the morning of the conviction, F. Don Miller, executive director of the United States Olympic Committee, immediately characterized the conviction as "blatant, outrageous, and unwarranted." Two weeks later Charles Neinas, chairman of the American Basketball Association, USA games committee, personally supported Knight's decision not to return to Puerto Rico.

From this reconstruction of events, Knight emerges as hero, the leader who rallies his team under adversity to defeat not only another team, but the forces of iniquity and injustice. Yet even those writers who admit that the events happened as the American team insists believe Knight's cause was injured by his comments at the heady moment of victory. John Papanek in Sports Illustrated points to Knight's remark: "Their basketball is a hell of a lot easier to beat than their court system. The only thing they know how to do is grow bananas . . . I didn't have any friends in Puerto Rico when I came here, so I don't have any fewer when I leave."[1]

Given what Knight had been put through, let alone how the incident has been distorted for a decade since, Knight's remarks seem, if undiplomatic, incommensurate with the injustice he had suffered.

The press coverage, both during the events and later, distressed Mike Krzyzewski: "Finally, when we did have a press conference a few days later, and we told our version," Krzyzewski was shocked to discover, "it was we who were the ones who were lying. I graduated from West Point. I was coaching at West Point. The one thing I don't do is lie. I don't lie. I'm not going to lie for Coach Knight. We're very close friends, but I would never lie for him. I've never lied for anybody. When we had the press conference, I thought truth and justice would come out and they [the press] would rally around us. Forget it . . ."

In September, Knight wrote a letter to Puerto Rican Governor Carlos Romero-Barcelo in an attempt to clarify events, which were continuing to be distorted in the press. Knight refers to comments he made "with a humorous intent . . . as well as some things said in the heat of the moment after the game that I should not have said." In this apology he makes reference as well to "several statements of an inflammatory nature attributed to me that I just simply did not make." The remarks he did make were meant for those involved in the incident.

In this letter, Knight speaks of his experience in Puerto Rico as

1. July 23, 1979.

a positive one and declares that he never had any intention to offend "a warm and friendly people." And he offers "most sincere apologies" if anything "I have done or said has been interpreted as being offensive to the people of Puerto Rico." That Romero-Barcelo did not have the matter dropped then and there, and allow Knight to pay the fine, may only be attributed to his own political agenda.

No matter where the facts lay, however. For most of the American press committed to the fable that had already seen its way into print, retraction or clarification might have seemed a blight on their original reporting, a doubt cast on their tough-mindedness, on their very manhood. By the time the Olympic Committee allowed Knight to speak to the press, the "facts" had been writ in stone. The slugging of the Puerto Rican policeman, no matter that it had never happened, had entered the litany, that series of tales about Bob Knight that seem destined for immortality.

III

"I think I anticipate the consequences and then I let my sense of saying exactly what I think run away with my ability to anticipate . . . at that point I think that the son of a bitch is wrong, that's unfair, that's unjust, that's not the way it should be, and goddamn it, I'm going to tell him."

"Sometimes I regret it when the chair's half-way across the floor."

Rarely do the chanters of the litany forget either "the chair" or the "stuffing" of the Louisiana State University fan into the garbage can.

"No excuse," Knight says of the occasion when, protesting a foul early in a game against Purdue, he picked up the orange plastic chair on which he had been sitting and sent it across the court.

Most of the litanies make it sound as if he threw the chair at someone or in the direction of someone, neither of which is true.

Or that he threw it so violently that you couldn't be certain where it would land, or whom it would hit, also untrue. He picked up the chair at its bottom and sent it spinning. It skittered across the court. There was no one in its path, either along the way or at its ultimate destination. It was certainly not a sportsmanlike thing to do, but hardly was it the wild act portrayed endlessly thereafter.

Jim Crews, a Knight assistant coach at the time, argues that Knight's throwing the chair was a form of communication to his team, a calculated act. The floor was empty as the Purdue player was about to take his free throw. Knight turned around and stood facing his chair, his back to the court. He said nothing. Then, slowly, he lifted the chair and with a flick of the wrist sent it lightly across the court. His intention, as Crews interpreted it, was to bring his team together, even at his own expense. The score was 11–6, with fifteen minutes remaining in the first half, so he couldn't have been very angry at the officials yet. But he might have been communicating his disgust with a team whose play, as the season would reveal, was unworthy of the effort their coaches had been making.

Mention of the chair is usually followed by the incident in which Knight supposedly "stuffed" a supporter of the LSU basketball team into a garbage can. "Bouncing the Bayou Bengal loyalist into a trashcan," Bill Conlin writes in the Philadelphia *Daily News*.[1] Reporting on the 1987 NCAA tournament for Sports Illustrated, Curry Kirkpatrick reminds us that the LSU "loyalists" "hadn't forgotten the 1981 Final Four, when the Indiana coach slammed the LSU fan into a trash can."

For Knight, the Final Four has served as a reunion for old friends (particularly the fourteen of his former assistants who at the start of the 1987 season were head coaches elsewhere). On the particular Saturday afternoon in question, Indiana had defeated LSU to advance to the finals. A group was on its way through the bar to the special area of the restaurant set aside for them. In the group were Knight, Mike Krzyzewski, Ed Gottlieb, who had been the manager of Knight's Ohio State basketball team, and Ralph Floyd, Indiana's athletic director.

For two days LSU fans, staying at the same hotel where the Indiana players were staying, chanted their favorite slogan. Or

1. November 24, 1987.

they would walk through the lobby and yell in the students' faces: "Tiger bait! Tiger bait!" When the Indiana players went for their team walk after the pre-game meal, there was an LSU contingent calling after them, "Tiger bait! Tiger bait!" Knight said nothing, did nothing—other than defeat LSU that afternoon.

Witnesses are unanimous about what happened, so it might be best to hear Knight's version. The scene is the bar beside which stood an empty trash can with a plastic liner used to hold ice, but at this time empty. As Knight attempted to pass, an LSU supporter had a few words for the Indiana coach:

> *"The fan is standing. He's got on a purple T-shirt with all sorts of buttons and emblems and bullshit. With a drink in each hand, he conversationally says, 'Nice game, Coach.'*
>
> *" 'Yep, yep, we weren't tiger bait after all, were we?'*
>
> *"Just as conversationally and I just kept right on going. And the guy screams, 'You're an asshole, Knight, you're an asshole!'*
>
> *"And with that I went back to the guy, and I said, 'You know, you people can walk around here just sticking it to our kids for two days with all this 'here comes tiger bait,' and then we beat your ass and it seems that you can't handle that. What's wrong with you people?'*
>
> *" 'Well, you're still an asshole.'*
>
> *"I just took the guy by the shoulders and with the heels of my hands I shoved him back up against the wall. He hit the wall and he just slid down. On the way down he hit an ashcan that spilled over on top of him."*

Knight grabbed the man by the shirt front, pushed him against the wall, and then abruptly let go so that the man slid and staggered sideways. On his way down, the empty garbage can fell on top of him. No damage having been done, Knight and his group proceeded to the restaurant, where dinner was already in progress. Happily seated at his table, Jim Crews heard the commotion, figured it was exactly what he had predicted, and went on eating his soup.

Knight did indeed grab the drunk and thrust him out of the way. "I'm an activist," he says.

In fact, most of the time when Knight is harassed in this manner, he does not retaliate. At a Michigan game three years ago, Indiana was one point ahead at the buzzer when Michigan put up a twenty-five foot (then) two-point shot and it went through.

Knight sank back into his seat with his head down as the Michigan crowd exploded. Suddenly a fan walked right up to him and began to scream obscenities in his face. Knight looked up, then rose and walked away.

During the 1987 regional final in Cincinnati against, again, LSU, a spectator stuck his pom-pom in Knight's face each time he passed. At the Duke game and then at the LSU, Knight silently endured abuse from the stands. Whenever he passed the spot, the same thing happened. Finally, at halftime during the LSU-Indiana game, the fan got closer and took a swipe at Knight with the pom-pom stick. Indiana team doctor Brad Bomba, following Knight, grabbed the pom-pom and reported the fan to a policeman. Bomba didn't hear Knight say anything in reply to the obscenities that rained down on him from the stands. But Knight does remember:

"I haven't said a word. The eighth time that I go through there, I look up and say, 'Hey, why don't all you people take those pom-poms and just stick 'em up your ass!' "

At the press conference after the game, talking about whether the final basket would count, Knight said, "I watched the officials and as soon as those sons of bitches left the floor, boy, I was right with them." Later he was asked to explain to the NCAA tournament committee why he had "cursed the officials." His reply to this suggestion is in keeping with its absurdity: "Hey, you and I may choose different pronouns . . . in my language 'son of a bitch' is a pronoun!"

(It's one he'll use with no small amount of creativity. Teaching students to look for good shots, to pass the ball, he says, "Ricky, the son of a bitch won't go off. Have you ever all the time you've been here heard the son of a bitch go off?" The "son of a bitch" in question is, of course, the 45-second clock.)

Profanity often appears on the litany of sins, but in fact Knight uses it in its strongest manifestations rarely. Nor, probably, are there many coaches who choose never to address players in the language they themselves use. "I use 'choice words' when I'm talking to my players about drugs," Bob Wade, the Maryland coach said one day on national television.[1] Indeed profanity as a tool of persuasion is useful because, irreverent, it demands

1. ABC-TV News, January 6, 1988.

attention; its defiance of the norms of language evokes a similar emotion in those who hear it.

Another item that turns up in the litany involves Joe B. Hall, former Kentucky coach. The bare facts are these: Knight slapped Hall on the head during a heated exchange at courtside. A Kentucky assistant rose from the bench and demanded combat with Knight over this injustice.

What happened is somewhat different.

In a game against Kentucky, Indiana was way ahead, once by as much as thirty-four points. The incident occurred toward the end of the game. Indiana's substitutes, who had been in for some time, were now playing very badly, and the lead was shrinking. Steve Ahlfeld was then called for a foul.

"All right, Steve, that's all right," Knight called out.

"Way to go, Bobby," yelled a Kentucky assistant named Lynn Nance.

"Why don't you guys coach your end and I'll coach my end," Knight shouted and walked back to the Indiana bench.

At once Hall got up and walked over to the scorer's table and the two coaches met at center court. By now both were smiling.

"Let's get this game over with so you can get home and I can get home and we can get on to the next game," Knight said. And he reached over and hit Hall on the back of the head, as he will one of his players or a friend. Perhaps he hit him a little harder than he meant to because Hall was jolted a bit and his glasses moved, but both men remained smiling.

On the Kentucky bench Nance now popped up from his seat and called, "Do that to me, Bobby," and the press had its story.

The incident might have ended there had Hall told the reporters that Knight didn't mean anything, that Knight had been kind to him. Knight had recently praised Hall on national television for the fine job he was doing, having taken over from the legendary Adolph Rupp.

But instead, following Indiana's victory over Kentucky that day, Hall let the incident build so that it joined the litany, his motives for doing so unclear.

"If it was meant to be malicious," Knight says, "I would have blasted him into the seats."

But in the insular world of college basketball we find little evidence of the fellowship of coaches. LSU coach Dale Brown in a national magazine uses language fit for Idi Amin, Pinochet or Jaruzelski in a grotesque, unmotivated attack on Knight, to which Knight did not reply: ("What he *really* is," Brown declares, "is a despicable human being . . . who the hell appointed the self-righteous son-of-a-bitch judge anyway? Who is he, Barabbas?"[1]) Florida coach Norm Sloan charges Knight with misusing his influence to further his own recruiting during the tryouts for the 1987 World University Games. According to Sloan, Knight, without justification, arranged tryouts for Todd Jadlow and two potential recruits, George Ackles (who ultimately chose Nevada/Las Vegas) and John White. "Let me tell you," Sloan told whomever would listen, "there are a lot of different ways to cheat."[2] Meanwhile Sloan's own Florida player, Vernon Maxwell, failed the drug test during those tryouts.

In 1979, ironically, the press had chastised Knight for dismissing three students from the team for smoking marijuana during the team trip to Alaska for the Great Alaska Shootout. Counterculture sympathies among the press had Knight the "volatile adolescent" out of touch with contemporary youth, contemporary problems.

Out of fashion though it might be, Knight took the matter seriously. He questioned each student individually and discovered that there were eight students involved. Then he called each parent, told them what he had learned and received their support for what he planned to do. Cox, Roberson and Baker were dropped from the team; the other five were put on probation for the remainder of their stay at Indiana.

When David Israel, then of the Chicago *Daily News,* defended Knight, pointing out that most coaches were looking the other way on the drug issue, they became good friends, Israel's long hair and blue jeans notwithstanding.

For those who would perpetuate the litany still, it might be instructive to remember how another coach handled his team infected with a drug problem. When Rollie Massimino of Villanova heard reports about Gary McLain's drug taking, and by no

1. Sport, February 1988.

2. *The Sporting News,* June 22, 1987.

means were either the rumors or the facts confined to McLain alone, he chose not to pursue them. According to McLain, and he is supported in this by his high school coach Bill Donlon, Donlon warned Massimino during his very recruiting visit that McLain had already been caught with drugs.

Nonetheless McLain was recruited by Villanova. Later, when Massimino heard rumors of McLain's taking cocaine, he did nothing: "He had me in his office," McLain writes in Sports Illustrated,[1] "and he said 'I hear you're on cocaine or selling it. If I find out, you're gone.' " There was no urinalysis, only several more confrontations, concluding again with no consequences to McClain other than Massimino's saying, 'If I hear it again . . .'" Neither Massimino nor anyone at Villanova has disputed McLain's story, which Sports Illustrated courageously reported. With McLain, Massimino went on to win his national championship. Following his own 1979 problem with marijuana-smoking players, Knight went on to win only the NIT. He had to wait until 1981 for another national championship, but he did it without the marijuana smokers. Some may insist that Knight cares only about winning. In fact, in any conflict between winning and a principle that affects the moral development of his students, winning comes in a distant second.

If there is a common denominator in the litany where Knight would have been wiser to ignore a provocation, it is in his impulse always to teach someone a lesson. From anyone, strangers no less than players or assistant coaches, he will invariably demand acceptable behavior, whatever the circumstances.

One day Knight and then dean of the Indiana University Law School, Harry Pratter, were driving onto Kirkwood Avenue in Bloomington, traveling at about five miles an hour. At the same time a student on a bicycle was approaching the intersection. The student stopped; Knight slid through. He was probably in the wrong, he admits, because he should have waited for the cyclist to cross.

Suddenly, however, without recognizing the driver of the car, the student began to scream obscenities.

1. "The Downfall of a Champion," by Gary McLain, as told to Jeffrey Marx, March 16, 1987.

At once Knight jerked the car, backed up, jumped out and confronted the rider.

"Coach, I had no idea it was you."

"What difference does it make? I'm not an asshole. The man riding with me is acting Dean of the Law School. He's not an asshole. Maybe we were at fault, but you stopped and we proceeded on. What did it cost you, four seconds?"

When a photographer appeared on the scene and was about to take a picture, Knight just picked him up and set him into the hedges. (The next morning, however, Harry Pratter apologized to the photographer on Knight's behalf).

"I wanted to teach the kid a lesson," Knight says. At such moments the cost in energy, time and misunderstanding matters not a whit.

A final example: one day before a game, Knight received a telephone call from a referee who was to officiate that night. All officials receive tickets to games, but this man complained about the seats he got and wanted more tickets. Such a request implied how the game would be called.

Knight's reaction was instantaneous. "I'm going to turn you into the head of officials for the Big Ten and tell him what you did!" That such a response might cost him the game at that moment of indignation obviously did not enter his head.

IV

"Nobody likes hassles less than I do. I'd just like to go through life without another hassle. But it will be unavoidable because I'll take certain stands on things and somebody will make some comment, and I'll say, 'That's an idiotic thing to say,' because it is idiotic to say."

The entire litany was revived at the opening of the 1987–88 season in the widely-reported "Russian incident." Unanimously, reporters wrote that in protest against the officiating Knight took his team off the floor. Yet this is not what happened at all. After Knight had protested against leaving, referee Jim Burr had raced over to the scorer's table and written that the game was forfeited before anyone realized what was happening. Only then did Knight and his team leave.

This sequence of events might be contrasted with the December game in which Manhattan College coach Bob Della Bovi did indeed pull his team off the floor after he received his third technical. The referees had not signaled the game forfeited; Della Bovi, unlike Knight, simply removed his team. Yet the Della Bovi incident was reported and then duly forgotten with no one stopping to underline the significant difference between the two events. With Knight, normal standards of accurate reporting don't seem to operate.

Some background: the Russian incident was not the first time Bob Knight received three technical fouls. In 1974 at a CCA tournament, one of the consolations for those who are not invited to the NCAAs, Knight received two technical fouls (the limit then) only to remain in the stands and coach the game from there. Earlier in the tournament Tennessee coach Ray Mears and his assistant Stu Aberdeen had tossed off their coats and thrown clipboards onto the floor, yet had received no technical fouls. Now in the final game between Indiana and Southern California, an SC student palmed the ball.

Knight rose from his seat and shouted, "He carried the ball, he carried the ball!" He received a technical from the same referee, who had stood silently watching Mears throwing the clipboard. When Knight added, "You don't have any idea what the hell you're doing," he received technical number two and was supposed to leave. The game resumed with Knight in the stands offering advice to his assistants, a practice that has since been outlawed. The incident is significant only in that it had so profound an effect on Knight—it was his third season at Indiana—that he seriously considered resigning.

Knight's players rarely receive technicals. They are instructed that he'll take care of representing them should there be an unfair call. "I'll be your lawyer," he says. During that CCA tournament in 1974 Steve Green received a technical for raising his hand for a foul directly in front of the official's face and only then straight up. It was the first technical a Knight player at Indiana had ever gotten and Green did it intentionally to express solidarity with his coach sitting up there in the stands.

"Keep your nose out of it!" Knight told Green after the game.

The following year in that superb 1975 team's 92–90 loss to Kentucky in the regional final, Green got another technical. "Oh, no," he said to himself, "if I'm going to get a technical, at least let me say something." He hadn't said a single word.

After the game, the referee told Knight that Green had slapped his hand. In fact, when the referee had extended his hand to Green to help him up from the floor where he had landed, Green had waved him off, as if to say, "I don't need your help." There had been no slap, only simple disdain.

Although Indiana had played the Russians in exhibition games in the 1976, 1978, 1979, 1980, 1983 and 1987 seasons, this time Knight went on the record saying that in an Olympic year it was questionable whether the Americans should compete with the Russians and so help to train them for the summer games. Yet despite what some of his Indiana supporters believed—his supposed dislike of the Russians, his supposed right-wing politics and anti-communism—none of these beliefs had anything to do with what happened.

In fact, Knight would more accurately be labeled a democrat with a small "d," a midwestern populist restless with ideology, a proponent of hard work and the rights of the individual man. Loyalty and friendship seem to govern his political choices; he believes he has been labeled a Republican because of his long friendship with Otis Bowen, former Indiana governor and Secretary of Health and Human Services in the Reagan administration.

Knight supported liberal Senator Birch Bayh because Bayh called during the Puerto Rican events and offered to fly down to Puerto Rico to help. Knight refused the offer. "They'll just make a big issue out of your being here, it'll be worse," he said, a predictable response from him.

During the 1980 campaign, Bayh was singled out as a target by right-wing groups. Bayh's campaign workers telephoned Knight to request that he make a commercial.

"Will it put you in a bad position?" the Bayh campaign worker, hesitating, wondered.

"Hell, no," Knight said. And then he wrote the commercial himself:

"Hey, when it comes to politics, I vote for the guy that I think will do the best job. I've voted for Republicans and Democrats, and in this case I'm going to vote for a guy that I think has done a great job for Indiana and will continue to do so, Birch Bayh."

Mail poured into then-IU President Ryan's office. Indignant, Knight held his ground: "As though I haven't a right. Because I work for the state of Indiana, that denies me the right to have a political leaning? Well, I just blistered their ass."

("It's instructive that Knight's language seldom goes beyond the anal stage," Frank DeFord wrote in his 1981 Sports Illustrated profile. Instructive to what end? At times the attacks on Knight are as subtle as this, slipped into a seemingly innocuous discussion of his profanity.)

Knight went on to note that no Democrat complained when he spoke on behalf of Governor Bowen, a Republican. To those who attacked him, he replied in a letter which said, in effect, "After the way I've supported Doc Bowen and now I do something positive for another guy whom I happen to like, that tells me if ever I have a party affiliation, which one it will be."

Oliver North was not a favorite with Knight for a simpler reason than Iran-contra politics: he lied. When people, schooled in misconceptions about Knight, came up and told him, "You must have loved Oliver North," he replied, "Hey, I'd have fired him in a second if it would have been me. I mean, he lied and he lied and he lied."

His politics? "I like people."

The game against the Russians was badly officiated. Jim Burr, who had worked the LSU game in the tumultuous 1987 regional, might still have been reacting to charges that he wasn't tough enough on Knight at the LSU game after Knight slammed his hand down on the telephone at the scorer's table. He may have felt it cost him an appearance at the Final Four: none of the referees in that game went on to work the championship games.

Early in the game, the Russians suddenly had six people on the floor with the ball in play. "Just give them the ball back," Knight told the official. "Forget it, let's go."

By this point the Russians had a twelve- or fourteen-point lead.

Indiana cut it to eight. Then, with five minutes gone in the second half, six Russian players once again appeared on the floor. The matter was straightened out with no technical foul assessed to the Russians. A minute later as the Russians were shooting a free throw, one of their players stepped out of the lane and began to run to the other end of the floor, which should have meant Indiana's ball out of bounds. Referee Burr led the errant player back to the lane instead of calling an obvious foul lane violation.

Knight got up and walked down to mid-court. Up to this point the Russian coach had been out of the coaching box eight or ten times with the referees ignoring him or putting him back in the box, although, having played in America before, the Russian coach certainly knew the rules.

When Knight reached the scorer's table, Burr hit him with a technical foul.

Bill Wall, executive director of the Amateur Basketball Association/USA, was seated at the end of the Russian bench and Knight spoke to him.

"Bill, get these officials, the Russian coach and everyone together and tell the guy there isn't going to be any technical foul," Knight said.

"I can't do that. I can't interfere with the game," Wall said. "It's the official's game."

When Knight continued to complain, Burr hit him with his second technical. What could easily have been resolved soon became an international incident. Knight returned to his bench and play resumed. In a change of possessions, Burr was situated right in front of Knight for a few seconds, words were exchanged and Knight received the third technical.

Because of what he judged to be the bizarre way Burr had handled the game, frequently ignoring the rules, Knight refused to leave the floor. He did not take his team off the floor. Rather, Knight simply refused to go, as the rule demanded that he do. Burr went over to Wall to ask him to get Knight to leave the floor. But Wall again refused to intervene, although he might have demanded that play resume. Burr then ran over to the scorer's table and signed a forfeit. The game was over. It was then, the outcome of the game having been determined by Burr, that the Indiana team left the floor.

Weeks later, reporters, with the exception of Dick Vitale on

ABC television, still had Knight removing his team from the floor as if it had been a matter of his choice, his decision. As in the case of Puerto Rico, the original error was perpetuated in the press: Knight petulantly had led his team off the court. "Grow up," wrote Harvey Araton in the New York *Daily News,* adding, "punch a cop in San Juan, if you must, throw a few chairs, but do get us into the Final Four." Even Andy Rooney of "Sixty Minutes" had his say via the Tribune Media Services: "Knight decided, on the spot, to take his team off the floor and forfeit the game."

There is a profound difference between a team leaving the floor after a forfeit and taking your team off the floor and by so doing forfeiting the game. Further, it might be argued that without rules sports is no longer sports. Knight was not depriving audiences of fifteen minutes of basketball (the time remaining) because the unruly play permitted had amounted to no game at all.

Acknowledging this fact, the Amateur Basketball Association apologized "for inconsistencies in the official's enforcement of the Russian coach's box, substitution and free throw lane rules," an apology which never made the newspapers. When several months later, however, Bill Wall suddenly sent a two-hundred-dollar contribution to the Oak Street Playground Fund in Orrville in memory of Knight's mother, Knight had the check returned. There is no substitute for doing the right thing at the moment when you must.

After the game, Knight apologized to the fans. "I just should have walked away from it," he said, no doubt true. He did not help to set the matter straight when he added, carelessly, "As far as taking the team off the floor, there are things I wish I could do over again. That is one of them." He *hadn't* taken his team off the court, as he later acknowledged.

The next day, Knight telephoned Indiana President Thomas Ehrlich, requesting that the University issue a reprimand. Ehrlich suggested to Knight that he, Ehrlich, send the text over to Knight's office for his perusal, but Knight declined.

Knight had acted on behalf of his principles, which include playing the game as it ought to be played. He failed, Bob Hammel believes, to live up to the fundamental demand he makes of his players, to anticipate. With his last outburst, he provided Burr with ammunition he was obviously seeking. "Knight would reply to the view that at such times he should cease and desist," Hammel speculates, "by saying 'You don't understand the number of times when I don't do that.'"

For Harry Pratter with his legal mind the Russian incident is the only serious sin in the litany because it breaks faith with the structure of the game by flaunting its rules: no matter the injustice, the coach must depart after receiving his third technical.

"Pseudointellectual," Knight pronounces this argument. "I would agree with Harry, but for a different reason. I truly mistreated seventeen thousand people and a television audience. I had no right to prevent them from watching the game."

All coaches, in one style or another, communicate with referees, and Knight's open approach might be preferred to John Wooden's. Silent to the crowd, Wooden would hiss at a referee whose call he wished to oppose, "You'll never work again and I can make it stick." With Knight, there are no threats, just very loud outrage.

Did he make a mistake in not departing after that third technical in the game with the Russians? Of course he did. And he'll tell you so, quoting Churchill in the bargain: "I believe this and I don't think people have much of a grasp of this as far as I'm concerned: 'Eating words has never given me indigestion.'"

V

"They don't care."

From the chair to the LSU fan to the "Russian incident," Knight's behavior is not always right, wise or appropriate. Yet these incidents have been blown out of all proportion. For when other coaches misbehave either the press is not overly bothered, praises the coach for his tenacity, or reports the incident once and then lets it die.

In March of 1987 Bob Dukiet, the coach of Marquette University, hit a referee across the arm with a rolled-up program. The referee turned around and gave Dukiet a technical foul. Then he put his whistle back into his mouth, ready to resume play. Enraged, Dukiet threw the rolled-up program at the official, knocking the whistle out of his mouth! For this he received a second technical and remained in the game. The Milwaukee press called it the turning point of the game, an inspiration for a team which, in fact, went on to win.

In a game against Oral Roberts, Bill Harrell, coach of Moorehead State, threw a chair *into the stands.* When someone called out, "You can't throw Oral Roberts' chairs into the stands!" he threw another.

The 1987–88 season produced the following examples of inappropriate behavior, none of which involved Bob Knight. On Saturday, January 23, 1988, Billy Tubbs raises his arms and snarls at an official, demanding a three-pointer instead of a mere two as Oklahoma leaves the floor at the half, nine points ahead of Pitt. On the same day, his face contorted in a wolflike grimace, his jacket long since thrown somewhere, Dale Brown, as Jim Nantz of CBS puts it, "loses his cool" and is slapped with two technicals. According to observers, each time Brown awards the referee an obscene gesture.

A few weeks later Villanova's Massimino accuses Pitt coach Paul Evans of calling him "a very serious and dirty name." At a game with Temple, Lasalle coach Speedy Morris berates and grabs a player by the jersey.

This is not to justify Knight's throwing the chair. Rather, it is to suggest that Knight's violation of decorum should be viewed within a context where emotions run high, and that a double standard is at work when he is involved.

Art Spander in *The Sporting News* writes of John Wooden, "If given the choice he would rather be remembered as a good person than a good coach. Wooden, of course, was both. Bobby Knight? Well, one out of two ain't bad."[1]

And yet in Wooden's basketball program, students were persistently bribed and corrupted by their benefactor Sam Gilbert (amusingly indicted for racketeering and money laundering in connection with a Florida marijuana smuggling ring—four days after his death!) and his predecessors. Happily the UCLA players

1. December 14, 1987.

drove among the palm trees in their new Toyotas, since, no doubt, upgraded. Wickedly Nevada Las Vegas coach, Jerry Tarkanian once called Gilbert "the most important stone in Wooden's famous 'Pyramid of Success.' " As even the most jaded sportswriter will admit, there is no cheating in Knight's program.

Should the press focus more on this issue of the bribing of students? "They don't care," Knight says simply. "I don't think they have any interest in that."

"He's an isolationist," Mike Krzyzewski mourns, sorry that the man from whom he learned so much and who, he believes, has so much to offer, has absented himself from arenas of discussion within the sport. Because Bill Wall did not intervene to return a sense of fair play to the Russian game, Knight quietly resigned from the Olympic committee.

Meanwhile he builds his program—alone, scrupulously avoiding so much as a mention of the foibles, let alone the crimes, of any other coach—at least to this writer. "By your own soul learn to live," reads an unattributed plaque in his office. "And if man thwart you pay no heed/If man hate you have no care/Sing your song, dream your dream, Pray your prayer/By your own soul Learn to live." The warfare with the press provides an outlet for his not inconsiderable wit. In a 1981 commencement address he gave at Indiana, he told of how on the same day that the newspapers virtually ignored Lincoln's "Gettysburg Address," Edward Everett was soundly praised for his rhetoric. The press?—"An institution willing to praise undeserving people."

He's an easy target then, fair game. The exploits of the devil, real or ersatz, sell more newspapers than Adam, God, Christ and the angels put together. He's unfashionable, no matter that the atrocious plaid jackets have given way to red sweaters that do little to conceal extra pounds. It's also unfashionable for a teacher to be a stern disciplinarian and utterly to eschew democracy in the classroom.

Judging from appearances, there *is* something out of date in his style of masculinity, something anachronistic in an era of willed androgyny and the post-feminist view that men are no different from women. He's loud, strident and efficient, and the women I surmise he'd like best are those smart, competent, hard-talking women in the movies of Howard Hawks: Lauren Bacall in *To Have and Have Not* or Jean Arthur in *Only Angels Have Wings:*

women who stand up to men, talk their language and won't wilt in a crisis, women who can roll up their sleeves and do the work of men. (A cassette of *Shane,* however, with its paean to the domesticated woman played by Jean Arthur, sits in his living-room bookshelves.)

Finally he doesn't explain himself, stoic that he is. He'll tell you how tough he is ("Yea, though I walk through the valley of the shadow of death, I will fear no evil for I am the toughest son of a bitch in the valley"). He will readily defend others, but rarely himself. Judge him not by what you read, or by the persona viewed on television (the wire services have people at his games solely to photograph him at moments of anger), but perhaps by the fact that in the last five minutes of a game his students are less likely to make mistakes than those of other coaches. It's *their* grace under pressure that's at issue, not his.

He allows the press to misunderstand him and write that all he cares about is winning. In fact, his refusal to back down after a series of bad calls has nothing to do with the score, or whether the opponent is a Big Ten rival, or the Russians in the era of *Perestroika* and glasnost. If he grabs the shirt front of a drunk who vilifies him in a bar, it's *after* his team has advanced to the finals. You're your own man whether you win or lose.

Common sense decrees that you don't throw a chair to rouse a lethargic team. You don't grab someone who abuses you. And you resist those few more words to an official bent on your downfall, even if he thrusts his face right up to yours.

But for Knight, it would seem, the world is governed by rules other than the one that says that you cover yourself first, you don't get thrown out. In an era where the medium is the message, you don't put yourself in a position where you might be misunderstood. Meanwhile, to relieve the boredom that afflicts us all, but especially one whose commanding intellect might have led him to other pursuits, isn't it sometimes fun to play into the stereotype, to pretend to be what other people are so convinced you are—and so Knight quotes Bob Hope:

> *"I play in a golf tournament that President Ford has every summer. In 1984 I couldn't play, and a guy that's a Hollywood personality that's on a whole lot of things, Wayne Rogers, is there as the MC. Among people that weren't able to be there that summer, he mentioned me.*

And he said, 'As you all know, Bob's in Los Angeles trying to win the gold medal in basketball and keep us out of World War III.' And so everybody laughs at that.

Bob Hope comes on a little bit later. And he says, 'Wayne mentioned about Bob Knight being in Los Angeles and we all know that he's there doing everything he can to see that we win the gold medal in basketball. And those of us who really know him understand that he doesn't give a damn whether he gets us into World War III or not to do it.'

Which I liked."

PART TWO

CHAPTER FIVE

THE ART OF BASKETBALL

"It's like they're analyzing the participants in the Yalta conference, and I mean it just blows my mind. It's a simple goddamn thing. I just say, hey, kid, goddamn it, be the best player you can be."

IT'S THURSDAY, October 15, the first official day of practice. But other than a few remarks last night, addressed to last year's national champions ("The Bears beat the Giants before the strike; Detroit won more games than Minnesota; the same thing could happen to you!"), there is no lecture, no outlining of rules. "We just start practicing," Knight had said. Freshman players—and new assistant coaches both—are thrown headlong into the crucible with no guiding instructions. "We don't have any set working hours," Knight says. "We do what we have to do to get the job done."

(To his first full recruiting class at Indiana University in 1972, however, he said something else. "We're going to win the national championship," he told them. "That's everyone's goal. But we're going to do it with good people and do it the right

way." He wasn't "Bob Knight" then, but some coach from West Point. Nonetheless, they believed him.)

I am struck by the beauty of the room, the sparkling quality of Assembly Hall, pristine in every detail, from the highly polished floor to the seats. The colors red and white and blue alternate so that you feel as if you are sitting inside an American flag. Overhead, swaying to the breeze of the ventilation system, are the championship flags: 1940 and 1953 have been joined by the three flags of the Knight era: 1976, 1981 and 1987, for he won his national championships with three completely different teams, different personnel. The 1975 undefeated regular season team is represented by a flag from the NIT. Although he has won eight Big Ten championships, there is only one Big Ten Championship flag, for 1983 for the fans who never deserted that team. High above, flanking the American flag, are those two hard-won triumphs, the Olympic white and the Pan American blue.

The first person out on the floor with the players is assistant coach Ron Felling, lithe, limber and ready to go. But there's also a new assistant this year, Taylor ("Tates") Locke, who arrived yesterday at Indianapolis airport in hunting cap and blue plaid shirt. He's a strong-featured man with light eyes, gray-blond hair and a cleft in his chin. Twenty-five years ago as head coach at West Point he honored his predecessor's commitment to retain twenty-two-year-old Bob Knight as his assistant. (He himself was only twenty-five.) Today he remembers himself and Knight sitting with Joe Lapchick at a press conference in New York, two coaches in their twenties listening and learning as the older coaches talked.

The intervening years have not been kind. There were recruiting violations at Clemson, where he coached. These included changing the grades of players, an assistant coach's daughter taking a math test for a player, creating a phony black fraternity to lure black players to a small Southern town, and the usual cars and monthly spending allowances for players from a slush fund. In 1982 Locke wrote a book called *Caught in the Net.*[1] "Foolishly, I didn't listen to my conscience," he wrote. Having read the manuscript, Bob Knight wanted to pay off whatever money had been

1. Tates Locke and Bob Ibach, *Caught in the Net* West Point, New York: Leisure Press, 1982.

put into the project and prevent publication of the book. There was no point in dwelling on what couldn't be changed.

Now the Bob Knight who hates and detests cheating of any kind has hired his old friend as an Indiana assistant.

A contradiction?

"He was good to me," Bob Knight says softly when Locke is out of earshot.

On this first day of practice at Indiana, Locke stands quietly on the sidelines, dressed in a red shirt and white shorts. "I want to be with him," he has said, "I'll stay as long as he wants me to." In their telephone conversation as Knight invited him to come, Locke had brought up the past, but Knight had cut him off. Why should it be different for friends than for players? Knight's is a world of the clean slate, of starting over, of not giving up on people.

There are no reporters here today, none are permitted entry, but in the stands sit the professors: Drew Schwartz, the botanist; William Wiggins, of Black Studies; Harry Pratter; and Robert F. Byrnes, the distinguished professor of Soviet history who views Knight as the paradigm of the teacher.

As the players begin their drills, Knight is nowhere to be seen. But on the floor in his motorized wheelchair is Landon Turner, crippled for life in an automobile accident in the summer of 1981 and the recipient of the well-known Landon Turner trust fund created by his former coach.

(Not that Bob Knight will ever speak about this or any other of the acts of generosity with which he leavens his days. Once someone asked him for a ticket to a game, saying, "Well, I gave to Landon Turner's fund."

"If that's what it meant to you," Knight scathingly replied, "I'll give you your money back!")

Landon has been summoned to Assembly Hall today to be chewed out by his old coach for having quit his job at Indiana University in Indianapolis now that his lawsuit has been settled. He wants to become an agent representing athletes; his former coach is not so sure this is a good idea.

Last night at Valparaiso someone wanted to know what Landon was up to. One of the results of Knight's constant evocations of his former players is that they—and Landon Turner in particular—remain of great concern to the fans of Indiana basketball long after their playing days are over.

"Landon and I are a little bit at odds right now," Knight confided to that audience of two thousand, "because he had a good job with the university that he gave up to pursue a couple of things, reminiscent of some of the shots he took while he was playing. I reminded him of that the other day, and he said, 'You think it's really that bad?' I said, 'Yeah, you'd better get down here on Thursday.'

"You should have talked to me first if you weren't pleased with the job," Knight tells him today.

"The job wasn't me," Landon says. "I didn't think I had to come to you." But Landon knows—Knight would have tried to set him up with something he did like, if only he had spoken to him first.

Indeed, Knight is always in search of opportunities to help people. "I try to let people know that I'm always here," he says, "and that if there are things that I can do to help you, I'll be glad to. Let me know. I'll do anything within reason that people I know ask me to. Just give me a break and ask me."

It was Landon Turner, everyone agrees, who spearheaded the 1981 championship team, Landon who had started out that year in disfavor for not working hard enough.

During one of the 1979 Pan American practices, Knight sat down next to Landon Turner, who was watching from the stands.

"I talked with Buzz Kurpius [the director of Indiana's academic support program for athletes] the other day and she says you missed some classes."

"I haven't missed any classes."

"I know damned well you have because she showed me the figures. You know you could be the best player we have ever had; you could be better than Scott May was. You've got enormous talent. You simply haven't worked hard enough. If you do that, you'll make this a great team and you'll be a great player. You'll go on to an extraordinary professional career."

It was, thought Bob Byrnes, sitting there in the stands eavesdropping, like father and son. But Turner somehow wasn't listening. He kept saying he was doing as well as he could and Knight kept getting angrier and angrier.

Finally Knight stood up.

"Why am I wasting my time with someone as dumb as you?" he roared, storming off, kicking a wastebasket on his way.

But soon Landon presented Knight with his significantly improved grades.

Yet again Knight berated him, because he hadn't done better before, and he could do still better than that. Unrelenting pushing, unrelenting pressure: ask Phil Isenbarger, former Indiana player, now an Indianapolis lawyer who is here today in the stands on October 15.

"Was Knight harder on anybody than on Kitchel?" (about whom, more later).

"Landon Turner," Isenbarger replies without hesitation.

Did Landon appreciate this much attention, this much caring? "When I was playing for him," Turner remembers, "sometimes I couldn't stand him and sometimes I enjoyed his coaching, but his personality stung with me. But I knew if he stopped hollering, that meant he just didn't care, that he had given up on me. But it's just the way he does it, he just cusses you out, he makes you feel like a little ant. You feel that you're a man and he makes you feel like a little kid."

Not that Turner was entirely browbeaten. One day after practice, Knight sat on his chair with the team gathered around him.

"You really worked hard today, you did a good job. Let's come back and work hard again tomorrow," he told them.

Then Landon Turner slapped Knight on the leg and said, "I think you did a good job today too, Coach." And with that he walked away quickly before even the rumble of a repercussion.

Now Turner reflects: "He wants perfectness, which is hard to get from humans."

The former players agree: there was no one Coach pushed more, loved more. In the hospital, after his accident, depressed, Landon Turner had given up—until Bob Knight laid down the law: "You're going to recover. I'm going to insist that you recover. Do you remember when you were having a bad time last year and you weren't playing at all? You finally got into the Northwestern game and you played badly. I took you out and I gave you one more chance and you played very well. You played well for the rest of the season and you really made that NCAA team. Without you, we wouldn't have won. YOU'RE GOING TO GET UP AND RECOVER FROM THIS!"

For a time after his accident that summer of 1981 Turner sat in a chair, unresponsive. "I thought Coach was going to pick him up out of that chair and throw him on the floor," Joby Wright, once an Indiana player, today down there on the floor as a Knight assistant, remembers. "Landon had lost the money, the career, his looks." Joby gestures. "He lost all that, and Coach was so mad."

"What I got from him was love," Landon says.

At last, fifty minutes into this first day of practice in another post-championship season, Coach Knight, delayed by a telephone call, appears in red warm-up jacket and blue pants, his unvarying practice costume. He is speaking with two television people. One holds a steadicam. Beside the television man, another reporter is holding up a tape recorder as Knight gives an opening-day interview.

Knight thinks to himself, what the hell do the TV people need this on tape for if they're getting it on film? It doesn't make sense.

The interview lasts three or four minutes and then the man with the tape recorder introduces himself as a reporter from AP. Eric Ruden from the Sports Information Department of the University is there as well, and Knight says, "Eric, what's this guy doing here? I don't know him. I don't allow reporters in practice. You know that. What the hell is he doing here?"

It is not a matter of the man's point of view; Knight does not know what that is. But this is not how things are done. The man leaves. Ruden explains. The reporter had told him, "If the TV people can come in, I have a right to come in."

Has another potential mortal enemy in the press been hatched? There are probably more observers at Knight's practices than at anyone else's, but practice is Knight's classroom, something he takes very seriously, and he chooses his own guests.

Knight spots Turner. Why isn't he helping with the practice? "I can get lots of guys to come around and sit on their asses!" he yells. A moment later he stands beside the wheelchair, his arm around Turner, his irritation forgotten.

"What am I doing here?" Tates Locke asks Knight.

"Relax," Knight says, and he moves on.

He wanders from group to group. Nothing any one of his players does escapes him. He looks grim and they look grim. This is serious business because what they have to learn is hard: how never to abandon your effort, how to take pride in yourself, how to believe in your own value. He's an idealist, this man. He takes people nearly grown up and believes they can still learn character, if they choose to do so; there's still time. And he has figured out how to do it; if only they execute what he is teaching them in practice, they'll win against superior opponents.

They must concentrate every second, as he does, always moving from group to group. Under the generosity of his vigilance he never asks of a student what he can't give and is furious when one of them tries to do what he's not capable of. "These kids don't need a nice guy," he'll say. "They need somebody that's willing to say, I'll be the distraction, I'll be the pressure, I'll be what you have to play through." And so it begins.

"We've got a basket open and three guys here," he calls. He illustrates Todd Jadlow's run, slow and heavy. Some players have not spread out on the floor: "I could put a sheet over the three of you," he says in disgust. With Mark Robinson, the new junior college recruit from the same San Francisco program that brought him Dean Garrett, he is more patient: "One of the things you can't do is shoot it over someone six foot ten." Freshman Jay Edwards is taken aside by the arm for a talk. A moment later Knight is taking Jay's hand and twisting his head around: "Make sure you know what's behind you," he orders. Then Jay is awarded with a pat. Throughout, Edwards' expression does not change.

Knight is annoyed with his veterans for not having taught the freshmen the drills over the past month. He sure isn't "taking twenty minutes to do it." Jay indeed doesn't know the drills: four corners, three lanes.

"I was scared," he admits later. "After a week, I got adapted to it."

The issue of leadership has reared its head on this first day of practice: what Steve Alford did for Keith Smart, what Daryl Thomas did for Dean Garrett, what Quinn Buckner took on for his teammates from his first day of practice—as a freshman—who now will do these things for Lyndon Jones, who is even more frightened than Jay, and Jay himself and Mark Robinson?

Immediately Knight spots weaknesses, some old and some recently acquired. "I don't want any goddamned defense you developed over the summer," he tells Joe Hillman. Hillman, simultaneously animated and expressionless, doesn't miss a beat. Steve Eyl must use his advantage, defense, because, "unless there's been divine intervention over the summer, shooting isn't it."

"Good pass, Steve," Knight calls a moment later. "But be ready to take the shot."

Rangy Magnus Pelkowski, however talented an artist, needs to marshall all his forces when it comes to basketball: "Don't just stand. Make the play and get back into it. Don't let someone make the next play. If you don't want to play basketball, paint pictures!"

Knight increases his displeasure with those who will respond only to a firmer hand. Pelkowski is told he hasn't made a single play, "and on the basis of what I've seen tonight, you aren't going to."

Practice is made much more grueling than any game could be; stats are kept by the managers and films are made of each session, to be reviewed by coaches and players as a measure of how far they have come. Knight carries his famous index card, listing the drills he plans, and compares his card with Ron Felling's. Since Knight has arrived late, the players must repeat some of the drills while he leans against the basketball supports watching.

At practice, there are no stars. You are only as valuable as the last play you have made—and how effectively you have gotten back on conversion. If there are students today who come in for the most criticism, they are Keith Smart, Dean Garrett, Joe Hillman and Steve Eyl, members of that (so long ago) championship team. "The shot," as reporters have called it, which won the 1987 NCAA championship game against Syracuse has never been praised by Knight; that, Keith Smart hopes, will come after graduation. What Knight does talk about is how Daryl Thomas, not in a bad position to take the shot himself, nevertheless passed the ball to Smart on the baseline.

Meanwhile, Garrett is told, "You aren't playing as well as you did when you first came here. What do you think?" Garrett looks solemn. Then, quietly, sadly, he says, "No."

II

"We've got to set things up so that the kids can't screw it up. My feeling is that if we allow them to make the switch,

*we're not teaching. We're not setting up something that they
can do well. Let's set it up so they can do it the best way
possible. . . ."*

On Friday, 402 high school and junior college coaches gather
from around the country, and Taiwan, Japan, China, Yugoslavia
and Egypt, for a clinic. From Friday night through Sunday noon,
Knight will outline the principles by which he teaches basketball, the philosophy by which he understands it. There are no
"good evenings," or "good mornings," no time wasted on the
irrelevant.

On Friday night he goes over the schedule. "If you've got a
question, the only way it won't be answered is if you don't ask
it," he announces. And when they leave, the coaches will be told
that practice is always open to any of them. They are even wel-
come to bring their teams.

The young coaches are treated as equals, as colleagues. He is
anxious to share all that he has discovered about the game, all
the rules of play upon which for over twenty-five years he has
learned to depend. What binds him and the participants in this
clinic is their common enterprise: teaching kids to play the game
they all love so well. That Knight takes this clinic very seriously
may be measured by his stated aspiration. He hopes that they
will go away feeling "nothing you've ever done has been more
beneficial to you as far as basketball is concerned."

He speaks without notes, occasionally using a clipboard projected onto a screen, through a wireless microphone—until it
breaks down.

"I don't think I'm smart enough to operate this goddamned
thing," he says, his voice booming out into the far corners of
Assembly Hall without it. When the projector attached to the
clipboard won't work, he has an answer for that too. "Where did
you get this thing?" he calls out. "Puerto Rico?" The coaches, men,
but with a sprinkling of women too, laugh. They've heard the
litany, of course, but they're not victims of it. They're here for
something else.

At the scorer's table, dressed in a red cap and a green high
school jacket, Shawn Kemp sits with another potential recruit, a
skinny high school junior named Patrick Knight. Kemp's visit is
an official one, no small matter because he is the leading high
school senior in the state of Indiana; as a junior he had averaged

25 points and 14.4 rebounds a game, shooting 58 percent from the field. There was a game where he scored 42 points with 21 rebounds. By his senior year at Concord he had scored 1,483 points.

Joby Wright, in charge of most of the recruiting, had been worried. Kemp "wasn't doing well in his books." Should he not receive a score of 700 on his combined English and Math SATs, or pass the ACT, he would be the first Indiana recruit to be ineligible to play as a freshman under the NCAA's Proposition 48. (The average score of black students in general on the SATs is 745.)

For most of the weekend, Kemp will be entertained by the players; now he seems as absorbed in the clinic as the coaches. The clinic itself is a project of Knight's older son, Tim, age twenty-three, who was working this season as his father's business manager. He resembles his father much more than his younger brother, his eyebrows darkly shadowing his eyes, his eyes themselves deep set, although he is shorter and stockier and less graceful than Patrick. Unlike their father, who speaks in standard American speech, Patrick and Tim surprise you with their Southern Indiana drawls.

Tim was the student of the family, attempting to please his father with his high grades. He was never an outstanding athlete, although he played baseball in high school, incurring his father's displeasure by not working harder at it.

Because of a bout with mononucleosis during his freshman year at Stanford, Tim did not graduate on time. In September of 1986, as his final semester began, his father made him an offer.

"You're going to graduate at a bad time to get a job, Christmas. I have some stuff that you can do. You can work a few months for me. I'll pay you. Get that stuff done for me and then look for a job."

Knight had seriously doubted that his son would accept. There would be "no way. But I wanted him to know that I would like him to do that, that I thought enough of him."

A month later, Tim said, "I've been thinking and if you're serious, I'm going to come back."

Knight and Tim joke about their fantasy business firm, "Knight, Knight and Maybe." Patrick's interest at the moment residing exclusively in basketball, he is the "maybe."

"I enjoy it but it's not something I look to do for the rest of my life," Tim says. *"I'd like it to be a start for me to go on my own in the next six to eight years, move away and run my business somewhere else."*

At business he has always excelled, from the time he was twelve and ran the concession at his father's basketball camp. And he loves basketball too, having at the age of three sat on the West Point bench, being looked after by an assistant manager while his father coached the team.

Inevitably, the roles of father and son reverse. In part, Tim has accepted the job as a way of looking after his father. "The way I see it," Tim says, *"there are a lot of people out there looking to take advantage of him. Who could be more loyal to you than your son?"*

Knight explains the structure of his practices. He holds up a red notebook: these are kept by all the students in their lockers. They are taken on the road and emerge whenever coaches talk to the team. At the start of every practice, the team is taken off the floor to the locker room, where they are addressed by the coach about something important in practice, or a game, or a past game, or the season. Then they come back out and the practice starts. Always they begin with the four-corner passing drill, calling out each other's names, communicating.

The principle by which he teaches, Knight reveals, is to break everything down into parts, and then put it together as a whole. Basketball is broken down into its essence. He is teaching the game, not patterns, teaching people how to anticipate, concentrate and execute. And he attributes his methods to his mentors, Pete Newell, Clair Bee and Henry Iba, not so much because they are really responsible for what he is about to say, but because he sees himself as belonging to a living tradition, to which he is contributing. Most people who major in history in college, as Knight did, don't assume a historical approach to life as he does. But Knight approaches basketball and his participation in it as if it were living history.

The clinic becomes a clinic in teaching, its subject, basketball, at times almost irrelevant. A teacher, Knight explains, can never "assume."

"We have to teach what our kids can do and what they can't

do," he says. "Kids will do first what's easy and what you will tolerate."

"You leave it up to the kid. He comes down the floor and he makes the pass with two guys open. He's going to make the pass a lot of the time to the easier of the two to throw it to, although the other guy who's open is the much better shooter. . . ."

The solution: rules. And there is a rule for practically everything: "When you catch the ball, unless you can drive to the bucket, you must face the basket for a count of two. As soon as you catch the ball, 1,001, 1,002. Just to see what the hell is going on." There are two things to do to set screens, seven things a passer can do. At once he eliminates three of the passer's options: "I don't want him to go behind to get the ball back; I don't like him to screen for the ball and I don't want him to stand where he is."

Four alternatives for the passer remain: inside cut, cut to the bucket, screen away, replace yourself. There are three things to do to distort the zone; there are three ways to use the dribble effectively against a zone (penetrate gaps, take the ball off the top, employ the freeze dribble). And with the dribble you must reverse the ball twice on each possession.

You can't distort a zone with passing. You don't go to the basket unless you have been screened. On defense, the further the ball is from your man, the further you should be from the man. The center can't go anywhere that he can't score from. On offense there are three things you must immediately learn to do: pass, cut and screen. But never do you teach patterns: "You teach kids how to play and what to look for."

There isn't anything that can happen on the basketball court that he can't predict, defend against, distort or maneuver beyond. He's there to lead, and he's comfortable with the habit of leadership. He's not permissive. In Knight's experience, students just don't learn on their own. They must be followers in his classroom, mastering these rules he has spent his lifetime developing. Yet leadership is something they must assume.

Thus he instructs these young coaches in their alternatives, particularly where they must not allow their players to make decisions. "I never let the players call out a switch," Knight says. "They're not smart enough to do that."

Where it is likely to produce mistakes, spontaneity is eliminated. If self-esteem and self-confidence are the goals, the players must not be put in situations where they are likely to fail. There will be frustration when they don't get it right and self-esteem when they do. But a student cannot gain confidence trying to do what he is physically incapable of accomplishing.

The players have come out to practice now, going through their drills, seemingly oblivious of the unusual gathering as Knight continues to address the coaches:

"I never trust the sons of bitches," he confides. "Don't trust them. You trust them and they're going to say to you, 'Well I thought we should have switched.' Don't give them that option. Either they switch it every time on a high cut or they stay put every time on the low cut. That's as plain as it could be." The goal is to break basketball down into its individual elements so that his students can understand it, learn it, succeed at it.

"Keith Smart's a hell of a basketball player," Knight announces. He calls Smart forward and puts his arm around him.

"Do you think I have total trust in you?" Knight asks.

Smart, a quick-witted, modest young man with irrepressible high spirits, reveals the tail end of a barely suppressed smile. He shakes his head. No.

"The epitaph I want on my tombstone," Knight says, "is 'He didn't trust the sons of bitches.' "

In part, Knight's success is based on how well he perceives his players, who they are, and what they are likely to do. He is an astute student of their thinking. So his advice to the coaches is to get your players there on offense a second late—which may seem surprising until he explains:

"Never be on time because when they're on time they're always early. Kids are anxious. They cheat, they lean, they cut too soon. They think they're on time, but they're early. Being there a split second late is far more important to the timing of what you're doing offensively than anything I'm aware of."

He emphasizes the distance, the separation, between himself and them—which is the appropriate distance between all teachers and students. On the first day of his coaching class he asks his eighty students, male and female, "How many of you had a coach in high school that you didn't like?"

Every hand goes up; the students all smile to each other knowingly—for a moment.

"The first thing you people have to understand," Knight tells his student coaches in the classroom, "is we don't like all you little bastards either."

"So don't feel that they're going to think like you do," Knight tells the young coaches here today during this October Clinic weekend.

The cornerstone of Knight's teaching is making the students concentrate, the principle behind every practice. Only five minutes are spent on any aspect of play, then they go on to something else. "Four on four," he'll call, and they must immediately move into the next situation. "I really believe we can teach kids to be quicker by making them concentrate," he says.

Already on the weekend of October 15, problems that will plague Indiana during the coming season are apparent. Joe Hillman seems reluctant to take initiatives. By Saturday, Knight is complaining about the absence of communication among the players, the absence of leadership—which will be Indiana's greatest deficiency this season:

> *"Garrett's in white, and there was a red shirt up here with nobody guarding him, and that's the whole idea of communication. Hey, let's get somebody on him. Well, Garrett doesn't say a word. He just stands there. . . ."*

One of the freshmen doesn't pick anybody up. And so coach screams at Ricky Calloway. "We've got no leadership here! Why didn't you tell him to get out there! You've got to see what's going on, Rick. Get everybody in position!" (And when, later in the season, Calloway fails in this challenge that he lead, having been a starting player on a championship team, he is benched.)

"Move, you have to come to the ball, Joe," Knight screams. "How many years have you played here?"

His curly black hair and blue eyes making him the handsomest member of the squad, Hillman is also the one who concentrates hardest. And when Knight speaks to him, he answers. This time, however, his answer is inaudible.

"This is the fourth year? Give me within six months of the date that I ever talked to you about soft lob passes in the middle of the zone. I never have? OK. I just wanted to check. I thought maybe I was losing my mind."

Suddenly, on this Saturday afternoon, in the middle of the practice floor, Knight descends on Tates Locke and engulfs him in a giant bear hug. Overcome with emotion, in tears, Locke tries to express his gratitude to Knight for having brought him to Indiana. Abruptly, Knight waves him off. In this world of men, where the expression of emotion is viewed as antithetical to the purity of it, Knight abruptly silences his friend.

By now the philosophy at the heart of Knight's teaching has become clear: "You win with people," he says, not with offense or defense. You find ways to use kids; you find a role for each individual based on his particular talents. You demand what he can do; you never allow him to attempt what he cannot, no matter how hard he tries.

Shooting is never "an equal opportunity situation." In high school, Knight confides, he was plagued by a coach who thought everybody should shoot the same amount of times: it was a terrible experience for him as a player far superior on offense than defense. Ability alone determines how a student will be used; some are scorers, some feeders, some primary screeners.

He turns to the tradition of Indiana basketball for his examples. As a freshman playing guard, Randy Wittman turned the ball over less than twice a game, and he didn't score. Later, as a senior, when Ted Kitchel was hurt, he did. Roles change. No point would be complete, however, without Quinn Buckner marching to center stage.

Knight recalls once more Alabama, the first game of the 1976 regionals. He set up a delay game, and he told his two guards, Buckner and Bobby Wilkerson, there were two things they were not to do: cross and provoke a three second call.

"What do you want us *to do,* coach?" Buckner asked.

"Not one goddamn thing."

He didn't want them to go up and shoot free throws because they weren't good free-throw shooters. May and Abernethy would handle the basketball because they could make free throws. But, Knight says, he had never seen a kid leave a time-out as mad as Buckner was.

Roles in basketball, however, do change. And so Knight creates for the coaches an imaginary conversation with a potential recruit, a young man schooled in players being assigned, not only roles, but numbers to go with them.

"Coach, where would I play?"

"You'll play between the sidelines and the end zone."

"Would I be a one, a two, a three or a five?"

"You can be all of them, if you want. I don't care. What do you want to be?"

"Would I be a power forward or a small forward?"

"Well, you aren't real big, so you must be small. And you can't play unless you're a powerful son of a bitch, so you've got to be a small power forward. How's that?

"Hey, you come to Indiana and we'll teach you how to play the goddamn game. We'll play you anywhere. We'll play you in the post, we'll play you here, we'll play you there. You'll just learn to play and that's what basketball here is all about."

Students grow and develop new talents; and as they do, in basketball as in life, their roles correspondingly change.

As for the basis of offense, of course it's shot selection, along with everybody knowing who can shoot and who can't. After a week of practice, Knight confides, "I'll stop somebody on the red team and I'll say, 'Hey, Dean, who's the best shooter on your team?'

"And he better pick out the best shooter. If I say that to a kid who is the best shooter, he'd better say 'It's me.' and if I ask who the worst shooter is, he'd better look around and say 'It's me'—or he'd better pick one of the worst shooters. People talk about a kid's confidence. I don't give a damn about his confidence. I'm concerned about my confidence. When somebody goes up to shoot, I want to feel confident that the son of a bitch is going in."

The coaches in the stands laugh, although Knight is exaggerating here. Trying to do what you can't reduces confidence; achieving what you can builds it. His entire basketball philosophy is founded on the principle of developing in each student a recognition of his abilities and then an insistence that he realize them, consistently, efficiently, and without respite. Not that this always happens:

"One day in practice Wittman gets the ball on the break. He starts down the floor, crosses mid-court and sees a red shirt coming in from the other side and makes the pass. The red shirt coming in from the other side was our center, Blab, who had a tough time catching the ball and a particularly tough time catching the ball on the run.

"Now we have a standard rule here that you only throw the ball to big guys if you expect them to dunk. Never throw it to them if they have to put it on the floor. As soon as he throws the ball, Wittman looks to see who it is, and he says, 'Oh, no.'

"The ball goes right through Blab's hands, out of bounds, and sails out to the wall.

"I came out on the floor, and I said, 'Goddamn it, Wittman, how many years have you been here? This is your fifth god-damn year here. How long have you watched Blab play? How well does he catch the ball?'

"Wittman sat there and he was so mad. He wanted to say something back to me in the worst way. But he knew he was wrong, so he couldn't. If they're right and they say something back, that doesn't bother me. But if they're wrong, they better not.

"Wittman seethes, as if to say, all right, all right, I know. For Christ's sake, leave me alone. But when I get them at that stage, I just keep at them. I had Wittman and Wittman is mad.

"We've never had a smarter player than Wittman. But ten minutes later, the same situation occurs. Wittman throws the ball again, but Blab, instead of trying to catch it, just runs right past, doesn't even make an effort to catch the ball.

"That, temporarily, takes me away from Wittman.

" 'Goddamn it, Uwe, the least you can do is try and catch it. I mean, knock it down, maybe you can deflect it and somebody else can come up with it. You can't help it that Wittman threw it to you, the dumb sob. But try to catch it, will you?'

"Uwe, a brilliant student from Germany, looked at basket-ball a little differently from the way we do.

" 'Coach,' he said, 'I want you to know if Wittman is so dumb he throw me the ball, I'm not so goddamn dumb I try to catch it!' "

Knight draws another example from his coaching days at West Point:

"A player named Schrage, who was my best defensive player ever, gets a rebound twelve feet from the bucket right in front

of the free throw line. He goes up to shoot it. There isn't anybody within eight feet of him. He shoots it and misses it, which
is predictable.

"We get the rebound, I call time, and I have him by the throat.
I can remember my fingers slipping off his Adam's apple or I
would have killed him. I had his shirt in my fist in the time-out
and I said, 'I want to tell you something. Someday do you want
to be a goddamn general?'

" 'Yes, sir.'

" 'You've got no chance of being a goddamn second lieuten-
ant if you shoot that son of a bitch one more time. Do you
understand that?'

" 'Yes, sir.'

"He isn't going to make it. He isn't going to make the son of
a bitch the next one hundred shots he takes because he can't
shoot." (Knight demonstrates.) "He shoots the ball like this, for
Christ's sake, the worst goddamn looking shot I've ever seen.
Well, I don't want him shooting, he can do enough other things.
He was a hell of a player. But when it came to shooting, hell,
no."

In practice, Knight explains, there are times when he will in-
struct that the only person who can shoot the ball is the scorer;
he did this for Steve Alford, ordering the offense to get him open.
On another day, he would say, "Steve, I don't want you to shoot
today. Make everybody else score. You don't score today."

The lesson is literally "from each according to his ability."
"We'll do the same thing with Smart this year," Knight plans.
Knight envisions his post-Alford team with Keith Smart doing
most of the scoring.

What Knight is proudest of in his teaching is that he praises the
students inordinately for what they do right, but also never permits a mistake to pass unnoticed, no matter the score, or the
situation. (Jim Crews says he has broken it down: joking, teaching
and praising ninety percent, with ten percent devoted to yelling
and criticizing.)

Suddenly Knight puts his arms around two players, as if to
introduce them to the audience. "This is Hillman and Smart," he
says. Hillman keeps a straight face; Smart has trouble:

*"Let me introduce you to Hillman and Smart. They're both
fourth-year college students. They both played instrumental*

roles in our winning the national championship last year. They both played really well in the game against Nevada/Las Vegas and the game against Syracuse. We're going to have a little offensive change in about ten minutes where we're going to run triangle, post exchange and regular offense. Now with all you two have practiced and everything that you've done, as twenty-two-year-old young men, smart enough to leave Louisiana, smart enough to leave California, everything you've accomplished . . ."
and then comes the punchline . . .
"I hope I can trust you two not to mess up the next ten minutes . . . (pause) . . . you better not."

Out on the floor, Tates Locke begins to coach, using some rough language, rougher than what you would *expect* of Knight. Off the court during a break, Knight tells Bob Murrey, who has put together the clinic, that he hadn't said anything about his language to Locke in advance. But he'll straighten it out later. If an obscene word is used here, it is only by Coach Knight.

Meanwhile throughout the three days Knight's teaching is precise, self-explanatory, detailed and unrelenting. He takes extra time to help his fledgling freshmen:

"Lyndon, don't dribble him back to his position. When you dribble down the floor, notice a skinny black kid, number 20 [Calloway] playing point. If you see a short white guy, number 44 [Hillman], you know it's not the point man. Get a point of recognition, his knee pad, whatever you have to do to recognize him and then move him further off the point."

If you let the little things slide, Knight says, then the big things will slide.

"The leadership out here is nonexistent," he yells. "How can you let Edwards run a flare when he doesn't know what a flare is." If they don't master the screens, Knight turns to another new assistant coach, Dan Dakich, the sharp-featured young man who met me at the airport, once also a Knight player, "they're going to run the steps, and, Danny, you're going to run with them."

(Later one of the coaches will ask Dakich, would he really have made you run up and down the stairs? The answer comes back: yes).

Freshman Jay Edwards is made to feel at home. "He stole it

from you, from you and from you," Knight points. "And his last competition was a high school team. That's pretty good. He must think you guys are awfully easy to play against."

Keith Smart, in particular, should know better:

> "Keith, we need better penetration. I can stand here and do this. I don't need you to do it. I don't need you to be on the outside and pass the ball. I can do that. I think I can do it better than you can do it the way I've seen you throw the ball around for two days. What I can't do, Keith, is this."

Joe has the ball. Knight takes it back.

His voice grows louder.

"I can't penetrate like you can and pass like you can. But I can sure as hell do that garbage."

He is not tolerant, nor does he believe he should be. "I believe that kids are satisfied with what we tolerate," he says. "If we're intolerant, then they're going to be hard to satisfy." Intolerant people should coach a team, he insists. Nor does he want his own children taught by tolerant people. Demanding people are the efficient ones; they are the ones who get a job done.

This lesson has little to do with basketball. Rather, it returns us to Knight's larger motive, turning out effective, competent human beings who will succeed at whatever they choose to do. "I'm talking about turning out a kid that can compete with other kids a little bit better than they can compete with him—because of his association with you or his association with me."

And so he believes in pushing people to their limit, an approach that, inexplicably, seems to bother so many sportswriters. But they are not teachers; they do not understand how difficult it is to change the behavior of students, and how great and unrelenting a physical and mental effort it demands of the teacher. Knight finds an example that would please those of his critics who would stereotype him as one who peppers his stories with military analogies. He recalls Colonel Blaik, the West Point football coach under whom Vince Lombardi was initiated into coaching:

> "They've got Pete Dawkins on a two-by-four trying to get him up. He's got a torn muscle in his calf and they can't get Dawkins up. The colonel comes in and he gets behind Pete, and he says, 'Pete, get up! Get up, Pete! Damn it, Pete, get up, Pete!'

"Finally Dawkins turns and says, 'Goddamn it, Colonel, I can't.'

"You could have heard a pin drop. Everyone there was sure Dawkins would never play again, there would never be another play that Dawkins was involved in.

"But all Blaik did was turn and walk away. It didn't bother him because he knew he had pushed the kid to the limit."

It's clear that Knight loves to teach, to teach kids to recognize "what's going to happen." And he is no less fierce than he will be when there are not four hundred observers.

That Dean Garrett was picked "Big Ten Pre-Season Player of the Year" is sufficient cause alone for his coach to be hard on him: "Dean, where's the ball? You made no move to the ball. Come on, Dean, think, think, think. Come on, Dean, get the thing in play!"

"Garrett thinks he's a lot better shooter than I do," Knight confides, as if Garrett were not within earshot.

Those who know Indiana basketball only from the movie *Hoosiers* might be amused to hear the coach upon whom Gene Hackman's character is modeled demanding of his players what Hackman demanded of his. As the hero in *Hoosiers* instructs, so does the reallife model: four passes are crucial, especially with this team where there is no real shooter. Only with an Alford, a Woodson or a Wittman can one deviate from that rule: "Offensive play requires four passes on a half court," Knight instructs.

Another restriction he'll invariably insist upon is that they run the offense minus the dribble, which puts emphasis on cutting and screening. And he teaches the young coaches a game: four on four or five on five where, if the offense gets to eight passes, they score one point, and if they make a basket, a lay-up, they get two, while, if the defense gets a hand on the ball, it gets a point, and if the defense gets possession, no matter how, they score three.

"Dean, you've had the three worst practices since you came out of junior college," Knight tells him.

"That was really a good job of Hillman reading the screen," Knight calls. "He looked at the defensive man, not at the ball.

"If I look up again and see you walking back there, you're going back to San Francisco," this to Mark Robinson.

"Good move, Jeff, but come up with the ball. Good help. Come on, come on, who's got the ball? You're letting them take the ball where they want to take it." Smart hits the floor. Mark Robinson is taken aside for individual teaching.

Knight puts his arm around Lyndon Jones.

"Free throws," he calls, their rest period.

"Move, Mark, move," he yells. You have to move without the ball here or you won't play.

"The man isn't going to score," he calls. "I've never seen a man go through the bucket yet. It's the ball that's going in."

"Ricky, Ricky, see how far out of position you are. You're eight feet out of position."

Six on four. They must force the ball into the corner now. The corner man must take it as far as he can go. If the drive is stopped, he can throw it back out.

"Stance, Jay, stance. Move your feet. Don't play with your hands. Move your feet."

"Change!" Ron calls, and the five offensive men become defensive men.

"We're reacting slowly to making the change from offense to defense," Knight complains.

Pressure is kept up and everyone is playing hard. "Get back, get back!" Joby yells.

Knight asks Joby to demonstrate Jadlow's shot. Without hesitating, Joby moves into a perfect imitation. "I don't want that shot taken by you ever again unless you get your feet straight," Knight says.

Everything has been broken down into parts, what a coach can do in defensive play, what he can do in offensive play:

"First, let's take man to man. You're going to play man to man against my team. Here's what you can do and here's what I can do. You can decide who your players will guard. I don't have anything to do with that unless you're going to switch. And if you're switching, then I'll take your weakest defensive player and put him in a position where he has to switch to our best offensive player. We can easily do that in triangle or in post exchange . . . you decide who's going to guard our five players. But here's what I decide for you. I decide where they're going to play."

Against a half-court trap, he explains, he'll put his quickest player—Keith Smart—in the center of the court. Knight then discusses how he will use Smart. On offense, why not send your best scorer to set a screen twice to thwart the defensive player ready to shut him down on the first pass? Or—don't make two consecutive cuts in the same direction.

The day winds down. Knight shakes hands with Patrick Knight as he departs.

By Saturday evening, Knight has a splitting headache. Yet he remains into the early evening, signing autographs, posing for pictures, including one in which he holds a baby. Then he goes hunting. Grouse season started yesterday, but although he is out for two hours, he doesn't get a shot and returns home empty-handed.

III

"They get into those sessions with the pro players and pretty soon they start telling stories about me, and they become the focal point of attention. Because now it's, 'What was he like? What was it like playing for him?' Now they exaggerate. They forget the nine hundred and ninety-nine times I patted them on the ass, or patted them on the back, or said something good to them. Now it's 'Boy, I survived this, I survived Camp LeJune. I'm a green beret now for what I survived.' And they don't mean that."

Him and them: Knight's relationship with his players also partakes of myth, forms a litany of its own. Harassed and mistreated, the newspapers would have it, his players leave in droves. In fact, Indiana falls midway among Big Ten schools in the number of players who leave to play elsewhere. Among basketball freshmen entering in 1974, by October of 1987 more players left Michigan State, Wisconsin, Ohio State, Purdue and Minnesota than they did Indiana.

That even this many players leave (36.7 percent at Indiana as of April 1988 as against a national transfer average of about 29 percent) may in part be attributed to the down side of the Hoosier obsession with basketball. As the Valparaiso aficionados revealed, towns like Marion, which sent Knight Lyndon Jones and Jay Edwards, expect their high school stars to start as college freshmen and to play many minutes. When some don't crack the lineup early in their freshman year, they are made to feel as if they're failures. And indeed at smaller schools, or at schools attracting less talent, they would be offered more playing time, as Indiana's Delray Brooks was at Providence and Marty Simmons was at Evansville, neither of whom would be drafted by the NBA at the close of their senior seasons.

"The people here are really great," Dave Minor said as he departed in the fall of 1987. "I wish I could have contributed a little more to the team." Sometimes, too, as we will see with one starter from the 1987 championship team, parents intervene, their only concern their own child's playing time. And it takes a strong child to withstand the demands of a parent's ego.

"Great game," Ed Vreeswyck told his son Michael after a Temple loss to Nevada/Las Vegas in the 1986 pre-season NIT in which Michael had scored twenty-two points.

"What's that supposed to mean?" his son answered with cold disdain. "We lost, didn't we?" And the father, who tells this story on himself, learned something from his son and John Chaney.

Shooters who are recalcitrant about learning to be strong defensive players encounter resistance at Indiana (where, as Knight says and means it, the word team has no "I" in it). Steve Alford responded to Knight's insistence that he "defend someone," although it may not always have been easy. "He abused Steve Alford," Buddy Martin wrote in the Denver *Post.*

In fact, Knight forced Alford to be what Alford insisted he wanted to be—a creditable basketball player. "I love that man," Alford said at a press conference in the Market Square Arena in Indianapolis in the fall of 1987 as a rookie Dallas Maverick. When Delray Brooks played below the level of the rest of the team, rather than redshirting him, Knight encouraged him to transfer at once so that he would have two and a half more years to play.

Most of the defections came in one season. After the 1976 championship, everybody but Kent Benson had graduated, five of the top six players. In 1977 as the second best high school player in Ohio, Mike Miday announced he'd cut off all his hair to play for Knight. He started his second game, but not the third because he had already been missing class. He quit the following week with harsh words about his coach: "He dehumanized me."

That same season Bobby Bender, a sophomore, Billy Cunningham and Derek Holcomb left, disappointed in their playing time as Knight shuffled his lineup and began to rebuild. A football player named Trent Smock was allowed to come out for the team. When he complained that he didn't play in the first game, Knight called him in and said, "I don't need that. I think you're better off taking your time to do something else." A reluctant student, Mark Haymore, went to the University of Massachusetts because "Julius Erving played there." Later, he wrote to Knight, wishing he'd remained at Indiana, and Knight regretted it too: "We made a mistake in not keeping him."

Mike Giomi, the team's leading rebounder at a time when the team was struggling, was cut after having been warned about cutting classes. Ira Berkow has written sympathetically about Giomi's plight, contending that a student's development should be measured by means other than his attendance record. It's the more permissive approach to education, this view that students may choose how they are to learn, that the old-fashioned dictatorial approach, which includes a focus on discipline and attending class, has little place in education.

In fact, this permissive approach has few adherents in university education today. There is simply no student who doesn't profit from class attendance, from whatever level he begins, and athletes usually do not enter college with the best academic preparation or habits. (Only after Giomi left did Knight discover that he had left unpaid library fines, parking fines, bills owing to merchants all over Bloomington.)

At the end of that 1977 season, Miday's roommate, Rick Valavicius, also departed. One night he was coming down the floor with the ball; Knight screamed at him from the bench so that it unnerved him. He accused Knight of being "arbitrary and violent" and went off to Auburn.

When at the end of that 1977 season Bob Hammel in the Bloomington *Herald-Telephone* printed Valavicius's statement, a rupture ensued with Bob. Knight not speaking to Hammel for close to eight months. For Knight, coming as it did after a flood of defections, printing the words of still another disaffected student seemed superfluous and unnecessary. For Hammel, it was his responsibility to print what was happening in the Indiana basketball program, his biggest winter story. As two men of strong convictions, unyielding in their sense of what was right, neither would back down.

That summer, Hammel's son Rick worked at Knight's basketball camp. "It must be you," he told his father one night, "because he's pretty nice to me. You must be the one at fault."

In the autumn, Hammel greeted Knight's silence by writing pre-season columns about the players, not once mentioning Knight's name. Once the season began, Hammel believes, Knight responded to their feud by canceling all his post-game press conferences and having his comments distributed in mimeographed form so that he would not be accessible to Hammel. (Knight denies this action had anything to do with Hammel).

And then one day there was a telephone call.

"Do you want war?"

Hammel laughed. His going to war with Knight seemed ridiculous.

"No, not really. Why?"

"Because if you want it, you can have it."

Such a telephone call could only mean that rapprochement had begun. But Hammel was not yet out of the woods. There was a banquet celebrating the Indiana Classic at which the four coaches sang "Jingle Bells" and Knight made a speech "ripping the devil out of me, in the nature of what a bad job I was doing," Hammel says. "It was savage." At the end of that speech President John Ryan went up and apologized to Hammel. "There's no problem," Hammel assured him. "This is OK."

Hammel knew that Knight had made his second overture. But Hammel would have to endure a chilly reception on a road trip before, at last, it was over. And meanwhile he continued to report, neither permitting Knight's intransigence toward him personally to affect his writing, nor ignoring any aspect of a story he happened to be reporting.

Hammel ponders it now: "Given the opportunity to take the clay and remodel it, I would probably change some things. I don't know that in my reshaping, I would come up with as effective a person as there is right now. In some mysterious way these rough aspects that I find removable add in some peculiar way to the effectiveness."

Now the two men meet in a shared ideal that Knight more than any other basketball coach has realized: you can win without cheating.

Knight's reputation of being rough on his players may date from that 1976 photograph in which he is shown pulling a player named Jim Wisman off the court by his jersey. Wisman looks perplexed. Looking at the photograph himself, he decides that he looks "goofy."

It happened during that extraordinary 1976 season when Indiana would go thirty-two and zero. In a game against Michigan, Wisman threw the ball away twice against the press. Knight couldn't get the game stopped fast enough.

"I called time-out and I saw a white shirt out of the corner of my eye," Knight remembers. "I reached out and grabbed the shirt. I had no idea whom I had. It ended up that I had Wisman, who had just thrown the ball away twice."

At first Wisman didn't realize who was grabbing him. "Oh, no!" was his sudden reaction, and he was embarrassed. But what made him mad was that right then and there Knight benched him. The wire services had a field day.

The next day, Sunday, in practice, Wisman again threw away the ball.

"Wisman, I'm going to tell you one thing," Knight said then. "You're either going to have to learn how to get the ball in against the press, or you'd better get a tearaway jersey to wear." The whole team laughed. In the championship game of the Final Four, against Michigan, Wisman came in off the bench and played well.

Knight, however, does not apologize for pressuring his players. "Hey," he says, "what is this kid going to do when somebody gives him something to do when he's out working and he screws it up like that? He's going to lose his job. He better learn to do things right now. That's one thing we teach our kids here in basketball. You have a chance to leave here and do things right later because you know that's what's expected of you."

In 1978, a senior now, Jim Wisman played his last game for Indiana. It was an NCAA tournament game against Villanova. Indiana was one point up. Villanova called time-out, with possession. "If they score, you race the ball down here and call time-out," Knight told Wisman. Villanova scored. Wisman raced the ball down, and called time. Indiana took the ball in bounds—and then they lost.

And all the way down the ramp to the lockers, Knight followed Wisman, saying, "Goddamn it, Jimmy next time . . ." He was still coaching, still teaching, so intent on improving Wisman's basketball that he forgot that Wisman would never play another college game.

Indeed, to some players, Knight's unrelenting teaching is difficult to accept. "When you get down on me," Patrick Knight has told him, "it's hard to remember you're my father." Because Knight is never one to "explain" his motives—not to players, let alone to the press—the mythology grows that, motivated by the need to win basketball games, he manipulates and tortures students.

Many players, in fact, do catch on. "Sometimes he yells at you for something he says you did wrong," Rick Calloway confides. "But you did it right, just to see how you're going to react. Are you going into a shell and not want to play tomorrow or are you going to come back and not worry about what he said and just keep on playing?"

It's October 16 and the players are eating dinner together after practice.

Shawn Kemp, whom they are entertaining, listens intently.

Are you planning to come here? he is asked.

"We hope so," says Ricky, strongly, encouragingly.

Did Kemp enjoy the practice? He did.

It's always been the same: the players who can tolerate unrelenting criticism are criticized more. Ray Tolbert had trouble hanging onto the ball, but if he fumbled, Jim Wisman would be attacked: "Why did you throw him a pass like that?" If Wisman didn't pass to Tolbert, he would still be attacked: "Didn't you see him open? Can't you see out of your left eye?"

"I don't care if you don't score a point, just play your role," Wisman would be told. "You played forty minutes and you didn't score a point!" he'd then be chastised. "I can put guys in who can kick it in a few times." Angry at Bobby Wilkerson, he would yell at John Laskowski.

The year after the 1976 championship season, the season of the jersey, Wisman's excellent performance in the Final Four victory over Michigan was forgotten.

"You know something?" Knight told Jimmy Wisman. "You didn't even play so well in the championship game."

For Wisman the moment produced an epiphany. What counted in basketball as in life, was not what you once did, but what you are doing now. At the start of his own post-championship season, Dean Garrett grasps the same truth as he listens to his coach telling him he's worse than when he first came: "It's a motivational move for myself. What I'm thinking is, he knows you're out there, what he's trying to tell you is, just go harder. I want you to be better than you were before you came." Keith Smart sees that too: "He wants you thinking all the time, not only on the court, but outside in the rest of the world too, because there are a lot of people that can fool you and say things to you."

But no one rose to the challenge of Knight's motivational strategies more than Steve Green, now a dentist, one of Knight's first recruits.

"One year we got together in pre-season and decided we're not going to lose *any* games because we're not going to face him in a losing situation. We'd show him we were better than he said." It was a team that went into the NCAA tournament twenty-nine and zero.

At the end of that 1975 season after they had advanced to the regional against the University of Texas at El Paso, Knight stopped practice and demanded of his assistant, Bob Weltlich, "How bad are we going to get beat?"

"Hey, they're going to kill us."

The players then looked at each other and thought: don't you dare say that to us!

Motivation won out: Indiana triumphed in that game, losing later to Kentucky 92–90 in the regional final. The perfect season had been destroyed not, however, as it seemed, by one basket, but because of an injury to Scott May at Indiana's conference championship clinching game at Purdue with four games remaining in the regular season.

In the locker room, slightly raising his voice, Knight said, "Goddamn it, we should have won this game!" But then he said, "Why am I yelling at these kids?" Some had cried and Green had to console Tim Knight on the bench.

Knight was deeply pleased by that beloved 1975 team. He is a man light-years away in character from a Vince Lombardi, who after a victory could tell his team, "Don't think you're responsible for all this success . . . because I want you to understand that *I* did this. *I* made you guys what you are."[1] It is impossible to imagine Bob Knight speaking such words.

Because he did so many things well, as an Indiana player from 1979 to 1981, Isiah Thomas did not realize how much better he could be if he were more of a team player. Corrected, he would stare what came to be known as the "blank Isiah stare" and attempt to look right through Knight.

Was Knight too hard on Isiah? Piston coach Chuck Daly sometimes tells Thomas to control his game so he can play better with the other players. Isiah responds, as he confided to Bill Nack of Sports Illustrated: "I can't decide whether to play or to win." Winning means he must submerge his individualistic play, play Knight does not permit, not for the best player, and not for the weakest. In this sense Knight indeed runs an "equal opportunity" program. "I'm the only person in his life that's ever whacked him, ever," Knight says, "and I think he has a problem with that. No coach has ever gotten on his ass like I have."

Sometimes his teammates were perplexed by the degree to which Knight strove to shape Isiah's enormous talent to the team game, the winning game. But for Knight the team game alone justifies the expenditure of time these university students spend on basketball. Only the team game encourages the development of character.

One day in the student locker room Knight made an accusation.

"I think Isiah is throwing games. He doesn't care if the team wins."

And then he quizzed the team: how many disagree?

Ted Kitchel raised his hand. "How can you say that?" he demanded. "I think Isiah is giving one hundred percent, giving as much as he can. I don't know how you can say that."

Missing the larger picture—that Isiah was not accepting the Indiana style of play—Kitchel had taken Knight literally. Knight, being Knight, would not explain, knowing that the best teaching involves the student's discovering the truth of what he's saying for himself.

---

1. Michael O'Brien, *Vince: A Personal Biography of Vince Lombardi.* New York: William Morrow and Company, Inc., 1987, p. 248.

"We're either going to play in the NCAA tournament with you or without you. It doesn't make any difference to me," Knight told Isiah that spring of 1981. "If we're going to play *with* you, you're going to play my way. Period."

"The only championship team he ever played on was at Indiana," Knight says. "He had to be babied, he had to be coaxed, hardest guy to coach I ever had, and the most talented. He was a hell of a player. He was a tough, competitive kid."

Obviously there was a side to Isiah's recalcitrance Knight admired. Later came that well-publicized Fort Wayne awards banquet where Isiah, responding to racism among the so-called benefactors, behaved childishly, lacing his acceptance speech with obscenities, regretting it all the while that he was doing it yet unable to stop himself. And then out of the view of the audience he made a peculiarly lewd gesture toward Knight.

"If anyone would stand up for him," Knight searingly told Ted Kitchel that day he quizzed the team, "I figured it would be you."

Kitchel might have been the greatest rebel in the Knight corps. In Kitchel's memory Knight never praised him for a great game. But one day, before the whole team, Knight announced, "If I were going to war, I'd want Kitchel on my side."

Once in a game against Northwestern, Kitchel pulled a muscle so badly he could hardly walk. Practice seemed out of the question. The coach, however, thought otherwise.

"When I played at Ohio State, John Havlicek once had two pulled groin muscles and he didn't miss a minute!"

As soon as Knight walked away, Kitchel turned to Phil Isenbarger and said, "If you were Fred Taylor, what would you do? Play Havlicek with two bad legs—or start your sixth man?" (The "sixth man" was, of course, Knight.)

At times, a player will stand up to Knight:

"Uwe, you picked up swearing really well," Knight told Blab one day. "Why don't you teach me some words in German?"

"No, Coach, then you'd know what I'm calling you in practice."

In an earlier era after a Knight dressing-down in the locker room, Tom Abernathy would turn to Quinn Buckner and, slowly, wink.

In a season opener, Buckner was indignant with Knight, who yelled at him because he missed a practice (he was on a football scholarship, playing two sports). After he had scored eighteen points, he looked at Knight so pointedly that the coach was driven to bark, "Don't look at me in that tone of voice!"

On still another occasion, particularly annoyed with Randy Wittman, whom he accused of not working hard enough to get open, Knight enlisted eleven-year-old Patrick Knight to guard him in practice. Then he demanded that the other players set screens on Patrick. This went on for three or four plays.

"Dad, I held him!" Patrick gleefully asserted. "He didn't score!"

Wittman, of course, wasn't about to give Knight the satisfaction.

On still another occasion Buckner made a pass that Knight didn't think he should have made and which cost them the game. Buckner maintained that it remained a good pass, only the guy missed it. He wanted to discuss it, but Knight simply refused. Disturbed, Buckner told his father.

"Maybe you want to leave IU?" his father said.

And Buckner saw at once there was jealousy between the two fathers.

"My father could see there was a male influence other than himself," Buckner says. Knight perceived it too. When after graduation Buckner's father began to help with his contract with the Milwaukee Bucks, Knight quietly backed away.

Kitchel was told he couldn't count to four (four passes), Kitchel was given a kick in the butt, not, as some reporters have written, right after an operation but four years later. In a game against Iowa, Kitchel shot on the first pass and was promptly taken out of the game and benched for eight minutes.

"How could you take that shot?" Knight demanded.

"I wanted to get us off to a good start," Kitchel said, undaunted.

When Kitchel was a senior and the team had a ten and zero record, Indiana lost a game to Ohio State by one point. Knight threw all the seniors out and told them that for the next week they could dress in the visitors' locker room. They couldn't prepare for the next game by watching films. Finally Kitchel said, "If we're a team, this isn't going to work." And he went off to the coaches' locker room to confront Knight.

It wasn't easy. Knight made fun of Kitchel before the assistants and seemed unwilling to relent.

"I don't want you back in," Knight told him, according to Kitchel.

"We're moving back in!" Kitchel said, holding his ground. And they did.

"You can bet the absolute goddamn farm that Kitchel never said that to me," Knight now says. "I don't even remember the incident. I remember throwing Dakich's team out of the locker room. But I can guarantee that Kitchel never told me anything. They've found they can become the center of a big party telling stories about me.")

Mostly, however, the force of his will prevails, during their playing days and after. One day when he was giving a clinic in New Jersey, Knight called Jimmy Oxley, who had played for him at West Point, and asked him to meet him for dinner. Oxley was in medical school and very busy at the time, but he agreed.

At the clinic Knight asked Oxley to join him on the stage. He introduced his former player with many compliments, all the while discussing motivation. Oxley was in his late twenties, in street clothes, but as Knight beckoned him forward, demanding, "Walk faster, walk faster," Oxley found himself complying. "It made me so mad," he said later, "but I kept on going faster and faster. I just couldn't go slow. I almost ran across that stage when all I wanted was to go nice and slow." If this story sounds a bit like Thomas Mann's "Mario and the Magician," one might add that the commanding personality, that force of will, may be used, in the service of a variety of causes, some good and some evil.

After Knight's players leave, friendship begins. (Only a student's failure to graduate jeopardizes that relationship.) "The answer," Knight says in response to attacks on his methods, "is the product. The answer is all the kids that have graduated, the answer is their reaction to coming back to Indiana, the answer is their willingness to help us in any way they can." An annual summer golf tournament, which raises money for Indiana scholarships and for the library, draws nearly all of them back for a reunion. "If the product understands what was done to get it there and in every conceivable way," Knight says, "then that's the answer."

Playing basketball in Europe in 1977 and not doing particularly well, Joby Wright called Knight to say he wanted to finish school and perhaps coach.

"Come on back to school and we'll help you," Knight said. Joby arrived back in Bloomington only to receive a call to play in Finland. He slipped out of town without even telling Knight. Shortly after his arrival, however, Joby tore up his leg. He had to call Knight and ask for a second chance.

Joby, it was clear, needed a Knight lesson.

"If you want to play ball, play ball," Knight told him. "If you want to come back and rehabilitate your leg, come back. But there are no promises."

When Joby returned, he had to face the music.

"You're making an idiot of yourself," Knight said, "chasing a dream that's never going to materialize. If you haven't made it by now, you're never going to make it in basketball. Stop fooling yourself. If you're going to get yourself together, start by going back to school. I had it set up for you to go. You walked out on that. I'll help you get into school, but you've got to show me what you're all about."

The road back was slow. Joby first worked in Knight's basketball camp. Before he could be an assistant coach, for three years he had to mop the floors "if some kid puked," wash the backboards, do whatever Knight asked. "It taught me some things about myself," Joby says.

Each student is treated differently. When a former player accumulated gambling debts, Knight bailed him out—more than once. One day Jimmy Wisman, Wisman of that tearaway jersey, who had been working in advertising in Columbus, Indiana, appeared in Knight's office.

"I hear you're doing well," Knight began.

"I want to move to Chicago."

"You're not the most cosmopolitan son of a bitch."

"It's more than that . . ." Wisman began to explain, and even as he tried to tell Knight what it was he wanted, Knight was reaching for the telephone, calling the head of the School of Business.

"You remember Jimmy Wisman," Knight said to Dean Wentworth. "He would be successful at anything he does. I don't know anything about this business, but I'd like him to come over and talk to you." Out of this call came an interview with Leo Burnett in Chicago—and a job.

At their rites of passage, he materializes: funerals, weddings, illnesses, revealing concern that they might have anticipated while they were still at school. As a freshman, arriving for his first day of practice at the brand-new Assembly Hall, Steve Green was pulled aside by Knight and told that his Grandma Green had died in a car accident and his father wanted him home. Green hesitated. Couldn't it wait until after practice?

"Get dressed and get out of here!" Knight growled.

At times of personal crisis they may not notify him, but somehow he finds out. When Jim Crews' wife had a miscarriage, their unlikely early Sunday morning caller was Bob Knight. When Steve Green's baby was born with Down's Syndrome, the first person to call outside the family was Bob Knight.

"I'm doing fine," said Green staunchly.

"Hell no, you're not," Knight said, telling Green it was not necessary to maintain a brave front.

When Quinn Buckner's father died, he told Knight the role was exclusively his from now on.

And although he does not say so, Knight counts on their understanding, which explains why he could be incensed at an interview Kent Benson gave to the Akron *Beacon Journal*[1] in which Benson brags about having "survived that!" Knight recognizes that the remarks are positive in their intent, but misguided in their approach to helping him. Why didn't Benson admit that "for every time he hollered at me, there were twenty times when he patted me on the back"? In the article Benson remarks how Buckner and May, once yelled at, were lost for three weeks.

Knight shakes his head. "May and Buckner wouldn't break down in the face of the Gestapo," he remembers. "I've had Benson in tears out here over almost nothing."

"He swears at me more than at you two," Benson whined to Buckner and May one day. "I'm quitting!"

Buckner and May laughed. Member of the Fellowship of Christian Athletes or not, Benson did no small amount of swearing himself. After a visit to Father James Higgins, the unofficial team chaplain, Benson decided to stay.

And so they return, to be chided, encouraged, assisted in their careers, and, no less than anyone else, needled. "He's an impor-

---

1. "Count Cavs' Embry, Benson Among Knight Fans," Beacon *Journal*, Sunday, November 29, 1987.

tant person in my life," Ted Kitchel says of Fred Taylor's sixth
man. "I had to take being called the Dick Vitale of the Southside,"
Quinn Buckner says with ironic chagrin. No one seems to doubt
it's worthwhile.

IV

"It's the inefficient people that bother me."

On the day after Valparaiso, I wait for him in his office. I'm eager
to make an appointment for an interview, surely not too much to
expect after close to a year of negotiations prior to my arrival. He
saunters up the ramp and enters the office.

"How're you doing?" he asks, and abruptly turns away, making
it clear that he has no business with me. He seems darkly intimidating, inaccessible to rational appeal. I dare not follow him
into his private office.

"If you can," Bob Hammel advises, "treat it as if nothing has
happened. Just continue." I decide that Hammel is covering up
some truth too awful to utter, that he is being evasive.

But in the evening, after practice, as Knight sits chatting at the
scorer's table with the head of the board of trustees, I make my
way across the floor from where I've been chatting with Landon
Turner. I ask when I might talk with him.

"Tomorrow," he says, loud, unfriendly, dismissive. I say good-
night. He does not respond.

The following day he takes no telephone calls. I think he must
have changed his mind about cooperating for my article. I imagine that somehow on the plane ride to Valparaiso, or at the Big
Wheel afterward, I said the wrong thing. I join the audience at the
clinic, and chat with the fledgling coaches. I eat dinner with Bob
Murrey, his friend who is running the clinic and to whom I reveal
my disappointment. He's just busy, Murrey demurs, as if nothing
out of the ordinary had occurred.

The clinic is about to open its concluding session on Sunday
morning when Knight shouts my name across the floor. He takes
me aside, keeping the four hundred participants waiting. He allows me to accuse him of bad faith, only to accept no blame.

"You have to come after me, I'm not coming after you!" he states categorically. "I'm doing five things. You're only doing one." Unbeknownst to me, I think, we've been competing. It's also apparent that he's half amused by it all. He promises to talk after the clinic is over.

And so we sit down in the coaches' locker room, although I'm annoyed that we'll only have a few minutes, that I must be constantly aware of my impending flight. I feel as if I have nothing to lose. I demand an explanation. How can he justify his not having returned my telephone calls? Surely I have him on that.

"You may have called," he says, "but you have not talked to me. Now if I say, I'm not going to talk to you, that's entirely different. You just can't ever use intermediaries."

My sense that this is sophistry is mediated by my relief that at least we are, in fact, talking.

Joby Wright puts his head in the door with news. Shawn Kemp has told him his mother had said that morning on the telephone that she doesn't want him to visit Nevada/Las Vegas. He's easily the best high school senior in Indiana and one of the top ten players in the country. Indiana wants him. That his mother seems to view Indiana favorably is good news. As all college recruiters know, the support of a player's mother often makes the difference. It was, for example, the confidence of Mary Thomas in Bob Knight that ensured Isiah's choice of Indiana.

Knight turns to the subject of his own children. He really likes them both, he says, "Not every parent likes his kids. You love your kids, but you don't always like them." They're polite to people, which is important to him. It's clear he's proud of them both too- Patrick, who's shooting baskets outside at this very moment, and Tim who "works like hell" at his job here.

He feels a need to explain how inconceivable to him it is that a player and coach should be friends. This is something most teachers should know, but, he says, they don't. He acknowledges our mutual interest; we are both teachers at universities.

He waits. He offers me a grape. He is being friendly.

The issue for him is what makes teaching possible. Just as notion of wanting a student to be his friend is alien to him, so is the fear among some teachers that an antagonistic, adversarial relationship might grow up between a coach and his players. "I'm not sure how many coaches I've ever known that were anybody's friend." You might, of course, say the same thing about teachers in general. He is as sophisticated in his approach to teaching as any professor anywhere.

As for the military metaphors that are perpetually attached to him, he says he rarely uses those quotations to support something he has done, although it's easy to attach military metaphors to a tough-minded coach. The military figure he admires most is Ulysses S. Grant, who, after his western campaigns, checked into a Washington hotel as "U.S. Grant and son."

Who is *he?*

He finds an answer in Themistocles, who, asked whether he would rather be Achilles or Homer, said, "Which would you rather be, a conquerer in the Olympic games or the crier that proclaimed who the conquerers were?" With his eternal adversaries, he is always ready to do battle: "I could be hired tomorrow as a sportswriter and I'd be pretty good. How many sportswriters could be hired tomorrow as coaches?"

He judges everyone by their fiber, no more on gender than on race or nationality. "It's the inefficient people that bother me," he says, "male or female doesn't make any difference. I'm not intrigued by inefficient people, whether it be a housewife or the Chairman of the Board of General Motors."

I return to the subject of his seeming intransigence, and now he has his full explanation of what happened.

"Let me tell you exactly what you're doing. You're doing the very same thing these people do, you're assuming, taking it for granted [that he's unreasonable]. You're saying that well, this must be true. You're doing everything you're trying to eliminate. That's exactly what you're doing. You let yourself fall into the same trap that you've been reading about!"

He pauses. There's no question but that I've been outargued. I had come to challenge the stereotype only to behave as if it were the gospel truth.

He could leave it at that. But he does not, because, I suspect, at the core he's a generous man:

"You come out here for two days when we're practicing and you know now that all you have to do is say, 'Hey, goddamn it, I'm going to take you out to eat tonight. What time are we going?' "

CHAPTER SIX

SCRIMMAGING

*"When we start playing, and we're starting into games, part
of getting a kid not to make mistakes is getting him to a
point where he doesn't want to make mistakes. Because he
doesn't want to hear me when he makes a mistake, if that's
what it takes. Then, eventually, he understands how much
better he is when he doesn't make mistakes. Now his own
willingness not to make mistakes supersedes his reluctance
to hear me. Without developing that, I don't think you have
a chance to be any better than anybody else."*

ON THURSDAY, November 5, Bob Knight calls.

"Where's my note thanking me for my hospitality?"

"I'm angry at you."

By now, of course, I'm not; it's rather that an adversarial stance
seems appropriate.

"Just as long as you're five times as mad at yourself because
you blew it."

I'm willing to grant I had been intimidated, so he seizes the
opportunity to do what he does by reflex: develop your character.

"I hope I've gotten you out of that." He enjoys bringing up
people; it could be a player, or a TV interviewer, or me. We set
a date when I can listen to him give a talk in Indianapolis "which
might be interesting."

*   *   *

Noon on November 12: it's a luncheon benefit for Cathedral High School to raise fifteen thousand dollars for scholarships. He wears a blue nylon windbreaker over the red sweater, and, today, sunglasses: no coat and no tie.

He dresses this way, he says, without a tie, to be accessible to the people he speaks to; the red sweater bespeaks familiarity. So, he confesses, he'll come up to the podium and begin speaking before anyone can introduce him. Or he'll ask to be introduced simply as "The coach of Indiana University."

He drives a Mercury, with his credit cards in the glove compartment. He doesn't know exactly where he's going or what time he has to be there. Mary Ann Davis, his indefatigable secretary, has taped the directions on his door. At the last minute he grabs the paper and he's off.

On the hour-long drive to Indianapolis, his mind is on recruiting. Knight knows that other coaches recruit specifically against him, insisting that Steve Alford was in "a concentration camp" for four years. "Our only difficulty," Purdue's Gene Keady will say in the February 22 issue of Sports Illustrated, "is finding guys with courage enough to fight Knight . . . it doesn't bother me. Or I'm too stupid." In the recruiting wars among that fraternity it would appear there is little honor, little sense of fair play.

Yet Knight continues not to coddle potential recruits, and not to make promises he couldn't possibly keep. He will ask a recruit, "Is there anything I can tell you?" He will not, "Call a kid and say, 'How are you, baby? You'll play every day.' " If he enters a player's home, and finds no books there, no newspapers or magazines, he doubts whether the player will choose Indiana.

In fact, today's Louisville *Courier-Journal* has the story. Both Shawn Kemp and Chris Mills who, as another of the country's top high school players, has also visited Indiana, have signed letters of intent with Kentucky. And some facts are emerging. Mrs. Kemp, who said she did not have gas money to visit Bloomington, the trip from Elkhart being "too expensive" and her car too unreliable, turned up in Lexington, Kentucky, more than three hours away. And if we look into the future, there is Shawn Kemp driving a brand-new blue 1987 Z24 Chevrolet Cavalier automobile, and Chris Mills a 1984 Datsun 300 ZX.

Shawn Kemp's high school principal will confront him with a question: "Where'd you get that car?"

In Indianapolis at the door of the athletic club awaiting—or almost awaiting—his old coach is orthopedic surgeon Steve Ahlfeld. Only Ahlfeld doesn't have anyone at the door at the precise moment when the coach drives up. It doesn't matter that the coach is late. At once Ahlfeld is treated to a ribbing. Coach hopes his patients get out of surgery more efficiently than his car has been dealt with today. One of his first recruits, Ahlfeld, class of 1975, laughs. But he squirms a bit too.

Ahlfeld will not be the only recipient of needles today: the head table is filled with likely victims, from Dan O'Malia, president of O'Malia Food Stores and the chairman of the board of Cathedral High School to the Reverend James P. Higgins, pastor of St. Martins in Martinsville and former director of St. Paul's Catholic Center in Bloomington, that unofficial team chaplain who set Kent Benson straight about Knight's swearing more at him than at Buckner and May. They are already through their chicken and canned string beans when Knight arrives.

The master of ceremonies is Bob Collins, columnist for the Indianapolis *Star,* who functions today as a friendly adversary. At once the two old combatants go one on one in merciless ribbing.

Collins is attacked for his pink jacket. "Father Jim Higgins," says Knight, "a longtime friend of mine, has just given me a note to read. 'Bob, please don't make any more references to Collins' gay leanings. We're trying to introduce a more tolerant view of this in the church.' "

Collins, who can both dish it out and take it, chooses, for now, to address himself to the priest, who sits happily smoking his cigar at the head table.

"Father Higgins, I'd like to say that, like you, I'm celibate. This came not through preference, but through aging."

"You have asked me so many questions over the years, and my answers have supplied so many columns for your rather feeble pen, that I would simply like to ask you this question: Is your third wife merely a camouflage for all this?" Knight rejoins.

Collins' comeback contains a sharp, an unmistakable needle, biting and pointed and effective:

"Coach, I'd like to say to you, 'Congratulations on your recruiting season.' "

The audience—businessmen, former players, Indianapolis professionals, nearly all men, largely Indiana fans—roars with laughter. They too have heard the news about Kemp and Mills. Knight laughs too. Collins has him—for the moment.

The ribbing goes on: Collins calls Knight "a dear sweet man who teaches semantics," and begins a story about one day encountering a player doing twenty-mile laps.

"I asked him why? He said, for 'absolutely nothing.'

" 'Young man, that's not true. I happen to know for a fact that the penalty for absolutely nothing is twelve laps!' "

In deference to O'Malia, the food merchant, there's a typical male joke about what to do with cucumbers. Then Knight is awarded a plaque by Cathedral High School "for his unwavering leadership, dedication and love to the youth of our country for these many years."

"Thanks for coming, Coach Knight," Dan O'Malia says shyly.

But at moments of sentiment, within an all-male environment, it would be inconceivable for Knight to reveal his tender side.

"I would rather the hell have had Barlow," he growls. Ken Barlow, a former Cathedral student, and a fine basketball player, a few years ago chose Notre Dame over Indiana. "You can take that plaque and put it where your cucumbers are." His timing is flawless. He pauses, and then he drives the point home: "That's a hell of a thing," Knight says. "You send [Phelps] Barlow and you bring me here to raise money for you!"

Knight's affection for Father Higgins only ensures that the "Padre" will be the butt of several jokes which include an accusation that he used profanity from a seat just behind the Indiana bench when Tom Abernethy tipped in a basket against Notre Dame.

"I just don't condone that kind of language," says Knight.

After Knight relives some games for them, it's time for questions. He becomes serious as he discusses the game against LSU in the 1987 regionals: "That game expressed what I get out of coaching. You talk about patience and you talk about determination and effort and playing under control and reliance on one another, confidence in being able to get the job done under any circumstances. We were nine points down with 4:07 to play and we won. That's what I get out of coaching. Seeing all those things come together with those kids out there." The ribbing will resume in a moment—for now, unselfconsciously, he has stated his credo.

The supposed concentration camp victim, Steve Alford, consulted him about his present NBA chances only the other day. Knight went through the NBA roster team by team and found six players about Steve's size and athletic skills who have played pretty well. He was honest with his former star, for he is not one to flatter: They all handled the ball better than Alford did. But he shot it better than they all did! "What he had to do in my opinion was work on handling the ball better and getting it to people that were open. He's never again going to have the opportunity to score. His scoring is going to be secondary to everything else that he does."

Someone wants to know if Knight will be redshirting anyone this season, asking any players to postpone their eligibility. The speaker, however, has ignored the issue of tact and trust: the student might hear it first from a stranger or read it in a newspaper.

"Did it take you all morning to think of that question?"

Then Knight does reply. There will be a scrimmage tonight. "I want to see exactly where we are. Five or six players have already been redshirted. So we have only a couple of possibilities."

He behaves as if he's among friends, people with whom he can reminisce about his boyhood, when he listened to college basketball games on the radio, and knew the names of all the major league baseball players and all the football players. Thirty-one years ago someone had told him that there was a player better than Jerry Lucas and he couldn't believe it, because he had never heard of Oscar Robertson, although he was only one state away.

There has been another change, which he illustrates with an incident involving his son Patrick, who went to a basketball camp last summer with another coach's son. There the two boys posed for a picture with their feet on the bumper of a Mercedes Benz automobile:

"I heard about that and I went to the camp director and asked him if he wanted to run this camp next year. If you do, I better never see that picture anywhere." The corruption of kids has resulted in college becoming almost a stop to the pros. "Nobody even thought about this back when I was in school."

Now he introduces "one of the great people in the whole history of American college basketball."

"I think when he's right here among us we kind of tend to overlook this man. I don't think that if we were to rate a coach on the basis of what he has been able to do with talent, year after year, we could ever find a guy to place higher on the ladder than Tony Hinkle. Tony, stand up."

Hinkle, the retired basketball coach of Butler University, now a very old man, stands up at the head table, gratified.

"If they ever had a Hall of Fame for gentlemen in athletics," Knight continues, "the first two inductees in my mind would be Everett Dean and Tony Hinkle." It's Knight again showing respect for those in his profession who have preceded him; it's Knight participating in the living history of coaching.

And then, as if this were entirely too much emotion, he's off into a discussion of a Big Ten post-season tournament.

"You know, my feeling without knowing a hell of a lot about the subject would be the same as having women as priests."

The audience roars. Cathedral is a Catholic school, of course; no one enjoys the joke more than Father Higgins.

"How am I doing, Padre?" Knight wants to know.

Someone would like him to eat his words with respect to last season's predictions.

"Last year you said you didn't have a championship-quality team."

"Well, I was wrong."

"Are you going to repeat this year?"

"Nope!" But such a dumb question deserves a special needle: "I was speaking down at the resort hall in French Lick and some guy in the corner stands up and says, 'Coach, we want two in a row!' And I look and I said, 'You wouldn't have been happy with what He did with a couple of fish and a few loaves of bread either'!"

Then he must rib the many Indiana University graduates in the room; there are simply too many to leave this group unmolested. He remembers a telegram from the Indianapolis Alumni Association that he supposedly received when he first came to Blooming-ton. "Coach Knight, congratulations on being named head coach at our alma mater. We're with you all the way—win or tie!"

It's time to go, and Collins gently rises. "I've got a feeling for Collins despite everything I say," Knight concludes. "I don't like Welch worth a damn (former Chairman of the Board of Cathedral and Chairman of the Board of the Landmark Bank) and if they ever get another Barlow here, you just keep your ass out of it."

He's happy to be able to have done something to help kids, "because that's what I think it's all about for all of us. Did you ever see a bad four-year-old kid? Think about this. Did you ever see a bad four-year-old kid? I don't care what color he is . . ."

"I'm not difficult to deal with like these people think I am."

"But I know they don't learn more in chemistry than they learn here. I know that."

Steve Green: *"Keep your nose out of it."*

Before the Russian game, with Bill Wall: *"I can't interfere. . . ."* PHOTO COURTESY OF INDIANA UNIVERSITY ATHLETIC DEPARTMENT

At the Russian game: *"Just give them the ball back."* PHOTO COURTESY OF INDIANA UNIVERSITY ATHLETIC DEPARTMENT

Steve Eyl: *"Unless there's been divine intervention over the summer, shooting isn't it."*

Todd Jadlow: *"I don't want that shot taken by you ever again unless you get your feet straight."*

Tim Knight with Dan Dakich: *"I wanted him to know . . . that I thought enough of him."*

Ted Kitchel: *"If I were going to war, I'd want Kitchel on my side."*

Jim Crews: *"Joking, teaching, praising—with 10% devoted to yelling and criticizing."*

With assistant coach Ron Felling: "I'm doing five things. You're only doing one."

Dr. Steve Ahlfeld: "The answer is their willingness to help us in any way they can."

With Tony Hinkle, left, and Everett Dean: "If they ever had a Hall of Fame for gentlemen in Athletics, the first two inductees in my mind would be Everett Dean and Tony Hinkle."

With Bob Collins: "Did you ever know a bad four-year-old?" "Your mother did."

Seymour Scrimmage: *"Let's see what we can do."*

The Professors, from left: Harry Pratter, Bob Byrnes, Drew Schwartz.

Knight with Patrick Knight:
"I forget you're my father."

Patrick Knight, Joby
Wright: *"When we go out to
eat, he's my Dad."*

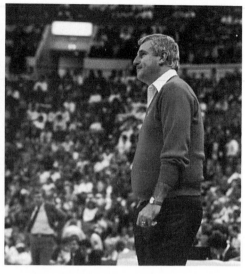

Ralph Floyd presents Professor
Byrnes with a check for $18,198.63
for the Library Fund. PHOTO
COURTESY OF INDIANA UNIVERSITY
ATHLETIC DEPARTMENT

Knight: *"They're all good kids."*
PHOTO COURTESY OF INDIANA
UNIVERSITY ATHLETIC DEPARTMENT

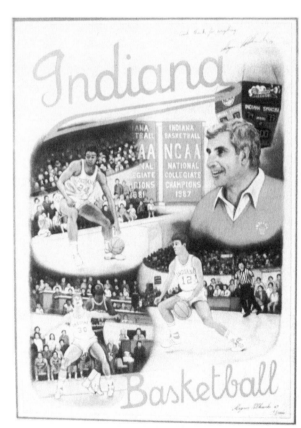

Poster by Magnus
Pelkowski: *"Coach,
thanks for everything."*

Patrick Knight:
*"Move it, Patrick.
Don't dance out there.
Move through."*

Steve Eyl: *"Eyl, were you ever told
to deviate from our rules?"* PHOTO
COURTESY OF INDIANA UNIVERSITY
ATHLETIC DEPARTMENT

Rick Calloway: *"Ricky, how badly
do you think these players care
about playing?"*

With Kreigh Smith: *"I think I made a mistake in not playing you against Kentucky."* PHOTO COURTESY OF INDIANA UNIVERSITY ATHLETIC DEPARTMENT

With Julio Salazar: *"I needle Julio a little bit."*

Former player Tom Abernethy:
*"If he needed anything on
the spur of the moment, all of us
would just jump at the chance
to repay him."*

Ryan White, right: *"I heard Ryan
was an IU fan. . . ."*

Mrs. Lingelfelter presenting
Coach Knight with a red and
white afghan. PHOTO COURTESY
OF INDIANA UNIVERSITY ATHLETIC
DEPARTMENT

With Don Fischer: *"The key word in this whole thing, Don, is bull. . . ."*

Dean Garrett: *"Dean, you're playing a lot better in practice the last two days. Why do you think that is?"*

PHOTO COURTESY OF INDIANA UNIVERSITY ATHLETIC DEPARTMENT

With Purdue coach Gene Keady.

PHOTO COURTESY OF INDIANA UNIVERSITY ATHLETIC DEPARTMENT

With Joe Hillman: *"It's very demanding. But that's what you're here for."*

Meeting the press: *"Questions?"*

With Dick Vitale (middle) and Dick Otte: *"Then you'll know I don't like you anymore."*

With Connie Chung: *"The one thing that intimidates me is intelligence and knowledge."*

With Todd Jadlow: *"I don't need anyone bigger than you or quicker than you or better than you."*

With Keith Smart: *"I want him to have a strong finish."* PHOTO COURTESY OF INDIANA UNIVERSITY ATHLETIC DEPARTMENT

With Steve Eyl: *"I want Steve to get the ball."* PHOTO COURTESY OF INDIANA UNIVERSITY ATHLETIC DEPARTMENT

New recruits John White and Michael Boykin, with Mark Robinson.

With Jay Edwards: *"He knew I was a good kid."* PHOTO COURTESY OF INDIANA UNIVERSITY ATHLETIC DEPARTMENT

Fred Taylor: *"Hell, I've known him since I was seventeen years old."*

With Bob Hammel: *"Hammel walks around Assembly Hall like he owns the place."* PHOTO COURTESY OF INDIANA UNIVERSITY ATHLETIC DEPARTMENT

With Smart and Garrett, last game of the season: *"We do it after the game."*

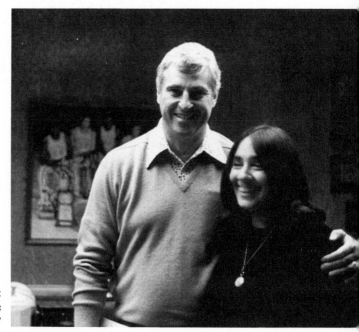

With the author:
*"This is this year's
Feinstein."*

But Collins has had enough; Collins isn't through.

"Your mother did," Collins says, and brings down the house.

Knight's final words are for education: "If we eliminated basketball at Indiana tomorrow, it would in no way affect the ability of the university to educate the kids in the state of Indiana," he says, "but if we took the chemistry department away, it would have a very adverse effect." Athletics is really only "the top of the tail of the dog."

He picks the winner of the door prize, an Indiana University jacket. (Collins calls it a Purdue jacket.) Knight, about to spend the next half hour signing autographs and posing for pictures, modestly hopes "that this season we'll give you a team you enjoy watching to play."

(At Cathedral's main fundraising event in February, called "the shamrauction," an uncensored videotape of his talk will be auctioned off and bring three hundred fifty dollars.)

Collins, returning to the *Star* office, is asked by one of his fellow writers, "Well, did you kiss His Majesty's ring?"

"No, but I'll tell you something," he retorts. "You'd kiss his ass if he'd say three words to you, and you'd walk all the way to Bloomington to do it, and everybody in this office knows it."

And with that he turns on his heels and walks out.

"Did you enjoy it?" Knight asks me on the way back. He gives more than a hundred of these fundraising speeches a year. What *he* enjoyed was Collins' comeback. Have you ever seen a bad four-year-old child? "Your mother did."

The Seymour scrimmage is tonight. "Dress casual!" he orders.

II

"I had a terrific time this afternoon."

The intrasquad scrimmage will be held tonight in Seymour, sixty-five miles south of Bloomington, in the gym of the high school attended by John Cougar Mellencamp. It's that Southern Indiana

Kurt Vonnegut calls "mean," where in the mid-1960s a sign still read "Black man, don't let the sun set on you here!" and the whole town boasted twenty-eight black households. "You'll find blacks in Clarksville or New Albany on the Ohio River, but not here," someone says.

Eighty-one hundred, a sell-out crowd, will watch Indiana play against itself, with nary a black face among them, not counting Professor William Wiggins, a member of the IU entourage. With the adjoining towns Seymour may be said to have a population of fifteen thousand.

Wiggins emerges from pre-game feasting into the lobby in front of the gigantic trophy case on the basketball side of Assembly Hall where he joins his colleagues. Professor Byrnes, the Sovietologist, is here along with Harry Pratter, the legal scholar, Drew Schwartz, the botanist, and Brion Mitchell of Comparative Literature.

Knight comes bustling down the ramp to decide who will go on the bus with the team and who will drive in the van with Ralph Floyd, the athletic director.

Driving the van, Floyd talks about how Knight "saved him, pulled him through" when his wife died three years earlier. And now, he still looks after him, seeing that he isn't left to eat alone every night.

After the 1985 season, as exhausted as he was, Knight took his team on a trip around the world. His final plans turned out to include Everett Dean, Indiana's first All-American who had coached Stanford to an NCAA championship in 1942 and also coached at IU, Henry Iba—both of whom were in their eighties—and Ralph Floyd. Each had lost his wife in the last year; each had been depressed. By including them on the trip he brought them out of their shells, back into the world, and as grueling as the travel was (it included Japan), they all felt restored and ready to go on with life.

The team enters the gym by a side door, cheered by a gaggle of waiting fans, but most of the applause goes to the coach. When he comes out onto the court after his team, by himself, his head down, his hands in his pockets, the applause is thunderous.

"He's lost weight," murmurs a woman in the third row.

Dr. Steve Ahlfeld is here tonight, still worrying about his temporary breach of efficiency in not having been outside the Indianapolis Athletic Club this morning so that coach would not have to park his car. Dr. Steve Green, the dentist, is here too, as is Steve Downey, their former teammate and now an assistant athletic director at IU.

Beside Knight on the bench sits Al Lobaldo, in 1965 Knight's assistant at West Point and before that the winningest high school coach in New Jersey. Now in his sixties Lobaldo is visiting for a few days on temporary leave from his part-time job as an assistant to Lou Carnesecca at St. John's. Knight calls him "Grandpa."

The coaching tonight will be done by Tates Locke and Ron Felling while Knight watches. Occasionally—since this is only a scrimmage—he halts the action and walks out onto the floor, puts his arm around a player and engages in talk, completely oblivious of the audience, of anyone's expectation that this be a "game."

"Sometimes it was hard," Steve Ahlfeld says, "doing pre-med and playing basketball."

"Post-exchange," Locke calls to his team. When Mark Robinson sits down, Julio Salazar, the head manager, advises him.

"Get the ball out and get it down the floor," Knight calls to the red team. "We're slower now than we are in practice." Then he moves over to talk to the whites.

"Good defense, Mark," calls Smart, sidelined by a groin injury, from the bench.

It's a teaching situation, with the score almost even throughout, 17–17 at 10:43, 39–34 with .59 to play in the first period. Knight even has one of the index cards he uses at practice. He tells Mark to give Lyndon some support. He calls Rick Calloway off the floor, puts an arm around his waist, and gives him a pat on the rear. He gathers the whole red group and talks to them, his arms raised.

No one is supposed to get tired. "If you think you are," he tells Todd Jadlow, "you'll be sitting next to me."

He begins to demand more intensity. "Judgment, judgment!" he calls to Steve Eyl, while Calloway yells to Pelkowski, "Get your feet set, Magnus." Will Calloway fill the role as the much-needed team leader? With the reds down 44–33 Knight comes over to tell Magnus, "You're only as tired as you think you are."

"Let's see what we can do," Knight tells the reds. "We're down eleven with three minutes to play." With 1.09 remaining, Knight takes the mike to thank the crowd for supporting the Indiana Basketball Hall of Fame, with which the Indiana Library fund will divide tonight's proceeds of around forty thousand dollars.

Does this scrimmage predict Indiana's season? Jeff Oliphant, who had been redshirted and then missed most of his first year with a broken foot, has scored three three—point shots and had nineteen points-. Knight worries that he is not accustomed to playing as hard as he can. Calloway, Garrett and Mark Robinson played on the winning team in both halves.

But although Calloway scored twenty-nine points, he has not pleased Knight because he put the ball on the floor too much (the Isiah sin). Garrett only scored ten points; Mark Robinson had seventeen and Jay Edwards twenty-two. Joe Hillman, back in Bloomington with a back problem, is still in everyone's mind as the team's floor leader.

Before they can board the bus, the team is besieged for autographs, not only by kids and nubile young girls, but by adults as well. Nor do they neglect Green, Ahlfeld and Downey, or Dan Dakich, all remembered as Indiana University basketball heroes.

As the bus wends its way back to Bloomington, there's a stop at a Holiday Inn for supper. Long tables have been set up in a private room, with a buffet of fried chicken, beef, corn, mashed potatoes, salad, cherry cobbler and bread pudding. Knight sits at the end of a table in the farthermost corner of the room; opposite him, in his customary seat, is Bob Hammel.

"I had a terrific time this afternoon," Knight tells Hammel, launching into the story of how he told O'Malia to stick the plaque in the place occupied by the cucumbers, how he had told them he would have preferred Barlow.

The target for ribbing at dinner turns out to be Steve Downey, at the far end of Knight's own table. He's too fat, his old coach decides, his cheeks are round and they stick out. Maybe he should grow his hair long so that his face would look "straight." And, more, Downey is ribbed about a free throw in a game against Notre Dame twelve years earlier.

"Is it like this traveling with Temple?" Knight asks me suddenly.

Then he turns to Professor Byrnes. What did the prof think?

"I never saw so many poorly chosen shots," says Byrnes.

"It's never as bad as you think or as good as you think," says Knight severely.

Brynes, whose gentleness belies his distinction (shortly he will be off to Washington to take part in the entertaining of Gorbachev), remains silent. But later he will think: I give him the answer that I usually do and he jumps all over me. He asks the question so he can destroy you.

"The last thing I need is another piece of chicken," Knight says to no one in particular. Then, impatient, perhaps bored, he rouses himself. "Is everybody done?" he yells. "Let's go!"

Ahlfeld, Downey and Green come over to thank him for including them in the dinner. However intense the needling, grace and good manners remain the natural form of their discourse with him.

"You got to sit near the throne," Harry Pratter says to me affectionately, half-enviously, as we head for the parking lot.

Boredom is the villain, the enemy, which is why, the next day, sitting in his office, he will talk to me and at the same time leaf through old clippings, alternately favorable and unfavorable, dictate letters, talk to his secretary, today B.J. McElroy make telephone calls and peruse sad stories of the death of kings. B.J. views Knight with an irony born of a worldliness which allows her to be amused by the anomalies of his personality. They are also friends.

He tells me he received a standing ovation at his annual talk to the student body. Thirty-five hundred turned up, five hundred more had been turned away, and so he told them, "You must be cheering because the university has done away with the school of journalism and we've made it a legitimate curriculum all the way around." As usual his remarks inspire a deluge of letters, from detractors and defenders both.

He believes he is emotionally close to those around him, to his coaches, to B.J., whom he insists upon calling Barbara, to all of them: "I want to get to know these people and I don't think I fail or am reluctant to get involved emotionally with people that I work around."

He asks B.J. to call David Ferrell at the library, one of the most important of his charities, and one for which he has personally raised hundreds of thousands of dollars since he began in 1976.

His friends are not hangers-on, or contributors, but people he plays golf with or goes fishing or hunting with—or whom "I just enjoy." Dinner parties with "mixed couples," by which he means men and women, are anathema and one doubts whether his marriage will alter this since what he objects to is the inane, the trivial, and the hypocritical and hence false attempts at intimacy. He did go to one "kind of a gourmet sort of a deal with little individual salt and pepper shakers and a spoon for everything. I went one more time and rented a tuxedo and wore it." Was he the only one in evening clothes? "Sure. I thought that went along with the whole scheme." His social life, he says, "is not built around bisexual groups."

"If I were to define my existence," he says, "it would be a fairly independent semi-solitary existence that I enjoy. Independent as much as a person in this job can be independent. I haven't ever held a party."

As for his favorite group: it's grandmothers. "They understand. They've been through it all. They know that not everybody can be perfect and not everybody can say what they think should be said. They look at everything with an air of indifference, an air of being set apart now." And, he says, grandmothers have been among his greatest defenders: One came up and said, 'I've got a grandchild in the third grade that knows more words than you do.' "

He laughs. "Maybe they all think they need to help me. They accept you for what you are and they understand why you are what you are. They're no longer competing with anybody for anything. See, most women are competing with other women for attention . . . and men compete too, and then you get to a point where you're really no longer a part of that competition for attention. I enjoy those people." (He has maintained a long friendship with the mother of those famous Indiana players before his time, Dick and Tom Van Arsdale.)

He seems a man with a lot of happiness in his life, enjoying the fullness of each day. "The last thing in the world that bothers me is somebody putting me down." He is thinking again of Collins, and that bad four-year-old his mother knew.

"I could have you in tears in about four minutes," he says to me suddenly.

How soon did he realize that?

"Very quickly."

Then he returns to his enjoyable life, "doing nothing, but the little bit I do. It certainly isn't an extravagant or opulent existence. It isn't full of cars and trips and glamorous people. I just enjoy from day to day. I just enjoy people, I enjoy going around and doing the things that I do."

He now asks B.J. to call Eddie Gottlieb. Gottlieb is attending a funeral, and Knight is concerned. He waits and returns to the subject of his sons, "the two people that absolutely mean the most to me in my life. I'm not sure how well I've done by them and that's a concern.

"Having Tim around is the most enjoyable single thing I've ever done."

"Tim has a more easygoing nature than you do," I say. He disagrees. "But, see, I think I'm pretty easygoing. You could not get in to see any other coach like you've gotten in to see me. They wouldn't have time for you. I don't think I've even asked you who the hell you're writing this for."

Tim Knight passes by outside. His father tells him I said he has a nicer personality than his father. Evading a potential confrontation, Tim turns to business. He and his father now engage in a long discussion about the items sold at Seymour and what will be taken to Fort Wayne, site of the next scrimmage. Tim is imaginative, as he holds up a shirt with the season's IU schedule on the back, the biggest seller, like a concert shirt.

Knight returns to his attempt to define himself with the story of how a woman in real estate turned up at their summer golf tournament: "Here's this little old gal sitting there and she's thoroughly confused because this is just a players' thing and yet she had driven up from Louisville and had a room at the Ramada Inn."

Knight managed to include her in some of the festivities. Later he sent her tournament tickets. A former teacher, "she had problems with her self-image and she was really working hard to overcome this." He said to himself, "Here's a gal who is trying like hell to do something, make a life for herself. If she gets some enjoyment out of following our basketball team, I don't think there's anything really big about that. I don't ever take myself as seriously as a lot of people do," he says.

If he talks a lot about sports, a fact which strikes me as surprising because of his far-reaching intellect, it's because "I don't know a hell of a lot about anything else." And if he prefers Hammel to other sportswriters, it's because he never misquotes. He would never remind you of something you said unless he can show where you said it. "Hammel is really the best sportswriter in the country, bar none," he says.

Being misunderstood, however, may be turned into fun. He recalls his response to the faculty council's 1987 statement on student athletes' rights, an implied attack on his treatment of his players. His retaliation began on his radio show when, asked as usual for the night's starting lineup, he said he didn't know because the faculty council hadn't sent it in yet:

"But they might be too busy since they are involved in a heated debate as to whether to plant petunias or daffodils in the flower bed behind the old library." Knight then decided for them: American Beauty roses, red and white, Indiana's colors. He instructed his television audience that those who think roses should be planted, should send their view to the faculty council. The council received ten thousand letters along with rose bushes of every description. And at the next game—the whole audience wore roses so that there wasn't a rose remaining in a single flower shop in Bloomington.

While most "Bobby Knight stories" are exaggerations, designed to earn the teller a laugh, this event actually happened. Other such anecdotes are less accurate. Someone insisted he once emptied his bag of golf clubs in the direction of a rabbit who appeared at an inopportune moment. "I honestly can't remember swinging a club. By the time the story is told, it's emptying a bag of clubs. It's great to call people on things and just let them know. It's great to make them squirm a little bit. It doesn't hurt."

He asks B.J. to send a package to David Israel—an NCAA shirt, a sweater, extra large, and a blouse and sweater to his wife. "What better wedding gifts than Indiana clothes," Knight dictates. "However, I don't think of these as wedding gifts. I think of them as humble efforts on my part to help clothe the downtrodden minorities within the borders of this great country. Sincerely yours."

"What size is she?" B.J. asks.

The answer is in good humor and B.J. takes it that way: "How the hell do I know?"

A last letter goes to a coach: "Just a note to wish you the very best as this season is about to begin. I hope that the trip you made this summer with your team paid great dividends. I thoroughly enjoyed the book that you sent to me. Best wishes for a most enjoyable and successful year."

*   *   *

And then it's time for practice. Tonight for a period of time Jay Edwards only is permitted to shoot. Jay is being groomed as a strong offensive player.

Eight passes, Knight calls, no dribble. Jay must learn to get open off a screen. "Jay, you haven't set a screen yet," he is told a little later, "you haven't even looked for one. This isn't the kind of basketball you've played. But it's the kind you're going to have to learn to play fast. So the faster you learn it, the better."

In the middle of it all Knight asks Tim to call his brother and ask him to come over.

"I wasn't a very good player," Knight tells Dean Garrett. "But I never missed a lay-up under the basket."

No professors drift in on this Friday night. Nor is there any profanity. It's all teaching, instruction in the complicated Indiana screens.

"Work, Jay, work off those screens," Knight calls. The other freshman, Lyndon Jones, must also learn to get open for the shot. "Flare for it, flare!" Knight yells. Jones makes the shot.

It's obvious that everybody's habit is the reverse of what their coach desires; they dribble instead of pass; they shoot instead of screen. "You want to be ball handlers, you want to be shooters," he tells them, "but we have to have screeners."

When they get it right, they are immediately rewarded. "Atta boy, Brian," he calls. "Good set up and good cut. Brian, get open off the screen! Here he comes! Brian, you can always get open off the screen. Keep that in mind!" Now Brian Sloan must get Dean open.

After practice, Knight tapes a television commercial, invariably beginning with an out-take. Tonight's joke: "When one of our players gets hurt, we get rid of the S.O.B. and find someone else who can play!"

Well into the commercial, a technician asks him to speak more rapidly. He's indignant, or pretends to be.

"That's the way I talk," he says. "If you want to go faster, get goddamn Paul Newman!"

Suddenly he shouts my name, his voice ringing out to the far reaches of the floor. But I can't imagine that he is calling me in the tone he uses to get a player's—or a coach's—attention. The assistants, however, seem to have frozen in their places. They cast sidelong looks in my direction, as if I had committed some breach of ethics or, at least, decorum.

I walk, slowly, over to where he's sitting on the floor, his back against one of the basketball supports.

"Well, what do you think?" he asks softly.

I remark upon the complexity of the screens.

"If you spend a lifetime, you'll never understand the screens!"

There seems no logical reply to this, so I change the subject, thinking that I might get the last word nonetheless. The impulse to compete, in whatever arena you can, becomes irresistible at Assembly Hall.

"Was that four seconds or four minutes you said it would take to make me cry?"

He suppresses a smile.

"Maybe I exaggerated."

III

"I could never really understand why a meeting has any significance if articles are written about people that aren't there. That's always boggled my mind. And yet I was really pleased to be required to come here today."

On Saturday he goes hunting in Southern Indiana, bagging twelve birds. And on Sunday morning he attends the Big Ten Press Conference in Chicago, a meeting he boycotted for the past three years. Now there will be a one-game suspension for any coach who doesn't attend.

On this warm November day he drives up to the little Monroe County airfield in his black Bronco dressed in the blue nylon windbreaker with the red sweater underneath. He carries a briefcase full of clippings, quotations and mail, along with Tom Clancy's *Red Storm Rising*. Bob Hammel is already there, and Eric Ruden of Indiana's sports information department, as well as Jorja Hoehn, the women's basketball coach, who must attend her own press conference.

"Let's go, girls!" Knight calls.

Jorja doesn't seem to mind; he's been exceptionally supportive of her efforts with the women's team, attending their practices, allowing her coaches to attend his, and mentioning the women's team on his radio program. She is adapting his motion offense for the women's team.

Unlike the other Big Ten coaches, he has not dragged one of his players with him. It is enough that his time is being wasted.

"What's in it for me?" he asks Ruden.

"It cuts down on interviews," Ruden ventures.

"I never give interviews."

"Is it worth a day of your life?" he demands of Hammel.

"I might get a good line," Hammel says.

"For one good line?"

"Some days you don't even get one good line," Hammel laughs.

Yesterday, Big Ten Commissioner Wayne Duke had blustered, "If he's coming to knock the post-season tournament, let him not come." This is not a world in which the normal rules of civilized discourse, of democracy, apply. There will be a vote, but the "wrong" position merits chastisement, even abuse. Knight weaves his way through, comfortable by now in being a lone dissenting voice.

In the corridor of the O'Hare Marriott, a reporter comes up with his hand outstretched: "I know I should be an objective reporter, but I just want to congratulate you on a great season!"

"An objective reporter?" Knight jests lightly and gestures toward the man's nametag. "What newspaper?"

In the grand ballroom the coaches address the reporters, each doing his best to be charming. "Make sure nobody tells Bob Knight that we led the league in defense," says Illinois' Lou Henson. Bill Frieder, Clem Haskins, they're all in favor of the post-season tournament. "It'll give us half a million or more," says Henson.

When Knight comes up to speak, he has the devil in him. At once he attacks the purpose of the meeting—and the requirement that the coach attend "regardless of what it costs the school."

"Wayne, are you here?" he calls. Duke, of course, is very much there. Knight asks, again, what he has asked before: "Is there any meeting that the athletic directors are required to attend?" There isn't.

"Tell me if I'm incorrect," he persists. "Obviously Wayne's

silence means that I am correct, but he doesn't agree with what I'm going to say." The money for these meetings, what it costs for the coaches to attend, Knight says, should go to women's athletics.

Abandoning his prey, he then turns to his audience—the press. Out of his bag come some clippings "which will reveal exactly what comes out of associations between coaches and the press and how much we're able to help you people and how much a lot of you know about what the hell is going on."

What he has brought are press predictions as to how the 1986–87 season was supposed to turn out: "Team most likely to come out of nowhere and win the NCAA: Western Kentucky. The Hilltoppers have a great front line." With great relish he announces what actually happened, lest they have forgotten: Western Kentucky got beat in the second game of the tournament by Syracuse, 104–86.

It gets worse: Virginia, picked to reach the Final Four, is beaten in the first game by Wyoming; who's hot? Georgetown, Missouri, Illinois and UCLA—only Georgetown making it beyond the second round. Who'll be in the Final Four? Iowa, Georgetown, Temple and Purdue. (None of these, of course, made it).

In a loud clear voice, devoid of emotion, he concludes: "The number one seed least likely to reach the Final Four: Indiana. The Hoosiers are the most overrated of the top eight seeds with the possible exception of Syracuse!"

At this the reporters cannot help themselves; they erupt in laughter. He, however, neither reacts nor stops reading: "Indiana has a virtual bye into the regional semifinals, but the Hoosiers will never get past Missouri."

He waits. He pauses.

"Well, we couldn't because Missouri couldn't get past Xavier!"

He can't tell them much about this year's team because he doesn't know a lot about it. So "it's just nice to share more time with my fellow writers." He refers to the columns he wrote about the NCAA tournament with Billy Reed, who had been forced out when the Louisville *Courier-Journal* was sold by the Bingham family to the Gannett organization. Wanting to help Reed, Knight dictated the information, and Reed re-wrote and edited the columns.

He used to feel sorry for reporters over the years, Knight tells them, but now he isn't going to do that, knowing "what your pay scale as daily writers has to be." (In fact, for their eight columns which appeared in forty newspapers Knight and Reed split a total of seventy-six hundred dollars.)

Who's going to play on his team? "I don't really know. Hell, you can get that out of Street and Smith. It'll only cost you about two dollars and fifty cents. It's a hell of a lot cheaper than a plane ticket all the way here. Anybody got a question?"

At first there aren't any. Then one brave soul, older than the others, who all seem in their twenties, does have one.

"Coach Knight, would you share with us your views on the proposed post-season Big Ten basketball tournament?"

"Don't you read Hammel's paper up here?" he asks.

"No!" says one of the Big Ten Coaches who have wandered back in and now sit in a little clump at the right rear corner of the room.

No one has asked the players, Knight says. His students prefer to play each school twice, which would no longer be possible were there a post-season tournament: "Our players can see no reason why they should miss three or four extra days of class to play in a tournament that really decides nothing." The Big Ten already has four or five teams in the NCAAs.

"We talked about exploiting kids," he says. "The only argument I've heard so far from anybody is financial, and now we're really exploiting kids. We're telling these kids you have to play another week of basketball; you have to miss three or four more days of class so we can make more money." The source of this financial argument? Those who are in attendance at meetings "when they aren't on fishing trips or hunting trips or skiing trips."

There is a question about how he will replace Steve Alford. "I don't think you replace Alford with another player," he says, adding, "I don't think we should lose sight of how much Daryl Thomas contributed to what we did." Deliberately he singles out the player who disappointed him, who didn't graduate, yet who was a leader of that championship team—which he will always be. By hearing he is still appreciated, Daryl Thomas just might set his life in order. (And indeed by the end of the season Daryl Thomas will announce his return to IU).

When Knight judges that he's talked to them enough, he suddenly demands, "OK?"

The taxi back to the airport is driven by a young man in tattered blue jeans. For a while he's silent, although he's well aware of who is sitting beside him in the front seat. At last he asks for an autograph—on his pants.

"There isn't enough thread for me to sign," says the coach, with seeming disdain.

But at the airport, as the driver is helping his passengers retrieve parcels from the trunk, the coach quietly, surreptitiously, leaves an autograph on the front seat of the taxi.

An article I had written about him for the sports section of the New York *Times* appeared today and I had raced to the Marriott newsstand to garner their last copy. On the plane back, I consider whether to show it to him. We're on the eight-seater, and his seat faces mine. Should there be anything he dislikes in the article, he might explode, or be cutting, sarcastic about my understanding of his methods. He might hit me with that favorite line of his distinguishing those who "see" from those who "perceive."

Then it seems absurd not to show it to him and so I make a motion with it in his direction. He, of course, is much too quick not to "perceive" exactly what it is I have in my hands.

"What makes you think I want to see that?" he challenges.

"It's your last chance, do you want to see it or not?" I say, pulling back my hand and the ungainly long pages.

"Let me see that," he growls.

He reads. I bury my head in *King Lear,* this week's assignment in my survey course in English literature. I'm watching him out of the corner of my eye. He finishes the article, puts it somewhere, and picks up his Tom Clancy novel, his face expressionless all the while. He neither says a word nor looks in my direction.

"You shouldn't have mentioned the Pan American games," he says when we are back in Bloomington, referring to my reference to the previous summer games in which Dean Garrett and Keith Smart participated. I realize that I have never once heard him criticize the coaching of anyone else. But if I had expected praise, I'm disappointed. That's all he says.

He heads for his Bronco. "You go with Hammel," he gestures as we make our way back to Assembly Hall.

He has arrived back in Bloomington in time for an hour of teaching, which will precede tonight's intersquad scrimmage.

When he walks out onto the floor, the students are already there, holding their red notebooks. Today he is trying to teach them to see the whole court and everyone on it, to anticipate what the others are going to do before they do it. He is also trying to teach them how to concentrate, knowing that it isn't nearly enough to tell them to do it. "We can't get beat because I don't look at the outside and here comes Ricky and I don't see him," he says. It's still pre-season. In short the lesson today is in seeing.

When they get down to mid-court, they must know who's there, what's outside, what's inside of you.

"As I'm coming back right there," he demonstrates, "I immediately look to see what's here."

He teaches defensive conversion by breaking the lesson into small parts so that each segment appears to be simple, possible, manageable: anyone can do it. As he breaks down the game, so he breaks down the floor, and as he completes each segment, he asks, "Now does anybody have a question on conversion?" No one has.

Part of the lesson is in communication: "Lyndon and I are coming along here. I'm not guarding Lyndon so I let Lyndon go and wait on who I'm guarding. It's Ron, but there's nobody to pick up Lyndon. So eventually Lyndon gets open for an easy shot."

"We don't play the man," he adds, "we're playing to stop the ball."

The other team sets up an offense, then the defenders must pressure that offense. We: Jump to the ball instead of waiting on what the passer is going to do *after* he gets rid of the ball. "I want everybody to write that down in capital letters," he orders. "JUMP TO THE BALL." Repetition reinforces his method; repetition has become so natural to him that it governs his conversation no less than his teaching: "Wherever the pass is made, anytime it's lateral or penetrating of any kind, jump to the ball, get to the basketball, the basketball is what we're trying to stop."

Once that principle is mastered, they work at keeping the ball moving toward the corners and taking away the reverse pass.

"Make him back up in reversing the ball; that's the hardest pass in basketball to complete, the back cut down the lane by perimeter play. Do you all understand what I'm talking about here?" He wants the opponent anxious about his offense because "the more anxious they are, the more mistakes they're going to make."

His voice rings out through Assembly Hall, clear as a bell, no microphone today. It's so clear, lucid, direct and overwhelming that it drowns out contrary thoughts; it drowns out doubts. It's the voice of authority telling them he knows this game better than anyone else has ever known it. As if basketball paralelled the labyrinthine plot of a Tom Clancy novel, he teaches them to maneuver, how to get the edge, how to outthink an adversary, how to find the loophole in an opponent's reasoning, how to beat him to the destination, all the while stretching the peculiar harmony of mind and body that is basketball.

In each coaching session these principles predominate: preparation, communication, self-discipline, competition, taking initiatives, hard work to anticipate any eventuality, taking responsibility. In his 1981 baccalaureate address he revealed he knew students sometimes come to college not knowing how to read and write. Unlike many educators, however, he admitted that there are some who *leave* "not particularly adept at writing and reading." Then he told the students that it was partly their own fault.

"We've got to be a team that doesn't make mistakes." Meanwhile "the more mistakes *they* make, the better we're going be." He pauses for an instant. "If you've got any questions at all, I want them answered before we go through this. Because if there aren't any questions, we're all done with the defense and we can get into the offense."

There are no mysteries. They must: recover short to take away the drive, recover to put pressure on the shot, recover to make the interception if it's there. They've eliminated the lunge. But what is brother to the lunge? It's leaving your feet on the shot fake! They've already seen a Pistons-Hawks game and he's pointed out the times Isiah Thomas got caught in the shot fake: "Isiah worked for years here on the shot fake. We can't have that happen to us."

The implication is clear: if they work hard, if they follow what he tells them, they can supersede even Isiah, whom they know has more natural talent than all of them put together. More: if Isiah went through this, and it resulted in his outstanding career, hard work might bring them a similar success.

He teaches the possible. The shot fake is something they all can do. Not everybody will be a great natural shooter. But they all can learn the shot fake.

Already he suspects what the season will reveal. They are weak in making it tough for a post man to get position: "We don't have anybody fighting the post man. We don't have anybody taking away direction." He tells them what will happen and what they can do about it. "If the ball moves, step back and establish yourself behind him."

Dave has the ball and he makes a pass to Ricky. "But *this* is not jump to the ball. *This* is not what we want."

"Now Keith," he adds, "you're terribly guilty of this . . . the move that we want is directly toward the basketball with the back hand to the passing lane." It is this degree of detail that they must master: "The ball is above the foul line extended, I am one step on the man side of the bucket. The ball is below the foul line extended, I am one step on the ball side of the bucket."

There are many areas where they're weak. "Wherever we are," he tells them, "we're not doing a real good job of taking away cuts." In blockout situations, they're turning on the boards rather than on the man. The break should be on one side of the lane or the other, not in the middle of the floor.

Keith, Ricky and Jay must learn to work off somebody every time they come down the floor because they have the best ability to score. They cannot just get open. They cannot catch the ball: "That's not what your jobs are. You people are to get open to score and you don't score by being a ball handler."

The season is only two weeks away; he has decided that his offense must come from these three: from Keith, from Ricky and from Jay. He cannot know at this point in the season that Keith and Ricky both will disappoint him, that Jay will almost be lost to the team.

Everyone has a role: Jadlow, Garrett and Pelkowski get the ball to somebody who can handle it (after the rebound). Or you come right inside and you're set for the shot. No one is expected to do everything.

As the hour winds down, worry seems to set in. He's speaking and then, suddenly, his patience is gone. "Steve Eyl," he says, "for whatever the reason, you do this worse than anybody we have. You just catch the ball. You don't even look. You're just here and you throw it right back. You're not in any way looking to see what's going on. When the ball is brought toward you, you're going to screen. When the ball goes away from you, you're going to cut.

"We just don't do enough things right yet, boys," he concludes. "You beat people through execution; you don't beat them because you outjump them, outrun them or outshoot them. You outthink them and you outexecute them." It seems to be the most difficult lesson of all: "If you stay down and screen, you'll get shot opportunities. You'll get tremendous shots because you're a screener that you won't believe." He looks at them and he knows them. "You obviously don't believe it because you don't do it," he says.

"Be hard to guard. The more they have to guard you, the more we can get people twisted around." He looks at Ricky. "You're not getting squared up. You're not taking the shots that you have." He knows the game so well that it seems he is looking through a crystal ball. "And you're taking shots that you don't have."

When the ball comes across mid-court what he wants is movement, but passing, and not that Isiah sin, dribbling. "I want it passed right now so that the cut is made from up there and then he replaces himself or he inside cuts or whatever." What he hates is the "comfort zone." "Boys," he says, "you cannot be a good team playing comfortable. This team has no chance of being good playing comfortable. I don't want anybody handling the ball where he can't shoot it."

He teaches them all he knows; it's all he can do. And out of the simplicity, the clarity, he hopes will arise from within all of them—the will to execute.

"Well, what do you think?" he wants to know.

Then he turns to Patrick, who is practicing at one of the baskets. "You're shooting way up on top of the ball," he tells his son. "It just looks awful. You can't hit the front rim and score. That's three in a row on the front rim."

Patrick continues to shoot from the same place.

"Pat, get the ball right off the top of your head. Don't get the ball stretched way down your arm. The ball is too high. Don't even jump. Right there, that's good, that's the kind of release we're after. Shoot the damn thing long. Now concentrate. Hold your follow-through."

Tates Locke has an idea. He pushes over a chair. Patrick sits down and shoots baskets from the chair.

"Hold your follow-through. Now go out at the white line and keep it extended."

Knight goes out and demonstrates, holding Patrick's arms. "I can't tell you how much better that is," he tells his son. Patrick keeps on shooting one jumper after another.

Knight goes off to eat with Tim while Patrick keeps on practicing with Dan Dakich. "That's it," Danny encourages.

"When we go out to eat, he's my Dad," Patrick says, "but when I'm out on the floor, which is ninety percent of the time we're together, he's a coach."

Assembly Hall is now deserted. It's only Patrick Knight with Dan Dakich guarding him, shooting over and over again.

Then Patrick and Danny repair to the coaches' locker room, where they watch an old high school scrimmage of Patrick's team, Bloomington North. Patrick says he's not good enough to play for Indiana; it's this, it seems, and not any problem playing for his father, that will determine where he goes to college. (Tim has another view: "I think it's best for the son to play for somebody else.")

The tape is stopped every minute or two for study. Tim and Bob Knight return and Tim offers his brother something red in a plastic container, chili or spaghetti. Patrick declines. The remains of a homemade apple cake are oozing in the pan, beside the diet sodas. The tape is so faint you can barely make out Patrick, except for his black-and-white knee pad. "Is that you?" his father has to ask.

Patrick is sent home to change his clothes; he is not permitted to wear shorts, a T-shirt, cap and sneakers to the scrimmage tonight. Patrick departs. "Any people coming?" Knight asks. "Go look outside. Were there any cars out there?"

"It's not filled up, but it's getting crowded," Danny reports.

"Get up there and sell some tickets," Knight jokes.

He's still preoccupied with that Big Ten press conference. "Somebody will write how surly I was, and my arrogant ways," he predicts. "That's just me. I talked to them today just like you and I talk. There wasn't anything surly about what I did. But I just couldn't resist that"—by which he means throwing their inaccurate predictions in their faces.

Patrick concerns him too. "I'm not sure how good I've been," Knight says. He is sad now. "That's the hardest thing I've ever had to do. Not to be able to spend more time with him or see him in the morning or see him in the evening since I've been divorced. That really bothers me."

He offers me a frozen yogurt pie from the refrigerator. And he returns to the game, to motivating students. Anger is not a great motivational device, he has found, because the student can't get mad often enough. There's so much starting and stopping involved in playing the game that overcommitment is a greater error than undercommitment. That's where anger has limitations; it will cause a player to overcommit. Since his days coaching Army, he has believed that basketball is a game where the mental is to the physical as four is to one. "The great players are the guys that think constantly with good talent."

That the students didn't have many questions did not surprise him: "It's easy to get people to ask you questions," he says. "Don't explain things very well." At his summer camp he talks to the kids about not behaving, saying " 'The first kid that tries me, I'm going to pack your ass on the next bus home. All right, are there any questions? Good. I'm glad you all understand me.' And I just say it that way so there isn't time for a kid to raise his hand."

The telephone rings. What about a starting lineup for tonight's scrimmage? "How many do we have available?" he asks. "OK, put Garrett, Calloway, Eyl, Smart, Oliphant and Jones in one color and the other seven in the other color to start with."

He remembers a game against Wisconsin at a time when Indiana was in first place in the Big Ten and Wisconsin in last. He asked his team to draw a starting lineup among both teams and "they picked two of ours and three of theirs and they were absolutely right. Indiana won the conference championship and Wisconsin finished last. The point is that what separates kids is not talent. And it's not skill. It's thinking."

He recalls the scene a few years ago when, annoyed at the cheerleaders for encouraging a chant as Steve Alford took his free throws, he kicked a megaphone which accidentally hit a girl, whose father was a good friend of his, in the calf of her leg. Shortly thereafter he received a letter laced with obscenities from the sister of another cheerleader who was working in Dallas.

"What would have happened had I found out the name of the president of this company and sent the letter to him, asking, is this the kind of writing you want your employees to do on your stationery?"

Two cheerleaders came in to see him; the one who was hit was not really upset.

"Before you even start," he told them, "let me tell you how

unhappy I was. You cheerleaders are only out there for one reason—that's because I let you out there. You only go on trips
because I let you go on trips. Did you two go to New York last
year?"

"Yes."

"Which one of you sent me a thank-you note for being included
in that trip? Expense-paid trip to New York for five days. That's
a pretty good trip for an eighteen-year-old kid. I didn't get a
thank-you note from you and I didn't get one from you. The shoes
you have on I got for you. You get three pairs of Adidas shoes,
don't you?

"I sent you those three pair of shoes. I haven't gotten one
thank-you from one cheerleader as long as I've been here so don't
come into me with this."

He returns to the theme of other coaches recruiting against him,
even telling overt lies as a way of persuading students to play for
them. They were recruiting a student named Glen Grunwald out
of Chicago when an Illinois coach told Grunwald that at the half
of a game, Knight threw a coat and a soda can at Quinn Buckner
and hit him in the head. Buckner was a senior at the time, and he
called the high school boy himself. Buckner's message was: "If
you're too dumb not to see through that, then you're not smart
enough to come to Indiana." (Grunwald went on to play for Indiana from 1977 through 1981.)

This is not to say that he never becomes angry at a player. Then
it gratifies him when someone understands, as at a party a doctor's wife told the crowd, "Wait a minute. When was the last time
one of you people either paddled, grabbed or slapped one of your
kids? He's dealing with fourteen kids, everybody else's kids, and
he's spending more time with those fourteen than any of us are
spending with our own. And what the hell is so bad about him
getting upset with one of them?"

He sits chatting, oblivious of the time until the scrimmage is
about to begin, and the band has begun to play.

A moment later, he is taking the microphone, and addressing
the crowd: "We really appreciate your coming out tonight and I
think I would be remiss if I didn't tell you that the three officials
here tonight, all Indiana guys, Bob, Gary and Eric, have donated
their services to tonight's game. But I told them as we've paid
them a lot of money in the past for doing nothing . . ."

CHAPTER SEVEN

INTERLUDE: INDIANA CLASSIC

"I don't have a doghouse. I have a birdhouse. If you fly, you get into the birdhouse and you get to play. You don't put guys on the bench. You put other guys in the game who deserve to play."

IT'S A THURSDAY at two in the afternoon in the coaches' locker room. Wearing a gray T-shirt, the nondescript blue pants and white athletic socks, Coach Bob Knight sits in his favorite chair watching a tape of practice. Simultaneously he talks on the telephone to someone he hopes will hire the son of one of his friends as an assistant football coach.

"He's really good and he's really bright," Knight says. "He's smart enough to do enough things so eventually you begin to lean on a guy like him. I've known him since he was in junior high school. He's self-motivated and he would be very, very good for you."

The conversation concludes with Knight not only polite, but even humble.

"I appreciate your taking the call."

Indiana has already beaten Miami of Ohio, Notre Dame and

Vanderbilt. It has also lost to Kentucky in overtime 82–76, at one point in that game failing to score on six consecutive possessions. Nor to be taken lightly is the fact that Keith Smart had six turnovers, including one in which he dribbled the ball off his leg in the last minute as Indiana had a chance to tie. Jay Edwards forced an overtime with a baseline shot at the buzzer. But then Kentucky's Rex Chapman, who had been shut down for most of the game, going five for seventeen, clinched the game with a three-point shot. For Indiana, Rick Calloway was the high scorer with twenty-six points.

Now Knight is scrutinizing his team on tape, while Ron Felling watches with him. Jay's got "an all arms shot," Knight decides. "He doesn't get his legs into it." While perusing the stat sheet from last night's practice, he talks about a potential recruit: "Do we have a record of his games to date, whether he scored or anything?"

"What's going on in the literary world?" he suddenly asks me without taking his eyes off the television set so that for an instant I'm not sure to whom he's talking. "This is the worst thing that we can do, right here." Lyndon Jones "doesn't understand about dribbling in front of somebody." Something on the stat sheet does please him: Hillman was eight for nine from three-point range with one turnover and ten assists.

"What do your people think of this?" he wants to know, referring to the prospect of my doing this book about him, of this fascination with basketball.

"They say I'll get over it." I keep a straight face.

This evokes the barest trace of a Knight smile.

Ron Felling writes the names of the Indiana players who will start against James Madison tomorrow in the first game of the Indiana Classic tournament, and then the James Madison players against whom they will match up. Felling is asked to sum up James Madison's approach: "They'll bring in a big six-eleven white kid off the bench. They play a four-man motion around him. No screening. Just cuts and they play a little like the Kentucky back cut down into the post." The frame on the television screen is abruptly frozen as they decide:

Jones - Gordon
Smart - Ferdinand

Magnus - Green
Garrett - Brown
Calloway - Winchester

With Daryl Thomas and Steve Alford gone, there is no indubitable starting five this year. Now, in December, Garrett, Smart and Calloway seem certain. Lyndon Jones is being developed.

Tomorrow's experiment, however, involves the starting of Magnus Pelkowski, the Colombian player, who is not only an excellent student majoring in international business, but an accomplished artist. Last spring, he drew a poster of Knight, Alford, Thomas and Todd Meier, sold one thousand copies for ten dollars apiece and spent the summer in Europe. ("Coach, thanks for everything," Magnus had inscribed on the print he reserved for Knight.) Son of the owners of a toy factory, he had as a boy designed remote-controlled airplanes: at twelve he built a 25 × 15 A-frame house, a retreat which housed two beds and to which he escaped on more than one occasion.

As a basketball player, however, despite his 6'10", 220-pound well-developed physique, he lacks the quickness, the overall skill of the first-rank college athlete.

But this weekend, because he scored fifteen points from the bench in the first half of the game against Vanderbilt on Tuesday, Magnus is being given a start.

Magnus is summoned to view the tape with Knight and Felling. He arrives in his bare feet, sits down on the couch, and waits.

For Knight must now telephone the father of the job-seeker to fill him in and to send a message to the son: he should tell his son, "I'll be glad to call any of these people for him. But he should not be concerned with whether he gets this or not. All right. OK." The conversation concludes with a joke about changing the prospective coach's resume since, "I'm not sure anybody has ever graduated from Purdue with distinction."

Pelkowski laughs and waits for Knight to get to him.

"If we start you in the corner," Knight explains, "that screws you up. You have a really good knack for seeing openings. You have to learn to move your body a little bit. I want you really working at moving, like you start down low and maybe you flash up high, then if the corner is open, you circle it or drift out to the corner.

"But when we start you in the corner, that screws you up. You're much better moving to open spots. I really want you working to go into open spots when we're playing against a two-three zone. When we're playing against a one-three-one, we're going to set you on the baseline, but not against a two-three. Just watch what you're doing here a little bit."

The tone is gentle, matter of fact, the mood, analytical. Coach and player study the tape. As he observes his mistakes, Magnus shakes his head in disbelief.

"You did a good job against Vanderbilt in going to the offensive board every time. See, this is excellent right here. You have a really good knack for seeing openings. Just make sure that you keep working and looking to go to openings. You turn and shoot the ball well in the openings. All right, now you've got to learn to move your body a little bit. . . ."

Magnus watches intently, seemingly confident that he will be able to accomplish what the coach requests.

"Right there you just go up left-handed and lay that in. See, this I don't want against a two-three zone because you just stand."

"You don't want . . . ?"

"No, I don't want that. Not against a two-three zone because you just stand and then you throw up jump shots with guys running at you . . . if you were on the low post and he were dribbling the ball back on the white line toward the lane, then you can just slide up on the open baseline . . ."

"How about coming across where Dean is? If I move right now and go where Dean is?"

"Well, but you'll come underneath and you're all right. But you see you have no follow-through here at all, Magnus. That's what I don't like about you shooting this shot . . . See your follow-through? It's just terrible. You're doing a good job screening. You need to come up in the middle a little bit more because you've got a good shot in the middle. Keep Dean down low and you come into the middle . . .

"Learn to pass the ball right off your ear. That's good, see, that's good right here. Edwards should hit you right here, this is a real good slide that you make right here. You slide right back out, excellent! And then you're ready to take the shot."

Magnus must watch his arm and how it doesn't snap back in his follow-through.

Pelkowski again shakes his head in disbelief as he watches himself.

"OK," he says.

Dan Dakich and Julio Salazar have both come in. Dakich is asked to "get him out there holding his follow-through."

"Coach, he needs some high passes too," says Julio Salazar, an M.A. candidate in coaching, a Colombian who met Knight in Puerto Rico to ask permission to come to Bloomington to study Indiana basketball and stayed on to join the Knight staff. The coaching, no less than the playing, is a team effort, with everybody expected to do everything; again it's obvious that there is no distinction here, between those who recruit and those who coach on the floor.

After Pelkowski departs, Knight turns his attention to Jay Edwards: "Edwards should be told he made thirteen out of forty-two, so he's shooting thirty percent." Knight makes a call about tickets for someone for Saturday, and another to Ralph Floyd to arrange dinner. Joby Wright enters.

"Joby, how are we doing today?"

"We're doing all right, coach."

"Did we recruit anybody today?"

At practice, Knight sits on the steps while his assistants coach. He calls Ricky Calloway over to talk. Quiet for a moment, he then yells out instructions: "Jeff, don't let him come over the top of you. You can't let him do it!"

But today most of his comments are for Magnus. "Magnus, just rotate away and Jeff come up." An instant later he's annoyed: "You shouldn't act as if it's a new idea, Magnus! Who's guarding Eyl?"

It's two months since the beginning of practice and the freshmen have obviously improved dramatically. "Joe, Joe!" Lyndon calls. You can see the point guard in Lyndon Jones emerging, like a newborn bird pushing out of its shell.

If there are students with whom he's displeased at this early moment in the season, it's Garrett and Smart. "Instead of screening and posting," he tells Garrett, scathingly, "here you are calling for the ball." Knight shakes his head. "Keith, you just got caught behind the screen and that's no improvement over your defense!" In disgust, he lets them rest: "Free throws!" (Smart himself attributes his faltering start to his experience playing in the Pan American games last summer: "It was a different type of basketball played there. You weren't pushed every day." Does he like it better at Indiana despite the unceasing, unrelenting correction of every mistake? "Without a doubt.")

Watching from the stands today is Dean Garrett's (and Mark Robinson's) junior college coach from San Francisco, Brad Duggan, who recalls the day Knight came to recruit his prize center:

"We spoke for four hours. Dean's mom was there, Dean's sister, Dean, me and one of my assistants. There were no highlight films, which coaches usually bring, a projector, a screen, films of the most beautiful campus, girls, the team with every shot going in, and endorsements such as, 'Magic Johnson says,' a prefabricated scenario to which you couldn't say no. . . .

"He didn't do that. He just came in and the six of us talked about life, not about basketball. Where are you going to be in four years? he asked. You have to represent your family and yourself outside of basketball. What will you talk about to people outside of basketball?

"Dean pulled me aside and said, 'Tell him I want to go.' I said, 'You tell him.' At the end Dean said, 'Coach, I really want to come.' Bob said, 'You don't have to tell me now, visit some other places. See if you like them, and if you like them better, fine. If you don't like Indiana, I'll recommend places for you to go to.' Any other coach would say, 'Great, sign here.'

"When Dean said he was still sure, Bob said, 'Well, take a night, sleep on it, talk to your mom and Brad in the morning, if you still want . . .' and Dean said, 'I don't need that. I want to go.' About eighty schools were recruiting him; he was the number-one rated community college player in the country. Knight told him, you will never get any money, you will always go to class or you won't play, you will always act like a gentleman and I will scream and yell at you all the time. But I'll make you as good as you can be."

From the other players, Mark Robinson heard that he might be redshirted. In dismay, he called Duggan, who suggested that he talk to Knight directly. "You don't have to if you don't want to," Knight told him, "but I think you'll be three times as good if you do."

Now Duggan must listen to some tough words sent Garrett's way: "Dean, you can't just go constantly to the ball." Knight imitates Garrett, weaving through the players, his arms up. "That's your game!"

"Good help, Magnus!" he calls. "Look for the open spot. All right. All right. Good cut."

"Dean, come out and screen Magnus," he orders. Garrett is blamed for thinking too much about his own scoring. "That's obviously all you have on your mind!" Knight covers his face in dismay. He controls his energy, as he does his voice, raising it during an unsatisfactory play, lowering it as he talks one on one with a player.

As for Magnus Pelkowski today, every move he makes is doubly scrutinized:

"Magnus, he shot over you as if you were six-one. I don't want that foreign mentality on this team. If you're tired, we can't use you." He goes off muttering. "That's why they can't play the game anywhere but here."

We're into the season and they should be doing better. "Do you guys think you're going to play again and again and again?" he yells. "How many opportunities do you think I've got for you, Hillman? Do you think I've acquired patience all of a sudden?"

In fact, he's exhibiting extraordinary patience, and if he's hard on Garrett, he's gentle with Calloway. "Really good cut, Ricky," Calloway is told. "That's the way to help out, Magnus. Ricky come over on this side with Magnus. Pop out, Magnus. Pick him up, Dean, and come back. Go ahead, Magnus."

Now Knight sits hunched over at the scorer's table. "White triangle, white triangle," he calls. When practice is over, he's surrounded by his assistants for more discussion: Dakich and Felling, Joby Wright, Julio and the trainer, Tim Garl.

The game against James Madison begins. Magnus gets the first basket and the first rebound; it appears as if the practice devoted to getting him ready to play has paid off. He gets the second rebound as well, and then manages to slap the ball away for Keith Smart to turn into an easy lay-up.

But soon Knight is driven to yell, "Magnus, get into it!" At 11.39 Todd Jadlow is sent in to replace him. It's Jadlow tonight who excels, making three field goals (of seven), five free throws, getting three key rebounds and being responsible for the plays that enable the team to go ahead.

Garrett's ineffectual play, however, enrages Knight, and Garrett is soon benched. Before long, Knight strolls down for a few words: "If you don't get off your ass, you're going to be sitting there a long time." Lyndon Jones and Rick Calloway, however, are given a lot of court affection tonight, pats and embraces.

You can see, as he coaches, his search for a team leader, the player who, as Ted Kitchel says he did, takes the coach's character out onto the floor. "Joe, he's going to go right," he tells Hillman about the man he's to cover. "Joe, call that switch, Joe!" he yells as the team comes down the floor. "Joe, tell him to get a good shot," he calls after Jay Edwards has attempted the impossible. But unlike predecessors like Buckner and Todd Meier, players who were also less gifted than many of their teammates, Hillman does not seem willing to accept the leadership role. Soon Jeff Oliphant is sent in for Hillman.

At halftime Professor Byrnes is presented with a check for $18,198.63, the share of the proceeds from the Seymour scrimmage that Knight has assigned to the library fund.

Starting the second half, Pelkowski is given still another chance. When he misses two free throws, Knight bangs down his program. Then he marches down the bench to tell Garrett again that he got nothing from him in this game. He calls Pelkowski over to the sidelines for a long talk and a pat of encouragement.

Pelkowski, of course, makes the next basket—it's the overwhelming reaction of nearly every Knight player who goes back onto the floor after having been coached on the sideline.

The mistakes accumulate, however. Jadlow misses an easy lay-up: "You didn't even look," Knight tells him. Eyl still isn't staying down in his stance. Jay has double-dribbled, excusable, perhaps, for a freshman. In the midst of it all, Knight turns to a young man sitting in the first row behind the Indiana bench and asks, "Where's Tim?" With ten seconds left, and the outcome long since determined, he's still shouting out directions.

Indiana wins easily, 84–52. The high scorer is Calloway, with 16. Garrett, playing twenty minutes, has 7 rebounds, and 7 blocked shots, but only 4 points. Pelkowski has played twenty-eight minutes. But although he has come up with 10 rebounds, he has scored only 6 points, going 3 for 10, a disappointing offensive performance.

*   *   *

On Saturday Knight finds time between practices to spend with friends who have come for the weekend. These include his own high school coach in baseball and football, Bill Shunkwiler, and Ed Gottlieb, his college friend.

Lunch is at the Jiffy Treat; he eats a Sloppy Joe. The talk is of basketball: how many good players there are from the state of Michigan. With Joby Wright's help, the list is exhausted. The men exchange the names of favorite restaurants in a variety of cities. "Aren't you eating?" he wants to know when I can't manage the Sloppy Joe. He notices everything. He has chosen this place, it would appear, because it is deserted; he is left unmolested to enjoy his friends. Another favorite, the Third Base Lounge, also attracts patrons who do not disturb him at his meal for autographs.

On Saturday night, Indiana plays the championship game of the tournament against Washington State, the team that had eliminated Indiana State and a disappointing Eddie Bird in whom the crowd took only a mild interest.

The students eat their pre-game meal in the stately Federal Room of the Union Building high and away from curious eyes. Over the leavings of the pancakes and honey and toast and scrambled eggs, the baked potatoes and overcooked hamburgers and spaghetti and vanilla ice cream, he addresses them:

"The stands are full, the lights are on, TV, the whole thing, so you've got all kinds of added distractions. But it's the ultimate chance for an athlete to go out and play well. That's what every single competition that you go into is about. If you don't play well in competition, then whatever you do in practice just disintegrates."

Last night, he tells them, they played well. But practice, with somebody standing there and telling them to screen or move or pass isn't the ultimate. "That's playing the game." And, he warns them, he expects some improvement tonight.

As they depart, he is very annoyed with Lyndon Jones, who has appeared for pre-game meal without a necktie. Nothing escapes him, although he seemed to be too absorbed in talking with Shunkwiler to notice.

"My tie was broken."

"What you had was a bad goddamn necktie? Is that right?

Twenty-five years I've been in this business and I've heard every excuse, but I have never heard that one. Even Garrett hasn't come up with a broken necktie!"

From the beginning it is clear that the game against Washington State will result in no easy victory.

Garrett starts—and plays badly. Early on he loses the ball, while Knight settles back into his seat. Then the coach begins to pace, and then he sends Pelkowski in to replace Garrett, who gets a lecture. "You stood here, he came out . . . you've got to be ready for the ball."

It's a close game and with .34 to go in the first half, the score is tied at twenty-six. A seven-footer named Todd Anderson has occupied the low post, and it is only Jadlow with three key rebounds, drawing fouls and making his free throws, who will finally turn the game Indiana's way.

The second half produces its own challenges. Calloway turns the ball over twice. "Garrett, stay on the ground," Knight yells. His man pump faked and Garrett—left his feet! Smart did not shoot, he "threw the ball!" At 7.26 to go in the game, it's tied again, 44–44. "Four passes," Knight yells at Calloway.

When a Washington State player named Anthony Kidd tackles Keith Smart to avert a lay-up, and the new intentional foul rule is invoked, Knight calls Kidd over to tell him he knows he didn't intend to hurt Smart.

This is the turning point of the game. Indiana goes ahead 48–46 with 5.46 to go. By 2.09 it's 57–47, and with .55 to go Knight can yell at Jadlow for his shirt being out of his pants.

Nor because the game is virtually over does Knight stop teaching. Smart is called over to be chastised: "We took a time-out to diagram and then we don't do it. Then we get into the game and we don't do it."

With .15 left, Steve Eyl receives some harsh words. "He was on me," Eyl tries to explain. Knight wanders down the bench for a few more angry words to Garrett.

The final score is 63–56. Knight hugs Kidd and shakes hands with a few of the other Washington State players. Then he walks off the floor and heads for the coaches' locker room, too disgusted with his team and all its errors, its "mental mistakes," to remain to witness the awards ceremony.

"You don't belong in here," Brad Bomba would have liked to

tell him, as he did one year when Knight eschewed his usual role of addressing the fans at the season's closing game. But Knight is deeply worried about this team. With Daryl Thomas and Steve Alford gone, natural leadership had not arisen from their ranks to replace the vacuum. It is mid-December, yet the teaching, the motivating needed to make them a creditable basketball team seems barely to have begun.

Dinner is at a local Italian restaurant called Leslie's Italian Villa, a generous buffet of homemade ziti and fettucini, lasagna and pizza. Here Knight entertains the three visiting coaches and their assistants—and his own friends, including the "Over the Hill Gang"—Knight's friends from Orrville who make this tournament an annual pilgrimage. He obviously enjoys these good simple people who knew his parents. Knight's father was the boss of the father of the Demlow brothers on the Wheeling-Lake Erie Railroad. Their sister baby-sat for Bob Knight. Harve Linder managed a softball team in Ohio long ago.

Those occasions when his Mom employed the paddle come up since one of her victims, Danny Markley, is here.

"She paddled me once too," Knight says, with obvious approval. "All those ladies [by which he means schoolmarms] did that then." Discipline and concentration—both seem to have been passed down to him from his parents.

Dr. Donald Boop, the dentist who treated Knight when he was thirteen years old and became his lifelong friend, is here too. Boop is planning to move to California soon.

"You'll never go," Knight says. Then the devil gets the better of him: "Convince Pauline [Boop's wife] to go, and you stay home!" But his words are laced with affection.

He sits between Ed Gottlieb and Shunkwiler, opposite Harold Martin, renamed "Adolph" after Adolph Rupp, a man who once got him into a Kentucky high school game, and stayed on in his life. And the talk is of business, of golf, and of girls who turned heads at Orrville High School some thirty years ago.

He remembers a teammate on his high school football team. When he was fourteen, and weighed 150 pounds, he would walk home every day with this older teammate, cutting across someone's yard.

"I didn't know you were that friendly with him," Shunkwiler says, as if it had all happened yesterday. Long tables of men, former coaches, childhood friends, former classmates, colleagues in the coaching profession today—there isn't a woman in the room except the waitress, nor are women missed amid the reminiscing.

On such occasions it becomes apparent that a natural sense of continuity governs his life. Seamlessly he accommodates people out of his past. They are not to be cast out because he has moved on, or become successful. He lives strongly by values that have almost died out in our culture as he shares his success with the Orrville eight here tonight, with the college classmates, as with the parents of former players, former players, former assistants.

He assumes their trust; they're bulwarks against the corruption he otherwise finds endemic to the world in which he moves. With these people he can be direct, (maybe too direct?), uncompromising, and frank. He can say anything and they will understand. He can relax.

Each departing coach thanks Knight for his hospitality. "Thank *you* very much," Knight replies.

On his Sunday morning television show (taped the previous night after the Washington State game, making him late for his own party at Leslie's), host Chuck Marlowe asks who will be the new team leaders. And indeed the subject of leadership gnaws at him as he ponders his team early in the season.

"Popular people don't make particularly good leaders," he says. "Decisive people with judgment, who aren't afraid to tell other people who don't have such good judgment that their judgment isn't very good, make good leaders." He has named no names.

Jadlow, however, was the key to the Washington State victory with his four free throws in a row, tipping the ball back out, an offensive rebound, a couple of defensive rebounds, and good position all the way defensively. The television show becomes one more opportunity to praise his players.

Having returned from a day of hunting, in rubber boots and greenish canvas pants, he sits at the scorer's table on Sunday night surveying his team at practice.

"They're all good kids," he says. "But they're all followers. There's not a leader among them."

He asks me: "Do you know which one is best for enthusiasm?"

I guess Ricky Calloway. In reply to the same question, Ron Felling also names Calloway.

"It's Todd Jadlow," Knight says. "Look at last night's box: he played nine minutes, had four three throws, which he made, and three rebounds.

"Jay Edwards is going to have problems," Knight predicts. "His personality is too blasé, academically as well as in basketball."

He wants to know from his assistants whom Eastern Kentucky, their next opponent, has played this year. Marshall beat them 62–61, Ron tells him.

He looks over at his players again.

"This won't be a very good team," he says.

In the coaches' locker room he continues: "Do you know the best guy we have at talking to other players. I mean, it isn't even close? By far the best is Jadlow. He encourages them, comes up and says something to them, makes some comments that are pertinent to what's happening.

"You know who knows more about how we play than anybody? Oliphant."

The starting lineup against Eastern Kentucky is discussed. Knight suggests Smart, Hillman, Eyl, Calloway and Jadlow. He believes that if Garrett had played the rest of the game against Washington State, Indiana would have lost. He does not plan to start Garrett.

Now he decides to give the team Christmas eve off and let them come back to practice at seven in the evening on Christmas day. "We could overload Alford mentally," he remembers. "But I don't think we can these guys." Fondly he recalls these players now gone: Daryl Thomas, Todd Meier, who knew "how to talk to people."

"Maybe none of them individually could have done it. Obviously Meier and Daryl couldn't and maybe Steve couldn't without their help." He pauses. "But, boy, we struggle right now."

Two days later against Eastern Kentucky Dean Garrett scores twenty-five points, grabs eighteen rebounds and blocks seven shots as Indiana wins 103–75. He even makes seven of eight free throws.

Garrett did not, however, start the game.

"I was gonna make him keep me in," Garrett said afterwards,

accounting for his superb performance. But a difficult, an uneasy season appears increasingly likely.

And four days later there is an announcement. "IU freshman Jay Edwards is academically ineligible to play and probably will miss the entire Big Ten Conference season."

PART THREE

CHAPTER EIGHT

THE GAME'S THE TEST, AND THERE'S NO MULTIPLE CHOICE

"I don't want him, I want you."

CHRISTMAS FOLLOWS QUICKLY upon an 81–69 loss to Louisville, as Christmas night looks ahead to the remainder of the season. After the Louisville game, the team dispersed, the players returning home. Their coach, however, went hunting for four days, thinking all the while about what to say to them when they returned. Against Louisville, Indiana committed nineteen turnovers. It wasn't Louisville's free throws or their press. It was Indiana's own play that beat them. His Christmas present to his mother on Christmas Eve, a week before her death, is the best gift of all—not a chair, or an appliance but—a visit to Orrville.

Practice resumes at six P.M. on Christmas night for this team that has lost two nonconference games, to Kentucky and to Louisville. Between now and the Hoosier Classic in Indianapolis on Monday night, they'll be spending every waking moment at Assembly Hall, he has told them. It's a crisis early in the season for a leaderless team.

Friday night inaugurates the first of five practices as Knight and his assistants try to teach these players how to be a team. He must "give them a game they can win with." What he can teach them now will predict their season. They are not a good team, he insists. "I have parts of players." Now he must ready them for the Big Ten season, for which the Hoosier Classic is to be their dress rehearsal.

At five P.M. he walks out onto the floor with Ron Felling and waves. Joe Hillman comes out first and jumps rope. Jeff Oliphant follows. Lyndon Jones and Dean Garrett do stretching exercises. Ron Felling goes over to greet the players and wish them a good Christmas. Knight talks for a moment to his son Tim before they all troop into the players' locker room for the first lecture of this long five days.

It is my fourth visit, the first at which I'm permitted to attend the lectures in the players' dressing room. There are no outsiders here, no banter, no smiles, not among assistants, managers or players. It is not because the discipline is Draconian, but because everyone is taking himself seriously. "Don't wear perfume in the locker room," Knight tells me, an order for the next time. There is nothing I can do about the *Ysatis* today. In this perfectly ordered closed world there are rules of appropriate conduct down to every detail. They include no talking at practice, no matter that the classroom seats 17,357 and you might not be heard.

Each student sits in front of his locker, his red looseleaf notebook open on his knees.

There is a notable absence. There is no one sitting in front of Jay Edwards' locker. Jay has received an incomplete in one course, and a failure in another, a 1.6 for the semester, when he needs a 1.8, just less than a C. Knight has not waited for the official date when he will become ineligible to play. As far as the coach is concerned, the day the grades were issued was the day Jay would be suspended from the team.

Nor, as we saw after the Indiana Classic, was Bob Knight surprised that Jay did poorly his first semester. After the victory against Notre Dame, during which Edwards managed twelve points in ten minutes of play, blocking a David Rivers shot and stealing the ball from Rivers, which resulted in a Garrett dunk, Knight called him into his office.

"You're going to have a lot of nice things said and written about

you all over the country because of how you played last night,"
Knight said. "Three weeks from now those same people are going
to write about how you flunked out of Indiana unless you get
straightened out." Knight believes that Jay has not yet "looked
down the line to see whether a college education is important or
not. The other kid from Marion [Lyndon Jones] has."

Indeed, his words fall on deaf ears. Edwards does not believe
that it will happen to him. The heady excitement of starting in
big-time college basketball proves too much for many freshmen,
of course. At Georgetown, John Thompson permits no freshman
interviews or posing for pictures during the first semester. John
Chaney at Temple attempted to deal with the problem of Mark
Macon, a teammate of Edwards' during the Olympic Festival in
the spring of 1987, by forbidding him to give any interviews. "I'm
trying to keep my feet on the ground," Macon says when you meet
him. And, near the end of the season, Macon thanks Chaney: "I
appreciate what you did."

Edwards, however, falters. Given his autumn semester grades,
he has lost his eligibility. But by an NCAA technicality, he
becomes ineligible only on the first day of the spring semester, in
the middle of January. He could still play.

For Knight, however, he is ineligible. He has chosen the student, the individual, over winning.

There is, however, an escape for Edwards. Indiana runs be-
tween-semester independent studies courses that anyone can
take during the vacation period. Edwards signs up for "Self-In-
struction In Art" for non-art majors, although he has never taken
an art course in his life and has no interest in it. One project will
involve a collage that will "express his personality," and on
which he will paste a photograph of Mark Macon. There are eight
projects in all, for which he must receive a B-plus grade for the
group combined. Then he would be eligible to play in the spring.

Knight anticipates. He knows Jay's first thought will be to get
Magnus Pelkowski, who is a professional-quality artist, to help
him. "I put a stop to that!" Knight says.

Knight insists not only that the projects be done in the office of
Buzz Kurpius, the academic adviser, but that Kurpius, or one of
her assistants, deliver them to the art teacher. (On this point
Kurpius demurs. She phones the art teacher ahead and lets Jay
do the delivering himself, although Knight gives her "heck" for it.)

Meanwhile Knight worries. Edwards' mother is an older woman (he has a thirty-two year old brother) and perhaps he's spoiled. She has sent him to Indiana because "I know you people would really get after him and make him work. That's the only place he'll be forced to do that."

Now, no matter that even if Edwards flunked out completely, he would still be eligible to play until January 14, Edwards is gone, Knight's best shooter off the team. Had Knight allowed Jay to play out the semester, making sure he did the art course, there would have been no questions from the press and Edwards would certainly have helped the team in the losses against Louisville and the ones in the Big Ten season to come. But the student himself is at stake. And so while Indiana practices and prepares for the tough season to come, Edwards pastes up his collages, paints his pictures.

"Do I trust you, Keith?" Knight had joked during the October coaches' clinic. Smart hadn't been able to control his ironic smile. The teacher who cares, intervenes. In his own course in Methods of Basketball Coaching, a student who cuts once automatically receives a C. As for himself, yes he took Woody Hayes' course in Football at Ohio State, his absences always noticeable because his upright friend John Havlicek *never* cut. Knight got a B; the football players, no matter what they did, all got As. They should automatically have gotten As, he thinks now, without the pretense of their attending the class.

"The first thing is this," he begins now on Christmas night. "To be a team hard to play against you have to put in an effort. We're a bad team. There's not a guy here who makes the play the way he's supposed to." As far as the games in Indianapolis are concerned, he tells them, we aren't even going to prepare.

This, of course, is relative. In comparison, perhaps, with other teams, they're preparing as if the course were a combination of chemistry, psychology and military strategy. Seeing, thinking, anticipating, reacting—there is too great a disparity between what they know and what they do. In this simultaneous exercise of mind and body, the intellect, the will and the body, each falls short. There is only one with whom Knight is at least partially pleased—Ricky Calloway.

The teaching involves this: Each must be convinced of what he's doing wrong. Simultaneously, each must emerge with a sense of his own ability, a positive sense that there is much he can do. At this crucial moment when they haven't coalesced as a team, he must both expose their weaknesses and convince them that he believes in their individual strengths. Otherwise they will not believe in them themselves. What makes this task possible is the force of Knight's will, his ability to make others act.

Now each sits, each waits. Kreigh Smith is told he "has no idea" where the three-point line is, however hard they've worked on this. The lessons are amplified by the prodigious memory; he remembers every play they've made in every game without so much as glancing at the running plays. Whatever they've done has been burned into his memory.

But that loss to Louisville is what infuriates him today.

"Keith," he says. "You scored twenty-four points. I'm going to tell you what you were worth." He draws a number five in red on the white blackboard. "You didn't get the ball to anybody. You didn't guard anybody."

It's not only a team without true forwards, but it's also one with weak guard play. "We don't have a single guard here that gets us the basketball because he sees what the hell is going on," Knight says in scathing tones. "I'm going to tell you something. I'm not sure he can play. I'm not sure that he'll ever be as good as anybody in this room. But if I listed the eleven of you with Patrick on a list of who sees what out there, you know where I'd put Patrick? You know where I'd put him, Ricky?" It's Calloway, his hoped-for leader, whom at every opportunity he singles out.

"Close to the top," Calloway says.

"Maybe at the top," says Knight, as if to taunt them with the assertion that the skinny high school kid, Patrick, is better than they are.

"Only Lyndon sees more than Patrick does out there, and you go too slow. You don't go hard enough and quick enough. Hey, I have not worked as hard with Patrick as I have worked with you guys. But the son of a bitch sees what's going on."

Already he moves from the individual to the group. Lest they believe that their inadequate play was the result of a lapse by any single one of them, he addresses them all. "I don't know what you guys thought beat us. It wasn't the press."

Then it's back to the particular: "Twice, Kreigh, you're coming up the floor with the ball and you throw the ball back to Hillman back here . . ."

Perhaps more than many of the others, Kreigh Smith has disappointed him. He seems to be attacking Kreigh now. "If you want to transfer over Christmas do so, because you won't play much here. You'd better learn to play basketball."

It's a device he will use whenever he must: urging a player to prove him wrong by demonstrating that he can in fact play well. As the closing days of this season will demonstrate, it does not always work. But it remains a test of character and an opportunity for a student to reach down for the extra ability he did not know he possessed. Like all of us, these student basketball players draw upon far less of their potential than they might. The demand that they plumb these depths is at the root of Knight's teaching.

"The closest we got to it [a leader] now is Ricky, and Ricky's not blocking out cost us the game at Kentucky," he tells them. The coach on the floor, the student leader, is essential to the college basketball team. Now in December Knight offers Ricky Calloway this role outright and before the entire team. Someone else might, perhaps, be delighted with Calloway for his concentration, his effort, and the seriousness with which he takes himself and the enterprise.

But Knight can't afford this. He sees the moment and he looks into the future. Calloway seems to be doing well according to the stat sheets. But his mistakes presage disaster, and the coach knows it. To ease the tension, he turns to someone else.

"Eyl, were you ever told to deviate from our rules?" He who has achieved as close to perfect an understanding of the game as anyone who has coached it remains dependent upon students acting upon his wisdom. When they make mistakes, it infuriates him because he has taught them how to play without making mistakes. If only they would allow themselves to be taught, they could achieve perfection, the golden bowl without the flaw.

Dean Garrett has particularly displeased his coach.

"Garrett, for some reason, I don't know, leaves Ellison" (Pervis Ellison, the Louisville star junior forward). Garrett is summoned to the blackboard. "Draw for me where you should be." Garrett knows he hasn't done well. Garrett listens. "Now Dean," says Knight. "You don't have Daryl Thomas to lean on, to guide you . . . you've played three games out of eight, that's it. You've just been demolished."

There is nothing that happens in college basketball that he is not aware of, that he doesn't use to rouse them to perform. "Who in here can tell me the score of the Arizona–Washington State game?" He answers the question himself: it was 89–55 in favor of Arizona. The point is clear to them all. In the Hoosier Classic only two weeks ago Indiana had trouble beating Washington State. Now what does that say about their prospects?

"In the Louisville game, I absolutely lost interest." At the appropriate moment he will bring forth his ultimate threat, that he will no longer care. Do they appreciate the generosity of his vigilance? "The mature ones do," says former assistant Jim Crews. Students everywhere, in basketball as in life, resist change. They want the comfort of thinking as they already do. They're recalcitrant, stubborn and, left to their own devices, likely to sabotage themselves. The teacher who cares, however physically and spiritually exhausting it may become, never lets a student off the hook.

Knight directs his stare at Garrett and at Smart together, his junior college recruits, the "athletes" some sportswriters believe made the difference for Knight in the 1987 championship season. Replying to my suggestion that they would have come along more rapidly had they been four-year scholars in this program, Knight asserts, "No question."

"Here's where you are with your future," he tells them. "You two guys go ahead and say to this man in Orlando [Pat Williams, who has brought the post-season NBA showcase Aloha Tournament to Orlando this year], you're going to be gone out of class time for eight days. You think you're going to miss eight days and graduate? Do you think I'm going to let you?"

He has read an article from Orlando advertising this game and he doesn't like it. He addresses Garrett: "With the pro people you have dropped to rock bottom. I talked to five over the weekend. You're going to wind up a fourth- or fifth-round draft choice. You're either scared to play or you've been intimidated in three different games where you just quit. Your effort to rebound offensively in this game is the worst, bar none. You just back away. You never work to go to the offensive backboard . . . I don't think you can think. I think you're the poorest thinker I've ever seen inside here."

Garrett listens, expressionless. But Knight is not through, because Garrett must not be left believing he is incapable of being a good basketball player. "I don't think you're dumb," Knight says. "I think you're bright." Nor is it left at that. "We're going to be better next year, but where will you be?"

In fact, Knight is worried. For where indeed will Garrett be? Unless he improves at once, he will lose his opportunity for a pro career, for financial security.

"Ricky," Knight asks, "what did Daryl put into the game and what does Dean?"

"Daryl saw what was going on on the floor."

"Has he even come close?"

"Not very well."

Smart is drawn into the debate. Smart replies, "I don't think he's played well."

But Knight is not appeased. "Is the fact that you admit that an exoneration? I robbed the bank. I'm sorry?"

Now it's back to Smart. Knight saw Jack McMann over the weekend. He quotes others, quotes experts. "I can't believe Smart isn't playing any better for you," he was told. "You two can take that for what it's worth."

It's back to Eyl: "How many points have you scored in the two games we lost?"

"None," says Eyl.

"What are you going to do about it?"

For Knight, practice is the training ground; practice is treated as seriously as the games. "You don't play in a game anywhere like we do in practices." he tells them, and this is the key. Before each of the pratices to come in the next three days he will show them ten minutes of the Louisville game. There isn't a move any one of his players makes that will not be scrutinized. Now, their heads down, Knight tells them, "You people are working to defeat the purpose of putting a team together."

The promising play of freshman Lyndon Jones, and his serious attitude, have not gone unnoticed. But what will help Lyndon Jones develop is not praise, reminders of his glory days as Indiana high school state champion three years in a row. Lyndon must perceive the disparity between what he is and what he can be; he must develop the ability to play against his own potential.

"Dakich," Knight says, turning to his youngest assistant, "you tell Jones how well he listens."

Dakich knows what to say. He too has played here.

"I don't think he listens worth a damn." Dakich addresses Lyndon Jones directly. "You don't ever do it."

"We're talking about trying to concentrate to do what we did last year," says Knight. "That's what this next five practices will be about. I want you to see how badly this game was played." On the large screen always ready in their locker room, the Indiana-Louisville tape begins.

Every few seconds, the frame is frozen to point out to a student what he could have done, as opposed to what he did do. "Joe," says Knight. "You can be up on top of the guy. There's no effort to get on top of him." Repetition is indispensable to any teacher, let alone one whose students must coordinate efforts of the mind, the will and the body:

"You people are just not thinking well enough, working hard enough to beat good teams. We haven't denied a pass. You're just out there, Joe. You're not doing anything. You are the most average player to be playing here. You have five assists in this game. Was there any other than a pass to someone out on the perimeter? We can't have guards playing like this. Look where you are, Steve." Again the film is stopped.

"Steve, what would be your reaction if you saw this happen with a fourth-year player at the start of a ballgame? What goes through your head? What's our defensive rule here?" He answers it himself. "Be one step on the ball side. Why aren't you there? I don't know."

The lights go off again, the film goes on. The criticism is leavened by a sense of what might have been, what they can do if only they would think. "Just with a little simple effort, we're going to get some shots," he tells them. "We were standing around. . . . Kreigh," he wants to know, "how much trouble was it for Steve to bring the ball up against the press?" The answer is apparent. Looking at the tape makes it clear. It shouldn't have been difficult at all.

Perhaps because people predicted that Joe Hillman might be that leader the team sorely lacks, Knight is upset with him. "Joe," he says, "you see less than anybody in here." That his team lacks a leader is never far from his mind.

Nor is he pleased by Keith Smart's jubilation on the floor when he makes a basket; unselfish team play is so much a part of

Knight's ethic that it doesn't have to be mentioned. "I don't see you doing that when Ricky scores," Knight tells Smart. "I don't see you pat somebody on the back when he scores." Knight worries about Smart; he seems good only in open court play, and that won't be enough.

The film unfolds, the teaching intensifies. "Nobody contests anything," Knight says. "The ball is thrown around. It's a good thing Ellison walked because you aren't going to keep him from getting the ball. You had six turnovers within three feet of the basket." Nothing in Garrett's demeanor suggests that any of this is unfair.

It's constructive because with every criticism they are shown what they might have done, how they might have won the game. "Keith, you have to make a fake trap here. . . . Ricky, you don't go for the blockout. You just turn on the board."

Steve, however, whom Knight believes can do much better, is treated more harshly.

"What kind of athlete do you consider yourself to be?"

"Pretty good."

"Then why don't you keep anyone from getting the ball? You're not a good basketball player. You give the illusion of effort. There's no way you can count how many times Crook [Herbert Crook, Louisville's star senior] caught the ball against you. I counted four. What does that tell you? When have you ever made five jumpshots in a game?"

"Never."

"Then you better be doing something."

He teaches them the game. "You don't even think about the screener, Keith. They both jump to the cutter and you just throw the ball. If we take away open court play, you have no game."

He reverses himself.

"There's a bad call there, Ricky." Those who make much of Knight's supposed efforts to intimidate the officials ignore the many times on the floor he tells his players that a call against them was just, as here he informs Calloway of one that wasn't. To play the game at its height, which is the goal for them, they must approximate his understanding of it.

"See, this cost us a bucket later, Dean. I just told you about that in practice the other day." Here Knight isn't even as angry as most teachers would be when a lesson, only recently taught, turns out a few days later to have been forgotten.

"Joe, have you been taught to leave your hands at your sides?" Knight asks. "Joe, what on a scale of one to ten is your defensive value out on the perimeter?"

"A one."

"Are you above average as a player?"

"Yes."

"Why not go out and play differently tomorrow than you did today?" That this is possible Knight demonstrates through the film of their defeat. "We're ahead thirteen-four, and we aren't even playing well."

"Why don't we draw a charging foul," he demands of Garrett and Eyl, "instead of both of you leaving your feet?" He treats watching the tape with them as another opportunity to coach this game. "Pass fake, pass fake," he orders.

"Dean, explain to me the sense of this. The ball is inside the basket, it's so far in the cylinder. Tell me what goes through a player's mind that goal-tends that ball."

"He doesn't know what he's doing."

"That ball's on the way down. More of that ball's below the rim than above."

"How many passes were made here?"

"One."

"Have I ever told you to go ahead and shoot whenever you think you're open?"

"Ricky," the exasperated coach asks, "how badly do you think these players care about playing?"

"Real bad. They care."

"Then how can you not do what we want done? We stay up hour after hour watching this stuff. We're trying to give you a game you can win with. Do you think it's a coincidence that you [Keith] take a shot on one pass and throw up an airball? I don't."

On this Christmas night, he's far from finished with them. The teaching becomes even more detailed, exact. "Now Ricky, look where Garrett is, it must go to him. We don't see these things quickly enough. Joe, for what reason would you be running across the lane? Look where Ellison starts, Dean. Come up here, Ron. I'm Ellison, you're Garrett."

And he and Felling demonstrate. "Give Garrett a demonstration of the effort he extends to keep me from going into a low post position." Felling uses all the force of his body—no matter that he's a foot shorter than Knight—and keeps him from getting to the imaginary basket.

"You must not have enough determination, son," Knight tells Garrett. "You must not care about anybody in here. If you know we have no chance to win with you playing like this, why don't you do something about it?"

Garrett looks up at him. But it's still not over. "I have a friend of mine who really knows basketball and he told me it was impossible for him to believe you played as badly as you played. We're not going to rub something on your head [he rubs Garrett's head] and make you a better player. You play like you never listened to a minute of basketball teaching."

The point is that others have noticed, it's not just him, not just the coaches here. "I have no question about your being a good sincere kid, but that isn't going to get it done out here," Knight tells Dean Garrett. "You have to develop a game plan." It's Bill Russell who should be Garrett's model, Russell who "had a plan for every possession."

And there is more, words that will strike Garrett only later. "Do you know what pains me more than anything?" his coach asks him. "Not that Ellison got the ball, but that you're my center and you're my choice to play here. I don't want him, I want you!"

Allowing that to register, he goes on to the others. "Joe, do you think there's any chance we can get you out of slow motion? That slows down the pace of everybody."

"Keith, you're not guarding anyone. This isn't even a high pass. You jump up and catch this pass below your shoulders."

"How many passes have been made, Kreigh?"

"The first one," says Kreigh.

"That three-point line may be in Shanghai as far as you're concerned. You have no idea where it is. Tell me you're aware of the three-point line, are you or aren't you?"

But it's a lecture addressed to the team. No single individual is at fault. They look down, or at the film, and there isn't a trace of an argument. The evidence is right there before them. Failure awaits them should they not assume responsibility for themselves as individuals and as a team.

"You people may know there's a game going on, but you're not sure where it is or who's playing. You have no chance of winning in this league playing as you're playing." Each one of them must develop a basketball IQ, become a smarter player or they will have no chance. "We're the dumbest team that I've ever tried to coach right now. I can't coach players that play dumb. I have no patience with it."

There's also a threat. "If you don't make a hell of a commitment to doing what's right when it's right to do it, then this is going to be a goddamn long twenty games that we're playing, and I'll tell you another thing. I'll make it long for you and there isn't anybody in the world that can make it longer than I can. I don't intend to be playing dumb anymore like we are."

The session ends. Knight orders Ricky to sit there with them and find out who wants to play and who doesn't, who's going to come out of the locker room and play and who isn't. They have been "inside" for seventy minutes.

When they race out onto the practice floor into a particularly enthusiastic four-corner passing drill, calling out each other's names loudly, Knight orders Patrick Knight to join them. "We gotta have twelve guys. Let's go!"

II

"You have all worked hard. You have tried to do the things we want done. Let the other guy be dumb. Let the other guy lose."

Saturday morning in the students' locker room Julio passes out index cards. They are to write down the names of the two people, unrelated to them, whom they admire the most. First, two people whom you know. "I didn't say like the most, but admire and respect the most for what they are or for what they do." Then they must draw a line and write down the names of two they admire whom they don't know, a historical figure, living or dead, an athlete or a nonathlete. They write. Knight goes around the room, locker by locker and asks why each has listed the four he has.

The answers are predictable: the winners are competitive, committed, successful, mentally tough. He neither asks whom they have chosen ("That's private," he'll say later) nor do they volunteer the names, except for Keith Smart who has selected John Hope Franklin and James Weldon Thompson. "They came out on top."

"Apparently you have an admiration for people who are able to do the very things we want you people to do, and that's quite simply to get the most out of what you have."

The "we" is no accident; they are meant to see the assistant coaches as a team too. "Boys," Joby calls them. "Men," Ron says. Danny they enjoy; he played for Knight not long ago; he is closest to them in age, only three years older than the seniors.

It's the day after Christmas and Knight is making the speech of the season. He explores who he is and who they are, what he can do for them and what they must do for themselves. He asks if they believe the coaches are getting something extra for making them work this hard. "Not a dollar," he tells them. "We get paid the same whether we win, lose or draw. Do you realize that last year when we won the NCAA championship we as coaches did not get paid an extra dollar?" He believes they must be wondering about his motives, why he is driving them so hard. Is *he* getting something out of it? And he believes that if even one of them starts to think he's doing something *to* them rather than *for* them, he can no longer coach them.

"You want to know what the biggest difficulty in getting to the top of the ladder is? The biggest difficulty in getting to the top of the ladder is getting through the crowd at the bottom."

They are not being driven so hard "for some imagined benefit to the coaches. We're not pushing you for us. We're pushing you for you . . . there are a few of you in here who have to be pushed to excess, and that's not the way it should be."

Unselfconsciously, he tells his players that what he is doing for them is unique, and unlikely to be duplicated once they leave Indiana University. Once they're gone, "there isn't going to be somebody on your ass day after day; they'll just find somebody else." Always there's an example. It's Daryl Thomas, who failed to keep his commitments in the post-season and wound up a sixth- instead of a second-round draft choice, only to be playing in England for about ten percent of what he would make in the NBA.

"How many of you are reading a book right now?" he demands. He holds up the biography, *Vince,* which he is reading. "How many of you read books about people that succeed or fail? If you don't, how the hell do you know what's in success and what's in failure?" He takes from Lombardi an inspiration for his team, a "fourth dimension" determining success: "Selfless teamwork and collective pride which accumulate until they have made positive thinking and victory habitual." He searches for ways to motivate the leaderless team, the team without forwards, the team without a point guard, the team, unlike the legendary Knight teams which prided themselves on defense, which will have to succeed in high-scoring games. He does not give up on them.

Perhaps they are wondering why Coach Knight coaches. He tells them he "can't begin in the rest of my lifetime to spend the money I have." More, "there isn't any championship that a team I've coached hasn't won. There isn't any honor that a player I've coached hasn't had." He is not capable, he says, of influencing great multitudes of people. "But I think I can take a handful and influence them." And what does he want? "I don't just want you people to win in basketball," he says. "I want you to win in everything that you do."

He turns less soft. He looks at each of them hard, as if he were angry that they aren't doing as well as they might. "I only wonder why I coach when I have to get on *your* ass about catching the ball, or *yours* about applying pressure, or *yours* about thinking or *yours* about looking at what the hell's going on, or *yours* about playing intelligently." He hits every base.

The Louisville film comes on, exposing their errors once more: Joe has his hands on his knees. Smith's man "might as well be playing against a statue in the park as playing against you." He invokes Steve Alford with his "tremendous sense of wanting to win." On the wall facing them is a poem, "No one is beat 'til he quits, /No one is through 'til he stops /No matter how hard failure hits/No matter how often he drops . . ." And today on the bulletin board, photographs of the Pennsylvania players face them along with descriptions of their strengths, and clippings testifying to their abilities. The managers hung these posters the moment the Louisville game ended.

He leaves them alone in the locker room with Ricky again as his representative: "You people better talk again a little bit about what it's going to take to play. I don't know what you three, Eyl, and Garrett and Smart, want to be remembered for," he tells his seniors, "but we're a team of lazy players that does things conveniently and stays in a comfort zone and you can't beat anybody that way. If you have any questions about how to be good, ask me. If you don't know how to be good, then I'll tell you."

Out on the floor as they prepare for the Hoosier Classic, which Indiana University will host in Indianapolis in two days' time, it's practice as usual. At this tournament he will generally play the weakest team in the first game—unless a coach calls and asks that he not play Indiana that first night. Then he will play first, and, in all likelihood, be eliminated.

For lunch it's chicken wings at the Third Base Lounge, where all eyes are riveted on a movie-sized television screen and nobody bothers him. This lunch is on "the Eastern liberal establishment," he says.

"Move it, Patrick," he calls, once practice resumes in the late afternoon. "Don't dance out there. Move through." They must not attempt shots they are incapable of making. "You can make that shot, son, once out of a hundred times," Knight tells Keith. Magnus is also told, "How can you do something you've never done before? I never hit a golf shot left-handed so how can I do it?" It's the theme of the day, and the premise at the heart of his teaching: they will not be asked to do something they cannot. "What kind of shot is that for you, Steve?" he wants to know. "You have to know what you can do and what you can't do." That's their job—to know themselves well enough not to attempt the impossible, but to develop the abilities he knows they possess.

"Lyndon, everything was good, but you didn't see the cut. Tell him, Ricky." And so he continues to search for leadership, for a surrogate among them.

After a three-week absence with a back injury, Joe Hillman came back for one practice, only to have the team lose to Kentucky. It was at that point that Knight suggested he might become the team leader. With his intensity and determination, Hillman seems a quintessential Knight player, one limited only by his height: 6'2" rather than 6'8".

"I don't know if these guys will listen to what I have to say," Hillman replied, referring to a bad play he made in that Kentucky loss. Then he thought, you can't get on anybody if you're not doing a very good job yourself. He decided they should go out and develop some of their own leadership. But Knight thought otherwise, remembering Quinn Buckner, who had seized the reins of leadership, although he was far from being the best player.

"Get in there, Pat, are you going to play or not?" And then, "Dean, Patrick just blocked you off the board. Patrick can't block high school kids off, but he just blocked you off. Only Lyndon sees more than Patrick sees," Knight says, encouraging the freshman who had arrived so frightened. And then there is something more, a father's pride: "I have not worked as hard with Patrick as I have with you guys," he says. "But the son of a bitch sees what's going on."

Of course it doesn't end there. Pat's inexperience leads to a lesson for them: "Here's how Pat was playing the zone. Eyes riveted on the basketball with no idea of what's going on behind him."

The feel of these post-Christmas practices is: now or never. Dean Garrett seems incapable of improving. "When you get the ball at four feet, you've got to be able to score." And, later, "Where's the ball, Dean? You had no idea where the ball was. Why shoot a ball you fumble? If you can't catch a ball, you can't shoot it."

Always, they are told, the object is not a shot, but a *good* shot. It's nearly January, the start of their conference play, but the teaching remains rooted in fundamentals, as it will until the last day of the season. "Joe, you should catch, look at your feet and then shoot the ball. You should know where you are." It's that "sense of where you are," Bill Bradley's phrase, which makes a good basketball player.

If no mistake goes unnoticed, no good play escapes without praise. "Good leap, Ricky. That's good, Keith. Atta boy, Lyndon." That he feels affection for all of them is unmistakable. "Son," he tells Smart, "you don't begin to use your ability."

But there is also: "Patrick, when you drove right here, where did you have the shot?" and "Pat, you can't hold the ball over your head." Smart is asked, "What are you doing defensively?" Smart replies, "Nothing."

Finally, even Dean comes through: "That's good. That's the way to see. Come on, Dean. Every play like that!" Not that it ends there. "Lyndon, did you make that pass to Garrett?" he asks. "The next time he drops it, go over and slap his face. I want somebody out here that makes him pay the price."

A freshman chastise a senior? Nobody finds that unusual, not that shy, still slightly-in-awe Lyndon would do it. "Tell him, Ricky, tell him!" Knight urges. How well they bear up under this scrutiny is a tribute to everybody.

When Patrick Knight doesn't take a shower, his father notices this too. "How come you're not taking a shower?"

"I've got no clean clothes. I had to borrow underwear from you."

"Where are you going?"

"Home. Is that all right?"

As far as Patrick's career with Bloomington North High School is concerned, Knight has never interfered, not even to suggest that Patrick should first play on the *junior* varsity, which Knight believed would have been a good idea.

At five in the afternoon on Saturday they're back in their locker room. He tells them he has seen some "improvement in recognition." The tape comes on. "That big fat-ass beats us to the spot. That just can't happen. There's just no way that can happen." They are conserving their energy, something this team cannot afford to do: "Playing all-out means everything to this team, at both ends of the floor." He tries to reach Kreigh Smith: "Kreigh, you almost act like you don't want any part of the ball. You just throw it back as fast as you can get it back." Later in the season he will have little to say to this player: the focus now can mean only one thing. The coach is hoping Kreigh will be able to play.

It is not always easy, this scrutiny. "How many passes here, Steve?" "Two." "Would you consider this an on-balance shot? . . . Is this the best kind of pressure you can exert, Joe?" "No." "Then why are you giving it to us? That's my next question. If this isn't the best, then why is this what we're getting? Answer that for me!"

The issue again is leadership with nobody organizing any screening. They are not working to get open. He points out Keith's play: "You started in the middle of the lane, and that is it. That's all there is. You ought to just cry when you see yourself playing. You just represent yourself so badly. Watch yourself, Keith. You're back on the line again because of a bad pass and because nobody works to get open. Nobody screens. Ricky, you just stand out there and holler for the ball thirty feet away." As for Kreigh, "You don't even look to take the ball up the side. . . ."

"Play through being tired!" he calls out when it's obvious that they're exhausted. Later in the season practices will be only an hour and fifteen minutes. But not now. "You guys let the fact that you're a little bit tired dictate how you're playing. You're all feeling sorry for yourselves because you're a little bit tired. I can show you what being tired is like two hours from now. I have nothing planned for tonight." A few minutes later he announces, "I planned to stop twenty minutes ago. Every time there's something like that, it adds ten minutes!

"Concentrate on how you play, not on how long you play." They are to write this down in their notebooks, exhausted as they are now at ten of seven on Saturday evening.

"Be dressed and ready at ten in the morning," he tells them as they depart.

On Sunday morning he reviews the stat sheets that have been kept of these practices. Kreigh Smith has had the most baskets, twenty-six. But . . . he has been out-rebounded by Patrick Knight! In one practice there were forty-four rebounds, and Kreigh only got one! He goes down the line: In one there were sixty-eight rebounds, and he got zero. Steve Eyl only got two!

Practice is the paradigm of Knight's teaching. They are all equally involved, no one waiting on the sidelines to take part. Each has an equal opportunity to show what he can do. More difficult than any game, the Knight practice is an exercise in pressure. And as in no other classroom, the teacher monitors every move, every thought of every single student.

Now the test papers are being returned to the class graded: Jadlow went eight for seventeen one night, yet made only two baskets the next time: "We play today and we don't play tomorrow.

"Ricky is the closest player we have to somebody who plays with consistency." So the coach decides . . . now.

"Keith, you get tired, and we're going to start playing you in spurts," Knight says. There may be a medical reason for this because, although he does not have the disease, Keith carries the trait for sickle-cell anemia. Off the bench, only Lyndon has played consistently. "Kreigh," Knight says pointedly, "that's why we can't think about playing you. You don't rebound. Let me ask you something. How can a guy be six foot seven and there be sixty-eight rebounds out here and you get zero? How many of you guys think Kreigh really wants to play?" Ricky, Steve, Joe and Magnus raise their hands.

"What would you do with this if you were a coach?" Of course the coach has his own answer. "The way you play," he tells Kreigh, "we're limited to playing you against the zone. You're not going to rebound, you're not going to scramble after the ball: the spot I have to have for you is one where we got some guy out here that never goes inside." Brian Sloan, on the other hand, has earned "a real chance to play and you're going to play." Hillman, who averaged forty-one points a game in high school, doesn't shoot enough.

"Do you think we inhibit your shooting?"

"No," Hillman whispers.

The point has been made: they all have a chance; there is no single starting five, no one whom he has decided simply will not play. "I want open shots taken by anybody that can make them. I want the ball passed four times, that's it. You don't have any requirement on your shooting other than that."

Why four passes? It's to test the defense, to reverse the ball twice, to get a chance to take the ball inside, to draw the foul, to get the three-point play. "It's an automatic sit-down for a guy that shoots the ball other than off the break in a wide open shot in less than four passes. I'm just tired of this," he tells them. "We just don't do things without a reason." They are also shown a tape of their own strong, aggressive, successful play. The moral is clear: They *can* do it, they can play well. He believes it because they have demonstrated it.

"How are you, Keith?" Ron Felling affectionately asks on Sunday morning.

Smart smiles. "I'm living."

Knight sees the season before him. He realizes that this team must gain an advantage in the first five minutes of a game (he puts the number 5 on the whiteboard). Then it must not allow a comeback for the opponent in the second five minutes. For the last ten minutes of the first half they need "steady play."

All but Kreigh are writing in their notebooks. And there's the goal Knight is famous for, the one that's no myth—"We have to be able to play mistake free." He points to the sign on their wall: "Victory Favors the Team Making the Fewest Mistakes."

This is not a team that will dominate its opponents.

As for Kreigh, "When I recruited you, I thought you'd be as good as Wittman. I can remember the first time I saw you play . . ." This he means too: "It just kills us when guys come in a game and give up points or throw the ball away or don't see.

"We have room for a lot of people to play, boys."

Garrett remains far from the birdhouse. Nor is Knight beyond using the players against each other to drive the message home:

"Ricky, if Dean happens to be here, and he comes over the top to this spot, and the ball's over in here somewhere, and he moves to the ball, and the ball goes back to the other side, tell me what he's going to do. I mean, what he's going to do ninety percent of the time."

"He'll go right back the same way."

"How many guys in here could have answered that for what Dean's going to do?"

All hands go up, save one.

"You couldn't have?"

Lyndon, still shy, nods. Yes, he could have.

"Then you better get your hand up!" But Knight is gentle with this shy freshman. "How are you today?" he asks, obviously only pretending to be gruff.

It's Sunday and they're about to leave for Indianapolis. No one has been immobilized by the scrutiny in the locker room and today players are called aside for private teaching. "Atta boy, Todd, good position," Knight calls. "That was perfect." "Good, good, good," he tells Magnus, "but stay on your feet." It's obvious that they have dramatically improved in these five practices since Christmas night. It's almost palpable. You can feel their spirits rise.

In the locker room for the last time, he tells them, "I think we've made some progress. You people each have to be better, but you don't have to be any better than you are. We're not asking you to be any stronger nor any quicker. We're just asking you to be as good as you are. That's all it takes."

It's a speech they will hear again and again, but one they may not understand until long after they have left Indiana. "Play to win," he concludes as they practice for the last time before boarding the bus to Indianapolis.

Just before five, Everett Dean appears in Assembly Hall. Nearly ninety now, he is unwilling to miss this annual excursion Knight prepares for him. Dean, whom Knight had praised at the Cathedral High School fund raiser, coached Stanford to an NCAA championship in 1942, and also coached Indiana. He is one of the old coaches Knight looks after, as, in their wisdom, they looked after him when he was a young man.

As soon as the players arrive at the Marriott in Indianapolis, Knight begins to speak not about Pennsylvania, an easy win, but about the Big Ten season to come. They should be encouraged by games like Eastern Kentucky, when they played well.

In twenty-two years, there's never been a bedcheck; there's zero chance of anyone being out. The players, "dressed," holding their notebooks, giggle.

III

"If you were to ask me to boil this whole thing down to the simplest form, it might be this: in order to be any good, you got to know what you're bad at, and so you play to your strengths and play away from your weaknesses. But somebody's got to tell you what the hell your weaknesses are and somebody's got to tell you the mistakes you're making. If they don't do that, you have no chance."

While Knight lies on the couch of his suite listening, Dan Dakich telephones a potential recruit.

"Tell him who you are so they have some point of reference," Knight coaches while Dakich talks to someone. "I'm Dan Dakich. I'm one of Coach Knight's assistants. I used to play at Indiana."

Unflappable, Dakich keeps up his conversation, unmindful of the prompter. "How old are you?" he asks the potential recruit's fifteen-year-old sister.

"All those are good questions except you never ask anybody how old they are," Knight points out after Dakich has hung up.

With his players resting in this interlude, the lull before the conference season, Knight ponders the enigma of his team. "You develop a game for a team to play and the game we developed for this team is a quick-paced game both on the full court and the half-court." But they're playing a slow-paced game. "The game that we developed is based upon recognition which leads into anticipation and being able to stop things defensively or do things offensively, and we're not playing with any reading or recognition at all.

"We're playing a smart game with no thought and that's impossible," he says, looking forward to the fate of this year's Indiana team. "They've not yet developed their judgment.

"The problem that you have with most players at this level is that they all think that they're really good players. Well, they aren't. There are only a few really good players. The rest of them have to understand that they're going to get by learning to do some things and learning not to do some things. Our guys haven't really done that yet. They don't have a really good player among them that just tells them all what to do and brings them all to his level. The best players are those that make everybody else a little better, either through their own play or through what they do and say."

If there is one player who accomplished that in this post-Christmas interlude, it's . . . Patrick Knight, close to his heart, but more, one who played with fire and intensity all week. "Patrick in this five-day session had more assists than anybody else on the team, which really pleases me." He may be a father, however, but he must also be fair. "He also had far more turnovers than anybody else." Then Knight adds, "But that's not being used to this kind of play. Patrick is the kind of player who can make other people better because he's creative and he sees." The coach demonstrates. "If I go here, I can throw there. Our guys don't see that." Patrick's strengths, Patrick's weaknesses: "He plays well around the ball. When he doesn't have the ball, either on offense or defense, he doesn't play well."

Knight focuses his rational intelligence on his own son no less than on the others.

And then the father re-emerges. "I'll tell you one thing. He was a hell of a lot better at these five practices than I thought he would be. He made some absolutely great passes. Not only did he have more assists, but he saw better. Hell, he had probably a dozen guys miss lay-ups on passes he made. He's got balls. He's not afraid to make a play."

Will he then recruit Patrick?

"If he can play, that's where he is going to play. I'm not putting all this effort into him and then getting somebody else to coach him."

Who can excel? "It's not an easy game for them. You have to be able to find something that makes it easy, like just simply playing hard because by playing hard you don't make as many errors. And you get into position so that all of a sudden there's a play you can make."

He remembers himself as a college senior being asked to speak at high school dinners. He started out by talking right over the top of everybody's head: "So consequently I'm never interrupted in my thinking. I've never locked gazes with anybody. I'm never distracted by what anybody does. Then gradually I would look. Even today when I speak I never look at somebody because you could be distracted for any one of a hundred reasons. And you lose your train of thought. Well, a lot of people are petrified when they get up to speak. How many people have you heard get up and say, 'I'm more surprised than you are that I'm going to talk,' or, 'I had no idea I would be asked.' Well, why say that? These inane things don't mean anything. Just get up and say something and sit down!"

Do these reminiscences have a point; are they self-serving? In fact, they're about his basketball team. "That's what these guys have to latch onto as a basketball team," he says, "And I don't know where they're going to do it." He had hopes for Hillman, Hillman who had averaged forty-one points in high school. "But Hillman does not see the game well enough; he doesn't make enough things happen. He doesn't recognize enough; he's going to be cautious." Knight grants that Hillman's not going to throw the ball away. "I'll play him," Knight decides. "I'm not going to start him, but, I'll play him and we'll see if he makes five or six baskets in a night.

"The one thing that's disappointed me most about this team," he admits, "is that Smart hasn't been a good scorer. He's not a real tough-minded kid. He only does one thing to a superlative degree and that's play in an open court situation on offense when he has the ball."

Everything his team does interests him. "I would not have had them wear a coat and tie tonight, except they all had them on when I went into that room, so I didn't say anything about it." He is pleased by this, pleased by good behavior in which they've taken the initiative. With no bed check, he is certain they're up there in their rooms watching the Movie Channel. It's not that they're entirely on the honor system. Once, he remembers, at Butterfield's, a Bloomington restaurant, a player ran up a seventy dollar bill despite his eighteen dollar limit. "I told them, here's what we're going to pay, and I almost told him, 'You can pay the rest of it.' The key word there, of course, is "almost." "They've got the evening free, but they never go anywhere. There is no rule that they don't go out, but they never have."

In his hotel suite, resting between team meetings, his thoughts turn to the new Big Ten rule that decrees that a junior college player, who would not have passed the NCAA academic requirement under Proposition 48, would be required to sit out a year before playing. If adopted, it would mean, he predicts, that the Big Ten could never recruit a junior college player. He has had seven junior college players. Four would have been required to sit out the year, three—Jadlow, Smart and Courtney Witte would not.

As for the assistants that he hires, it's on the basis "of being able to teach, not recruit. There isn't a recruiter here, they're all teachers." Ron Felling, in particular, is an example of that. "He has a great way of telling people things," says Knight. "I really like the way Felling has great presence in explanation. He gets upset, but he doesn't get upset like I do."

This tournament, the Hoosier Classic, "isn't anything. What will tell us where we are is the month of January. If we could develop, we're in a great position. We couldn't be any better because they've already had to listen since they've lost. They haven't played well. The players that have to play well have not played well. If we had players who have to play well really playing well, and we're still getting beat, then we're in trouble." There is still hope for this season despite the losses to Kentucky and Louisville.

"We can't afford to lose one of these games. Then we have to get off to a reasonably good start in the Big Ten. Iowa could beat us, but we can't lose to Northwestern. We're in a good position to do some things, but we have to get better. My concern is, do we have enough kids for whom basketball is an easy game to be able to do that? Or do we have too many for whom the game is too hard?"

IV

"I think we're at fault to this extent. I think we should have played Smith a lot in the Kentucky game. We overplayed Eyl. Smith really did a pretty decent job in the Notre Dame game. I think he scored nine points in the time that he was in there. He threw the ball away a couple of times, but he was tired by then. Then we came back and didn't play him in the Kentucky game. So as fragile as his constitution is, that could have really screwed him up."

Venerable Everett Dean joins the team for breakfast on Monday morning, but Knight does not. At the Market Square Arena, where they have come to practice, Knight sits reading *Vince* while they dress and are taped. Knight's physical strength extends to his eyesight; although he is never without a book (it might be *The Reckoning,* by David Halberstam, or *Pentagon* by Allen Drury), in his late forties, he wears no reading glasses.

He sits in the empty gym and draws around himself a protective aura of unapproachability. It isn't hostile or directed against anyone in particular. It's more an assertion, a visible desire to be alone with himself. If someone assaults his privacy—this morning it's Don Fischer who does the Indiana play-by-play on the radio, and Knight's pre-game show—he's pleasant. A guest who does gain admittance to the closed practice is Jim Strickland, an Indianapolis physician who, certain that he is out of earshot, whispers how one year Knight walked five miles in the snow to the University of Minnesota hospital to visit an Indiana woman dying of leukemia. Knight remained an hour in her room dressed in a mask and gown.

Otherwise it's practice as usual: Lyndon Jones runs around the perimeter of the court to test his injured ankle; everyone else is immediately put under pressure. Todd pushes off, but Magnus makes a good move. "I don't think we're asking too much of anybody," he tells me. The implied question to them is always the same: "How much do you want to do the things you've worked at? Hillman, I'm going to isolate you and Smith because God put you on Earth to torture me." Smith's play has particularly attracted his attention. Smith is on his mind.

"Dean, you never moved . . . instead of getting over here and challenging him. Do you want to play?"

"Yes."

"You're not convincing me you want to play."

No one's place is assured. Knight turns to Ricky Calloway.

"Has Garrett convinced you he wants to play?"

"No."

Although Penn is probably the easiest team Indiana will play this season, he is infuriated at the lackadaisical practice. Suddenly he zeroes in on the culprit.

"L.J.," he calls to one of the managers, L.J. Wright, who is the best basketball player, "put on a white shirt!" And Kreigh Smith is banished to the showers. Revealing no emotion, sweaty with exertion, Kreigh departs.

The practice goes on, their effort up a notch. Keith is praised for a cut, Lyndon for anticipating, Brian for a good screen. But the hero of the practice is Ricky Calloway, Calloway whom Knight now sees as a creator. "Good, Ricky, very good," he calls. "Ricky, that was a really good step. You've got to create. You can't wait for something to happen. Atta boy. That's what basketball is all about. That's the way to play the game."

The others are told not to stand and wait to see what Ricky's going to do. And Ricky is given the highest Knight compliment: further instruction. "Ricky, when you hit him with the ball, come into the hole. Now you're posted. Don't let them match up to you. That was a great play, Ricky. I can't tell you how good a play that was." Now Ricky must "make the play. Think what you've got. Look at what you've got and have it register." A few moments later, Knight again praises Calloway: "Great pass, Ricky, that's the way to look." In his third season with Knight, having started on a championship team, Calloway is now treated as the team leader for whom Knight is desperately searching. Knight hopes Calloway will assume the role.

"What do you think, Jimbo?" Knight asks Strickland's wide-eyed thirteen-year-old son.

After practice a family comes up to Knight with their son, a boy aged eleven with his head shaved, obviously the result of chemotherapy. Knight takes a photo with the child. The father, a tall man with gray hair, tells Knight how someone, suggesting a resemblance with Knight, told him not to throw any chairs. Knight smiles weakly, and doesn't say a word.

The television interviewers have arrived, and their first question has to do with Jay Edwards. Is he ineligible? Will he come back? What happened? "Why should we talk about a guy who couldn't keep his grades up? We're talking about those who are playing," Knight replies firmly.

On the way back to the hotel in Strickland's car he sings: "Why, oh, why, did I leave Ohio?" The second button is broken on Strickland's brown tweed jacket. Knight reaches over from the back seat where he has chosen to sit with Jimbo and yanks it off.

"That was doing me for a long time," the doctor laughs.

"It's very hard to become something if you don't look as if you're already doing it," Knight answers emphatically.

Lunch is chicken and noodles, homemade biscuits and jelly, preceded by his inevitable bowl of chili, at Bob Evans, a restaurant he likes better than last night's mediocre Italian restaurant. His talk ranges from genuine pleasure at his national championships with three completely different teams—so unselfconscious that it is charming—to English history ("Anne Boleyn," he says, "not bad for a basketball coach") to the Russian game.

Autograph hunters descend, breaking into his conversation, as they invariably do when he eats at a restaurant. Today's shameless autograph seeker is a Baptist minister. We avert our eyes. No one says anything. The minister calls Knight "Bobby." Uncannily he knows the one right thing to say: he admires the team. The Baptist minister congratulates Knight for "building character."

Without missing a beat, as soon as the man is gone, Knight immediately resumes his conversation. He wants to discuss with Jimbo, a basketball player of course, which of three Indiana high schools would be the best for him. Knight becomes a parent: "At which would you be able to play the most?" Jimbo has demonstrated an interest in aviation, which provides the opening for a needle. Why isn't he coming to basketball camp? Does he want to be a pilot or a basketball player?

I can't argue him out of the check. Then he dons his pointy black-and-white checkered tweed hat which perches on the top of his head like a star on top of a Christmas tree and which functions well as a semi-disguise, and it's back to the hotel, to the team.

In his suite, the team awaits him. They are being lectured by Julio Salazar, who has done the scouting of Penn: "They run a regular UCLA cut. When they don't get it, they take the ball to one of the sides. . . ."

"Mark, are you here?" Knight teases the redshirted player who was given a few days extra off for Christmas because he is from California. "I thought you were transferring to the University of Trinidad. Look to your left, then look around the room, Mark, and then back to your left. Who do you think the guy in here most likely to fake an injury would be?"

They all laugh, slightly injured Lyndon Jones no less than the others. Knight goes on to tease Julio: "I understand exactly what Julio says. Todd, did you understand that? Julio, don't let these guys give you any shit now." Having excelled at scouting and research, watching endless tapes, weekends, evenings, boiling down an opponent to a series of cards, it is one of Julio's first walk-throughs and Knight is trying to put him at his ease. Julio, in turn, has an answer to each of Knight's questions. What is it percentage-wise, man to man versus zone? "It's ninety-five percent man to man, coach," Julio answers.

When the team is gone, Knight discusses Kreigh Smith with his assistants. (I ask him how Kreigh took being thrown out of practice. His reply is unrelenting: "The correct question from Kreigh's point of view is how *I'm* taking it.")

In fact, he is not happy with Smith's play because "everything he does is wrapped around his shooting, either positively or negatively. None of it has anything to do with the other ninety-five percent of basketball." Dan Dakich reports Kreigh told him, "I just have a real hard time. I'm supposed to be a shooter and I want to score because I think that's what I should be doing, that's what they want me to do." Kreigh cannot account for the errors in his play: "I don't know why I don't do that. I just don't know why."

Knight takes some of the blame. "I think we're at fault to this extent," he explains. Kreigh had scored nine points against Notre Dame, and had a right to expect to play against Kentucky. He should have played him instead of Eyl.

Dakich agrees. "Now his thinking is when he doesn't play in the Kentucky game, they're mad at me. What did I do wrong? Why are they mad at me? I don't know if he could have done any good for us," Dakich adds.

"Well, he certainly couldn't have been worse than Eyl," Knight says.

"He was sitting next to me in the Kentucky game, Coach," says Julio. "During the game he mentioned to me that he wanted to be ready because he'd played a big role in the game against Kentucky two years ago. He was really positive that he would be played again."

Dakich takes the opportunity to speak on Smith's behalf. "He played well this week. He shot the ball extremely well. In my opinion this is a game he'd play really well in."

Knight is sceptical. "This game? Well, that's the problem. He could score twenty points in this game and then where are you?" The point is clear. Playing against Penn is no test of anything.

But Dakich persists. "As far as getting him going a little bit, this whole tournament wouldn't be bad."

Patrick Knight telephones. He is exhausted after the five Indiana practices and won't be driving up for the first game of the Hoosier Classic. Today he just wants to sleep.

How did he do in his own practice today, his father wants to know.

"Awful," Patrick says.

Don Fischer arrives for his pre-game show to find a playful guest. Fischer, whose play-by-play is outstanding, (he's an unsung Tim Carver of basketball), enjoys the obstreperous Knight. As usual, he plays it straight. What about the field of the Hoosier Classic?

"I just don't know anything about it."

"How about Penn, the opponent tonight?"

"I really know very little about Penn. It's located in Philadelphia and it has a business school called the Wharton School of Finance which a lot of assholes have gone to and graduated from." Knight goes on to say something uncomplimentary about his own team. He is bored, trying to amuse himself and others. He would make life full, not boringly repetitive, as these pre-game shows invariably are, with the coach praising the best players of the opponent. He works at freeing life from becoming routine, as he demands that his players work at getting open on offense.

"What did you get for Christmas, coal and sticks?"

"Santa Claus forgot me."

Then he does get serious. Knight has invited two good California teams, California/Santa Barbara (which this season will go on to beat Nevada/Las Vegas twice) and Stanford to the Hoosier Classic. As for his own team, he turns the question back to Fischer. "What do you think?"

"I think the kids are working hard. I don't know if they've grasped what you're trying to get through to them, though."

And here comes the merciless Knight, the Knight who, if he so chooses, will not let anyone off the hook.

"What do you think it is that I'm trying to get through to them that they haven't grasped?"

Fischer ventures forward. He talks about their being alert, playing solidly. . . .

"Are you saying then that you don't think they're more alert, that you don't think they're playing solidly?"

"I still think there are a couple of people that have some work to do."

"Oh, I think there are more than a couple of people that have work to do," Knight slices in, "and I think that goes through all facets of Indiana basketball and that includes even the broadcast team."

Fischer reminds Knight that he's never had a team take this much time off since the last ballgame. They lost to Louisville on December 19, and didn't return to practice until the 25th. Knight wanted them "to get some rest and rethink where we were as players and what we had to do individually."

As all these pre-game coach shows do, this one ends with Fischer wanting to know tonight's starting lineup.

"If you pay careful attention to the introductions," Knight tells him, "you'll be able to pick it up."

With Fischer gone, and the game only a few hours away, he still wants to talk to me about his team, about Dean Garrett, who two years ago had "the worst run I had ever seen. He ran on his heels, didn't use his arms to run, just shuffled down the floor. He can't jump; he's not a very good athlete. He's just a guy who's been made to play because he happens to be six-ten. But what I know about Garrett is this: Garrett has to play on a team that's good."

His concern for Garrett extends beyond Indiana's own season: will Garrett be able to convince one of the pro people to draft him in the first round so he gets a good contract? "He isn't a forward and he isn't a center and he has a tough time moving from here to there with the ball and he doesn't see things very well."

As he speaks, one of the tapes of practice runs. He illustrates how Smart is looking the wrong way. "Now watch this whole thing unfold. See where Smart is. There's nobody close to him, nobody behind him, and the position he should be in is right where Smith is because that's the closest guy for him to guard. And Smith gets this uncontested shot."

He backs up the tape. "The guy for Smart to guard is right here. On that pass he should move across the line and look this way. All right, what is there for me? There's nobody for me to guard, so I look and I go right where Smith is.

"What can happen then is they can throw across court to Patrick, all right. But look at the bottom man here who has no one to guard either, so he comes out on Patrick's man. This is what you've got to teach in a zone defense. You've got to teach people where there aren't any players.

"Let me back this up for you and I'll show you. Now watch where Smith starts. He starts OK, they jump him. Now he can come back. But now Smart should be right on Smith. There's no one else. He can't expect a guy to cover the passer and the receiver both. You see what I mean? What Smart is doing is, he's expecting Hillman to guard the passer and the receiver and you can't do that. Now if the pass does come across to Patrick, then the bottom man comes out on Patrick, and Garrett comes over to play the bottom man, so Smart ends . . . this is what bothers me most about him. He just gives up plays like that because he really gets tired.

Knight does play zone defense, he admits, but only to affect the other team's play. What's more important is that his team really works well against a zone. "Like Calloway has to stay with the ball, there's nowhere else for him to go but staying with the basketball. I don't know why he thinks about going anywhere else . . . "

Teaching them is teaching them to see as he does, which is both an impossible and the only possible goal. Now we watch Calloway whose defender just stands. "There are more mistakes that can be made in basketball than in any other game," Knight says.

"Watch Patrick make a good move here. This is why I think he has a chance to be good. Watch, watch him, he's up on top of the screen. Watch how he starts in, then he slides back and steps right into the shot. Perfect footwork, he stepped right into it."

Did his father teach him when he was a child?

The reply is gruff. "Well, a little."

Even this conversation does not conclude without a glance back at the sportswriters and the double standard they bring to reporting about him. It seems not to occur to him that there may be a causal connection between *ad hominem* reporting about him and his attacks on them, range wars on the order of the Hatfields and the McCoys:

"Constantly last year writers would write things about how fat I was, or about how out of shape I was. Do I look like I'm . . . ? I would say to Hammel, 'Have you ever seen a normal sportswriter? They're little short guys, or they're bald-headed fat guys like you, or they're guys with some kind of a physical handicap, they've got a bent arm, they limp, they wear thick glasses.' It just amazes me that they could pick on that. . . ."

V

"Do you have stock in Pennzoil?"

We are on the bus headed for the Market Square Arena and the game with Penn, which he knows they must secretly believe will be easy: "Let's be as good on every possession that we can be. Let's anticipate. Let's don't react. Let's get a possession over with and win that possession and win the next possession. . . ." Tim Knight is on the bus and his father calls him up to sit beside him so he can discuss Patrick's success in practice. Has Tim talked to him? He has.

In the audience is Ryan White and his family, the sixteen-year-old hemophiliac with AIDS, an Indiana celebrity after his family had been hounded out of Kokomo by community pressure. Knight tracked him down and telephoned.

"I heard Ryan was an IU fan and would be interested in coming to a basketball game after January first," Knight told Mrs. White. Since Indianapolis is closer to their home, they chose this tournament. Now Ryan, a smiling boy in blue jeans and a blue-jean jacket, who looks more like thirteen than sixteen, sits chatting with his friends and Mom right behind the Indiana bench.

Nor can the game begin without a blind woman named Mrs. Lingelfelter presenting the coach with a red-and-white Afghan that she has crocheted, complete with the IU logo at its center. Knight puts his arm around her, pats her on the neck. Tim Knight takes charge of the Afghan, which will wind up draped over a sofa in Knight's living room not far from the Olympic banner reading "To Our Coach, WE ARE ALL BEHIND YOU," signed in embroidery by all those who participated with him in the 1984 Olympics.

Against Penn, the starters in this year without a starting five are Calloway, Sloan, Garrett, Jones and Smart. The game is coached with all the intensity that the conference games will be. Knight draws on the clipboard. He screams for Smart to move, move your feet, watch your feet on the perimeter. He calls for Dean to flare. He praises Brian when he dives for the ball. Dean is called over to be told, "You were in the right position. That's all it took," and to receive a pat. Kreigh Smith enters the game and is given extra advice.

At 7.55, with Indiana leading 22–9, after a time-out Knight once again offers Rick Calloway the leadership of the team. "Get 'em together, Rick," he says as play is about to resume. Then he calls Smart over. But Smart is already shaking his head. He knows what he has done wrong.

"This is the best defense I've seen all year," Everett Dean tells me.

But Knight is not satisfied. "Come on, Ricky, handle the ball," he calls. "Step up to the middle. We've got to have good shots." Hillman is told he has just done "the worst thing I've ever seen you do." And Kreigh, as he fouls, is told, "You've got to see it coming. That's a play you have to learn to make." In a minute and a half Steve Eyl scores six points after having scored hardly at all in the post-Christmas practices. It's the "I'll show him" response that Knight hopes will result from his announcement to a player that he's just about given up on him.

He's furious when Calloway loses the ball. "Ricky, he's just wearing you out," he calls. No matter that Penn has long since been blown away. The score is 61–37 with 12.23 to go. Calloway is taken out, to be followed down the bench by the coach.

"There's just no sense to that," he says. The issue, now as always, is their doing well, their having assimilated his teaching, their commitment to effectiveness—none of which has anything to do with the particular opponent, whether it be Penn or Purdue. And so he can scream despite a thirty-point lead: "Get on the board, Lyndon, look at what you've got there!"

It is also true that the moods of the man, those clouds blowing across autumn skies, are at the wellspring of his coaching. Criticism turns to praise, the change as swift as a change in the weather and the players know it. The students know that the criticism can and will, like lightning, turn to praise with the next play. All they need do, which is what they want to do anyway, is perform at the level of their talents. "Atta boy, Joe, good pass," Knight calls to Hillman.

Ryan White dons a heavier quilted jacket as the game nears its end.

With 4.04 to go, and the score 76–47, in a huddle he tells them: "Let's have four minutes of really good basketball!" Back onto the floor go Oliphant, Jadlow, Pelkowski, Hillman and Smith. At 2.50 Kreigh gets his third personal and is mad at himself. "He'll go left every time. You've got to see what's going on," Knight says. Although Kreigh plays fifteen minutes, he scores only three points. Hillman, however, is four for five, with five for five free throws, scoring 14 points.

Walking off the court, Knight puts his arm around the shoulder of a Penn freshman named Dane Watts, who has been involved in some altercations with the officials. "Hey, you have a chance to be a pretty good player if you'll just shut up and play and quit bitching." "Thank you, Coach," says the rambunctious Watts, now gracious in defeat. Then Knight grabs Phil Pitts, the Penn senior: "You could play for me," he tells him.

In the locker room Ryan White appears to meet the players. He has his picture taken, and receives a hug from the coach. Does he have four tickets for the championship game? Ryan White stands there, his voice eerie and high-pitched, his complexion sallow. His courage refuses to allow him self-pity or to reject life. He's a person this coach would admire. Knight instructs Tim to get him some sweaters.

"Keith, wear a sport coat tomorrow," Knight calls as Smart heads for the bus.

* * *

At dinner, he chooses lobster tails. Then it's more talk about
them, how they live no less than how they play. Dorms shouldn't
be coeducational: why make it easy? Churchgoing, midwestern
values of clean living (no gambling, no smoking, no alcohol define
his standard for them). Tonight he has a light drink, but this is rare
for him. When his players complained of marijuana smoke coming into the rooms via a phone-box which linked rooms, delighted,
he decided to allow them to live off campus.

He discusses the 49'ers football team with Tim; he shows respect to his son. Leaving Tim to deal with the check, he disappears before dessert only to have a sundae delivered to his room.

He joins his team for breakfast, ready to analyze last night's
second game in which Stanford beat Santa Barbara. Julio has
stayed up all night in his room studying the Stanford team, pro-
ducing the cards, the preparation.

"What grade would you give Julio on his scouting report,
Keith?" Knight wants to know.

"A-plus."

Magnus Pelkowski concurs.

"You're easy graders," Knight scoffs.

He looks at what they're eating. "It'll take more than coffee to
keep you awake," he tells Todd Jadlow. Knight eats Rice Krispies
and steals a last bit of bacon on his way out; he doesn't drink
coffee, but milk, and teases Ron Felling for requesting coffee just
to get a little closer to the waitress.

"A little bit of heaven," says Felling. It's his favorite line.

And then it's on to Stanford and Todd Lichti, to post exchange
and Stanford's endless efforts to punch the ball inside. The bus
ferries the team to practice, but suddenly it stops, and a tall man
in a blue jacket and a funny tweed pointed hat, clutching a
sweater, gets off and walks toward a building, a solitary figure on
the cold morning landscape. A sign reveals his destination: the
Indiana University Medical Center.

The team proceeds without him to a very grand facility opposite an Olympic-sized swimming pool, the joint Indiana-Purdue
sports facility in Indianapolis. Practice begins.

When Knight finally arrives, Bernie Souers of WTTV wants to
discuss the tip-off program.

"Well, you don't mind if we do a little practicing first?"

The television, the VCR, the tapes have been brought to practice, which, this morning, is a lecture. The students sit on the floor, their notebooks open, as each Stanford player is examined. "He's right handed and likes to go to his right. . . . Butler is just like the kid from Washington State. . . .

"Most everyone will play zone against us," he tells them. "We have to take the ball one way and pass it back the other way. Don't take the ball with the pass the same way you're dribbling the basketball. Reverse pass and look to get the ball inside." Ron Felling lectures, with Knight chiming in: Taylor took four shots last night and they were all three-point shots. Lichti was nine for fifteen.

McSweeney, Wright, Butler, Taylor, Lichti—the names are repeated so often they become second nature, as do their achievements: Wright scored thirty against UCLA, twenty-four against USC. Stanford is treated as a formidable opponent. "I can't impress on you enough that these people are very, very good at what they do," Knight says.

"They work to get Lichti open like we work to get Ricky open." It's Lichti who will receive the lob pass, who will be screened for. "You got two things with Lichti in the corner. The ball comes to Lichti—which it shouldn't. We should be able to prevent that. The ball goes opposite and Lichti comes out of the corner. There he is on the drive. What's happened here is that they've been forced to switch it. . . . We want to make it tough for Lichti to go through here to the basketball. When the pass goes opposite, Ron picks and Lichti goes off of him. You can easily recognize that. The ball goes opposite and Lichti comes out of the corner. . . ."

The tape rolls. "You have to see that switch coming on or they'll just bury you there with Lichti. Lichti comes toward the ball again, and there he is. He finally gets it. . . ."

Knight anticipates the press: "I believe we can score against anybody that presses us," he tells them—as indeed the closing game of the season will reveal.

They return to the floor. He sits right under the basket, watching, the ultimate distraction. "That's good, Dean," he says. Or "Post, Steve, post." He uses his voice in all its range. "Downscreen, Ricky, downscreen and post. Good. Good. Screen, screen, that's good, Dean." Then, suddenly, he screams. "SCREEN,

DEAN." Then, very softly, "Ricky, go outside and put the defense out." Then, louder, "HOLD IT, KEITH, HOLD IT. GOOD, DEAN, BE READY TO SHOOT, DEAN, DON'T HAVE TO TAKE THAT EXTRA STEP. . . ."

The value of his being a master is that he can predict what the other side will do. It is to a large extent this expertise, proven time and time again, which allows them the confidence, the poise to stop an opponent. They believe they have an edge because they will not be surprised as to who goes right and who goes left, who will pop out from where. No one can emerge from these sessions without the feeling "I can do it!", however formidable the reputation of the opponent.

All they have to do is what he tells them. "Under pressure they look to give Lichti the basketball." He has analyzed Stanford psychologically no less than physically. He knows what they will do in a crisis and what adjustments they will make when they can't follow their usual patterns. He warns how they will get open. "I want us to be able to make it tough for Lichti to get the ball out on the perimeter and keep the ball." They watch a tape of Stanford playing Iowa and then they get up and walk through.

"We've got eighteen of these coming up," he tells them. "We've got to be well prepared. We have to take it away. This is a challenging game. It's going to be a forty-minute basketball game. All right. Let's go."

Practice over, he motions to Kreigh Smith.

"What do you think it is?" Knight asks his student. "I just get disgusted. Just like yesterday morning" (the morning Kreigh was thrown out of practice). "You took a shot after one pass, or last night your foot was right there instead of right here."

But it's not all criticism. "I think you're a very good player," Knight tells Smith. "You're also your own worst enemy. It's entirely up to you. This team needs you. I think you played very well against Notre Dame. I think I made a mistake in not playing you against Kentucky. You've got to keep your man off the boards. You've got to do all those things in order to be able to play. All right."

And Kreigh runs off—happy.

*   *   *

If you imagine that he's grown tired, you'd be wrong. He's not too tired to tease the television crew that has set up in the gym. "Bernie wanted me to start out tonight's pre-game show by talking about last night's game," he says, ostensibly on the air. "Look, I said, I'm going to talk about whatever I want to talk about. He also told me to talk about tonight's . . . , I don't know what's going to happen. How the hell do I know? The goddamn game hasn't been played yet. I have no idea what we're the hell going to do until the game starts. We do things that I don't see, that I don't know about . . . "

"Damn." "Hell." He ensures this will be an outtake. And, as he often does, he assumes both roles: host and guest: "We'll be back in just a moment after these words from our goddamn charming . . . sponsor."

"How would that be?" he asks Bernie, as if it were conceivable that they would broadcast the tape as is.

"People would really love it."

The real show includes compliments to the Stanford coach as well as to Everett Dean: "It may be the best start Stanford has had since Everett Dean was coaching there thirty-five to forty years ago." He warns the audience that zone will be played against Indiana. "I'm not sure that we have the kind of shooting that we usually have against the zone." With Steve Alford gone, and Jay Edwards ineligible, not by the NCAA regulations but by his own, Indiana lacks a three-point shooter with whom to beat the zone.

I try, I pester him three times, without success. He won't reveal whom he visited in the hospital this morning.

On the bus back to the hotel he has a question for trainer Tim Garl: Has he left the four tickets for Ryan White?

By one-thirty he's back in his suite, teasing Ricky Calloway about the fancy leather gloves he's now wearing indoors. Does he have stock in Pennzoil? "When was the last checkered flag?" And a moment later, "Do you use Pennzoil?"

Before the tapes are started, the lesson is repeated: "Two things can happen when Lichti goes to the corner. They throw the ball to him and it's a two-man game. They don't throw the ball to him and it's a reversal and a downscreen. He can go either way off of it. It could be a 'bak pik,' as Julio would say."

Knight puts his arm around Julio. "Your grammar is perfect, but we have trouble understanding you," he says. "You do awfully well with English, but we have to needle you a little bit. Here, Julio. That's part of being here." He hugs Julio. "Felling's grammar is such that your grammar overrides Felling's grammar so that the two of you are really a good team."

And now throughout the session they will hear about the "bak pik." "It's going to be a back pick . . . and there it is." Knight discovers that the remote control device is missing, and several people are blamed. "I want to tell you guys something," he says. "I needle Julio a little bit. The first time I met Julio he couldn't speak a word of English, not one word. He just worked like hell and I think you know how hard he works on your behalf. If anybody worked like he does, you'd be a goddamn all-American. Just keep that in mind."

The telephone rings and it's a Channel 13 commentator. "What the hell do you want?" Knight asks. "I want you to understand one thing. My whole team is sitting here. We're going through a scouting report. Do you know what Garrett just did? He just turned to Smart, and he said, 'Keith, that's that asshole from Channel 13 again.' " He hangs up. But he's not finished. "That's called public relations," he tells Julio. "As you get older and you're head coach at Indiana, I want you to handle public relations just like I do, OK?"

Is there anyone who can escape the needle? My camera rewinds automatically, and he pauses, about to turn on the television again. "Is our TV thing interfering with your camera?" he wants to know.

"Fake trapping, three-man stack against the zone, triangle, I want them in foul trouble in the first ten minutes of the game," he orders. Will they remember all this? (Dan Dakich confesses he remembered only his own part.) "Ricky, you be on the baseline," Knight says. "Read what that guy does like I'm you, and I'm the bottom guy on the baseline and the ball's brought off the point. Maybe he releases and that bottom man comes up. As soon as that happens, you replace the bottom man over here, coming right to get the basketball. Then if it's reversed, you can always come back the other way." All they need to do is read their maps and they will emerge victorious. Victory will be sweeter against a worthy opponent, and he has guarded against their contempt for this Western team, although they have been schooled in the belief that the Big Ten conference is the toughest.

"This becomes a hell of a test for us tonight," he tells them. "A really good test. Let's get to the point where good teams have real trouble playing against us. That's where we have to elevate ourselves. You guys better get together down there and talk things over a little bit." He likes the idea of their conferring without him, discovering leaders among themselves, maybe even conspiring against him, if only to prove him wrong about someone or something.

Now he does the show for Channel 13, although his best remarks are not those that will appear on the air. Again a reporter wants to discuss Jay Edwards and again he's told, "Keep one thing in mind when you're dealing with me. Talk about the goddamn kids that are playing and not the ones that aren't. If a kid's hurt, that's one thing. But if a kid screws things up, let's talk about kids that aren't screwing things up."

There's time for still another walk-through. Dan Dakich's pants are too long, in the coach's opinion, so he's told to put brushes on the ends of his pants and sweep the floor. "We'll play each of you a few minutes on Lichti just to keep somebody really fresh on him. I don't want you to go in there if you're not going to work to keep him from getting the basketball. That's the whole purpose in our playing him." He tells Keith he'll be relieved after playing Taylor; by now, Smart's lack of stamina has been taken into account. They take copious notes, freshman Lyndon Jones neatly, conscientiously, although no notebook is as elegant as Magnus Pelkowski's.

They must get used to the idea that "as we go down through the season we're going to have a different starting lineup almost every time we play because we just don't have enough people who have shown us we can play them in every kind of situation. And that's what we've got to have. One night we might need somebody to play defensively. Another night we might need somebody to shoot against the zone. Another night it's our man-to-man offense. So don't worry about whether you started last night or don't start tonight. If you start thinking like that, then all you're going to do is get the thing screwed up." Joe Hillman will start on Lichti, then Steve Eyl. Keith will go in and "bust your ass" for four minutes. Even Lyndon may later go in on Lichti. In fact, although Calloway, Garrett, Smart, Hillman and Sloan will start, nine of them will play, Todd Jadlow for fourteen minutes.

By now there can't be anyone who hasn't conjured up the image of Lichti moving to his right, or who hasn't seen the ball being lobbed into the post. When the game begins, it will be almost a shock to see the real Lichti, flesh and blood, a handsome 6'4" 200 lb. guard. The instructions, even so close to game time, are minute, exact and spoken with the full confidence that they can and will be carried out: "Ricky, read what's happening. If you're over here, Rick, and you're being covered, let's say by McSweeney, and you see that when the ball's reversed, Wright has to go up and play the ball, then get over there as soon as you see both guards have rotated in your direction. Then go out. You're playing opposite the guards on the baseline." Above all they are warned about Stanford's post play. The post man might be standing there lethargically and then "all of a sudden the guy steps in, he's got the ball." He would hate it if they were fooled, a post player pretending to be asleep and then winding up with the ball.

They are warned. If they don't play as well as they can, they'll get beat. Always there are goals. It is December 29, their last game of the year. "Let's get this year ended with this tournament," he says. On the bus, he tells them, "Let's go out ready to play and let's come back with the championship."

Former players dot the crowd: Courtney Witte, Todd Meier, Steve Green and Steve Ahlfeld and Steve Downey, the old reliables, Phil Isenbarger, Ted Kitchel, Tom Abernethy sitting between his twin eight-year-old sons. Abernethy confides: "Anyone who played, who went through those four years here, any one of them would do anything he possibly could for him. If he needed anything on the spur of the moment, all of us would just jump at the chance to repay him." Not, of course, that Knight would ever ask.

Professor William Wiggins offers a holiday message to the crowd, thanking the fans on behalf of the parents of Steve Eyl, Dean Garrett and Keith Smart, this year's seniors, "for helping their sons mature into fine young men." It's Knight's overriding theme: the development of his students into effective human beings who have transcended difficulty through hard work, who have come through.

*   *   *

Stanford, of course, plays zone against them. It's clear Indiana would do better with Jay Edwards. But teaching the young man a lesson about his studies came before winning basketball games. At 9.25 Lyndon is brought in against the mighty Lichti, while Knight chastises the team for dropping their lead from sixteen to ten. Immediately Calloway and Garrett score, a process repeated over and over. The harsher his criticism on the sidelines, in the huddle, the more likely you will see an immediate result: a rebound, a bucket, a steal. If they forget what they've been taught, he reminds them: "We told you fake left and drive left."

At the half the score is 41–31. Knight has a pile of IU T-shirts delivered to the White group. Ryan immediately puts one on, while his mother, a sweet woman whose courage seems to match that of her son, holds the rest on her lap.

Stanford closes to 59–53. Knight screams at them. Smart replaces Smith. Ricky is called over for instructions. Indiana keeps its lead, but only marginally. Eyl draws a fourth personal foul, then loses the ball, then is the victim of a steal.

"You threw the ball away twice," he screams at Steve Eyl. "You just can't throw the ball away like that. You can't play like that." And Knight shakes him by the shoulders. There's 1.16 to go and the score is 79–68, but that's never the point. And, like Jimmy Wisman, if Eyl will be mad at anybody, it will be at himself.

"Atta boy, Kreigh," Knight encourages as Smith makes a free throw. But when he misses another, the coach says, "For Christ's sake, how can you miss free throws?" And with less than forty seconds to go, he's still furious at their forgetting the preparation. "The ball goes in and we stand there waiting when we know what he's going to do. He's going to go to his right hand."

With .28 left Knight wants an intentional foul. "Read the rule when you get home!" he yells at the official. "He wasn't even trying to get the ball!"

The final score is 83–73. With 27 points Rick Calloway is names the Most Valuable Player of the tournament. And the all-tournament team is: Pitts ("You could play for me"), Lichti (who has finished with only 15 points!), Garrett, Smart and Calloway.

"Todd [Lichti] had to work real hard for what he did get," Stanford coach Mike Montgomery tells the press. "They denied,

they took him out, we just have to find ways to win without him."
Knight has kind words to say about Stanford, toward which he's
"a little prejudiced because I have a boy that went there [Tim]."
And he praises Garrett for "the best defensive job I've ever seen
him do. I think he was absolutely outstanding."

Kreigh Smith in his eight minutes scores three points, no rebounds, no assists. Taylor, for Stanford, hits four of five three-
pointers, as predicted. And, in a statistic that no one mentions,
Stanford commits nineteen turnovers to Indiana's nine.

It would appear that the players have indeed passed their test,
the one, Knight says in the locker room after the victory over
Stanford, on which "there is no multiple choice." Even without
Jay Edwards, Indiana seems ready for the Big Ten conference
season, which will begin on January 6 at Iowa City.

CHAPTER NINE

LEARNING AS YOU'RE PLAYING

"I'll get five guys whoever they are, like I've always done, to pass, to listen to me, to work hard."

THOSE LOSSES TO KENTUCKY and Louisville, however, turn out to be harbingers of Indiana's season: a 1–4 opening to Big Ten play. They lose not only to Iowa, but also to Northwestern, that game Knight said they could not afford to lose, in a bitter 66–64 defeat. After missing six games, Jay Edwards returns on January 14 in a squeaker of a win against Wisconsin, which precedes a 75–74 loss to Michigan State, one of the sisters of the poor. A January 24 loss to Michigan, 72–60, comes as no surprise.

This Michigan game also generates a torrent of newsprint. After Steve Eyl throws away two passes with seven minutes remaining in the first half, Knight seems to push him down the length of the bench. A caller to Indianapolis radio station WIBC claims to have heard on ESPN that Knight is about to resign.

Jim Crews, now coaching at Evansville, is said to be ready to take his place. But Eyl apologizes to the coach for anything his parents might have said to reporters that had been misconstrued. On the radio Knight congratulates Don Fischer on resigning from *his* job to cover the bullfighting circuit in Montevideo: "The key word in this whole thing, Don, is 'bull.' "

As the Big Ten season roars into full swing, something else is happening on this team. It's Ricky Calloway's play, Calloway who had only two points well into the first half against Michigan. His failure to work with weights the previous summer, his resting on the laurels of the national championship, have resulted in his not being strong enough to contest for the basketball; at 6'6", he should weigh more than 186 pounds. The ball skitters out of his hands; he's playing forward and he can't hold onto a rebound.

In the first half against Michigan, Indiana commits nine turnovers. Meanwhile, Keith Smart is revealing the weaknesses of junior college players entering Knight's system. On defense, Smart is costing the team games. Early in the second half against Michigan, he picks up his fourth personal foul.

As Knight told them in Indianapolis, there is no starting five: Pelkowski had been started, unsuccessfully, against James Madison. Against Iowa, Calloway, Eyl, Garrett, Smart and Hillman start. Against Northwestern, Sloan replaces Eyl; Jones starts rather than Hillman. Against Michigan State, Calloway, Eyl, Garrett, Jones and Smart start the game.

The turning point of the Big Ten season comes on January 27, with the game against Ohio State. The team is now 9–6 for the season, 1–4 in Big Ten play. On the Wednesday of game day against Ohio State, during practice Ricky Calloway stands around chatting with Lyndon Jones, clearly not taking the drills seriously. For setting a bad example, he is thrown out of practice.

Later that day, the team is gathered in the ballroom of their hotel for the walk-through. Knight turns to Garrett.

"Dean," he says, "you're playing a lot better in practice the last two days. Why do you think that is?"

"These guys," says Garrett, pointing to Edwards and Jones, "are easier to play with than Ricky and Keith. *These* guys are looking to pass. *Those* guys are looking to score." Garrett is reminded of last year when "If things were going bad, I would say, 'Hey, Steve [Alford], you've got to help us out here.' That's how I think Jay and Lyndon might look at me right now. They're depending on me. That gives me more confidence. Helping others makes you a better player."

Smart, Garrett's best friend on the team, listens, remembering himself being asked one day, "How do you think Ricky played today?"

"Poorly," Smart admitted.

"Well, you tell him," Knight had said.

Knight, of course, is not shy about informing Calloway of his displeasure: After three Big Ten losses, he has sent Ricky to sit alone in the locker room and think, only after fifteen minutes to go back in and get him.

Listening to Garrett now, Knight is pleased at the honesty, if disheartened at the demise of "certain expectations" he himself had. He has examined the stat sheets comparing this year with last. After four big ten games last year, Garrett had twenty-eight points; this year he has sixty. But both Calloway and Smart are doing more poorly than they were last year. The "I'm gonna be a star," mentality has engulfed them. Shooting at sixty percent last year, they're down to forty. Against Michigan State and Michigan, Smart has scored a total of eight points. And meanwhile their ratio of assists to turnovers is appalling; Calloway is 35–35, while Knight expects a modest 3:1 ratio.

Is there really a choice? Smart and Calloway are both benched.

Smart is gracious. "Even when he got on me and made Dean and me run fifty or sixty sprints down the floor," Smart says, "I never did get upset. He didn't put me there [on the bench]; I put myself there." In Garden City, his junior college coach Jim Carey is less reasonable. He accuses Knight of not playing Smart because he doesn't like *him*. Knight telephones Carey's assistant with some sharp words: "Did you ever stop to think Smart wasn't playing because he didn't play well?"

Unlike Smart, an impressive person with a sense of perspective, Calloway sulks. He seems not to remember his own words spoken on October 15 at the special supper at which the team entertained Shawn Kemp: "You gotta listen to what he's saying, but don't take it and just fold up into a little shell. My family background was pretty good, so I already had that type of attitude going before I got here. Anything he says is just like a repetition of what my parents have told me over the years. He's telling us, never give up, always play hard. When you want something bad enough, go for it." And on that evening Calloway had remembered when Knight yelled at him "for something he says you did wrong, but you did it right, just to see how you're going to react. Are you going into a shell and not want to play or are you going to come back and not worry about what he said and just keep on playing?" He had seemed to understand as the season opened. But his failure to play well after being Most Valuable Player of both pre-conference tournaments seems to have unsettled him.

With Calloway's deterioration as a basketball player, the absence of team leadership is even more glaring. Knight had taken Joe Hillman aside and asked him to be their leader. But Hillman had been uncertain. And now there is no one.

Although he does not become a team leader, Garrett improves; he scores 22 points as Indiana defeats Ohio State, 75–71. The victory is not overwhelming, but it is significant, made more so in retrospect when four days later Indiana defeats Purdue. With his coach's confidence, Garrett improves. Now Knight reassures Jay Edwards that he does indeed want him on the team: ("Hey, there are a helluva lot of people who thought you couldn't play for me when you came, that you wouldn't work hard enough, that I wouldn't work with you," Knight tells Edwards. "Let's just you and I prove all of them were wrong.") Edwards at once becomes a player, on his way to becoming Big Ten freshman of the year.

Against Purdue, Edwards scores sixteen points in the first half, twenty-two in all. Jones and Edwards play forty minutes, side by side, effortlessly aware of each other, as they played to those three state championships for Marion.

Calloway remains benched; Smart plays less than two minutes. The winning basket against Purdue is scored by Garrett, who has thirty-one points in this game, the high point of his season. The player who sat there on Christmas night, his head down, as his coach told him he thought less well than anyone on the team, but that he was still the one the coach wanted ("I don't want him, I want you"), is coming into his own.

Ryan White again watches from the stands, as do the usual company of former players: Wayne Radford, Todd Meier, Stevie Ahlfeld, all of whom gather to be interviewed on television by Steve Green about old contests with Purdue.

"I screwed up," Jay Edwards tells Quinn Buckner, in town to do color commentary on the Purdue game.

*   *   *

Indiana goes on to struggle through its Big Ten season, winning against Minnesota, Illinois and Northwestern, then losing again to Michigan.

Pete Newell, a Knight mentor, is in Bloomington on February 4 for the game against Minnesota. He praises his student for creating a team where there wasn't one before. Garrett continues to excel.

But Smart does not bounce back; he scores only eleven points against Northwestern, his very average on the Steve Alford team when he was not expected to assume the burden of the scoring.

Knight continues to coach fundamentals to a team that cannot, as he puts it, "see." Against Northwestern on February 11 they commit twenty turnovers! With such play, Indiana cannot win and Jay Edwards' 29 points against Michigan on February 13 is meaningless in a 92–72 loss.

"How's the health of the team?" Don Fischer wants to know as Indiana is about to play Michigan State. It's mid-February and the flu has overtaken Garrett, Jones and Eyl.

"I'm more concerned about *your* health, Don," says Knight, never one to make excuses. But it has not been an easy winter. Hazel Knight has died on New Year's Eve, and the only solace her son has is that Christmas visit he decided to make. A rich man, he had allowed her the independence of spending her own money, figuring he'd take over when hers ran out. In her eighties, Hazel Knight still enjoyed life and was about to go out to dinner with friends when she was found dead. The friends from Orrville at once help to make the funeral arrangements; Bob Knight attends alone, gracious to those who have come to pay their respects. These include "Adolph," the Kentuckyan he has adopted, Chuck Marlowe, with whom he does his television show, his secretary, B.J.

The loss to Michigan has eliminated Indiana from the Big Ten championship. Knight readjusts his goals. Now Indiana must "get in position to play in a post-season tournament." Calloway is given his first start in six games and goes eight for fourteen, leaving the game to a standing ovation. (Smart, however, comes in only off the bench.) Jay scores 24; in his last five games he is averaging 22.4 points, 20 for 32 from three-point range. He is the team's best shooter.

Both Calloway and Smart start against Purdue now on February 21, in a poorly officiated game. With Garrett in foul trouble early, Indiana falters. Calloway plays poorly again. Knight receives a technical, at first for stepping out of the coach's box, and then, when it's clear that he hasn't, for "unsportsmanlike conduct." Meanwhile, Gene Keady rants and rages at his end without penalty.

Purdue wins 95–85, but it's a closer game than that, close all the way. On the bench for much of the game, Garrett has only 10 points. Edwards has 20, but Calloway—only 8. It's a definite setback, one unmitigated by an 84–74 victory over Wisconsin on February 24.

II

"Did you see Smart put the ball behind his back down there? That's one of the most athletic plays I've ever seen on this floor."

After the victory over Ohio State, Knight announced a thirteen-game season in which Indiana could still do well. The losses against Kentucky and Louisville, the 1–4 start in Big Ten play, could recede as if they never happened; he had set them a new, a realizable goal. And, as always, he played whomever contributes to realizing that goal, and benched whomever did not.

If you expect anger and temper and impatience because this team has been disappointing, you won't find it. They prepare optimistically for their February 29 contest with Illinois, boasting a fine seven–two record in their new thirteen-game season; by this reckoning Indiana is only one game out of first place in the Big Ten. Only Purdue has a better record, he tells them, and Indiana beat Purdue, and then almost beat them again. "It's important that people think we're the second best team in the Big Ten," Knight tells his team.

On the practice floor he stresses fundamentals, adding an emphasis on their communicating with each other. Hillman is playing better, trying to lead. As his play has improved, he has become more relaxed with his teammates.

Knight is more irritated by Indiana's victory over Wisconsin than he is over the loss to Purdue. Smart, dazzling as he was, committed five turnovers. By not contesting a pass, he allowed Wisconsin a three-pointer, and then another three when he interrupted the shooter who had been stupidly moving in exactly the direction most likely to thwart him: toward the corner.

There is more praise than criticism in practice as the season winds down. Keith is told he's "as good as anyone in coming in hard and going up for the shot." He is chastised for a bad pass: "Is there a hole in the roof that would allow God to take that pass? Because I've never seen Hillman make it." This remark is much enjoyed by the contingent of professors. Knight tells Hillman, "Right where you caught it, there's the shot." The implication is that if Hillman would only see his opportunities, he could score.

The ball bounces out of bounds. "All right, all right, all right," Knight says. Joe is patted for taking the ball in well. "Keep it off the dribble," he tells them. "Every time we get into that goddamned dribbling, we get in trouble."

"You weren't even looking at the ball, Steve," he says.

He raises his hands in the air, exasperated. Then, walking away from them, to no one in particular, he says, "Patience, patience, patience." Seconds later, his hands in his pockets, the blue pants, the red warm-up jacket, everything the same, he turns and walks back to them.

Tates Locke tells me the new patience is a result of the happiness in his personal life. When I test out this theory on him, the coach raises an ironic eyebrow: "He hasn't seen me practice for twenty years!"

Preparation now begins in earnest for the February 29 game against Illinois, leap year evening. On Saturday at one in the afternoon they're in the locker room being instructed on how to handle the ball against the press, against Illinois' skill at making conversion baskets. As always, he knows exactly what will happen to them. "Don't get trapped down low where Kujawa can hang onto you and keep you moving up the lane," he tells Garrett. Only a few elements are stressed each day: today it's slipping the screen and preventing conversion baskets. "You're not a dribbler, Dean," he must say still this late in the season. "Stay with what you can do." Joe is told: "Think, think, think."

The team does not have a good practice. "You guys make a comfortable adjustment," he tells them once more. "Why not say, don't let him get the ball." Back-cut passes are going to be made against them. "Yet every time you prevent them from making the pass they want, that's just another nail in the coffin."

"You're relaxed down there," he tells Garrett. "They're eating you alive!" Joe Hillman is not in a contesting stance.

"Joe, where do we want you?"

"On the high side."

"You were all the way down here."

Yet the earnestness of Hillman, the effort, the dedication to excellence make him a paradigm of the Knight player. Hillman doesn't sulk, retreat, curve in on himself or allow his classwork to suffer. Garrett and Smart seated on one side of him in the locker room, Eyl and Calloway on the other, Hillman—the slow, short white kid—would be an asset at the heart of any team, and one to be measured without reference to games won or lost, or to stat sheets. If earlier in the season he had told Knight he wasn't sure he could be a team leader because "some of the guys wouldn't listen and hadn't listened to me at that point," nonetheless he has gone about "doing what I had to to be a leader."

Hillman admits: "It's awful hard to play here, I'll say that. It's very demanding." But then, he adds: *That's what you're here for.*" Knight indeed demands the analytic ability to master the system while simultaneously making the utmost physical demands on yourself. Not every player aspires to so high a standard of excellence. What some fail to perceive is that all college basketball players have a lot of natural ability; maybe most teams are equal. Something more must separate them. Knight appreciates natural athleticism, but he knows that it is not enough.

Suddenly he strides over to the scorer's table and says, with excitement in his voice, "Did you see Smart put the ball behind his back down there? That's one of the most athletic plays I've ever seen on this floor!"

Patrick enters Assembly Hall with two of his friends and sits down on the removable stairway. Tonight his school, Bloomington North, will lose its regular season finale to New Albany. Pat will go five for ten with nine rebounds, however. Who are you recruiting, he keeps asking his father? Any guards?

And then Knight's patience begins to wear thin. Magnus should have made a shot he failed to make: "All you had to do was catch the ball and lay it against the glass." "Strength, strength," he tells Ricky. "You're a twenty-one-year-old guy with the strength of somebody fourteen." That summer without his building himself up has cost the team dearly.

Dean takes a shot he has no chance of making: "I'm not bringing you out there [up high] to be a shooter." Jadlow loses the ball— and Indiana suddenly seems to be a team of people all with suspect hands, hands that can't hold onto the ball and so can't rebound. "Hold it," Knight yells, loud now. "Eyl, if I hadn't watched you for four years . . . you haven't had a shot from fifteen feet all year. Then when you have a shot, you reach for the ball with one hand!"

"Get out of here!" he tells them. "Go take a shower!" He appeals to their sense of fairness, how much more he is putting into their common effort than they are. He went to a high school game to recruit last night. This morning he has been here since ten looking at tape.

"Get out of here!" he repeats, and he means it. "You started the Big Ten season one and four and if you want to finish one and four, go ahead. This isn't playing, this mishmash."

He had warned them in October how difficult it would be to come back after the championship, but it appears they haven't believed him. It's as if that national championship has burrowed into their souls, the worm in the apple. They have been paralyzed by the disparity between what they think of themselves and how they're actually playing.

"Turn out the lights!" Knight orders the managers.

When they return at six, they hear a lecture by Tates Locke. He draws an analogy between their sloppy play and a pretty girl who doesn't take care of herself, so that after a while she ceases to be pretty.

"Ricky, how much time did you spend last summer squeezing rubber balls?" Knight wants to know at the next practice. "That's why you can't catch the ball." A segment of the practice is devoted to four people above the foul line getting the ball in to Dean, who is not to leave his position when the post man comes around him. "Ricky, don't make a move unless you come up with the ball," he adds.

And then suddenly Knight stands and claps his hands, applauds: "That's a great play, Keith!" he calls.

But when they practice working against the trap, Keith loses the ball. "Set it again," he calls. This time Jadlow infuriates him, Jadlow backing away when he caught the ball, Jadlow who's been here for three years and isn't set to shoot.

Anticipating a comment he will make on television after the season is over, Knight reveals his thinking to Jadlow: "That's why I say to myself I have to find a better player. That's why I have to get someone other than you. You could have told me otherwise. You can't make excuses night after night for three years and expect to play. I don't need anyone bigger than you or quicker than you or better than you. I need someone who'll do what I say." The words are meant to urge Jadlow on, yet Knight, in fact, has done exactly what he says: he has recruited Michael Boykin out of Atlanta, a big strong player to work inside, a student who played only eight games in the last two years because he had changed schools. But Knight clearly hopes Boykin will play an important role in the building of his new front line.

At 4:15, they're back: P A T I E N C E it says in Magnus Pelkowski's notebook. Inside play will be Illinois' strength. "None of them want to get it back out," Knight warns, as they scrutinize the tape. "Dean, I swear to you," Knight tells his center, "if you get up on his left shoulder, he's not going to make a bucket."

Julio has a baby son! "Raise him right and give him soul food," Keith advises. Then he turns to Dan Dakich: now it's his turn to get married. Dakich laughs. Dakich demurs. At this moment in the season only Joby and Julio are married.

At six-thirty on this Sunday night, after dinner, there is still more tape, "directed and produced by Julio." "Duke got beat today," Knight tells his team, "because they missed the block-out, a simple block-out." On the board he writes their record and Illinois'. "There's a hell of a difference between nine-six and eight-seven," he tells them. Out here in the heart of the country, only your record in Big Ten play counts. Illinois has very good athletic ability, but Indiana can neutralize that with its basketball ability.

"This has to be us playing at our best tomorrow, boys," he tells them. "Get a good night's rest." There's the sound of car keys jingling as they get up.

About to go out to dinner with Lou Henson, Knight is glued to the last scene of *The Vikings*. The heroic exploits of men fascinate him. He has brought with him an interview with Ted Williams, of note because it stresses how the man who had more natural talent than anyone else still stressed hard work and effort. "Do you think that you played up to your potential?" the interviewer asks Williams. "HELL, no," comes back the reply. As for people in other sports whom he admires—"Bobby Knight. I love his intensity. I love his discipline. I love his devotion."

On game day Knight sits on the sideline with two of his oldest friends, Dick Otte, of the Columbus *Dispatch*, who covered Knight as a college player, and Fred Taylor, his own college coach. Otte recalls how Knight, either a sophomore or junior, upset at the amount of playing time he was receiving from Taylor, asked Otte for money for the plane ride home to Orrville from Champaign, Illinois.

"Do you know how long it would take to go from Champaign, Illinois, to Orrville, Ohio, by plane?" Otte countered. The crisis blew over. Like so many players who don't believe they're receiving enough playing time, Knight was ready to bolt. Instead he was bolstered by his natural sense of the absurd, and his awareness that he wasn't as good a player as John Havlicek and the other Ohio State starters. Otte still wants to know if it was Knight who threw Otte's typewriter into the toilet nearly thirty years ago.

"I would have claimed credit by now if it had been me," Knight counters persuasively.

The friendship has continued over the years. When Otte's son developed a passion for West Point, he was entertained there by Knight. Today, his proud father announces, he's a major in the army.

Knight points to Taylor. "He's been all around the world and do you know where he says he had the best strawberry shortcake?" He's prescient, or he knows people, for Taylor has already told me about Knight's grandmother Sarah Henthorne's strawberry shortcake. Yet how could Knight know that?

Knight dispatches the two gentlemen off to a Bloomington steakhouse called Zagreb. "Order the tenderloin!" he demands and proceeds to offer extensive directions, left at the second traffic light, right at the old Southern Indiana courthouse, and it's a block down on the left. Otte and Taylor suppress smiles; they have been here before. Knight walks them upstairs to the door, repeating the instructions. And then, mocking himself with a straight face, he adds, "Unless it's one street further!"

Smiling fondly at the two older men as they leave, Knight says, "I wish we didn't have to win tonight."

In the coaches' locker room before the game, Fred Taylor tests out Knight's new set of golf clubs as if Knight didn't have a care in the world. The talk is of fishing: walleyed pike. "I bet they were three or four pounders." Trying to take his fish off the line, Otte's wife let them fall back in the water. The men laugh. It's not so much that women are not respected; women no less than men would do better not to venture where their competence does not warrant.

When Taylor retired as basketball coach at Ohio State, the ceremonies at his last game at Indiana were far more elaborate, grander than those in Columbus. Knight presented him with the traditional rocking chair. Now Knight recalls his days as a player. One day Taylor put up a sign, "Players Only," at practice to keep out a pesky booster, only for the booster to march right in. A brash Bobby Knight couldn't resist a needle: "Coach, either he can't read or you can't spell." (Was he always like this? I wonder. Well, so it seems.) And Taylor was so mad he didn't even say anything to Knight.

"What kind of steak did you have?" he wants to know. Fred had the tenderloin, Otte the strip. "Was it good?" The presence of these old friends soothes him. Their reunion is interrupted, however, by the entrance of Dick Vitale. "Dick, don't listen to anybody out here. Just talk," Knight advises.

"I want to come one time when you don't bust my chops."

"Then you'll know I don't like you anymore."

Tip-off isn't until 9:38, a fact which infuriates Knight. "If they truly cared about the kids they would play all their games on Friday night and Sunday afternoon."

And then he reveals he knows exactly what will happen in this game with Illinois.

"We can't play when every rebound is a struggle," Knight says quietly, seated in his favorite chair.

* * *

Just before tip-off, Quinn Buckner slides into a seat beside his old teammate Steve Ahlfeld.

Attending the game tonight too is Connie Chung, here to interview Knight for a documentary on stress. *Sixty Minutes* had called earlier in the season on behalf of Diane Sawyer, several times, but Knight did not return their calls. He suspected what their approach would be: the pro and the con. In fact, they had called Norm Sloan, the Florida coach, having read that he had attacked Knight. Sloan told them he didn't think they'd find a good coach in the country willing to say anything negative about Bob. They had called Isiah Thomas too, telling him they understood he didn't have a very good relationship with Coach Knight.

"You want some guys to speak positively and some to speak negatively about Coach Knight and you want me to speak negatively, is that right? Well, I think you have me on the wrong side," Isiah said, and he let Knight know he said so.

That Chung had called herself ("although she doesn't know me from a jar of Vick's"), leaving both her home and office number, that she had answered the phone herself when he returned her call, ensured her the interview. "All these other people get some leg guy who calls. I don't do that. If I want you to do something, I call you," Knight declares.

The Illinois team is strong and big and athletic. They crash the boards; they come up with two or three offensive rebounds every time down. And they move out to a 8–0 lead.

They're a step ahead of Indiana on everything so that it's three and a half minutes into the game before Garrett scores the first Indiana points. When Eyl replaces Garrett, he immediately grabs a rebound, only to lose the ball. And meanwhile if Indiana scores at all, it's only as a result of Jay Edwards' three-pointers.

The game goes exactly as Knight predicted. Nick Anderson scores on conversion twice in a row, while Battle outmuscles Indiana on the boards. Fast and strong, Illinois excels in post play, taking Garrett completely out of the game. Jones replaces Smart, Jadlow replaces Eyl. All Knight can do, short of going out and playing himself, is shuffle his lineup. Nothing works.

Calloway has started this game, and early on Knight takes Keith and Jay aside to say, "Ricky gives us more movement in ten

feet than you two have the whole goddamn game, now move!"
(But Calloway will have only an average game, scoring thirteen
points in thirty-eight minutes of play.)

"That's ridiculous," Knight tells referee Tim Higgins at one
point. "He warns a guy not to push and then the call's the other
way."

"You've made your point," Higgins says.

The coaching is calm, and measured, intense only where appropriate. "He didn't get up a couple of times where I would have
gotten up," Buckner tells me.

Meanwhile, Indiana cannot hold onto the ball. Calloway loses
it and Garrett is benched. In a run-down for a loose ball against
two of Illinois' best athletes, hustling Joe Hillman, of course,
doesn't have a chance. Illinois out-rebounds Indiana 48–26, and
with that goes on to win 75–65.

Having won his five hundredth game in this unlikely venue, at
the post-game press conference. Lou Henson is gracious: "I never
dreamed we could get boards the way we did." Knight too speaks
about the rebounding. "Questions?" he asks abruptly after a minute or two. He pauses. "OK," he says and walks out. There hasn't
been a single question.

In the morning Connie Chung awaits him all set up on the court
of Assembly Hall. "I wish I'd lost forty pounds," Knight says as
he strides out to his seat. He is dressed in a nondescript brown
sweater, the ubiquitous grey corduroy pants and moccasins, a
man who would not stand out in a crowd.

But if personal vanity is alien to him, sharpness of mind is not,
not even on this morning when his team is on its way to failing
in its new goal of a four-game season. At once Knight attacks
Chung's premise, quietly, softly and brilliantly.

The subject of the documentary is stress. But "stress" is not
what he feels when he coaches. Stress belongs to people in life
and death situations, such as a doctor performing a heart trans-
plant. What *he* feels is pressure, some anxiety and frustration,
which can be alleviated by preparation. It is hardly the flamboyant answer television would elicit to sell soapsuds or cars. "What
are the stakes here?" he persists, returning to his challenge of
Chung's definition of stress. "The NCAA tournament?"

"But what happens when you're yelling at the referee?"

Knight explains that, with seventeen thousand people yelling, you can't say softly, "John, John." It has to be "John goddamnit!" But if he allows himself to officiate, "the rest of the game slides away from me."

But does he feel better? she persists.

"I don't feel any better. I feel he now knows something he should be doing."

Quietly and methodically, he resists every attempt to sensationalize. Does he *ever* feel better? "I only feel better when the whole thing is over and I look back at how our preparation worked in the game." He mentions David Halberstam's book *The Best and the Brightest,* which describes how the Kennedy administration devoted three years to planning for its re-election. "If I coached like that, it would be chaotic."

But does he have headaches, migraines?

"I make the decisions. If they're wrong, I have to figure out how to make them right the next time."

The entire interview is a microcosm of the disparity between the man and how the world perceives him: angry, irrational, out of control, while he talks about how control, analysis and research have led to his success. These ideas, however, do not make for an exciting program. Talk about "preparation" is not what audiences expect of "Bobby Knight."

Chung persists.

"What's happening when you throw a chair, when you take the team off the floor . . ."

"I didn't," he says quietly. And he is willing even to talk about the chair. "I'm not saying that was a great and thoughtful action. I think it was frustration. Stress would be if I had thrown the chair at someone. I slid the chair away from everyone. It was something I had control over."

He admits to not holding things back. "In a position of leadership, you can't worry about hurting people's feelings."

"So, instead of eating nails for breakfast, you let it all hang out?"

"People who know me feel I have a lot more patience than people think."

"But you intimidate people." And she wants to know if *he* is ever intimidated: "The one thing that intimidates me is intelligence and knowledge. . . ." This important truth about himself, however, is not pursued.

Chung presses forward: "What about your intimidating look?" And so she finally forces him away from any serious exploration of the issue:

"I can't help the way I look! I don't look like Robert Redford!"

In the course of the interview Knight has also used a cliché to describe how, perhaps, he would do better to behave when he becomes the victim of bad officiating: rape's inevitable, so why not relax and enjoy it?

At lunch, Sloppy Joes at the Jiffy Treat, Connie Chung forgotten, he has a test for Quinn Buckner: "Explain Keith Smart to me as a basketball player."

"I don't think I'll play Smart anymore," he decides. (Smart had eight points against Illinois, starting and playing thirty-three minutes.) "And I don't know about Garrett. You know who's the player who understands what we do best? Edwards!"

III

"Where's the newspaper? I've got to have something to read until these guys figure out an answer."

Tuesday, March 1.

Day by day with only three games remaining, he tries to salvage the season.

At Tuesday afternoon practice Knight is in his street clothes. With three games to go in their new four-game season, Indiana is 0–1.

On the board he writes: Garrett, Eyl, Hillman, Smart, and beneath that, 114 minutes, 57 percent, 21 points, 13 rebounds. The 57 percent represents the amount of playing time out of the possible 200 minutes available to all the players that these four used up.

"I just want you to look at that," he tells them. "That's your total for 114 minutes of play, the four of you. I want to know why." He pulls up a chair. He is prepared to wait until they can come up with an answer.

"There were a lot of kids in here that didn't get beat last night," he says quietly, "but you four just got pummeled."

That they have failed their exam is obvious. But this is not a teacher who will simply pass out the atrocious exam papers, having recorded the abysmal grades, and be done with it. They must account to him and to themselves for their failure.

The four culprits look straight ahead. No one says anything.

"You got absolutely buried in the biggest game that we played all year or that we will play. I've never seen people less ready to play. I've never seen people do less in a game. I've really never seen people get beat worse." ("I thought we were ready to play," Joe Hillman told Quinn Buckner after the game.)

Three of the four, of course, are seniors. Joe Hillman is an academic senior with a year of basketball eligibility remaining. A finance major, he plans to study for a master's degree, an MBA, while he plays next season.

"I looked at the tape last night and I can't pick out one rational thing that you did in the game, Keith. It was as if we picked you up from a schoolyard somewhere, inserted you in the lineup and just told you to play."

Knight speaks softly, as if he were divulging the obvious. But he is not yet ready to let them off the hook. Three games remain. He is not yet ready to give up on them. He owes that to them, however human it might be to indulge in thoughts of the new recruits coming next season, or how dramatically redshirted Mark Robinson has improved.

"I want to know why. I'm prepared to sit here all afternoon. It doesn't make any difference to me. It was a game that means the whole season to us, and you four people let somebody come in here in a big game we're playing at home and just pound us. You hid the whole game, Dean. You never once flashed to get the ball, never moved once to get up into the lane."

He folds his arms. "Where's the newspaper? I've got to have something to read until these guys figure out an answer."

The only sound in the room is the ventilating system and the pages of the newspaper now slowly turning. No one stirs. On the wall the photographs of the Ohio State players, their next opponent, stare down at them.

He looks up. "Well, what are we going to do?"

Still no one speaks. As they can't realize what they did, so they lacked the superior basketball intelligence necessary to combat the unrelenting brawn of Illinois. The team is sent out onto the floor, minus the silent four, who must remain in the locker room to think. Practice begins. Teaching begins.

"Lyndon, what you've got to do is come in hard. Good plays don't just happen. You see them. You create them. You make them happen." Knight is quiet, patient. He tells Kreigh to stop and make himself available. Mark has faked himself into a bad shot. He criticizes Magnus for not practicing what he *doesn't* yet know how to do well.

Knight moves over to the free throw line and, as he talks to them, makes one free throw after another, a dazzling performance. "I can stand here all night making free throws but what good would it do me?" The lesson today is in what isn't enough. "Let's have a purpose to everything we do."

There are hints of preparation for the coming season. Mark Robinson is told to "dunk it as often as you can and let him foul you." Lyndon is told: "You've heard that possession is nine-tenths of the law. In basketball it's position. I don't have wings, but I have feet." Lyndon and Mark, part of the future: "You're dribbling while Mark is open," he tells Jones. "We missed one cutter after another last night."

But the defeat rankles. Keith Smart, who dribbled right into two defenders in the middle last night, made "the most ridiculous play I've ever seen in college basketball"; Smart came down the floor and picked up someone to defend who had already been picked up by someone else! "We need Calloway to score some points," he thinks. "I just don't know if he can. He's three years into playing; he should weight 205 and be a lot stronger, but he isn't."

Wednesday, March 2.

Knight walks purposefully into their locker room. "I'm going to get some players. It's never going to happen again. Calloway, you lose the ball seven times when it's in your hands. Seven times it's jarred out of your hands. There isn't one of you who could jar the ball out of my hands and I'm forty-seven years old. "He looks at Calloway, who alone had five turnovers against Illinois." I don't know if anybody has come in and looked at the tape. I'm going to get me some players that are going to come in here and work at playing, that are going to lift weights to get better, that don't have to be pushed and shoved and kicked in the ass every time we turn around. If you people want to play like you just want to finish out the season, that's how we'll coach. Four corners!"

Out on the floor, he's exasperated. "I've coached five years before you were born," he tells Magnus and Brian, "and here's a guy that doesn't pay any attention to what you want [four passes]. What would you do?"

"Isn't coaching a lot of fun?" he asks me as he passes the scorer's table.

And then it's back to fundamentals. "Good cut, Ricky," he calls. "Now Ricky was wide open, but Brian didn't make the pass because he had the ball over his head instead of going around him for a bounce pass."

"How many buckets does Garrett have?" he calls to the managers keeping score. He's one for four with two rebounds. "I have managers who could have scored more," Knight snarls.

If we had won that game against Illinois, he agonizes, we would have had a pretty good season. He still believes Hillman would have made the ideal team leader, although he will acknowledge that players will respond only to superior ability among each other. Smart? He couldn't lead because "he couldn't control himself."

Today Knight has found a job for Winston Morgan, a former player back from two years of basketball in Argentina, with a chemical company in Indianapolis owned by a friend, Ames Shuel. He has not forgotten the night he had told Morgan he had no room for him on the team only for Morgan to transcend his own pain sufficiently to congratulate Jimmy Crews on landing the head coaching job at Evansville. Knight muses over what they learn here. Not one former student whom he has gotten a job has ever been fired. After being with him, they are not afraid of difficulty, of hard work, of competing.

"I don't think I can afford to bench Garrett," Knight murmurs. "I am going to bench Smart. Do you know who the best player is?"

Edwards?

"Yes, Edwards," he says impatiently, a man with no time for the obvious. "But Mark Robinson is really going to be a good player. He wants to learn."

And still the Illinois game rankles. At 54–57, if only Garrett had made that play. . . .

Then he's off to watch Patrick play basketball, an agonizing experience because he cares too much. "It's hard for me to watch him play. I get too upset."

Thursday, March 3.

Indiana and Ohio State are now tied for fifth place in the Big Ten, competing for the last open spot in the NCAA tournament, since six conference teams will surely not be chosen.

"Joe, we're never going to confuse you with Magic Johnson," he calls out.

After practice, Patrick is weighed and measured: 6'4¾" tall, 182 pounds.

And a new thought takes over that will not leave Knight until the season ends. He wants Keith Smart to have a strong finish. Could things have been different? Maybe, he even wonders, it shouldn't have been Smart who made the game-winning shot against Syracuse in the 1987 NCAA championship game, but Steve Alford. It put too much pressure on Smart. He tries to analyze the incredulous look that comes over Smart's face when the ball is stripped from him. Is he mad at himself, or is he surprised because he doesn't know the game well enough?

"Yes," he says sadly, "but I want him to have a strong finish."

Friday, March 4.

His eyes fixed on a tape of Ohio State, Knight is on the telephone in search of former player John Ritter's telephone number. "I've got some people lined up to help him." As soon as he's off, Tom Abernethy calls with an offer of another job for Winston Morgan. That they should be taking care of each other gratifies him. He produces a long list of telephone calls since February 24 from people in the media that he has not returned. They range from newspapers to television and radio stations everywhere. Tim Garl enters to suggest teams for the 1993 Hoosier Classic: Texas Christian, Western Kentucky and Princeton. "That would be great," he approves.

Fred Taylor arrives, inspiring more stories of Knight's high school days in Orrville with his baseball coach Bill Shunkwiler. It's as if only keeping the past alive makes the present tolerable.

Shunkwiler would allow you only four pitches, not four swings, he remembers. And he'd stand back there and yell, "Get him out of there, that's it!"

"One day I was a junior and he had a kid pitching, a football player that I didn't like anyhow. I stand up there and I get four pitches and that is it. 'Get out of there, goddammit, you don't get any more pitches than anybody else.'

"So I slam the bat down and I walk away. It was cold and windy, the wind is blowing like hell, and I say, 'Well, if the son of a bitch could pitch . . .'

"And the wind just stops so you could hear me all over the park. Shunkwiler started throwing baseballs at me, he just started and I ran and he ran me right back to the high school. I can still see him standing throwing baseballs at me, running down the path. So I go up to the gym and I start shooting baskets. And he came in and played twenty-one with me and he never said one word."

His tone softens, turns gentle. "He was a really good coach. I was at Ohio State before I ever beat him at twenty-one. He's working for Gil Brandt of the Dallas Cowboys now." (Brandt is one of several men in sports other than basketball whom Knight admires.)

The telephone rings constantly. To one of his callers he confides, "At this point in time it matters not what you think, but just that we get the thing over with." That he must coach a team unreliable on defense is alien to him, painful, preposterous.

When the team enters, they are given photocopied clippings of their Illinois loss. "Why weren't *we* hungry?" he demands. "We're playing for the same thing they're playing for." He reads: Garrett "doesn't like the contact." His tone is scathing. Indiana "found itself overwhelmed in the category of intensity."

He faces them, furious: "We've played like good players and we've played like poor players. Which are we? What are we? Who are we? Where are we? It's running out. We have three games left to show who we are and what we are and this year's team will be in the book. And some of you will be more responsible for this year's team than you were for last year's team. [Calloway again, Calloway who was needed this year so much more than last.] Two different books and two different teams. But there's still time to write a good concluding chapter. That's up to you people!"

And so he coaches to the end a team without cohesion, without leaders, a team without a point guard, a team without forwards so that he's forced to play Hillman and Smart inside a lot of the time, a team without a ball handler who makes it his business not to turn over the ball, a team without players whose satisfaction may come from the unglamorous role of handing out assists.

In the stands at practice today is an invited crowd of donors to Knight's special library fund for which in the most recent drive he has raised nearly three hundred thousand dollars. They have come to present him with a little plaque. Trooping in from one of the balcony doors, on tiptoe, they have been warned to be silent. Professors, local businessmen and their wives, a diffident group compared to those down on the floor, they sit like stones in a little cluster, as if huddled together for comfort, waiting for the moment when he will join them for the little presentation.

But Knight ignores them, totally absorbed as he is in coaching his team to a finish they can remember with dignity. It is Fred Taylor he talks to, Taylor sitting at the scorer's table preparing for his television commentary.

"You said the only thing I could do is shoot," he says, putting his arm around Taylor's neck. "But I could get the ball to people." He sits down and watches his team take free throws. "They just don't look."

"I think the potentially best player is number 10 [Mark Robinson]," he tells Taylor. "I'd like to play Magnus, but he gets us into so much trouble." He wants Calloway to be a third ball handler against the press. (Unbeknownst to him, Magnus has signed up with Pete Newell's summer camp for pros; he wants to give it one more chance; he wants to improve; he wants to play.)

Up to the scorer's table now marches . . . a cowboy, complete with white Stetson, a weatherbeaten, bowlegged man of about sixty.

"Do you think it's going to rain?" Knight asks his Montana hunting and fishing companion Jim Galt, who sits down to chat with Fred Taylor while Knight returns to the team. A moment later, Joby Wright comes over to ask Galt to please be quiet. Then the coach himself reappears.

"This is the first time Galt has ever seen a black guy, let alone talk to one!"

He turns to Fred Taylor:

"Well, coach, are they any better than Monday night?"

And there is still another visitor, a burly, quiet man named

Gary Eiber, who played for Knight when he taught that season at Cuyahoga Falls High School. Eiber couldn't catch the ball. "You couldn't catch Marilyn Monroe in a telephone booth," his twenty-two year old coach told him. And Knight proceeded to blast one basketball after another at him, and he couldn't duck and had to catch them, and it hurt whether he caught them or not.

A few years later Knight recruited him at West Point, where he was in Mike Krzyzewski's class. One night Gary was hit in the eye during a game, but Knight told him, "It serves you right, you shouldn't be behind your man like that." And once when Eiber came up to Knight, who was talking to a major, Knight turned to him and said, "Didn't you forget something. This is Major ——— You're supposed to salute." "Oh, don't bother," said the major.

But Eiber's arm was already going up and of course the major saluted back. Eiber resurrects: the twenty-two year old high school coach taking his team out for hamburgers after sending them door to door to collect money for the team, and correcting them in the proper form of introducing themselves to their elders.

IV

"If you're waiting on me to pull out a miracle, I'm all out."

Saturday, March 5.

Saturday morning, the day of the Ohio State game, and Knight is delighted with Patrick's play in his sectional against Martinsville. He scored sixteen points, rebounded well and handled the ball well.

"We can't have watchers," he tells the Indiana team, which assembles at 9:40. "We have to have five people rebounding. Getting beat on the boards cost us the game Monday night. The thing is going on like a battle and you're standing with the best seat in the house and you're a spectator, not a participant." This time they better fight for loose balls.

His voice rises. "I don't want to lose a goddamn possession out here today." Now he is at the top of his lungs. "If you don't understand that, don't come to play! I don't want to get our ass whipped one more time!" His voice grows still louder, reaches its absolute top pitch: "I don't want to see one guy stand while a post man moves under him instead of coming right in on him. I don't want to see that once!"

How could they not want what he wants? "I want to win this ball game!"

As they prepare always, so do they now: Burson, the short white Ohio State shooter, prefers to go to his right. Francis "will exhaust every move known to man to get the shot off." Knight warns them, as always. "They're going to be competitive. They're going to be cocky coming in here to play. . . . When we start well, good things happen. When we get behind 11–2, it's a long time trying to catch up." Endlessly he repeats the same things, in the hope of reaching them. "Boys, individually you've got to give it everything you have, mentally and physically."

Again he appeals to their sense of fair play, to what they owe him as well as the other coaches, to what they owe themselves. "If we can't get our best effort after what happened on Monday, I don't know where to go, boys.

"If you're waiting on me to pull out a miracle, I'm all out. What I'm waiting on is for you people to play like you're capable of playing for forty minutes. I'm waiting on that."

At pre-game meal this ten-thirty A.M., a message awaits each of them at his place. "Play like champions!" He usually doesn't eat with the players, but this time he has joined them for spaghetti with meat sauce and vanilla ice cream. His address is: "There isn't anything we have to do that we aren't capable of doing. We've played a lot of basketball that's good enough to beat any-body—individually and collectively. It's just a matter of playing that kind of basketball. That's your responsibility. You're good enough to beat anybody, but you have to play that way and you have to think that way.

"You can win," he tells them. "You can do well." Achievement lies within their grasp.

After a brief nap in the coaches' locker room, he's in the stands in his stocking feet discussing Big Ten officiating with Ohio State coach Gary Williams. There ought to be a summer camp for referees, they agree. The referees ought to be accountable for their errors. He illustrates a play he noticed on the tape of Ohio State's game against Minnesota. A few people surreptitiously take his photograph. Otherwise he blends into the steadily filling stands, almost unnoticed.

Tates Locke has donned a pair of outlandish plaid trousers, almost as garish as Knight's old plaid jackets. Knight sits back in his armchair, raises an eyebrow: "He won with them once."

The starters are Calloway, Hillman, Garrett, Edwards and Jones. He does not start Smart. Indiana begins weakly: hands that don't hold onto the ball cost rebounds, with Garrett an offender. Hillman, alert, struggles with great intensity for every rebound. But Calloway has trouble with the Ohio State press and is called for a five-second violation. Meanwhile Ohio State has roared out, absorbing the lesson of the Illinois game. They play rough, testing Indiana, believing Indiana will not retaliate. Unfortunately, Ohio State begins to pick up fouls in the process.

At half time, with the score 39–35 in favor of Indiana, scholar athletes in each sport are honored. His A— average earns Magnus Pelkowski the award for basketball, while Joe Hillman wins for baseball. Each student has been asked to invite his favorite professor to a luncheon, and Magnus has chosen his professor of German literature in a 400 level course. But Hillman and Pelkowski must be praised in absentia. They are in the locker room being told by their coach that the next twenty minutes will determine the turning point of the season, that if they want to go on at all, they must win this game. A hopeful sign is that Indiana is leading Ohio State in rebounding 26–14.

Neither Garrett nor Smart start the second half. Jadlow does start, having earned the right by fierce play in the first half. Not being able to exert good pressure, they have few steals (Illinois had ten to their two), but they did shut down Burson in the first half: he had only six points.

Jadlow puts them up 57–52 and then Garrett misses a pass, and has the ball stripped from him. "Read the defense," Knight yells. "Triangle!" Jay is called over to the sidelines. "Get away from White, Jay, so he can't bump you on that screen."

It's only in the last two minutes that they solidify their lead. Having managed only three of twelve field goal attempts, Jay Edwards puts on a clinic in free throw shooting, going twelve for twelve, cool and calm, revealing the presence that will place him on the AP's all-freshman team along with Mark Macon, Kenny Miller, Livingston Chatman and Dennis Scott. As Indiana wins 85–77, Knight shakes hands with Ohio State player Jerry Francis, whom he thought had played well in the game.

Have the guards rebounded, as Knight had demanded they

should? Hillman has had seven, but Smart and Edwards only three each, and Jones and Calloway, who played seventeen minutes, two. Calloway has scored only three points. Garrett has had seventeen points; Knight excuses his less-than-dazzling performance on the grounds of a lingering flu. Smart is "up and down," making, as usual, some good plays and some bad ones. He did draw one charging foul and one they called a block. "It's been a roller coaster for us," Knight says. Jadlow, who came in off the bench, gave the team a lift. And Hillman, less reluctant to shoot than usual, has gone four for seven.

The press leaves the students' locker room, having crowded around Jadlow and Edwards, ignoring the others, a cruel display repeated game after game, and up go the Minnesota clippings and photographs.

"You did a hell of a job here in the second half," Knight tells his team. "They're a pretty good basketball team, pretty good players who came to play. We wouldn't be easy to beat if we played like this all the time."

It's six P.M. There's still time to drive to the Seymour High School gym to watch the sectional finals where Bedford North Lawrence will play Seymour. Knight sits high above the crowd on a chair catercornered over the wildly cheering crowd of eighty-one hundred, a totally white crowd which cheers frantically at every possession.

He talks about two things: first, Daimon Bailey, his discovery, a baby-faced fifteen-year-old, who wipes his hands on his sneakers like Larry Bird, scores magically both inside and out, fights for rebounds and blends in with his team. Bailey, still a sophomore, still only six foot three inches tall, may in two years drive down the road to play at Indiana. Tonight, Daimon Bailey scores forty-seven points; on the road to the state finals, he will score in another game—fifty-three. But Knight thinks also of Jay Edwards who, despite his cool demeanor, "has more heart than you think."

At ten P.M., it's chili and chicken with noodles at Bob Evans, and tea laced with lemonade. He grills Jim Galt, still wearing his cowboy hat, about next summer's Montana fishing prospects. In the car, he sings a song about Jesus wearing a Rolex while he saved souls, a satire on the television preachers, as he drives out of Southwest Indiana. This, he confirms, has been one of the last bastions of the Ku Klux Klan.

* * *

Sunday, March 6.

Parade magazine lists its All-America high school basketball team, and there on the fourth team is Daimon Bailey. Knight returns from very early spring fishing. As he scrutinizes a golf tournament on television, I remark, if Daimon and his team had enlisted all that intensity, intelligence and concentration, they could cure the ills of this planet, cancer, world peace, the homeless. It's one more facet of that down side of the Hoosier obsession with high school basketball.

"I think they'd settle for the regional championship," says the man with no illusions.

The team arrives. They've played five months and now only two games remain, one on the road against Minnesota and the last at home against Iowa: "It's going to all boil down to eighty minutes of basketball that we play this week. And every minute that everybody plays has got to be a good minute. Let's just make that our objective for the entire week. Let's make up your minds that you're not going to have a bad possession, that you're not going to have a thoughtless play, that we're going to have four hundred minutes of good individual basketball this week. That's really all I want to tell you." Then softly, he concludes: "OK. See you tomorrow."

V

"I've never felt worse for a kid than I feel for Smart."

A week remains, two more games, and he is still viewing the Wisconsin tape of February 24. Although Indiana won 84–74, at one point five straight Indiana turnovers and a few three-pointers for Wisconsin took the lead down to 73–70. Knight gets home from the movies only to watch the entire Wisconsin game one more time to see if there were things Smart did positively. Afterward, he thinks, I don't see how we won this game with Keith making all the mistakes he makes. Either he can't discipline himself, or he doesn't think quickly enough.

The next morning, Knight asks Dan Dakich to view the tape purely from the point of view of how Smart played.

"Don't watch anybody but him."

A few hours later Dakich reports back.

"He just gets lost. At the end he made four plays that very easily could have cost us the game."

In the coaches' locker room Knight illustrates the one play in that game that obsesses him: "We're trying to force the ball to the corner. Here's the man with the basketball and his first move is to the corner. Smart's guarding him and instead of keeping the ball going in the same direction, he tried to take away the direction we wanted him going in in the first place. He actually shuts that off. And now we've got three to block out four!"

Last year would have been the right moment for Smart to graduate, he thinks. "I just hate to see the kid wind up not having the kind of year that I envisioned he would have." Realistically, he concludes, "He'd be much better off playing in Oklahoma and I feel awful right now because he isn't suited to the way we're playing."

Keith Smart reflects upon that moment in the Wisconsin game when he moved ahead of that player heading for the corner:

"Sometimes I rely on anticipating where a player will go. He may seem to be setting up to go this way and pop back the other way. I'm thinking, 'Maybe I can make him think I'm going that way, and he'll go back the way I want him to go.' He reacts one way and I go the other way and the whole play is dead. But if he reacts the way I'm thinking, it's a great play!"

Resilient, intelligent, realistic, Smart admits that he hasn't worked with Knight long enough. "If I could get two more years here, I would love it. You need one year to learn things and the next year you're more comfortable with the system. If I could have started the year again, I don't know if I could have been the leader the team needed, but I would have tried. I never thought of myself as a guy people looked up to. If I had one more year, I would be able to make up for all that."

Meanwhile, with only two games remaining in the regular season, Knight wants Smart to have a brave finish. Watching tapes in the coach's locker room, he examines his team as he does every day and concludes he has "a lot of hunters. But we don't have any warriors." He has also "a bunch of guys out there who are in their fourth year and can't play at this level and they've had opportunity after opportunity to have demonstrated it." Calloway, however, is improving. He's "finally putting forth an effort which he should have been doing since October 15. But he wouldn't listen, didn't listen, didn't comprehend. Now it's almost midnight."

Monday, March 7, final week of the season.

Today there's a team meeting rather than practice. At this point of the season the practices are short, no more than an hour and fifteen minutes. "To save our legs," Joe Hillman explains. They view Minnesota's offense on tape, commentary by Ron Felling, then go out on the floor in their street clothes for a walk-through led by Julio Salazar.

In his last words of the afternoon Knight says he has heard (from Tates Locke, although he does not tell them this) that some of them have been running around late. Now he does something rare for him: he imposes a nine o'clock curfew. "If I call or someone comes by after nine and you're not there, you won't play. I've heard of guys running out all kinds of hours. That isn't how we run basketball here." He's been told that whenever anything is going on on campus, Calloway is there.

The curfew is a measure of how desperately he wants the season to end well and how uncertain he is about this team. The motivation for the Knight player has always been expected to come from within. But this has not been a typical Knight team. And even after their last game he will not stop searching for the reasons.

Tuesday, March 8.

"Let's set a tempo for our play for the week in what we do today," he tells them. "We've got our whole season riding on how we play this week."

Never does he forget how much he wants Smart to finish well. "Get Keith open and Magnus back pick for Keith," he calls. "Get set for the shot down there," he tells Keith. When Joe doesn't see Keith open, he's yelled at.

"Joby, was Keith open?"

"Wide open," Joby says.

Keith plays inside and outside both, as Knight looks for opportunities for this player to excel.

After practice, Smart reveals how surprised he was that Knight devoted so much of the practice to his offense, his surprise a measure of how the Knight players seem to understand him only in retrospect: "Today when he put me on the court and every play was Keith do this and Keith do that, I couldn't believe it! What I take away from here is knowing that if one day goes rough, another day will bring a smile. Coach would get on me, but a couple of days later, or the same day, or ten minutes later, he'd say, 'Great play, Keith!' I wouldn't trade places with anyone. I love it here."

Brian Sloan, with his double major in English and history, walks by, his Chaucer under his arm. He is a fine student despite his agonies with Spanish (he was put in Spanish honors by mistake). Like Magnus, he could graduate. Obviously not the best players, with no guarantees about playing time, nonetheless they choose to remain to complete their final year of eligibility because they too want to be here.

Tuesday, 6:00 P.M.

Patrick arrives for extra practice.

"Do you have a tape of the game against South?" his father wants to know. On Saturday, South defeated Patrick's school, North, for the sectional championship. The tension of watching Patrick play prevented his father from attending the game. South's leading scorer was Chris Lawson, whose thirty-two points, however, did not prevent North's almost winning at the buzzer.

Wednesday, March 9.

Former Knight assistant Royce Waltman, now a head coach himself, at DePauw, drops in. I am introduced.

"This is this year's Feinstein."

By now I should be accustomed to the needles, but I'm not. I wince, and can't manage a word for Waltman.

"We've got three days left," Knight tells his team, "Thursday, Friday and Saturday, and there isn't going to be an easy minute out of the eighty."

At Monroe County airport, they depart the bus onto the tarmac while he remains in the traditional head coach's right-hand front seat. He gives them each a pat on the back. Jay is complimented on his haircut, which looks more as if he's shaved his head. Jay can't resist a smile as soon as he thinks he's out of Knight's view.

On the plane Knight reads Golf World and passes around to players and coaches alike a big tin of homemade cookies and brownies "These are really good," he says. Throughout the flight he's obsessed because he can't remember the title of a self-help book. Was it by the author of *The Peter Principle?* I ask.

"Don't talk! Think!" he orders me.

The plane is met out on the runway by "Jake," a favorite driver, who's a Civil War buff and who presents Knight with a book about the Civil War each year as the team plays its road game with Minnesota. Today it's *Great Battles of the Civil War.* Jake announces that he has named his new cats Jeb (a grey) and Beaufort (a black).

On the way to dinner Knight jumps out of the car and rushes into a bookstore, emerging with the title which perplexed him. It's *Winning by Intimidation.*

Dinner is at Vescio's in Dinkytown near the university, an Italian restaurant of New York's Little Italy quality and then some. Knight and a long table of coaches, sportswriters, and two executives from Northwest Orient airlines are fed a banquet fit for Mafia dons. Sid Hartman, an old friend from the Minneapolis *Star and Tribune* is there, along with John Gutekunst, the football coach of the University of Minnesota and Jerry Burns, the Minnesota Vikings coach. Football coaches obviously are sitting targets for the Knight needle: who was at the bottom of Watergate? A football coach!

Could Lombardi coach today? Burns thinks he would have made the necessary adjustments. Knight is not so sure. The Northwest Orient president is a tourist here, wanting to know how being at Army influenced Knight's coaching. He solicits the obvious, only, obviously, to be disappointed. At Cuyahoga Falls high school Knight "blistered" the fifteen-year-olds at halftime. And they won. The next time he talked to them quietly and they went down 45–40. Knight *always* knew coaches had to be aggressive.

Corruption in coaching: the stories include one about a coach who fed his starters steak and the subs hamburger and pocketed the difference. Leadership? Black players respect ability. Talent? You need superior thinking more than athletic prowess. Coaching salaries? How much has your salary risen since 1970, Knight demands to know from the president of Northwest Orient airlines. His has increased twenty times. He was offered a job by Ohio State, but told them they would have to raise Woody Hayes' salary first. He refused to be paid more than the legendary football coach, who not only went home with a pittance, but never asked for a raise. There is neither self-consciousness about how Hayes' career ended nor so much as a reference to it. Glib comparisons to the contrary, however, it seems inconceivable that Knight could ever strike a student, as Hayes did.

Seated at the far end of the long table away from Knight, Tates Locke turns to Ron Felling: "Read my lips," he says. "I'm having a hard time." Then without a word Locke gets up and slips off into the night.

As for the food, it's out of Fellini: garlic bread spread with melted mozzarella, mounded hot and cold salads laced with hot sausage and red peppers, delicate many-flavored pizzas in long pans, and then the main courses, shrimp and broccoli over linguine, breaded chicken with peppers and spaghetti, flank steak roll-ups with cheese inside and a dab of fresh tomato sauce on top. Everyone eats a lot. The coaches drink beer, Knight, iced tea.

"What's that?" Knight calls down the table, spying the turtle pie, ice cream layered with caramel set in a chocolate nut crust.

In his suite the team awaits him.

"We're down to seventy-two hours," he tells them. "That's going to determine the whole outcome of the season for us. We have our fate in our own hands. We don't have to rely on anyone else to do anything. To borrow an old phrase, 'We are the masters of our fate.' People right in this room will determine what happens to Indiana."

What they talked about on October 15 is just as true today. "We've got to play hard and we've got to play smart." The opponent is never underestimated. Coffey is tough-minded; Burton, a fiery little shooter, is a hell of a player.

The Minnesota team has given everyone they've played real problems, Knight says. The Indiana players are not permitted to believe they are dealing with one of the sisters of the poor, although in fact Minnesota is hardly at the top of the Big Ten, coming into this game ten and sixteen overall, eight and seven at home and two and nine on the road.

After his players have gone to bed, Knight contemplates Indiana's tournament chances. He compares Ohio State's record with Indiana's, knowing that tonight Ohio State has defeated Purdue. He wonders where they are with Sagarin's computer ratings. Where would we be if we win these two games?

Ron Felling goes around to check on the players, but it isn't necessary; the Monday night curfew was unnecessary too.

At breakfast, Knight talks to them again about the opponent: Gaffney, Coffey, Hanson, Burton. He reads a clipping: "They hope to have effected a nothing-to-lose atmosphere." The players look up over their pancakes, eggs, sausages, potatoes, orange juice and milk, only to hear a lesson culled from last night's basketball. "Purdue goes into Ohio State, there is no way Ohio State can beat Purdue, none. What you had was a great inequity in attitude. Attitude can carry us a long way or it can keep us from going somewhere. This game tonight's going to be determined on that. OK. Ready to go?"

On the way to practice, the bus crosses a trickle of a river. He wants to bet me that it's the Mississippi. My sense of geography utterly deserts me. Could the Mississippi run this far north?

I bet him ten dollars, as much to test whether he would bluff as to stand behind something I know. Of course he wins. I pass him the ten dollars (he's sitting directly in front of me). But he adamantly refuses to take it and tosses it back to me.

"It would be like taking candy from a baby," he says.

Post–pre-game meal walk-through takes place in a mirror-lined mini-basketball court, part of the hotel's health club. They line up against the wall, Dean in his white jacket, Lyndon elegant in double-breasted grey, Magnus and Joe in college tweeds. Help and recover. Match-ups once more repeated. "Don't let Maxey or Shikenjanski get away from us," Knight adds presciently.

*   *   *

Williams Arena is the oldest in the Big Ten. Built in 1928, it still features the raised court, so that the players must go up a little flight of stairs to get from the bench to the floor. The benches are old wood, painted purple and yellow. Inside the scent of popcorn is so pervasive that, like Proust's madeleine, it calls up childhood memories, of the circus.

"Let's go red!" says Joe Hillman. "Right from the start. Right from the start." Off they race up onto the floor, the starters Garrett and Jadlow, rewarded for his effort against Ohio State, Jay, Keith and Lyndon. It's that team that must win on offense, the higher the score the better for Indiana. It will be another night for the freshman Jay Edwards, cool, oblivious to pressure and deadly accurate from three-point range. Jadlow begins with two quick rebounds while Smart, missing his shot, loses the ball.

As Jadlow grabs rebounds three and four, it's as if he were remembering his coach's words: "I would have been happy with you, I wasn't looking for anyone else." Jadlow makes two free throws.

Otherwise they are predictably themselves: Garrett has trouble catching the ball and trouble anticipating where a rebound will come down. Smart doesn't screen. Eyl is sent in with the command: "Let's get some strength." Soon he will be replaced by Jadlow. And all the while Knight keeps teaching: "Dean, work higher. Don't let him pin you against the baseline."

A 37–31 lead at the half ensures them nothing. What Knight feared now comes to pass. Having scored eight points in the first half, Jim Shikenjanski does indeed "get away from them," keeping Minnesota in the game. They're learning as they play once more. Lyndon is no match for Gaffney, and Knight brings the whole team up higher so that they've got the baseline to work with. Calloway goes in, but is reluctant to shoot, even when the shot is clearly his to take.

Meanwhile, the sophomore Shikenjanski, fierce and scrappy, begins to pour in the baskets, as if he were taking the opportunity tonight to prove that slow white kids can be basketball players too. And, having scored only three points in the first half, Burton wakes up to score eleven in the second.

But by 7.37 Jay Edwards has accumulated thirty-two points, while Burton picks up his third and then his fourth fouls. Unable to contest for the ball, weak as Knight angrily said he unnecessarily was, Calloway picks up three fouls too.

In the huddle, they're told: "Your whole season boils down to four and one quarter minutes." Victory is still not certain as Shikenjanski keeps answering, no matter that his previous career high was twelve points. (He'll wind up with 26 points). At 3.09 Willie Burton picks up his fifth personal.

In the huddle again at 1.46 with the score 86–76 in Indiana's favor, it's "Don't leave your feet and get around Shikenjanski! I want everybody blocked out!"

"For the season!" says Dean Garrett as they go back out. "For the season, let's go!"

At 87–80 with 1.01 to go, Steve Eyl is shooting one plus one. "Be a senior, Steve!" Knight whispers. Eyl makes the front end. Knight winces as he misses the bonus.

Smart makes six of eight free throws in the final minute and a half of play, going twelve for fourteen for the game and having made his first nine to set a Big Ten record of thirty-seven straight free throws. He has had a splendid game, beginning the finish his coach so desperately wants for him. In thirty-four minutes, he has scored twenty-four points.

Jay has scored eight three-pointers to break a Big Ten record of seven held by Steve Alford. Indiana has turned the ball over only nine times. The final score: 91–85. And through it all he's aware that I'm sitting right behind the bench: "The next best place to being next to me on the Indiana bench," he'll say the next day.

On the plane back after the game he eats a banana and reads *Pentagon* by Allen Drury. At one in the morning, the plane taxies down the mini-runway at Monroe County airport. A man is there not to speak to him, but simply to greet the team in silent approbation: it's a weatherbeaten man in late middle age named Charlie Deckard.

Once a service station man and a rather wild town character, and now a tree-trimmer, Deckard met Knight sixteen years ago. A friendship bloomed. Once a month Deckard wrote to Hazel Knight; he had visited her three weeks before her death. Of course he attended the funeral. A Pentecostal Christian, Deckard's religion forbids him from attending the games or even watching them on television: the attendant worldliness is alien to the spirit of his beliefs. But for every departure and every arrival as the team journeys back from the road, he is there, a lone figure in the darkness.

Outside Assembly Hall, another solitary figure greets the Indiana team. It's redshirted Mark Robinson. How did he know he was expected to be here? "No one told me," he whispers, "but I knew what happened to Steve." Alford is already a legend among them, as Quinn Buckner became to the classes that followed his. Robinson recalls Alford appearing even when, having been suspended for a game by the NCAA, he would not be traveling with the team.

Their uniforms deposited in the locker room, the team assembles in the lounge to wait for him. By now it's nearly two. "You make damn sure you're in class in the morning," he tells them. "We have one more forty minutes. One more. One more."

And they disappear into the night.

Will he be sad on Saturday when, after the Iowa game, the seniors say their farewells?

The answer is gruff: "I'll be in the locker room drinking a Coke!" There's a clue in that: he *never* drinks Coke, believing it's worse than cigarettes!

VI

"I want to see these three guys go out of here winning tomorrow."

Friday, March 11.

Good screens, good cuts, squaring up and taking the ball to the bucket—the lessons sound as if they belong to October and not to March. "They don't have anybody that can guard Keith," he announces. "If you'll work to get Keith open, you can cause so many problems for these people."

Iowa is assessed: they are a very good team offensively. But open court play, driving to the basket, exactly what Indiana, what Smart does well, will be effective against Iowa.

"I don't want happenstance," Knight tells them. "Think it out."

The tapes help. "Most of what they got out of us was in conversion," he reminds them of that 84–70 loss on January 6 to Iowa which began their Big Ten season.

Danny narrates as the film rolls. "Why don't we do that?" he asks them. Then he has to laugh. "Because it's Daryl!" They've been watching a highlight from one of last season's games!

Listening in the students' locker room is Robert Quay Norris, Knight's high school principal, in Bloomington from Orrville for the weekend with his wife.

Watching from the scorer's table is former Celtic player and coach, Tommy Heinsohn, in town to do the game for CBS. "I've known him since 1962," Heinsohn says proudly. Knight joins him to help with his broadcast. "I rarely use superlatives," he says, referring to Jay Edwards. But, he adds, "No one here can be a partial student and a complete basketball player." He compares Jay to Mike Woodson. After Knight is gone, Heinsohn explains to a young assistant: "This is the way they're gonna beat the press."

Locker room instruction focuses indeed on the Iowa press. On the whiteboard Knight outlines the cuts he wants, and who is to be in every position. In these last two days he sums up their season. "Last year was not full of thirty-four easy games," he reminds them. "You're being driven and demands are being placed on you." He is fully conscious of Calloway's pain at having been benched, Calloway who did not come back to make the kind of spectacular plays Keith Smart did.

"Guys get benched. That's the way basketball has been here and will always be here. When you overcome what you've been benched for, then you play. This season had some rough spots because of that and now we're down to the last game."

His primary focus of course is not Calloway, who will play only one minute against Iowa, but on those who are playing their last game at Assembly Hall.

"We've got three seniors. And I've been on Smart's ass and I've been on Garrett's ass and I've been on Eyl's ass. But I've been on the ass of everybody who's ever been a senior here before them, all the names on those lockers and they all went out of here pretty damn good people. I want to see these three guys go out of here winning tomorrow and a lot of it will depend on you three people yourselves."

Nor, despite going two and one in their four-game season and nine and three in their thirteen-game season, are they out of the woods as far as the NCAA tournament is concerned. A bid is still not certain. But the tournament is not their purpose; their goal is "for a team that didn't do some things and individuals that didn't do some things they should have been doing to come back." They have a chance to go ten and three in their thirteen-game season, "which is remarkable."

The game is at four in the afternoon "and we just don't have anything left after the game tomorrow."

A word remains for Eyl, Garrett and Smart. Without sentimentality, he tries to explain to them what their experience at Indiana has meant. "You three guys have done a lot for basketball here, but I think basketball has done, just as it has done for everybody that's ever been in here, far more for you three than you've done for it. I have and the coaches have a great appreciation for your having been a part of what we're doing here." He is telling them, he is not leaving it to chance for them to know: he appreciates them.

He wants only one more thing: that they take advantage of their opportunities to create "a hell of a memory for the three of you tomorrow."

After a six-thirty meeting they're sent home; "Whatever you've got planned for tonight, cancel. Let's get home and get to bed." They look exhausted; they yawn. They're young, but the late return from Minnesota last night has worn them out. Lyndon's head droops. Jeff Oliphant rubs his eyes. Jay leans against the side of his locker.

"Who's yawning?" I ask Magnus Pelkowski.

"Everybody," he laughs.

And still the coach is explaining: "Any time the ball is on top, his pass is across."

"Let's really be proud of what we do tomorrow!"

Saturday, March 12, final day of the regular season.

In the early A.M. he's there to watch Iowa on tape once more.

"Are you going to start Eyl?" Dan Dakich wants to know, as if there could be any doubt. That Dakich, who played for him for four years, and was a graduate assistant and now a coach, could ask such a question is a measure of how successfully Knight conceals his feelings, the enormous affection he feels for his players. Eyl has been an inconsistent player at best. That he would not start today as a graduating senior is inconceivable.

"Yes," is the complete reply to Dakich's question.

Robert Quay Norris wants to know if Knight will be coming to Orrville in the spring. There is Hazel Knight's house to see to. . . .

"Where'd you eat last night?" Knight wants to know. Certainly this is the most important basketball day of the season, but he doesn't relinquish the impulses of the host.

The team arrives to be reminded of the match-ups. "You can't make straight cuts against the press," he repeats. "You've got to make a V-cut on every single press cut."

Charlie Deckard wanders in and takes a seat in the stands to observe this last regular-season practice.

And now during this last practice Knight begins to run plays for Steve Eyl.

"I want Steve to get the ball."

It will also be Steve Eyl who will be bringing the ball in from out of bounds.

("That's because he's good at it," Phil Richards of the Indianapolis *Star* says when I mention this to him. The implication is that Knight would not do anything to enhance a senior's last game. But even Dakich wasn't sure.)

"When they've got this half court trap, Steve Eyl," Knight says, "you're on top. You cannot dribble into a trap. Reverse the ball. I don't care if you charge five times, I want you taking it to the bucket."

Expressionless, in keeping with the austerity of the moment, Eyl takes the point.

("We understand him," Eyl tells me. "We try to get his point, we don't sit in a room and cry about it. We just bounce back. That's one of the things he wants us to do; it's to be able to bounce back from adversity.")

Knight's message to them on this last day sums up everything he stands for, and his deep feelings. "If it were in my power to do so, I'd make this the best day any of us has ever had. I can't do that. That's up to you people." But it's not the impossible that's being asked of them either; they are not being asked to be Larry Birds, Earvin Johnsons. "Nobody has to play better than he can play. Nobody has to play smarter than he can play. And nobody has to play harder than he can play. But each guy has to play as smart, as well and as hard as each of you can play." And he sends them off to their pre-game meal.

> At each place is a card:
> "We started the season as champions—
> *Let's End Like Champions.*"

The starters are the three seniors, Smart, Eyl and Garrett, and the two freshmen, Edwards and Jones.

"Let's go white!" says Hillman, the player to whom Knight is grateful because he doesn't mind not starting, knowing that he will play the same twenty-four minutes whether he starts or not. And so Knight can start the younger, more psychologically fragile Lyndon Jones.

Although it's spring break, the stands are full. Seventeen thousand three hundred fifty-one are here, including Professor Robert F. Byrnes and his wife Eleanor, who have postponed their Florida vacation.

Smart and Eyl go to work at once, but Eyl begins to make mistakes. He isn't looking for Lyndon, as he was supposed to do, and Iowa is playing hard. But then Smart begins to score, eight points in the first five and one half minutes, while Hillman cheers from the bench.

As early as 13.13 Indiana has begun to break away. When Eyl makes a basket, he receives a standing ovation, as does Garrett's dunk at 5.41.

Smart will score twenty-four points in the half. All seems to be going smoothly, except for one contretemps.

With a minute to go in the half, it isn't Eyl bringing the ball in against the press, but Todd Jadlow. If it's particularly difficult to bring the ball in against the Iowa press, it's in part because the Iowa players have obviously been coached to get as close to the baseline as possible to harass that inbounds pass. Not infrequently, their feet are on that baseline, taking advantage of the fact that officials rarely call this violation.

Putting his arm back behind his head, suddenly Jadlow bounces the ball off the forehead of Iowa player, Kent Hill. This play is not illegal in college basketball, although usually the ball is bounced off a leg. Jadlow's action is taken in the context of Iowa's persistent violation of the rule.

Hill's reaction, however, is one of instantaneous rage. He swings in anger, ready to deliver a blow that would send Jadlow into the seats. Fortunately, he doesn't connect. At once Hill is assessed a flagrant foul, an intentional technical, and is ejected from his last college game. The Iowa bench, led by a fiery assistant, is now assessed a technical of its own and the free throws are shot by the icy calm Edwards. Was it Jadlow once more remembering Knight's "I didn't want to look for anyone else"? The halftime score is 53–34.

But Knight wants to leave nothing to chance. He's on his guard against the enemy—complacency. In the locker room during the half he writes on the blackboard 0–0. Let them start again, win again, lest they, this team which depends on offense, blow their lead.

Iowa player Bill Jones passes the Indiana bench and Knight calls to him, "Jones, you could play for me," while Knight tells Steve Eyl, "Don't get in a position to let them make that lob pass."

"Dean, you've got to move," Garrett is ordered. And meanwhile the Keith Smart highlight film proceeds, basket after basket interrupted only by a Garrett dunk, an Eyl rebound, another Garrett stuff.

On the bench, Coach Knight is tense. "Let me handle the rest of this," he tells Ron Felling. He's alert to every mistake. "If you want to finish the game, get the ball inbounds!" he screams at Eyl. When Jadlow is scored against, he's frantic. He walks down the bench with a clipboard to explain to Garrett what he did wrong, while on the floor Indiana has passed the one hundred–point mark.

At 5.58 Eyl fouls out. He leaves to a standing ovation while Knight bites his lip. This was not what he had in mind. At 108–86 with 2.31 to play, he's still demanding, "Why won't anybody commit to help?"

But when at .41 Garrett and Smart go out together, brothers as they've been, the junior college players who have had to work so hard to play here, Knight embraces them in a gigantic circular hug. Never one to do one thing at a time when he can do two, Knight simultaneously motions to manager Greg Burton to collect the basketball.

The final score is 116–89. Smart has scored 32 points and Garrett 26. To ensure that all would go well, Edwards, the future to their past, has contributed 24.

Everyone remains seated, everyone here knows what is coming. It's a tradition of Indiana basketball that the seniors say their farewells to the fans, introduced by the coach who has not (yet) retreated to the locker room for a Coke.

"It has not been easy in Steve's case to be told not to shoot the ball," Knight says. "There have been times when if he would have, he would have been a dead man!"

"With Keith, he and I differ on when to use his great talent and when not to use it." And now he grows serious, frank. Smart, he acknowledges, has had to use his talents within the framework of the way Knight wanted them to play. And as for Garrett, "There were coaches out West who never believed he could play at Indiana and there he was, playing for the national championship."

On October 15, Smart had told me "he hasn't talked to me anything about making the shot, he hasn't said anything about that, not yet, so I look forward, when I finish here, ten years when I come back . . ."

It turns out, however, that Smart will not have to wait ten years.

"After Keith made the shot in New Orleans last year . . ." Knight goes on. And the crowd erupts once more.

"They have all carved a special place for themselves in Indiana basketball on and off the court."

The floor is theirs now and he walks off, indeed to retreat into his locker room, not, one suspects, because of the reason he gives, "I wouldn't listen to my own speeches, let alone theirs," but because he cannot abide being praised.

Flash-forward: he's about to leave for the Final Four, to cheer on Mike Krzyzewski and the Duke team. But he calls to see how I am. "You must be a good teacher to have so brilliant a disciple," I tell him, and in a second he's off the phone; he can't bear to hear it.

Steve takes the microphone first, immediately to invoke: Kitchel and Wittman and his coaches, Wright, Felling and Dakich, all of whom have remained on the floor to listen. "Every move we make out here," he confides to the seventeen thousand, "they told us what to do."

Dean Garrett takes the audience back two years to his and

Keith's wondering "how it would be, what we were going to do, how long we would be here. . . ." to a roar of laughter. Indeed there have been some, and there will be others, who choose to eschew this struggle to excel.

Garrett's special appreciation goes to coach Joby Wright, "the first one to come to me to tell me what I did wrong and what I did right." It goes secondly to his "biggest buddy, Keith Smart."

Eyl and Garrett are both gracious, but it's Smart, who sheds a tear, who is the most charming. His mother, watching him from the stands today, has told him he lost weight. He thought to himself: "I guess coach Knight has taken the best out of me." And then Smart adds, "By the same token he's instilled in me some of the greatest qualities a young athlete could ask for."

Smart invokes campus life too, students meeting him when he was benched and telling him to hold his head up high. He recalls the day he and Garrett were made to run fifty sprints after practice and still his teammates waited in the locker room until they were finished. That was his greatest moment.

As for Garrett, "we'll always be together, just like brothers. Who knows," quips Smart, "we may get married!"

A model young man, Smart goes on to thank even more people than Steve Eyl did. Smart's list includes last year's assistants Kohn Smith and Royce Waltman as well as Ron Felling, Dan Dakich and Julio Salazar, saving for last Joby Wright who "represents what Indiana is all about." Nor does he forget his trainer, Tim Garl, and doctor, Brad Bomba.

Mom is saved for last, a short, plump, beaming woman who has brought along Keith's six-year-old brother. Keith remembers complaining about Knight to his mother only for his mother to reply, "He **needs** to be on you." And she, who Smart believes had to give up college when she became pregnant with him at nineteen, had told him, "I don't care what you do. I'm gonna be at your graduation in May."

"So, Mom," says Keith Smart, "I'll be there too." With that he brings down the house.

"We started the season as champions. Let's end like champions." And so they have.

Sunday, March 13.

They have been seeded fourth in the East to play Richmond at Hartford, Connecticut.

Having come to Indiana for the Iowa game, Michael Boykin and John White are taking their leave. "Get on those tests," Knight calls to Boykin, the student's ACT and SAT scores on his mind. Boykin leaves Assembly Hall, his future coach's arm around his shoulders.

Knight returns to peruse the NCAA pairings with Bob Hammel. "I can't believe that Indiana is seeded," he smiles.

VII

"Boys, we've got to play a hell of a basketball game."

Four days of preparation against Richmond begin in Bloomington. On Tuesday, Rick Calloway is asked to leave the floor because he is not playing hard. After practice, Dan Dakich shows him a tape he has compiled of three or four possessions where Calloway has played badly. Calloway looks down. "That won't happen again," he says.

On Thursday, the team flies to Hartford directly to practice. For the coach there's a press conference where, inevitably, a reporter must ask him about LSU coach Dale Brown. Brown's team has also come to Hartford. But LSU is on the other half of the slate. The two can play only if both make the East Rutherford regionals.

Knight brushes the question aside, as if Brown, who in print has called him "despicable" and a "cheater," were no more than a pesky fly attempting to alight on the hide of a bemused elephant: "When you ask questions about him, you should direct them to a psychiatrist, not me."

A reporter in the audience sports a striking fedora that attracts Knight's attention, anything to escape the tedium: "Reminds me of one my Dad used to wear when I was a little kid. Brings back good memories." The next morning the Hartford *Courant* reporter will launch into panegyrics of how Knight is "nurtured by memories of his father," how he "worshipped his father."

Knight shakes his head: more absurdity. "All I meant," he says, incredulous at the reporting, "is that the hat was out of date."

"We'll let them relax," Knight tells Ron Felling while the team eats dinner, meaning only that there will be no tapes tonight.

He greets me as "the female John Chaney," asks when I arrived and sits down to bouillabaisse over linguine and orange juice mixed with Seven-Up. And then he is off for his ritual walk with Bob Hammel, indeed his closest friend, the person he turns to for solace amid the tensions of big-time college basketball.

"North Carolina A.& T. beat Syracuse on the boards," Hammel says with a chuckle.

"Really?" Knight answers. Hours out of Bloomington they are immersed in the texture of the happening. More properly, their concentration on the tournament began the moment the seedings were announced by CBS Sports. Having been one of the sixty-four teams is an achievement in itself; now the players and coaches must enter the crucible of real life raised one notch by the tournament, testing their concentration and their ability to play as a team.

At ten-thirty the team awaits him in a third-floor meeting room, part restaurant, part screening room, with a section of parquet floor where basketball plays may still be demonstrated. Here Knight reads from the scouting report, and conducts one more walk-through with tomorrow's starters, Keith and Jay, Lyndon and Dean and Steve. As in his Bloomington classroom, teaching is founded upon repetition: "The diagonal pass and the step-in post we have to take away . . . the reverse pass to the high post we have to take away . . . the post cross screen, the screener be ready to switch, we went through that. . . ." Keith is told he will be the help-side wing man; they must all work to keep Atkinson, the feisty Richmond point guard, under pressure. Knight is at the blackboard, one last review before tomorrow's test.

"What's he going to do, Steve?"

Eyl murmurs, but he's not made to hang in the wind. "He's going to step right out here and back pick," Knight predicts. "Now their guards will cut quickly inside too. They might have Kratzer and Stapleton in a stack. Stapleton pops out, Kratzer comes up and Rice will flash quickly to the low post on the other side. So just be constantly aware of their coming toward the basketball. Kratzer comes up, Atkinson with the ball, Stapleton has come out, Rice and Woolfolk, and Rice is right up there. So with you in here, Jay, you have to be really alert with the ball being over here, because, all the more important, Steve, that we really fight the ball right here. They are not a team that really looks to lob the ball. They're a team that wants to work through here from one side to the other. . . .

"They could play a box and one against you," he warns Jay, "and then we'll just start you on the high post and almost play a triangle inside.

"You can anticipate everything that's being done," he tells them. "You can read their defense and react against it." The lesson, of course, is also part psychology. "Here's a team that will approach this with, 'Hey, we're little Richmond and this is gigantic Indiana.' They have everything to win and nothing to lose. Let's don't give them a chance to think they have a winning approach."

As he broke their year down to a thirteen-game season, as he offered them the goal of making the sixty-four team field, now once more he adjusts their goals: "If we could win today and Sunday, there are only sixteen teams left. That's a good point of accomplishment." He sends them away to confer together, to "think about where we are, what we're doing."

One last trump card remains. "We're still the champions," he tells them, "and let's play like it. Let's make everybody that's in our path pay a helluva price. Let's just start that out on the first possession tomorrow."

Back in his room, he confers with Ron Felling one last time: "Is there anything else? I think we've impressed on Garrett all we can. . . ." Garrett has had bad practices all week. Garrett, essential to their offense, worries him.

In the morning, George Vecsey's characterization of Dale Brown in the New York *Times* delights him: "When he saw LSU and Indiana in the same subregional, Brown leaped off his sofa and brandished a fist, like Elmer Fudd about to catch that Wascally Wabbit." Knight chuckles. "That's pretty good," he says.

Friends from Orrville arrive, Dick Rhoads, who arranged Hazel Knight's funeral, Tony Yanto, who heads one of the foundries for which Orrville is famous. Only there is no room at the inn. Knight summons Tim Garl; within minutes the old friends have rooms and their wives can be rescued from the car out front. There is none of the tension of game day you might expect, or certainly none that takes precedence over seeing to the well-being of old friends. Knight reaches for the telephone to call Bloomington, to have a janitor open the basketball office so that someone can read him Mike Krzyzewski's home and office numbers. He watches the fate of his disciple's team, Duke, gaining ground in the other half of the Eastern subregional being played at Chapel Hill.

Suddenly there's a loud knock on his door. Without waiting for a response, in bursts a man in a rumpled tweed jacket, incredulous at the spectacle of Knight lying on his hastily made-up bed. "I can't believe this! Get your . . . !" Knight is being given orders; Knight doesn't mind, not from this man.

Has his visitor arrived on a "chariot of fire?" "Where's your halo?" Knight asks softly.

"Tapes, tapes, tapes. Get them to play ball. Forget the goddamn tapes," the visitor retorts, no neophyte at administering the needle.

"Do you have enough tickets?" Knight asks with concern.

And he retreats with Red Auerbach to the living room of his suite for a private chat, basketball talk, those sentences that invariably begin, "We were playing . . ."

Don Fischer's pre-game show is preceded by the lecture that follows the team's eleven A.M. pre-game meal. Ron Felling is called upon to read an article from the morning's newspaper: "We're going to attack Garrett, get him off his feet and in foul trouble and that will be one less worry we'll have." This is to arouse them, fire Garrett with the spirit to prove them wrong. "We've got to pressure Atkinson and keep Kratzer from handling the basketball and we've got to make it tough for the ball to go inside to Woolfolk," Knight repeats.

Julio produces his painstakingly researched cards and a surprisingly long lecture ensues, as if the game were not just two hours away. Again they are told what they must take away: the diagonal pass, the step-in post, the reverse pass to the high post. "When the pass goes inside, we have to go inside with the pass. They're not going to throw it back out. We have to make it difficult for them to do anything with it inside."

As always, he combines infusing them with the confidence arising from their having played well, with an accurate appreciation of the other team's strengths. "You have to take this as a challenge to play smart and to play well," he tells them. "They have to guard you and that isn't like playing against Humpty Dumpty." He reminds them of their fine play in the first half of their splendid victory against Iowa when they did such a good job of taking away the diagonal pass and the step-in post. Now they must do it again.

Auerbach's needle notwithstanding, there are tapes, even now. At first the television set does not cooperate. "Here in the United States, Julio," Knight needles, "we don't have magic. We use electricity." Could he have read Gabriel García Márquez, is he aware of the magic realism that defines the culture of Julio's homeland?

No matter, off he goes into the details: "They want to go against you. Let's just turn that around and make it something they cannot handle. What they do offensively should really not cause us any problems. They move quickly, they get into things very quickly, *Rice is a very good shooter* . . . but one thing Rice does is come out of the stack on a reverse of the UCLA cut for the shot. Rice will line up on the bottom of that stack, and if they split it and Kratzer comes up opposite, and Stapleton goes out, Rice may quickly flash to the other side in the low post. . . ." How could the game not evoke déjà vu with this kind of preparation?

"But if we handle people, beginning with Atkinson on top," he goes on, "we have to be alert to switching the low cut, which is what we normally don't do. . . . One of the real things we have to be alert to, Steve, is not allowing Kratzer to handle the basketball. The less he handles the ball, the better we're going to be."

It's not only a question of what the others will do; there is much they can do, as he illustrates on the parquet floor. "We pass away from their movement. Woolfolk and Kratzer are really going to come at you hard. Look to lob the ball above Woolfolk and Kratzer. We can take the ball to the bucket and score with it. . . . I get it. I dribble hard away, and I pass back hard," he shows them. "Fill the baseline versus the isolated post. . . . We're going to start out playing with a three-man stack with Keith and Dean and Jay in a stack. Steve can then step right up and get the ball or start away and come back to the outside. Remember if that wing man stays down, and the point man takes Lyndon, then you just shoot into the gap right up there at the top of the key. That's the gap we want you in. . . ."

Whatever he can predict, plan, organize is done while he repeats over and over that "everything they run depends on these three things: Atkinson handling the ball, Kratzer handling the ball or their getting it into the post.

"Boys, we've got to play a hell of a basketball game," he concludes at last. "We aren't going to get by this game without playing well, and we won't get by the next game without playing well, and that's just the way it is, and that's the way it was last year." He reminds them. In the Auburn game during last year's tournament, they got behind by fourteen. Against Duke, they had trouble in the second half. Against LSU, they were down by eleven. Against Vegas, they gave away two good leads. Against Syracuse, they let them get eight points ahead.

"We know what has to be done 'cause we've done it," he tells them firmly. "And that's how we have to play. Let's be playing Sunday."

He sits down at a table where vanilla ice cream sits melting, the spaghetti, rock-hard hamburgers, pancakes and scrambled eggs having been cleared off. It's as if he's thinking aloud, reinforcing his own sense of where he is, concentrating. Since 1975 he has failed to make the regionals only twice, "and it's hard to get out of the regional. When you get down to the regional, now you're down to the last sixteen teams in the country," he murmurs. "Then you're down to the last eight. That's a really good accomplishment. I think it's great for the kids. If we can win today and Sunday to be able to go home on Sunday thinking there are only sixteen teams left and we're one of the sixteen teams. I think that's a good point of accomplishment for a season. And I don't honestly know that we can."

In the elevator I tell him I'll be driving to the Meadowlands next weekend. His reply is stern. "Let's win today!"

Out they come and again everything he has predicted comes true. Richmond plays a box with one player chasing Jay Edwards, so that in the first half he will score only seven points. Richmond, coming out on fire, takes the lead, 3–0 and then 5–0, and 9–4.

You can see it in their play. From the beginning Richmond believes that they can do it; they can win. Meanwhile what Knight feared most comes rapidly to pass: Garrett has been neutralized so that by the half he will have scored only one point with two rebounds. Reflecting that he has been entirely taken out of the game, Richmond leads 44–38. Meanwhile, Jones and Edwards both seem nervous, freshmen at the tournament. Atkinson is as flashy a guard as Knight warned he would be; Kratzer has five rebounds in the first half, and Woolfolk is a presence. Rice, whom

Knight warned was an excellent shooter, has scored fifteen points. It's only Smart's seventeen points that have kept Indiana in the game, and then Smart doesn't screen, loses his man. He makes all the mistakes that led to his being benched in the middle of the season.

As the second half begins, Garrett both takes a bad shot and bobbles the ball. He leaves his feet, as Richmond had predicted they would make him do.

"Come on, men," Felling encourages. But Richmond smells victory. Smart continues to keep Indiana in the game, and Jay Edwards makes three three-pointers in a row. Yet Indiana still cannot take possession of this game. With fifty-four seconds to go, the score is 70–69 in favor of Richmond. Then, with twenty seconds to go, Smart has a chance to give Indiana a 71–70 lead. He goes up for the shot, an acrobatic move, but lightning does not strike again. "The shot" does not repeat itself. Smart misses, and Atkinson, seizing the rebound, races off for a lay-up.

With scarcely two seconds to go, Hillman puts up a shot that would tie the game, but, off-balance, he too misses. It's over, 72–69, an upset. The press proclaims Richmond a "Cinderella"!

Rice has scored twenty-one points. Kratzer has had twelve rebounds, Steve Eyl having been unable to keep him from handling the ball. Pesky, ungainly Woolfolk has been dominating in the low post, scoring sixteen.

In the post-game press conference Knight is gracious. "Dick Tarrant was a good coach before I ever started coaching," he says. He praises the Richmond team for playing "patiently" and "smartly," exactly what he had hoped his own team would do. Why didn't he call time at the end? He never does under those circumstances: "That's what we practice for." Why didn't he play Calloway? "Because obviously I must have thought other people were better."

"Is everybody surprised that we lost?" he asks the reporters. "I thought there'd be a few people smart enough to know it was going to be a tough basketball game. I'm not surprised that we lost."

But the prize for the dumbest question must go to the elderly gentleman sitting stiffly in his seat who calls out, "How many times did you see Richmond play this year?"

"On tape . . . ," Knight answers mildly.

"Not personally?"

"How the hell would I get from Bloomington to Richmond during basketball season or for what reason? I think Tarrant's a helluva coach, but the son of a bitch isn't my brother!"

Moments later he is sitting in his dressing room. It looks like an actor's backstage dressing room with its mirror surrounded by lights. John Ryan enters with a word of solace. "You took us to the heights many times," he says. Knight is not consoled. The only person he wants to talk to is Bob Hammel; the only subject that interests him is the game. His eyes are small, set deep into his head, and his face is flushed, blotchy as he sits under the bright lights. He looks small, as if he's shrunk.

"I felt awful for Smart taking that shot," he says. "I told him he had kept us in the game until then."

"How many seconds were left when Hillman took the last shot?" Knight wants to know.

"Maybe two," Bob Hammel reports.

"Should I have taken a time-out? I don't know what else I could have done."

And he's back to them. "Eyl is . . ." "Garrett can't . . ." He speaks of the seniors in the present tense, as if he would still coach them, help them to overcome deficiencies, exactly as he had continued to coach Jimmy Wisman down the ramp after he had played his last college basketball game.

Then, obsessed as he is, he transcends his obsession. His natural sense of the absurd comes to the rescue.

"What's worse than a basketball post-mortem?" asks Coach Bob Knight.

Amid talk of weight-training, improving, within the hour they're off to Bloomington. As soon as he learns that the plane awaits, Knight orchestrates the seating arrangements on the small plane and the big. Then he slams his bag shut and races out the door, leaving Ron Felling and Dan Dakich to wait for the next interminable Ramada Inn elevator. It's the ninth floor, it takes forever, and then they realize . . . and bolt for the stairs lest he leave without them. In fact, the bus has begun to pull away as they rush out into the street. The driver hits the brakes, backs up . . .

"I'd like to see you on Monday or Tuesday," Knight tells Rick Calloway.

On Sunday morning, as usual, he is on television, if without

Chuck Marlowe, who was not quick enough to arrange a taping before the team's departure. Knight calls this "my least enjoyable year of coaching." His reasoning: he has not been able to depend on his team's defensive skills, something on which he had prided himself throughout his career.

Being Knight, he is not interested now in assuaging his players' egos. He's Knight, and so he says exactly what he thinks. "We have players who are returning who will have to do an awful lot of work, players who really didn't work as I think they should this past year." It's Calloway of course he's thinking of, Calloway who was pushed out of the way time and again by a stronger defender, Calloway who had the ball knocked out of his hands. It was not Calloway's lack of ability his coach complained about, but his not doing his best with what he had. "You can lift weights and work your ass off, and he just hasn't done it," Knight had said time and again during the season.

Knight announces on television that he plans to offer an opportunity to two or three of his incoming players (Eric Anderson, of course, for sure, but also John White, Matt Nover and Michael Boykin). Some who "have played a lot for us in the last year *or two or three* . . . have got to make some changes in their approach to how they're going to play." Richard Calloway in Cincinnati takes note.

On Monday morning Knight indeed meets with Rick Calloway. In December he had asked Calloway to lead, leaving him in the locker room in charge of the team. "Now Ricky, you talk it over with them . . . ," he had said. And then when Calloway had been too weak to hold onto the ball, his failure to build up his skinny 186-pound body over the summer coming back to haunt him, Calloway had been benched.

"It's more fun playing with them," Dean Garrett had told Knight before the Ohio State game which marked the season's turning point. "Them" were Jones and Edwards; Calloway had failed not only to provide leadership, but to play the team game. After he had been benched, he had started and played an average of thirty-three minutes in wins against Michigan State and Wisconsin and in losses to Purdue and Illinois. But in the team's best games, the victories against Illinois and Ohio State on the road, and Purdue and Iowa at home, he had figured scarcely at all.

This Monday morning, forbidden now by NCAA rules to practice again, as it had after they had lost to Cleveland State in the first game of the 1986 tournament, Indiana has time on its hands.

Knight and Ricky Calloway meet.

"I think you ought to quit because I don't think you can make this a commitment. If you think you can, that's where we should start from," Knight tells him. So he had told Landon Turner in January of the 1981 championship season. "I've given up on you. Go to the NBA." At that point Turner had been transformed, sparking the team to play at its best, determined to prove Knight wrong.

But Calloway is not Landon Turner.

"What I came in here to tell you was that I was going to quit," Calloway says.

"That's entirely up to you. A lot of things happened to you here. There are possibilities, a dedicated weight program . . ."

But Calloway has listened, perhaps, to his father, distressed by his son's not playing. Calloway fears he will sit on the bench for another year; the same thing that happened to Keith will happen to him. He does not take the measure of how Smart came back with that superb game against Iowa, with late season triumphs.

Much more importantly, he seems not to believe that the transforming power of hard work would result in his being a starter next season. (And later his father will talk to the press about how many teams recruited him out of high school and about how his son still has the ability to help somebody win an NCAA championship. He does not acknowledge that Knight wanted nothing less than the full development of his son. . . .)

"I'm just not happy here," Rick Calloway says.

In the press Calloway replies to Knight's criticism that he hasn't built up his strength sufficiently to contend for the basketball: Knight, says Calloway, "harped on me about not lifting weights during the summer and I really didn't do what I was supposed to do." With this admission, he goes on to blame his teammates: "But I wasn't planning on coming back and having to play Daryl's spot. Jadlow and Eyl and Sloan, they knew the position was open. They should have worked on their games also, so they could play it. None of them came in ready to play there so I had to do it."

In fact, when Calloway was benched, it was 6'2" Joe Hillman who moved into his position, and later Keith Smart would play forward. And of the nineteen games Calloway started over the year, fifteen were in a lineup with a bigger forward: Jadlow, Eyl, Sloan or Pelkowski. Further, as Knight had told his clinic audience in October, there are no number ones, twos or threes or fours writ in stone on his team, only players.

After that Ohio State game when Calloway was benched for the first time, Ohio State coach Gary Williams said, *"That* was Indiana basketball!" Although Calloway claimed he was benched and then forgotten, in fact he returned to start and play more than thirty minutes in four straight games in February.

His teammates having been attacked by Calloway in the press, some of those not mentioned now step forward. Joe Hillman tells a story of how Calloway ordered a manager to get his shoes. "Get your own shoes," Hillman told him. Magnus Pelkowski remembers hearing Calloway say, "A player like me shouldn't have to work in practice like that." Magnus, considering, realizes: "He was only happy when *he* played well."

It is still the week of the NCAA regionals. On Monday, Calloway tells Bob Knight that he will leave Indiana. On Thursday, Calloway receives a telephone call from Pontiac, Michigan. It's Larry Brown, coach of the University of Kansas.

In search of a new basketball coach, and having failed to lure Jim Valvano out West, UCLA announces a press conference for Saturday, April 9: Larry Brown has decided to rejoin the fold. The next day, however, Kansas announces that Brown has decided to remain in Lawrence.

And on this Friday morning another story has its origin in Lawrence. Rick Calloway is coming to Kansas, Richard Calloway Sr. is quoted as announcing. (At Kansas, of course, Rick Calloway will not find Larry Brown, who will have gone off to follow his fortune with the NBA and the San Antonio Spurs. He *will* find a school being investigated by the NCAA for recruiting violations. And indeed there were rumors of a car, of money having been offered to Rick Calloway).

In a week, Chris Lawson, that skinny 6'11" redheaded junior from Bloomington who averaged 22.7 points and 10.2 rebounds for South (18–7) this year, will make his oral commitment to attend Indiana University.

*   *   *

Flash-forward to March 31: a diligent Emery Worldwide air freight inspector in Los Angeles rescues a poorly wrapped package that has fallen to the floor and broken open. Out of a videotape box emerges an envelope containing twenty fifty-dollar bills. The origin of the package? Dwane Casey, Kentucky assistant coach. The recipient? Claud Mills, father of Chris, who, like Shawn Kemp, had preferred Kentucky to Indiana.

Mills is telephoned when the package breaks. "I've got a package for you with one thousand dollars in it. What do you want me to do with it?" the Emery worker asks. A conspiracy? "When you try to stuff a VHS tape into one of the eight-by-ten envelopes, comments Chuck Bullerman, head security agent for Emery in Los Angeles, "you're asking for trouble. They just break open."

"Did you send the money?" a reporter asks Casey.

"I would say 'no comment,' " Casey responds.[1]

Lacking subpoena power, and hence the power to obtain the truth beyond a shadow of a doubt, the NCAA nonetheless begins one more investigation of the Kentucky basketball program, the second in two and a half years. His son "could have gone anywhere in the country for fifty thousand or one hundred thousand dollars," Claud Mills says. "Chris Mills ain't no one-thousand-dollar player."[2]

At once the recruiting of Shawn Kemp is reviewed. Kemp's mother, Barbara Brown, had traveled by air to Lexington from Elkhart, Indiana, on October 31, although she had told Bob Knight she could not afford the gas money to come to Bloomington. Yet she paid cash, over four hundred dollars, for her airline ticket and over one hundred dollars in cash for a night at the Radisson Plaza Hotel. The NCAA learns that on October 28, three days before her visit to Lexington, Mrs. Brown received one of those Emery packages, one marked "urgent letter, next morning delivery."

The NCAA discovers that both Shawn Kemp and Chris Mills were suddenly driving automobiles within weeks of their signing letters of intent in November with Kentucky.

Claud Mills says he paid for his son's car out of a $24,000

1. Philadelphia *Inquirer,* April 15, 1988.

2. *USA Today,* April 26, 1988.

Workman's Compensation settlement, although he has not worked consistently since 1984. Mrs. Brown, who works at Elkhart General Hospital, says the $11,000 car Shawn was driving was a birthday present from her. She put down $1,000 in cash and agreed to pay the balance in monthly payments of $225 over five years.

It is in such an environment that Bob Knight must recruit players for Indiana.

At Indiana, Chris Mills was specific in his conversations with the players who were his hosts.

"I have no money. I have to have a car. I have to live in my own place," he told Mark Robinson.

How much did he need, Robinson wanted to know.

"Thousands."

At Kentucky, they would accuse Knight of leaking the story about Kemp and Mills. In fact, the Lexington *Herald-Leader*, which won the Pulitzer prize for exposing recruiting violations at Kentucky in 1985, and had been the recipient of local harassment ever since, had known about Kemp and Mills since November. Only hard facts, which came with the Emery exposure, led to their resuming their investigation and publishing their findings.

On June 28th, NBA draft day, Knight's Christmas concern about the basketball futures of Dean Garrett and Keith Smart becomes a reality. Both players are selected only deep in the second round: Garrett at number 38 by Phoenix and Smart at 41 by Golden State.

But it's still only Tuesday, March 22, four days after Indiana has lost to Richmond in the first round of the NCAA tournament. The hard recruiting necessary to rebuild his team still incomplete (he will add one more player, an Illinois guard named Jamal Meeks), Bob Knight closes the door to his office. He has coached nearly seven hundred games. But now an idea new for him seems to dawn, a tribute, perhaps, to the degree of peace and personal happiness which has settled over his private life.

"Well, I've just made up my mind," Bob Knight declares. "If you're a coach, you're going to get your ass beat now and then."

CHAPTER 10

REPRISE: THE LITANY

"If rape is inevitable . . ."

THE CRUELEST MONTH? On April 25, Connie Chung's documentary, "Stressed To Kill," airs on NBC. Barely a moment into Bob Knight's segment, almost his first words are "If rape is inevitable, relax and enjoy it." It's as if the subject of the program were sexuality in the eighties, with a basketball coach a peculiarly unlikely commentator. Completely gone is the context in which the coach made the remark: Knight himself immobilized by unjust officiating, rendered as helpless as a rape victim, attempting to perceive what it might feel like to be completely and hopelessly vulnerable.

Recognizing that the figure of speech, no matter its origins in Voltaire's *Candide,* might be misunderstood, Knight goes on immediately to qualify: "That's just an old term that you're going to use. The plane's down, so you have no control over it. God, I'm not talking about the act of rape, don't misinterpret me there. But what I'm talking about is something's happened to you so you have to handle it. You have to be able to realize that there's nothing you can do about it."

The wire services alter the text, adding an emphatic "now!" after "so you have to handle it," whereas the "now" came later, after "nothing you can do about it, now . . ." as the transition to Knight's next thought.

But no matter, there it is—too charged in its overtones to be wise, because it might be misconstrued. And indeed how could it not be since no question precedes the remark; the viewer is left entirely in the dark as to what issue Knight is addressing. From the program you could not guess that Knight was responding to a question about officiating.

After the interview, which took place on the floor of Assembly Hall, Knight returned to the coaches' locker room and said to me, Bob Hammel and Quinn Buckner, "I just spent two and a half hours with these people on a morning after we got beat. It doesn't mean anything to me. I only made one request to them, that they not use that remark. Now let's see what they do." A few minutes later, at lunch, Knight asked me, "Did you think she was intelligent?" as if Chung's brightness would determine the outcome of his presentation on the air. But hadn't he told her he was intimidated by people of greater knowledge and learning?

Chung, of course, had every right to use his remark. Yet it took those of us who had been there aback when we saw the program. None of Knight's challenges to her terminology made it to the final cut, although over and over he had explored her premise that what a sports figure feels is "stress." Knight had devoted the lion's share of his two hours to defining what, exactly, is meant by "stress" and to whom it applies. He had offered analogies ranging from a surgeon to a state trooper. He had drawn on literary references, including a book by David Halberstam. Yet his segment amounted to little more than the one remark—and a clip of the chair making its inevitable slide across the highly polished basketball court of Indiana University three years earlier.

And then I forgot it. The remark had not seemed offensive to me as I heard it, although as a feminist my antennae had throughout the season been adjusted toward discovering in Knight any evidence of the sexism of which he has been accused. I listened and I heard the coach speaking about himself being raped, being the victim of injustice on the basketball court, mauled by inept officials. Ironically, he was speaking to one particular rape victim, himself! He was instructing himself to do what he rarely does: remain silent and so avoid that technical, "relax and enjoy it." A passive stance was one he neither could nor should adopt, any more than could a victim of criminal assault "enjoy" a violent attack.

In short, he was being ironic. In an absurd world, an unjust one, irony becomes the intelligent person's weapon. Should he indeed, Knight asks, any more than any other victim of abuse, relax and enjoy being attacked and humiliated? Knight is constantly and un-selfconsciously ironic, although most people fail to register this because he keeps that straight face. And irony, of course, makes no one comfortable.

Knight was attempting what few men will: putting himself in the role of the rape victim, and speculating, ironically, on his options. Far from being insensitive to another person's being raped, he was suggesting that in his own small way he understood the frustration of being rendered vulnerable and powerless. Far from suggesting that anyone could "relax and enjoy it," he was enlisting his entire career, his whole stance in all its aggressive activism, its rejection of passivity, to demonstrate that the only possible response to rape is to scream, both literally and figuratively, as loudly as you can. Indeed hasn't he done just that?

Should he have trusted Chung? Knight should have expected, given the litany held over his head by a hostile press, that the crudest and most literal construction would at once be placed on any figure of speech he chose. He had immediately asked for a tape of the entire interview. The producer agreed to send it. And then he never did.

It's that sound of Orrville again, with Knight the last provincial. He saw no insensitivity in the remark because he did not mean for there to be any. He had thought Chung was in good faith because she had telephoned him directly without employing an intermediary, because she had left her home number, because she had picked up the telephone at home herself. She had told him that she and her husband were fans of Indiana basketball. On this slender evidence, he had believed she would represent his views fairly.

Even before Chung's documentary aired, Malcolm Moran of the New York *Times* telephoned President Thomas Ehrlich for a comment. Without having seen the program, without talking to Knight, Ehrlich gave a statement to the *Times:* "Coach Knight was not speaking for the university. His reference to rape and his coarse language were in very poor taste. Period. That's all I really want to say." Then Ehrlich told the *Times* to hold off printing his remark until the program aired.

That Ehrlich did not ask Knight for an explanation, or at least explore the context in which the remark had been made, was not surprising to those who knew that Ehrlich seemed to have arrived at Indiana the previous summer hostile to Knight. Richard Stoner, president of the Board of Trustees, and vice-president of Cummins Engine, had given him a copy of *A Season on the Brink;* that one-dimensional portrait was all Ehrlich knew about the man, the book about which Knight's player Todd Meier had told him, "Coach, it made you look as if you were crazy."

Contrary to popular opinion, there was no conflict around the Russian game. Knight had telephoned Ehrlich the day after and suggested a reprimand. Ehrlich had offered to send the text to Knight's office, and Knight had declined.

The overreaction to the Chung program was ludicrous when it was not vicious. If it resembled any of the other items on the litany of Knight's supposed sins, it was Puerto Rico. It was the misinterpretation we witnessed over Puerto Rico, but here doubly distorted by the wonders of modern technology where a remark taken out of context and then interpreted literally, when it was meant ironically, can seem to be the opposite of what it is. Yet if Knight could expect some public misunderstanding, and a great deal of press drumbeating, he had not anticipated that the president of the university would join the crowd in its antic furor.

Three days after the Chung program aired, Ehrlich sent to Knight's office a dozen anti-Knight letters, along with a copy of the letter he sent to each respondent. He thanks the writer and repeats that he found Knight's language coarse, adding that Knight did not speak for Indiana University. Ehrlich still had not spoken to Knight.

There was no covering letter.

In all her nearly twelve years at Indiana with Bob Knight, Mary Ann Davis, his secretary, said, she had never seen Knight so

upset as when he saw that. He was offended and he was hurt.
Insofar as any individual could speak *for* an institution, the principles of uprightness and integrity Knight instills in his players
has granted him that right. His influence on them continues long
after they have left him too; this spring, Bobby Wilkerson is
graduating, one of four Knight players who played for four years
who had not done so. Wilkerson is thirty-four. He played last for
Knight in 1976. "Now maybe my name won't come up when somebody writes a book about Coach Knight," Wilkerson, in Bloomington for graduation during these tumultuous post-Chung days,
says impishly. Daryl Thomas has enrolled in summer school,
hoping also to graduate and thereby reduce the number of non-
graduates who have played four years for Knight to two.

On the same day, Thursday, April 28, Knight attempted to explain the remark in an interview with Bob Hammel in the *Herald-
Telephone:* "All I can say is that if this did, even through misinterpretation, focus attention on a very serious social problem, then
I'm happy to have assisted." He suggested that anyone who
thought fairly, who knew him, would know that his remarks could
not in any way have been "tolerant of rape that is criminal assault." He spoke of the uses of the word rape, as indeed, meta-
phorically, we speak of the rape of cities, the rape of the minds
of the innocent. But the matter did not die.

On April 30, the New York *Times* ran an editorial condemning
Knight, quoting only the remark itself, "If rape is inevitable, relax
and enjoy it," as if this were what Knight was advocating. It bore
the style of Ira Berkow, who has attacked Knight so often and so
intensely.

Cries of foul echoed as well from zealots in the office of Indiana's dean for women's affairs, seizing on the issue for their
own ends. On Sunday, May 1, a rally attended by about two
hundred people was held on the campus, its rhetoric devoted to
turning Knight into an instrument for an effort to obtain funding
for a Rape Crisis Center, which the university had denied the
group only shortly before the Chung program aired. The goal of
course is admirable. The ugly use of this particular man to pursue
that goal seems unconscionable.

At that anti-Knight demonstration, the signs read, "Rape is
Every Woman's Knightmare," and, "Rape is No Game." One
woman demanded that mandatory rape awareness be taught

Knight's players, as if they were more prone than other young men to be involved in rape, so ludicrous a turn had the rhetoric taken. The leader of the campus caucus of the National Organization for Women admitted, "I think Bobby Knight helped as a catalyst to bring out more reaction." The Indiana University women's movement had indeed learned a political lesson, if one they borrowed from less liberal origins: the utility of the scapegoat. Meanwhile the crowd, a mob as mindless as any mob, cheered while a rape victim said that if Knight had suffered her attack, he wouldn't be able to say "relax and enjoy it."

Nor were the zealots through. On Saturday, May 6, during commencement-day festivities, some feminists of the IU/Bloomington Women's Collective built a shanty near the center of the campus. On one wall were spray-painted the words, "IU supports rape," on another, "Rape Crisis Center." Six women and a large, black dog stood around the shanty as dusk fell. An organizer said she hoped they could capitalize on the momentum created by Knight to hasten progress toward opening a rape crisis center. A legitimate and important goal had been married to an outrageous attack on Bob Knight for insensitivity to violence and abuse. So these women expected their noble end to justify their spurious and deeply dishonest means.

The next day, Sunday, May 8, President Ehrlich telephoned Bob Byrnes of the history department and asked that he serve as an intermediary between himself and Knight. "I'm going to make mistakes," he told Byrnes. Amazingly, he had come to Indiana believing that he would find there the abuses endemic to college athletes, unaware that if there was one program in the country built upon honesty and integrity, a refusal to exploit students, it was Indiana's.

Byrnes found the conversation alarming. Ehrlich spoke of Knight as if he were a member of a different social class from himself, a blue-collar person whose behavior was bound to be different from his own. He made a remark about Knight's children and his personal life, which Byrnes found appalling.

Ehrlich, however, wished now to defuse the situation. And so Byrnes advised him to write a letter to Knight the following morning, saying, "I made a mistake. I hope you stay. I appreciate all you've done for the university." Ehrlich agreed on Byrnes' formulation, according to Byrnes, more than once in the course of their conversation.

Knight had told Bob Byrnes there were five schools for which he would consider leaving Indiana: New Mexico was one of them. Once New Mexico knew it had a coaching vacancy, they had discussed alternatives with Knight for two hours on the telephone. Four days later they had called again. Was *he* available? The idea seemed appealing for personal reasons that would have prevailed had there been no Connie Chung documentary, no feminist hysteria, no failure in collegiality on the part of the president or, in fact, had he just won the NCAA championship. Knight decided to inquire further into the basketball program at New Mexico.

On Monday morning, May 9, Ehrlich's letter, hand-written, was hand-delivered to Knight's office. Neither "I made a mistake" nor "I hope you stay" had made it to the final draft. Only "I appreciate all you've done for the university" remained. Disgusted, Knight threw the letter in the wastebasket.

Later that afternoon, Knight retrieved the letter from the wastebasket to show it to Harry Pratter. He told Pratter he was concerned that New Mexico Athletic Director John Koenig had been looking for ways to explain the rape statement. Nonetheless the next day, May 10, he flew to Albuquerque on the private jet of Rick Galles, an Indy-car owner.

"Never tackle a folk legend," Bismarck is reputed to have said. On Wednesday, a full page advertisement, headed "We Feel it's Time to Say THANK YOU BOB KNIGHT," appeared in the *Herald-Telephone,* paid for with $1,026 by the "Friends of Bob Knight." A coupon encouraged readers to send Bob Knight an expression of their support. The text begins with a quotation by Abraham Lincoln, "To consent by silence makes cowards of men," and is an expression of Hoosier pride, Hoosier integrity. "These are not people who want to win at any cost," the Friends write. "Midwestern values run far deeper than that."

The Friends also take the opportunity to respond to those purveyors of the litany against Bob Knight: "It is not just troubling to read experts from afar, experts whose access to public opinion is as gigantic as The New York *Times* and Sports Illustrated, repeatedly sneer at the Bob Knight phenomenon in Indiana as love of victory run amok. The people of Indiana whom we feel we represent have personal ideals at least as high as those of anyone from journalism's aristocracy."

Indeed, the Chung special unleashed more chanting of the litany against Bob Knight with the usual mixture of truths, half-truths and misinformation.

On May 3, *USA Today* was ready with a list of "Bobby's Nightmares." These included the 1976 grabbing of Jim Wisman by the jersey, a "pushing match" with the policeman in Puerto Rico, and a "shoving match" with the LSU fan "who tells reporters Knight stuffed him in a garbage can." There are eleven items to this litany, the penultimate of which is Knight's pulling his team off the court with fifteen minutes to play in the exhibition game against the Russians.

Sports Illustrated weighs in on May 9 with a column that includes two paragraphs about Knight's "insensitivity toward women, particularly those who invade his sacred basketball realm. He has ridiculed women reporters and has drawn obscene pictures when he knew they were watching."

I was, of course, one such invader; I witnessed no obscene pictures, experienced no such insensitivity. This litany includes Knight "assault[ing]" the policeman in Puerto Rico, "stuff[ing]" the fan into a trash barrel and of course pulling the team off the court. It implies, incorrectly, that Knight's problems with Ehrlich stem from the reprimand issued by the president after the Russian game, the reprimand Knight solicited.

Ira Berkow calls his May 14 New York *Times* column "The High Priest of Hoop Hysteria," a headline borrowed from the previous day's *USA Today*. The policeman is "punch[ed]." Knight takes his team off the floor. And Knight is "disturbed" that Ehrlich chided him after the Russian game. Knight is also attacked for "wearing red sweaters with the name of a manufacturer clearly emblazoned above the heart, like a man wearing a billboard in front of a sandwich shop." Berkow does not mention that fifty percent of that money goes to the Indiana Foundation for scholarships and grants for research. That Knight's students go to class and pursue degrees? "Knight is doing no less than a college educator is ideally supposed to do." That in Knight's program, as opposed to a large number of basketball programs, players are not bribed or corrupted? That's not mentioned.

Nor would any litany be complete without a contribution from

Mike Lupica of the New York *Daily News.* "Bob Knight should talk to some rape victims before he opens his mouth on national TV and makes a fool of himself," Lupica writes on May 1, followed on May 15 by: "Bob Knight is trying to make it out like it was the president of Indiana University who made the dumb remark about rape. But I do think a change of scenery would be a good idea at this point in Knight's career."

To those journalists for whom the litany is bread and butter, no opportunity is foresworn, nor will evidence to the contrary ever matter.

On Wednesday, May 11, President Ehrlich releases a statement through his office: "I believe Bob Knight is an outstanding coach and I certainly hope Bob Knight will spend the rest of his career at Indiana." On this day Knight returns from Albuquerque with public praise for the people and for "an outstanding coaching situation."

Thursday, May 12, there is a "keep Knight" rally. Although the university is in summer recess, twenty-five hundred supporters gather outside Assembly Hall. In conjunction with the rally, the Governor of Indiana, Robert D. Orr, says, "I would hate to see Bob Knight go. He is someone who is so closely identified with the state of Indiana, someone who really exhibits what it means to be a winning Hoosier—bright, tough, loyal, a little stubborn, confident. He is not perfect, but I've yet to meet anyone in seventy years who is." So the governor suggests that Knight, in fact, does indeed speak for a larger constituency than himself.

It is a day Knight meets with his sons. You do what you have to do, they tell him, appreciating that this is a moment in their father's life when he is starting anew, and that it might be a good thing for him to begin his new life somewhere other than in Indiana. We'll get it straightened out at this end, they tell him. The appeal of starting over in his personal life in a new and hospitable environment is the strongest argument for his taking the job in New Mexico. He is pleased at this show of affection and understanding from Tim and Patrick.

And then he's off to Gary, to a little town called Merrillville, for the Hank Stram–Tony Zale Polish-Americans' scholarship banquet, where more than forty thousand dollars is raised.

A woman on the athletic committee for hiring at Albuquerque

says in regard to Knight's hiring, "We're not happy about it." Meanwhile, Harry Pratter tells Knight what a personal loss it would be for him were Knight to depart. "I very much appreciate that," Knight says. "It may make me decide to stay."

Friday, the 13th. Knight flies to New Orleans for a basketball clinic. In Muncie, Thomas Ehrlich, sensitive to the hostility of those who want Knight to stay, says, "I think I'm doing everything that I can to urge that Coach Knight stay in Indiana. Of course I don't like it, the suggestion that I'm not doing all that I can to see to it that he stays at Indiana University." Knight's statement today is designed to lessen the anti-Ehrlich tide by speaking of his decision as a personal one, not "because of people now at Indiana."

On Saturday upon his return at nine-fifteen in the evening from New Orleans, Knight spends from ten to after one in the morning discussing what to do with Bob Byrnes and his wife Eleanor. He has decided not to go to New Mexico, not only because of the expenditure of energy it would require to build a program there, but also because the extra money for his salary would have come from people outside the university. "I don't want to get into that situation," Knight says. At Indiana he is not dependent on anyone for money, those boosters who might attempt to speak on behalf of the basketball program.

During this long evening Byrnes advises Knight to tell Ehrlich exactly how he has spent the last week. That Ehrlich seems to have little sense of the man has become painfully apparent as the days wear on.

At eight on Sunday morning Knight speaks to Richard Stoner. "I'm delighted you're not going to New Mexico," Stoner says. Stoner believes it is not a good idea for Pratter and Byrnes to accompany Knight to this evening's meeting with President Ehrlich. The professors had thought they might attend as character witnesses.

A full-page ad in this morning's *Herald-Telephone* from well-wishers in New Mexico welcomes Coach Knight to Albuquerque. Should he choose to accept the job, supporters would be awaiting him there.

Six months earlier Knight had promised a nun he would speak